COURAGE IN THE SHADOWS

COVENTRY SAGA BOOK 9

ROBIN PATCHEN

For my launch team. Your kind words and reviews encourage me when the work is hard. I thank God for you.

CHAPTER ONE

When the bearded stranger stepped into the hospital room, a chill slithered down Summer's spine.

Though nobody else seemed bothered by the newcomer's presence, she brushed her fingertips against her holstered sidearm, pushing off the wall to stand closer to the children she'd been hired to protect.

His deeply tanned skin and black curly hair made her wonder if he was related to their client. He was about five-ten—a little shorter than herself—and trim, though the biceps that stretched the fabric of his sweater were anything but skinny. A slight bulge at his hip told her he was carrying, unusual in Massachusetts, where concealed weapons laws were strict. Was he in law enforcement?

Or a criminal?

The man barely gave her a glance as he set a laptop bag on the floor inside the door, draping a wool jacket over it. He headed toward the woman on the bed. "Maritza." He bent down and hugged her for a long time. They spoke in quiet tones, loudly enough for Summer to hear, but not slowly enough for her to translate. She picked up a few random words—*tabla de surf*. And he mentioned Montauk. Wasn't that in New York?

Was he suggesting they go *surfing*? Obviously not sincerely, considering the woman was barely able to walk to the bathroom on her own.

Maritza Hidalgo patted his cheek like one might a child. Based on her affectionate expression—and the lack of concern on the part of her husband seated at her side—this was a relative. Summer compared their features and ages—they both looked to be in their forties, though Maritza's skin was pale and pasty and more wrinkled, probably thanks to the tumor or the treatment she'd already undergone. Summer guessed Maritza and this newcomer could be brother and sister.

After they spoke for a few minutes, he turned to the others in the room, offering handshakes and hugs. Finally, he approached the kids, Summer's charges.

Nobody was worried about the newcomer getting close to the children. The fact that his proximity sent adrenaline to her veins was utterly irrelevant. She worked to keep her face blank, to keep her jaw from clenching, her hand from hovering over her handgun.

He crouched down before them and held out his arms.

"Uncle Vasco." The girl threw her arms around his neck, her voice breaking on his name. At nine, she understood enough of what was going on with her mother to be afraid.

The boy was only seven and didn't seem to grasp his mother's prognosis, the reason why they and so many of their family members had flown up from Mexico, and why his big sister seemed so sad. But he followed her lead and hugged his uncle.

Their mother was about to have a very risky surgery to remove a tumor from her brain. Her chances of survival were favorable, but less favorable were the chances that she would come out of the brain surgery the same as she'd gone in. Apparently, the doctors had warned that there might be permanent brain damage.

A risk indeed, but it was either that or the tumor would kill her. They'd mitigated as many risks as they could, which was why this high-profile family from Mexico was at Boston's Massachusetts General Hospital.

After the man talked to the kids for a few minutes, he stood, barely sparing a glance at Summer. Not surprising, considering her job was to manage security behind the scenes, to blend in unless danger presented itself. Señora Hidalgo was the governor of a Mexican state and had made herself an enemy of the local cartels. Unlike her predecessor, who'd profited nicely from drugs and human trafficking, she fought against the illegal activities.

The cartels, predictably, didn't like that.

Summer's job was to make sure Señora Hidalgo and her family were safe while they were in Boston. This was an easy assignment compared to some she'd had recently. She could go home to her apartment in the evenings and live a relatively normal life. And it could be a boon for the company she partly owned. High-profile people talked to other high-profile people. If Summer and her teammates performed their duties well, this assignment could lead to more like it. Good for Summer, her partners Jon and Bartlett, and the growing number of bodyguards they employed. It was exactly the kind of work they needed to keep their business afloat.

The man—Vasco, his niece had called him—settled against the wall near the door and joined the conversation with the other family members as if he'd been there all along. He asked the questions all the other visitors had asked, Señora Hidalgo giving the same optimistic answers. They spoke Spanish, but Summer had heard the words enough to get the gist of them.

There was no reason for Summer to believe Vasco was a risk. Obviously, everybody in this room trusted him.

Her partner was standing by the door, shoulders back, gaze straight ahead. Grant didn't seem alarmed by the newcomer. She and Grant had worked together for years, and he rarely seemed alarmed by anything. On the job, he was serious and focused, the consummate professional.

Summer couldn't relax back into the routine, not with the way her heart still pounded.

She chanced a longer look at the newcomer's face. It wasn't that she recognized him. He didn't look familiar, but then, she hadn't seen her kidnapper's face. The man who had haunted her dreams for seven years had possessed a strong grip, pulling her out of the room in darkness caused by the hood over her head, but he had only been a voice—a deep voice giving commands while men scrambled to do his bidding.

The newcomer's voice... Her fingers tingled, suddenly chilled. She allowed herself to go back in time, to remember the things she had tried so hard to forget.

That voice. Her kidnapper.

This was him. Summer was almost certain. As certain as she could be under the circumstances.

She quickly looked away, her gaze snagging on Grant's. He must have seen something in her expression because his eyes narrowed, crinkling the skin at their edges. She shook her head. The last thing, the very last thing she needed, was for Vasco to recognize her.

He stood not ten feet from her, chatting as if all were well while she fought conflicting urges.

Take him out.

Or flee.

She was ashamed of that second thought, but she couldn't deny it. Deep down in places she didn't like to acknowledge, fear pulsed with each heartbeat, the instinct to stay alive, to stay *free*. To never, ever allow herself to be taken again.

She fought the impulse to hide her face so he wouldn't recognize her. She kept her chin up, her attention focused on the children as it had been since she'd arrived that morning. She wouldn't give herself away.

Her life depended on it.

The next hour was pure torture.

Finally, it was time for their shift change. The fresh guards' arrival interrupted the awkward stand-around-and-pretend-all-is-well conversation going on in the room. Before Summer could approach Señor Hidalgo for any final instructions, Grant stepped in. Not his job, as the junior agent on duty.

He'd love that, being called *junior*.

But he'd sensed something was wrong. He didn't look Summer's way or even acknowledge her as he spoke to the family, introducing their replacements.

Summer took the opportunity to head for the door, passing just inches from Vasco and managing to keep her gaze forward. She didn't meet his eyes. She couldn't arouse his suspicion.

She walked down the hospital's sterile hallway at a normal pace, refusing her feet's desire to hurry. She stepped into the restroom and stared at herself in the mirror.

"Get a grip, Summer Lake."

Had she gone completely insane, or did her body remember something her mind had tried so hard to forget?

Surely, Vasco wasn't who she thought he was. What were the chances that she'd run into a man in Boston who was responsible for her kidnapping in Mexico seven years before?

She'd investigate Vasco whatshisname, figure out if he could possibly be the mastermind behind the most traumatic event of her life.

If he was, she'd make him pay.

When she felt calm enough, she made her way to the private room the hospital had provided for the family, where she'd left her personal items, figuring she'd run into Grant. He must've still been updating their replacements, even though, aside from the arrival of Vasco, it'd been a routine day.

She'd just put on her jacket and left the room when she caught sight of Vasco stepping into the elevator on the far side of the nurses station, coat on, phone pressed to his ear, laptop bag in his other hand. A gray-haired couple shifted to make room for him.

As soon as the elevator doors closed, Summer bolted for the stairwell and scrambled down six flights to the lobby, yanking her jacket's hood over her blond hair. It wasn't much of a disguise, but it was all she had.

This was probably a bad idea.

No *probably* about it.

When she reached the ground floor, she stepped out and looked around the huge, light-drenched lobby. A few people milled about. No sign of Vasco, but the gray-haired man and woman who'd shared Vasco's elevator were making their way toward the door.

If Vasco had come by car, he'd likely have parked underground. She hurried back into the stairwell and down, where she pushed open the heavy door at the highest level of the garage.

And there he was, about fifty yards ahead of her.

She eased the door shut, moved to an adjacent row to keep cars and concrete barriers between them, and walked the same direction, quietly hurrying to get close. He was still on the phone, but the few words she was able to pick up weren't spoken in English.

She really should have paid more attention in high school

Spanish. Her short stint in Mexico hadn't exactly heightened her love for the language.

Vasco gave no indication he knew she was there. And anyway, with her black jacket and the hood over her head, would he recognize her as the bodyguard of his niece and nephew?

She could hear her cousin's voice in her head. *"Gorgeous women don't blend in. Always assume that you'll be remembered."*

At just shy of six feet with naturally blond hair and gray eyes, Summer stood out from the crowd.

She hated that about herself.

But Vasco didn't seem the type to be nervous about his own personal protection. He seemed like a man who could defend himself, and there'd been that telltale bulge at his hip.

Of course, those things could also indicate a heightened sense of his personal protection. She needed to proceed carefully.

He finished his call and made his way toward the farthest corner of the garage. There, he leaned against a post, tapping on his phone.

Summer stopped behind an SUV and watched through the vehicle's windows.

If he was waiting for a ride, why not do that outside in the hospital's pickup area?

Maybe he was expecting someone who'd driven with him? Maybe that someone had the keys? She glanced at the nearby vehicles. A red Prius. A blue minivan. A silver Honda. Any of those could be his, especially considering he probably drove a rental.

But if one of the cars was his, why not lean on that instead of the post?

At the far end of the garage, a heavy door slammed. Footsteps echoed, getting closer.

Summer crouched between the SUV and the concrete barrier, glimpsing a man's back as he passed. He was average height. Thin brown hair. He wore trousers and a long wool coat. Probably a hospital visitor or employee.

But no.

He went straight to Vasco. "You have it?" His voice was clear, slightly high for a man's.

She stood to look through the SUV's windows.

Vasco pulled something from his bag and held it toward the newcomer.

The man took the object, carefully unwrapped it from tissue paper, and held it up. It was some kind of sculpture. Gold, or gilded, anyway. It seemed to have the likeness of a man, though not a great likeness. It was maybe eight inches tall and narrow enough to grip in a man's fist.

It seemed very, very old.

"Hmm, yes. Maya. I'd guess maybe five to eight hundred AD." The newcomer had a local accent with a JFK-esque Brahmin flair.

"That's just a taste," Vasco said. "The lot is yours for the use of your property and dock. With each delivery, you'll get another piece." He handed his phone to the stranger, who shoved the paper under his armpit, took the phone, and scrolled through what she assumed were photographs. After a minute, he handed the phone back. "The first delivery?"

"Sometime next week. I'll be in touch with the details."

The man stepped back. "I don't want to know the details. I don't need to know anything. We won't be there. Just give me a window, and I'll ensure the house is empty."

"Yes, yes, that seems best."

Yes, yes... The way Vasco said those words, as if he uttered them just like that all the time.

So simple. So familiar.

"Yes, yes. You will all be released, as soon as we get our money."

"Yes, yes. You keep the girls under control, and nobody will get hurt."

That voice.

Summer forced the memories aside. There'd be plenty of time to relive the nightmares later.

Vasco continued. "Better for us to be alone for these operations. We wouldn't want to disturb your family."

The man lifted the sculpture. "I'll appraise this. If it's authentic, then we have a deal. And you will leave an item of equal or greater value, or multiple items, if necessary, with each delivery."

"You tell me where you want the items left, and they will be there. We can put them in Amazon boxes if you like, eh?"

The man laughed as he rewrapped the sculpture in the paper and tucked it inside his jacket. After they shook hands, he turned on his heel and headed back the way he'd come.

Summer ducked again, wanting to get a look at his face but not willing to risk being seen.

When the door at the far end of the garage opened and slammed, Summer peeked around the SUV to see that Vasco was on his phone again, walking away. His voice was too low for her to hear.

She stayed crouched behind the van while his footsteps faded. A car engine started and drove off.

Only then did she breathe easier.

She was right. Not only had her client's relative been involved in her kidnapping seven years before, but here he was, involved in other nefarious dealings.

If Summer played this right, she could finally bring to justice the man who'd nearly destroyed her sister's life.

~

Waiting to be sure Vasco was gone, Summer typed notes into her phone so she wouldn't forget anything she'd heard.

The sound of an approaching engine reminded her where she was. She had no reason to believe Vasco whatshisname had known she was there, but she ought to go someplace less deserted. She stood and started toward the door. She needed to let Grant know she was all right. Her phone had vibrated in her pocket countless times since she'd left the hospital. She pulled it out and saw texts and missed calls from her partner. Not surprising. She didn't usually take off without letting him know where she was going, even if their shift was finished.

She wasn't much of a talk-to-texter, but she didn't want to pause, and after what she'd just witnessed, she didn't think she ought to take her eyes off her surroundings.

The door to the parking garage opened and slammed, and she looked up, slipping her phone into her pocket, senses on alert. She'd call Grant when she was back in the hospital.

As she approached the door, a figure stepped out of the shadows just beyond it.

A second figure came into view from behind a post.

Two men. One a little taller than Summer—probably six-one—slender, straight black hair that hung past his ears. He wore black jeans and a black jacket.

The other was moving at her, fast. He was shorter and stockier, arms so thick they bulged at his sides. He had a shaved head and a chin-curtain beard. He wore clothing similar to his friend. A bulge at his hip told her he was armed. They probably both were.

They were coming for her.

The stockier one smiled.

Summer was a good shot, but she couldn't take out two assailants before one of them returned fire.

She took a couple steps back. The ramp leading down to the next level was thirty yards away. It was her only hope. She turned and bolted.

The men followed, their footsteps gaining on her fast.

They shouted to each other in Spanish. She didn't even try to translate. She could tell by the amusement in their voices that they were confident in their mission.

The ramp was just ahead.

The sound of running came from her right.

He was trying to get in front of her.

She was not twenty feet from the ramp when the taller of the two stepped into her path.

"What's the rush?" His Spanish-accented tone was casual, as if this were a normal interaction.

Summer skidded to a stop and backed toward the cars lining the concrete wall of the garage. The second man was closing in from the other direction. She was trapped.

In one swift move, she pulled her Sig and fired at the taller one.

He cried out, the sound echoing off the concrete walls, and dove behind a car. Had she hit him? She couldn't be certain as she ducked between two vehicles, expecting a gunshot aimed her way.

But it never came.

A volley of Spanish words flew between the two men.

The second attacker was closing in. She couldn't see him over the van, but his voice was too close. "If he dies, you will be sorry."

So she'd injured the second man. One down.

She moved backward, thinking she'd skirt behind one of the cars. But they were parked too close to the wall for her to shimmy past without standing upright. "You should check on your friend," she called, "make sure he's not bleeding to death."

"I know who pays me." His voice came from behind her.

She turned, braced herself. But she was too late.

He barreled into her, pressing her against the concrete wall, her gun hand pinned above her head.

He left himself wide open. She jabbed her knee into his groin.

"Oomph." He backed away but didn't let go of her arm, twisting her wrist to get her to drop her weapon. She wouldn't give it up. She couldn't.

But the man punched her in the stomach and squeezed her wrist hard. Rather than fight a losing battle, Summer released her grip and dropped her gun. She elbowed the man in the chest, sending him off balance. He stumbled back between the cars, and she lifted her foot to kick him onto his back.

He saw it coming and straightened before she could get in a good blow. She barely got her balance, backing away, before he came toward her again.

"Stop this," he said. "Ramón said I don't kill—"

She kicked him in the stomach. It felt like her foot met a wall.

The man was barely fazed.

She tried to crawl over the sedan beside her, but he grabbed her wrist and yanked her back down. She pretended to be off balance when she fell, bent away from him, and jabbed her foot behind her into his knee.

With a stream of Spanish obscenities, he stumbled back, barely keeping his feet.

She needed to escape. But she was trapped between the van and the car. Wall behind her. Him in front.

She scrambled onto the hood of the car, but he got a handful of her hair and pulled. She slid down the cold metal, and he punched her just above her ear.

Her head snapped to the side. The pain traveled down her back. For a moment of strange numbness, she feared he'd broken her neck. She couldn't move, couldn't think.

But then the pain returned, jarring but not deadly.

Her attacker grabbed her hands, lifted her to her feet, and dragged her out from between the vehicles. She wanted to fight, to struggle, but she had no strength.

In her periphery, a figure rushed into view.

He barreled into the man in front of her, propelling them all forward before the attacker let up his grip on her.

She fell, banging her head on a car before she collapsed. Her head throbbed. She couldn't make out what was going on, who was there. Friend or foe, she had no idea.

Words that she couldn't understand floated over her head. She tried to reach out, to grab one and make sense of it. Maybe they'd been spoken in Spanish. Maybe she'd simply lost her ability to think.

And then a man was there shaking her. Yelling.

Her instincts kicked in, and she shoved him away, blinking to bring the scene into focus. She struggled to her feet but needed to hold onto the nearby car to keep from falling.

Arms snaked around her from behind. She tried to turn, to get away. When she couldn't extract herself, she jabbed an elbow back.

The man grunted. "Stop it! It's me!"

That voice. Deep.

And deeply annoyed.

The sound of running faded. Far away, a car door slammed. An engine roared.

Grant let Summer go and bolted toward the sound.

Good. She needed a second to process. She closed her eyes, sat on the concrete, and laid back. She let the cold seep through her clothes and soothe her aches. She would get up. Soon.

She would face what had almost happened. Just...not yet.

Someone stomped closer, and she opened her eyes.

Grant glared down at her. "If you'd just not fought me, we could have captured them."

"I had them." Her words were slurred. She struggled to sit up. The fuzziness was receding, the world gaining sharp edges again. "I didn't need your help."

She'd told her share of lies in her life, but that might have been the biggest.

And Grant knew it. She hated—hated more than anything—needing to be rescued.

But she was grateful that she hadn't just been molested or kidnapped or murdered. Maybe she ought to say so. She would. Eventually.

Grant blew out a long breath. "You looked like you had it well in hand before I got here. Never mind that the guy would have had you unconscious in about three seconds, thrown you over his shoulder, and hauled you into that van. Or killed you. But yeah, you had it all under control." He brushed himself off and then sighed again. He reached toward her. "Come on."

She took his hand and let him pull her up. "There were two."

"I'm guessing you shot the other one." Grant backed up a few steps and pointed at a small, shiny stain. Blood. "If you'd just..."

She'd fought Grant rather than helping him. She'd let them get away. "I didn't know it was you."

"I know. I didn't realize..." His Adam's apple bobbed. "They're gone now. You're safe."

Because he'd rescued her. Which meant that now she owed him. Again. "What are you doing here?"

"Looking for you."

Oh. Grant's protectiveness could be annoying. Maddening. But today, she wouldn't complain.

He looked at her a long moment. "Do you want to call the police or—?"

"Not even a little."

He scanned her, his mouth twisting. "We're going to the ER."

"I'm fine."

"You took a blow to the head. I think—"

"Absolutely not."

He glared, seemed about to fight her, and then gave up. He wrapped his hand around her back to support her, an intimacy she shouldn't allow. "Come on."

Summer might've argued, but she didn't have it in her. Her ribs ached, her head pounded, and her wrist... She cradled it with her other arm. It wasn't broken, just sprained. She limped beside Grant. A bruise on the shin, she thought. It would heal on its own. She vaguely remembered a well-placed kick.

He led her to the elevator and pushed the button.

"I can handle the stairs." Maybe. Or maybe that was the second giant lie she'd told in the last three minutes.

He ignored her.

She patted her empty holster, stifling the curse word that wanted to come out. "My gun. I don't know if he got it, or if it's over there."

"Where I found you?"

"Maybe around the gray van or the car beside it?"

Grant propped her against the wall. "Do not get on that elevator without me. Understand?"

She didn't take orders from Grant. He worked for her, not

the other way around. She'd tell him that, too, as soon as she mustered the energy. For now, she just nodded.

Grant sprinted away.

She rested her head against the cool wall, barely resisting the urge to slide down it, and only that because she didn't think she'd be able to stand back up.

The elevator dinged.

"Hold it!" Grant called as he ran into view. He reached the open door before she managed to push herself off the wall. He took her arm again and helped her into the empty car.

"Did you find it?" Summer asked.

"Yup."

The single word brought immense relief. At least she hadn't lost her weapon. This was embarrassing enough without having to admit that.

Grant pushed the button for a lower floor.

"You drove?"

His only answer was a quick nod.

The elevator dinged, and they stepped out and made their way to Grant's pickup.

As she settled into the passenger seat, she came to terms with the fact that he had probably saved her life. Certainly saved her from what would surely have been a torturous experience. She'd had enough torturous experiences to feel an overflow of gratitude welling up inside of her.

Grant reached into the backseat, then laid a scratchy wool blanket over her.

"I'm fine." She wasn't in shock, was she?

"Humor me." He tucked it close, ensuring it covered her from chin to toes. Only as its warmth penetrated did Summer realize how cold she was.

After Grant started the truck and clicked on his seatbelt, she forced the words bubbling in her throat out of her mouth. "Sorry for my... Obviously, I needed your..." But she couldn't seem to finish either sentence. She shouldn't have acted like she didn't need his help. She shouldn't have attacked him when he'd probably saved her life. Again.

She knew all her shortcomings. Knowing them and overcoming them were two very different things.

When she didn't finish, Grant said, "I'm just glad you're safe."

"Thank you."

"Anytime." He drove out of the parking garage and onto the busy Boston street. She was surprised when he headed not toward Storrow Drive and her apartment but toward downtown. "Where are we—?"

"I told Bartlett there was something wonky about that Vasco guy, and he wanted us to meet at the office."

"What do you know about him?"

"Absolutely nothing except your reaction."

"I didn't react. I was perfectly professional."

His laugh was not amused. "Perfectly professional people would have asked for help, not gone off on their own, following somebody they suspected of... You were following him, right?"

When she didn't answer, he grunted his frustration.

"That's what I thought. Perfectly professional people know how to work with a team."

"I had no idea that was going to happen."

"Really? You can't see into the future?"

"I don't need your sarcasm."

He yanked the wheel, turning toward South Boston. "We work with partners for a reason, to mitigate risks, because sometimes bad things happen that we didn't see coming. You willingly, *stupidly* followed a...a stranger you obviously didn't trust. And almost got yourself killed, or kidnapped and *then* killed."

"I see what you're—"

"I'm your *partner*." His words were low, vehement. "A quick text, a quick, *hey, following that Vasco guy into the parking garage.* That would've killed you?"

Summer's heart was pounding, not just from the attack she'd barely survived. Grant wasn't a jerk, not as a rule. And yet...

Okay, he was right. She should've told him. She shouldn't have gone off by herself.

"It all happened really fast. I figured I could just get his license plate number so I could learn his last name."

"And did you?"

"No plate number, but I think it's Ramón. Vasco Ramón." She swallowed, wishing she had a bottle of water. Some caffeine. An Advil...or four. "I got something much better." She could hear her words slowing, almost slurring.

She would explain everything to him and Bartlett, as soon as she could get her thoughts together.

But the adrenaline had drained, everything on her body ached, and she couldn't focus for one more second. She settled her head against the cool window. "I'll tell you everything. For now, just let me rest."

CHAPTER TWO

G rant Wright focused on bringing his heart rate down.
He was ready to kill.

He'd known when the newcomer walked into the hospital room that Summer recognized him, or thought she did, anyway.

Grant had seen her reaction, though he'd had no idea what it meant. She'd seemed nervous, maybe even a little scared. It had been a long time since she'd allowed either to show in her expression.

Her taking off so fast during shift change only confirmed his suspicion. He'd hurried through the update, hoping to catch up with her. But Señor Hidalgo had wanted to discuss the following day's events to ensure that there would be sufficient security to protect both his wife in surgery and his family, who would be in a waiting room down the hall.

Grant had assured him that they would have more guards on duty, that they'd all be safe.

The conversation had taken too long.

When he'd finally left Ian and Greta to the job, he looked for Summer in the room where they'd left their things, assuming she'd be waiting for him. But she wasn't.

He'd texted her. No response. He'd called. No answer.

After taking the elevator to the lobby, he'd debated jogging toward the T station to see if he could catch up with her, figuring she'd take the subway home. He hadn't believed she needed his help. If any woman could take care of herself, it was Summer Lake.

Without any clear idea where she'd gone, there was nothing he could do. He'd started down the stairs toward his truck and had nearly been to the level where he'd parked it when he'd heard the gunshot.

He would swear his heart had stopped.

He'd bolted back up the steps two at a time and run toward a scuffle in the far corner.

He got there just in time to see a man punch Summer on the side of the head.

Fury, fiery and red, clouded his vision. He'd itched to pull out his handgun. Fortunately, he was trained better than to fire at strangers when he had no idea what was going on—and when he could take out the enemy with less violent means.

He'd attacked, rung the guy's bell pretty good.

He hadn't realized how injured Lake was. He should have just let her rest and dispatched the attacker himself. But fear had clouded his judgment. He'd had to know she was all right.

And he knew her, knew she wouldn't want to be rescued. He knew she would want to take part in the takedown of her assailants if she could.

That was his downfall, caring so much about Summer's well-being. Had been since the moment he'd met her.

Not that it had done him one iota of good back then or in the years since.

At least he hadn't screwed up too badly. But if he could get a redo, those men would be in custody.

Stupid.

How many people would pay for that one?

He reached the office and his spot behind the building. When he shifted into park, Summer sat up, wincing. Some of her blond hair had escaped her tight bun and framed her angular face. Her skin was pale, her gray eyes narrowed as if fighting pain.

"You should go to the hospital."

"I'm fine," she snapped. "He hit me in the head. Of course it's going to hurt."

"What else?" He should've asked that before. He shouldn't have assumed that, just because she moved okay, she wasn't seriously injured. Now, she cradled one arm in the other. "Your wrist?"

She reached across her body and pulled the handle with her left hand. "It's just a sprain. I'm sure we have a brace inside." She climbed out and slammed the door.

When he'd been looking for her, he'd called Bartlett, one of the firm's partners, and told him that Summer seemed concerned about one of the family members. After the attack, he'd sent a quick text.

Summer attacked. Seems okay. We're on our way.

She wouldn't like that. In typical Summer fashion, she'd be embarrassed that she'd been attacked and unable to defend herself—though how she could possibly have prevailed against two armed thugs, he had no idea. When Summer got embarrassed, she got defensive. When she got defensive, she went on the attack.

It was her least attractive quality.

Maybe her only unattractive quality.

Or maybe Grant was biased.

He hurried to get ahead of her and opened the door, which earned him an irritated glare. She stepped past him without saying anything. She was not accustomed to being treated like a lady. One of the things he hoped to change if she could ever get over her disdain for him.

He followed her down the hallway, past the storage closet, the break room, and two private offices to the conference room of the Green Beret Protection Agency—GBPA, as it was usually known. When Bartlett, Jon, and Summer had started the business, they'd been counseled to choose a name that would highlight the fact that two of the three founders—and many of the guards—had been in the Army's Special Forces. Apparently, people were impressed by that.

Summer stepped into the conference room doorway and froze, then cast a hurt look at him over her shoulder.

Jon said, "Come on in and have a seat."

He wasn't in the city, but his upper half was displayed on the monitor affixed to the wall at the end of the room.

Bartlett sat on one side of the table, Hughes on the other. Hughes wasn't a partner, but he'd been with the agency as long as Grant.

Grant tapped Summer's back to urge her forward. With a low voice, he said, "I had no choice."

She stepped away from his touch and plopped down at the end of the table, where she could stare at her cousin on the screen.

Grant sat beside her.

Worry wrinkled Jon's brow. "Are you all right?"

"It's nothing." She probably didn't realize that she touched the side of her head when she said the words.

"Why aren't you at the ER?" He glared at Grant. His voice held barely contained rage. "You were already at Mass General."

"Have you met your cousin?" Grant kept his tone calm despite the frustration humming in his veins.

Jon's lips pressed closed, and he returned his glare to her.

Not needing to witness the family squabble Grant predicted, he hopped up and walked out, hurrying to the break room, where he rummaged through their supply of first aid equipment until he found three braces that looked like they could work. On his way back, he heard Jon peppering Summer with questions about her injuries.

"Did you lose consciousness?"

"No."

"Get dizzy? Faint?"

A slight pause. "It passed quickly."

Jon blew out a long breath. "If you have a concussion—"

"I'll heal. I'm fine."

Sure she was.

Back in the conference room, Grant sat and slid the wrist braces across the shiny table toward her. She selected one and slipped it on without a word.

Jon waited until she was finished. When she looked up, he said, "You want to tell us what you were thinking, going off by yourself?"

"I was off duty."

"Not if you were following our client's family member."

Summer didn't say anything, just lifted her chin.

Jon leaned onto the desk in front of him and crossed his arms, holding Summer's gaze.

Grant recognized the room behind his friend. Jon was in the office at his girlfriend's house in Coventry, New Hampshire.

Jon and Summer were having one of their epic staring contests. Grant resisted the urge to fill the silence. He'd learned in years of working with these two that it was never a good idea to get between them when they were arguing.

Summer broke first. She sat back and touched her head again.

Which elicited a worried look from Jon. "Are you sure you don't need—"

"I'm fine."

"Okay, then. Explain."

Summer's gaze darted around the room. She focused on Bartlett, maybe figuring she'd find a better ally in him. "I'd rather not discuss this in front of Grant and Hughes. It's private."

Hughes pushed back in his chair. "No problem. We can wait—"

"I'm not leaving." All eyes turned to Grant, but he focused on Summer. "I'm your partner. If you don't want to work with me, fine. You can find somebody else. But if I'm going to be your partner, I need to know everything."

His heart thumped double-time as the words left his mouth. If she sent him away, he'd be blind. How could he protect her if he were assigned to a different team member? But he couldn't exactly have her back if she wouldn't tell him what was going on.

Would she dump him as a partner a half hour after he'd saved her life?

This was Summer he was talking about. Summer, who hated to be vulnerable. Hated to need help. His having saved her would probably be a strike against him.

He was taking a risk, a big one. If she demanded he leave, he'd fail at the one job he'd sworn he'd never, ever give up.

But if she didn't trust him, if she didn't want him... Well, that wasn't the answer he wanted to the prayer he'd been sending skyward for seven years, but maybe it was the only answer he was going to get. Maybe it was time to accept it.

After a minute, she said, "Fine. He can stay." She looked at Hughes, who still hovered over his seat as if hoping to be told the same. "Sorry. It's just... It's personal. Grant already knows a lot of it."

Hughes stepped away from the table, lifting his hands. "No worries." He turned to Bartlett. "You want me to hang around or—?"

"No need," Summer said.

"Sorry I kept you late." Bartlett forced a thin smile. At nearly fifty, he was the oldest person in the security agency. Though he, Jon, and Summer owned equal shares, he'd been running the office, dealing with customers, and assigning posts for a couple of years, not wanting to be in the field. Jon had become more of a silent partner since he'd moved to New Hampshire, so Bartlett and Summer made most of the big decisions themselves.

The door had barely closed behind Hughes when Jon focused on Summer. "Start from the beginning."

She explained why she'd followed Vasco, whose last name was probably Ramón, to the parking garage. Grant could see her struggling to contain her defensiveness and irritation, to be straightforward and honest about her own failings. It was impressive, really. She seemed to be maturing in that area.

The thought warmed his heart, but it cooled when he realized what she was saying, what she suspected.

"You're saying that you believe..." On the screen, Jon's gaze was hard. "I thought you didn't see any of your kidnappers' faces."

"I didn't." Summer seemed to struggle to explain. "It was his voice. But even before he spoke...it was his presence. I know that doesn't make sense. I know that it wouldn't stand up in court. But I'm telling you, it was him."

The cousins looked at each other for a long moment, and then Jon's gaze flicked to Grant. "What did you think?"

"I wouldn't have thought anything if Lake hadn't reacted the way she did."

"I didn't react."

Grant managed to keep himself from smiling. Sometimes it was fun to press her buttons, but now wasn't the time. "Nobody else would've noticed it. I just know you well. Your shoulders stiffened. Your lips got tight around the edges, like they are right now."

Summer looked away, hiding whatever it was she was attempting to do to her lips. It bordered on funny.

Jon wasn't amused. "He didn't seem suspicious to you?"

"No," Grant said, "but I didn't know what she knew."

Jon turned back to Summer. "Okay, go on. You followed him to the garage, and then what happened?"

"I didn't think he saw me. I was hiding behind an SUV when he met with another guy."

"In a car?" Grant asked

"On foot. Came through the hospital doors. I hid. I didn't think he saw me, either."

"Somebody saw you." Bartlett had been quiet for most of their exchange. That was his way, to sit back and let everybody else battle it out, especially when Summer and Jon were involved. Before he could say anything else, though, his phone vibrated on the desk. He flipped it over to look at the screen, scowling. "I'd better get this." He walked out of the room, closing the door behind him.

"Go on," Jon said. "We can fill him in later."

Summer explained the conversation she'd overheard between the two men, the little statue that had changed hands, and the deal they'd made.

While Jon took his copious notes, Grant tried to make sense of it. "So they're making a deal, access to his property for more of whatever it was he gave him. And you think that little statue was...what exactly?"

"The guy said it was Mayan, dated to around five hundred AD. Obviously, it's worth a lot, worth breaking the law for."

Jon tapped a keyboard. "Mayan antiquities..." He was reading off his screen. "They come from Mexico, Guatemala, Brazil. Something like this?"

An image popped onto the screen, replacing his face. It was a stone statue of a man sitting on a throne.

"Does it say how tall that is?" she asked.

Jon checked. "Eight inches."

"Right size. But it was gold. I think the one I saw was standing, maybe wearing a crown."

"Okay." Jon removed the image, and his face showed again, though he was focused elsewhere. Researching Mayan antiquities, Grant figured.

He leaned toward Summer, his voice low. "Only you could stumble into something like that." He couldn't help the frustration in his tone. "Sheesh, Summer, you're lucky—"

"Lake. You call me *Lake*." She practically hissed the words. She was ridiculously defensive about that. Hers had been a great name when she was a cover model, but he supposed it was a little lighthearted for a personal security agent.

What was wrong with lighthearted?

He managed not to roll his eyes. "Fine, *Lake*." Everybody knew her real name, but nobody was allowed to use it. The truth was, when she wasn't scowling, the name Summer suited her, thanks to her blond hair, those eyes the color of storm clouds. If her past had been different, if her life had been different, would she have fit the name? Maybe, if she could get over all her hang-ups, she still could.

Over the speaker, Jon said, "Mayan antiquities are often stolen from dig sites or even graves and traded on the black market. You're sure there was going to be some kind of illegal deal at that dock?"

"No question." Summer punctuated the words with a nod, her eyes squinting the slightest afterward. She was hiding her pain well, but it was there.

"Drugs?" Grant asked.

"They didn't say, and the local man didn't ask, but knowing what I do about this guy, I wouldn't be surprised if it was people he was trafficking."

"You didn't see the second man's face," Jon clarified.

"Nope."

"Do you think you could remember the statue if you saw it again?"

Summer pressed a hand to the back of her neck. She really needed to get some ice packs and heating pads, to rest. Not to be grilled. "Maybe. It was about eight inches tall, gold. I saw what I guessed was a head and a weird headpiece or crown, but I didn't get a look at the rest of it."

Bartlett returned to the room. He looked furious.

"I take it that wasn't good news," Jon said.

Bartlett focused on Lake. "It was Hidalgo, the client's husband. He found out you followed his brother-in-law. He's furious."

"Got a lot of nerve considering what happened."

Bartlett ignored Grant. "He swears Vasco Ramón had nothing to do with those guys who attacked you."

She scoffed, shaking her head. Again, she squinted as if the action hurt. "Considering one of them used his name—"

"Ramón is a common name. Nothing to do with him."

"Obviously, he's lying," Grant said.

Again, Bartlett acted as if Grant hadn't spoken. "He wants you off his security detail and nowhere near him and his family. He threatened to fire us if there are any more 'indiscretions.'"

The way the color drained from Lake's face now, after everything that had happened, told Grant a lot. Why, though? What was the big deal? The agency had plenty of work, didn't it? He'd worked almost nonstop since Jon had left. But...oh. Because he, not Jon, was Lake's partner now, so of course he'd be busy. As an owner, Lake would always have work. But had Hughes been working full time? Had Marcus? Had Ian, as their newest hire?

Maybe work was slowing down. Maybe this job *was* a big deal.

While Jon filled Bartlett in on everything Summer had said, Summer interjecting her comments now and again, Grant considered the implications. Was the business in trouble? Having a high-profile client like the well-known governor of a Mexican state could only have been good for them. Had Lake's actions jeopardized the business?

Grant should care very much. He cared about the people that he worked with, and he had great regard for all three of the owners. He didn't want their venture to fail.

But he sure wouldn't mind if Summer weren't strapping a gun to her hip every single day. Couldn't she find some normal profession? Couldn't he? He was good at this, but did he like it, standing against a wall eight hours a day watching other people live their lives? It was not his dream job, but it came with his dream woman. He'd considered quitting. Moving on with his life and giving up on Summer. But how could he leave her when she might be in danger? How could he leave her in somebody else's hands?

He'd trusted Jon as her partner, but could he trust anybody else?

Would anybody else have sought her out after their shift, rescued her?

No, he'd left someone he loved behind once before. He knew how that worked out.

So maybe, deep down, he wouldn't mind if the business folded. Except that Lake would probably just go get another job as a personal security agent, and maybe he wouldn't be able to follow her.

That would make it a lot harder to keep her alive.

Bartlett interrupted his ruminating. "Absolutely not." He looked at the screen, clearly waiting for Jon to agree with him.

What had Grant missed?

"I know what you want to do, Lake," Jon said. "I know you want to take this guy down, and I don't blame you. But it's not our job." He turned his focus to Bartlett. "You know anybody at the FBI?"

Yes, that was the right move. Alert the authorities and then step away.

But by Summer's thunderous expression, it was clear she was not on board with the "step away" portion of that plan.

CHAPTER THREE

S tep away? They had to be kidding. Not only had this man kidnapped Summer, her sister, and twelve other models, one of whom had ended up dead, but now he was involved in some sort of smuggling operation. Probably people. After all, he'd been planning to sell them seven years before. Obviously, he wasn't above working in the sex-slave market. But it could be drugs—marijuana, heroin, cocaine, fentanyl. Something worth more than the little pieces of history Ramón was willing to part with.

Bartlett grabbed the conference room telephone and dialed. It took a few minutes to reach somebody at the FBI field office in Boston who could be helpful, and when they finally did, Bartlett gave Summer a confident go-ahead nod, as if all had been decided.

It ticked her off.

She glared at her cousin on the monitor, hoping he'd step in. But Jon said, "Tell him what happened."

No help there. When she shifted to Grant, he held her gaze but said nothing. At least *he* wasn't telling her what to do.

Her head was pounding, her wrist aching, her stomach roiling. She was having trouble thinking straight. But though she racked her brain, she could think of no reason why she shouldn't tell the FBI agent what had happened.

She explained what she'd heard in the parking garage, answering the questions posed by Agent Golinski's disembodied voice on the phone, a man she had never seen and knew nothing about. Neither Jon nor Bartlett seemed concerned, and she trusted them. Grant's expression said he thought she'd made the right choice. He was giving her that look she sometimes caught. She'd name it affection if she didn't know better.

She finished explaining what she'd overheard and would have been content to leave it at that.

"Tell him the rest, Lake," Jon said.

She glared at the screen. "The rest is irrelevant."

"No, it's not." Jon communicated his intentions with a determined, slightly annoyed grimace. Either she told Golinski, or he would.

Fine.

"After Ramón walked away," she said, "two thugs came at me." She explained the assault, her cheeks burning with shame even as she tried to brush off the attack as if it'd been the least important part of the afternoon.

When she was finished, Golinski sighed into the phone. "Look, I don't know much about this, but we were informed of Hidalgo's surgery. From what I can tell, she's working closely with the US, a true ally. If her brother is into something illegal, there's no indication of it in her file. We're going to need to tread very carefully here, maybe get State involved."

"I don't care who she is," Jon said. "Her brother's thugs attacked one of our people. And he's clearly involved in something big."

"I know, I know." Golinski sounded tired, not long-day tired but disappointing-life tired. "I'm just warning you that the powers-that-be might not want to ruffle any feathers."

"That's not acceptable," Jon said.

Ignoring that, Golinski said, "I'll look into it and get back to you."

When Bartlett hung up, she pushed back in her chair. "Are we done here?"

"You need to get out of town," Jon said. "Somewhere Ramón can't find you. Why don't you come up here until this blows over?"

"I have a job. I can't just—"

"Actually," Bartlett said, "you're on leave."

She swiveled to face him. "I'm *what?*" Rage vibrated beneath her skin.

Bartlett held up his hands, palms out. "That was the deal I made to keep the client happy. The family is not comfortable that we have a bodyguard they don't trust. They insisted I fire you. I promised them you would be removed for the duration of our contract, and they agreed. It's not for long."

The last thing Summer wanted was to jeopardize her business. These people—Jon and Bartlett, Grant and Hughes, all the bodyguards... These were her family. They were the only family she had nowadays. Her sisters weren't far away, but they might as well have lived on the other side of the country for as often as she saw them. Her relationship with them was strained at best. And she rarely saw her father.

If the business fell apart, the people closest to her would suffer. It would be her fault.

She'd been so sure the job protecting Denise Masters would turn things around for them, and it had. But they had more people on staff now, some of whom they'd hired full time for that assignment. They hadn't wanted to let those people go. There'd been plenty of jobs, but few required the manpower the

Masters job had. When they'd taken Hidalgo as a client, it had been with the hope of expanding their client base.

If they alienated Hidalgo, it could be disastrous for the agency.

But Vasco Ramón needed to pay for what he'd done. Lake had recovered from the kidnapping, but she'd never be the person she was before. There was a reason she carried a gun for a living. There was a reason she spent her life training and preparing to defend herself and others.

Misty had needed counseling and therapy for years.

There were eleven others still dealing with the trauma of that event. And one family grieving the loss of their daughter.

All of that, *all of that,* was Vasco Ramón's responsibility. And he needed to pay.

She would do what she could to protect her business and coworkers, but those models had been her family too. If she could bring the mastermind behind the kidnapping to justice, she had to do it.

Maybe, if she brought him to justice, she and Misty could be sisters again.

Summer pushed back in her chair and stood, focusing on Bartlett. "I'll make myself scarce. You let me know when you want me to come back." She marched to the door, trying to ignore the pain in her shin, the pounding in her head, the throbbing in her wrist.

She was halfway down the hall when footsteps came behind her. It wouldn't be Bartlett. She didn't even turn when she said, "What do you want, Grant?"

"What are you going to do?"

"What Jon suggested. I'm getting out of town." She was nearly to the door now.

In typical Grant fashion, he hurried to get ahead of her so he could open it. Only this time, he didn't. He stood in front of it. Arms crossed over his wide chest, brows drawn low over his dark brown eyes. His strong jaw was clenched. "You're not going to let it go, right? You're going to figure out what Vasco Ramón is up to."

"Move." Remembering that he'd just saved her life, she added, "Please."

"Just answer the question, Summer."

She gritted her teeth and ground out, "It's Lake. Do not call me Summer."

He rolled his eyes. "What's your plan?"

"It's none of your business."

"We're partners. That makes it my—"

"Your *partner* was just banished. So for the time being—"

"I'm taking vacation time," Grant said. "I already cleared it with Bartlett and Jon. They're both on board with this."

She gestured between them. "There is no *this*."

"Do you really think they don't know what you're up to? That you're not letting this go? You can't investigate this guy on company time and with company resources, but that doesn't mean you're not going to investigate him. I know that"—he pointed past her—"everybody in that room knows that. As you've already demonstrated once today, you can't take on the entire world by yourself."

She shouldered past him to the door and into the cold evening, ignoring the twinge of pain that bumping into him brought. She limped, shivering, across the pavement toward the edge of the building. She didn't want to think about Grant rescuing her. That everybody knew it, everybody knew she'd needed help.

Jon never needed help.

Except that wasn't true. On their last assignment, Jon had seen the danger Denise Masters was in and brought in more bodyguards. He hadn't fooled himself into thinking he could handle it alone.

She was just being her typical stubborn, stupid self. She heaved a deep breath of damp, chilly air and blew it out. She didn't have to turn to know Grant was on her heels as she walked through the alley toward the sidewalk ahead.

"You can take the T if you want," he said matter-of-factly. "I mean, those guys know your name and where you work, but if you want to risk running into them again tonight, I guess that's on you. If you prefer the subway to my warm pickup, we can go that route."

We.

Of course he wouldn't leave her alone.

Truth be told—though she'd never actually *tell* it—she didn't want to be alone. Jon had been her partner before he'd met Denise and moved to Coventry. After that, Bartlett had allowed her to choose her new partner. She'd chosen Grant. Aside from her cousin, Grant was the easiest to work with. The most easygoing. Considering she was probably the hardest to get along with, he was the best option.

And she trusted Grant.

The rest of what he'd said registered, and she slowed. She definitely did not want to run into those guys again tonight.

He lowered his voice and softened his tone. "Whether you like it or not, I *am* your partner, and that means I take your protection seriously."

She turned to face him, preparing to tell him that she didn't need his protection. Which, obviously, would be another lie.

Her conscience gave her pause. She should speak the truth. She knew that. But knowing it and doing it when she was angry and afraid and embarrassed...

"Like I assume you take my protection, right?" Grant added. "We're supposed to have each other's backs. I'm coming with you, whether you want me to or not." At the end, his words got hard. Stubborn.

As much as she wanted to take down Ramón, she definitely did not want to end up his captive again. And there were no extra points awarded if she worked alone. Jon had been trying to tell her that for years.

"Fine."

"Do you want to ride the T, or do you think it would be simpler if you got in my truck now?"

Rather than give the obvious answer, she swiveled toward the parking lot.

Grant was smart enough not to smile.

CHAPTER FOUR

G rant had barely stopped in front of Summer's apartment building when she opened the truck's door. "I'll be back in five."

Exasperating woman. He took her wrist—the uninjured one—before she could step out. "Stay there until I come around. Not a chance you're going in without me."

He cut the engine and hopped out. By the time she stood on the sidewalk, he was at her side. She steadied herself on the open truck door before looking at him.

Most people had to look up. At six-three, he was nearly a foot taller than the average woman. But there was nothing average about Summer Lake, including her height. If she wore high heels, she'd be nearly as tall as he. Or so he assumed. She wasn't exactly the stiletto type.

"I don't need a babysitter."

He glanced at the brownstones that flanked hers. Cars were parked tip-to-tail along both sides of the one-way street. Trees rose from some of the small front yards, their budding branches swaying in the chilly wind and casting weird shadows from the streetlights at every corner.

Too dark. Too many places to hide. He urged her toward the stairs leading to her apartment in the converted five-story brownstone. "You don't think there's any way those thugs know where you live?"

"How would they?"

"People like that don't play by the rules." He would wrap his arm around her back to support her if he didn't think she'd punch him.

She hobbled forward. "Seriously, Grant. I'm fine."

"Seriously, Summer. Someone tried to kill you today."

"Don't call me—"

"Do I really have to pretend I don't know your name? It's just the two of us."

He expected her to give him one of her famous *I could kill you with a butter knife* looks, but she seemed focused on putting one foot in front of the other. She made it to the top of the steps, unlocked the door, and stepped inside, where she stopped and stared at the winding staircase.

Grant had dropped her off here more than once, even swung by to pick her up a time or two, but he'd never been invited to her apartment. "Which floor?"

"Third."

"No elevator?"

"Not that works." She started to climb.

When they reached the landing halfway between the second and third stories, he whispered, "Stay here," and continued to the top. There were two doors, both closed. A TV played inside one apartment. Since she lived alone, he figured that wasn't hers.

But the other... Something wasn't right. He crept toward it, taking a penlight from his pocket, and studied the door. Though it had been pulled closed, it wasn't latched. Which meant either

Summer hadn't locked it properly when she left, or somebody was in there.

And Summer would definitely have latched it properly.

Silently, he returned to Summer and pointed in the direction of the first door, mouthing, *That one?* Just to be sure.

She shook her head.

Meaning the door that stood partially open was hers. The thugs had been in her place. Maybe were still there.

If he were alone, he'd barrel in and take them down. If he were alone, he'd do his best to get one of them in custody and talking.

But he wasn't alone, and Summer could hardly walk, much less fight.

He leaned in very close and spoke in her ear. "I think they're here. You need to be silent."

She nodded that she understood.

He swept her off her feet.

She gasped, but to her credit, made no other noise. He'd have warned her of his plan, but that would have caused an argument they had no time for.

He hurried down the stairs as quietly as possible, careful not to let her feet hit the wall. In another circumstance, he would very much enjoy having Summer pressed against his chest.

But right now, all he wanted was to get her to safety.

He pushed out the front door, jogged to his truck, and had her inside in seconds. He climbed in beside her, started it up, and was on the next block and dialing his phone in less than a minute.

Summer seemed to recover from her shock. "What the—?"

"Not now." As soon as the operator's voice filled the cab, he said, "There are intruders at..." He looked at Summer, who supplied the Back Bay address. When the operator promised to send a car, Grant hung up and dialed again.

"What are you doing?" Summer demanded.

Before he could respond, Bartlett answered with, "What happened?"

"Someone broke into Summer's apartment. Just called 911. I'm going to get her somewhere safe and go back."

She said, "I'm going—"

"Absolutely not." Bartlett's tone invited no argument. "I'll send a team. Get her out of town."

"Wait," Summer said. "I'm not leaving. We have to go back. How do you know someone broke in?"

Grant ignored her, staring at the speaker as if Bartlett were right there. Everything in him wanted to return to Summer's and take those guys out. But he'd have to leave her alone to do that. And if he knew her, she'd follow him, put herself in danger. "You can handle it?"

"We're on it," Bartlett said. "Let us know when you're safe."

Grant ended the call and braced himself.

"Tell me what you saw."

"Your door wasn't latched. Unless you're in the habit of leaving it open—"

"You know I'm not. Take me back. I'm not running away."

He headed toward the expressway. "Ramón knows you overheard him in the parking garage and sent his thugs after you. My guess is, this was his second attempt to take you out. Maybe, if we're lucky, those two guys will be captured, but people like Ramón can always hire more manpower. If you hang around, they'll find you."

"That's my home. I need to know—"

"There's nothing in that apartment more important than your life."

She slumped on the seat. She looked exhausted. Injured, wrung out.

"I need some things." She sounded dejected, defeated. He hated that. "Clothes, a toothbrush. My computer."

"We can stop on the way. Let's just put some miles between us and them."

He'd expected her to argue, but she didn't seem to have it in her. "Fine." A few moments later, she said, "You're probably right."

Huh. He was pretty sure she'd never given him that much credit before. Not aloud, anyway.

They were heading north on I-93, the Boston skyline fading in the rearview mirror, when she spoke again. "Thank you for... If you hadn't been with me, I don't want to think about what could have happened."

His hand itched to cross the console between them and grip hers. Something else she'd probably slug him for.

"Just doing my job, ma'am."

A quick peek in her direction showed her smile. "You're pretty good at it." Her voice was fading, and she yawned. "You should be a bodyguard or something." Her eyes closed.

A joke? Had she told a joke? That was new.

The blanket he'd given her earlier was lying on the floorboard. He grabbed a corner of it and tugged it over her.

She pulled it to her shoulders and curled up in the seat. Her breathing evened out within seconds.

Gaze flicking from the road to the rearview mirror, Grant kept watch for more thugs. He hadn't been followed—he was sure of it.

But if their offices had been watched—or maybe even the street in front of Summer's house—there was a chance Ramón knew the make and model of Grant's truck. And his license plate number.

He wouldn't let his guard down until they reached Coventry.

And not even then.

Grant would have carried Summer into Jon's condo if she hadn't awakened the instant he put the truck in park. She'd slept the entire drive.

"You all right?" he asked.

She stretched and yawned. "I could use an aspirin, but otherwise, yeah."

"You sure?"

Rather than answer, she opened the truck door and climbed out.

Jon must've been watching for them because he hurried down the porch steps. He slid his arm around Summer's waist and walked her inside.

Sure, she let Jon help her.

If Grant had tried that, she'd have elbowed him in the ribs.

Once the cousins were safely inside, Grant backed out again, wove among the narrow roads of the condominium development, and parked on the far side of the clubhouse. This far north in mountain country, pickup trucks were a dime a dozen. It should blend in there.

He jogged back to Jon's place and found the door locked. He knocked, and his friend pulled it open. "You disappeared."

"Hid the truck. Just in case."

Jon's eyes narrowed. "Explain."

"I could use some water—and food." It'd been a two-hour drive from Boston. He'd planned to stop along the way to grab dinner or at least a snack, not to mention the things they would need, but he hadn't had the heart to wake her up. His stomach had been growling so loudly in the truck that he was surprised the noise hadn't woken her.

Jon led the way through his sparse living room into the kitchen, grabbed a cup from a cabinet, and handed it to him, nodding to the fridge. "Help yourself."

After the ice clinked, Grant said, "She's resting?"

"I gave her two Tylenol and sent her to bed." He disappeared around a corner.

"She hasn't eaten either," Grant called.

Jon returned with a sleeve of crackers and a jar of peanut butter, which he tossed on the peninsula separating the kitchen from the eating area. "I offered. She said she wasn't hungry." He handed over a butter knife. "There. You have food and drink. Now talk."

"Gosh, you really know how to make a guy feel welcome." Grant took his time spreading peanut butter on a couple of crackers and eating them.

Jon blew out a loud breath.

Grant chased the crackers with a gulp of water. "I took her to her place to grab some clothes. Her door wasn't latched. I got her out of there."

"That much I know. Bartlett said the police didn't find anybody or anything indicating someone had broken in. They left it at that, but we have a team there looking for evidence."

"What have they found?"

"No prints that don't match hers yet. If they find something, they'll pass the information along to Golinski."

"But you don't think they will," Grant guessed.

"The intruders must've worn gloves. Maybe someone left a hair or something, but we don't have the resources to do DNA testing, and even if we hired a lab, it takes weeks, sometimes months."

"It's a dead end."

"'Fraid so. The truck?"

"I was worried someone saw us get into it, either at the office or at her place. I made sure nobody followed us, but better safe than sorry." Grant ate a few more crackers with peanut butter, contemplating ordering a pizza. "How'd she seem to you? She was hurting earlier."

"You should have taken her to the hospital." Jon looked none too happy that he hadn't.

"She didn't want to go. At some point, we have to respect people's wishes. Even those of pigheaded coworkers—and cousins."

Jon grunted, the only acknowledgment that Grant was right.

He was the best friend Grant had ever had, but this angry, glowering man didn't seem exactly happy to see him. He sipped his water, trying to figure out what Jon's problem was.

"Why are you here, Grant?"

He set the glass down a little too hard, the sound echoing off the bare walls. "Would you have had me leave her alone?"

"Not that I would've preferred it, but she's capable."

"She's injured. And she's my partner."

"You've delivered her," Jon said. "We can get you a new partner. I guess my question is, why are you *still* here?"

Grant had thought Jon would appreciate that he'd gone out of his way to take care of Summer.

"You want me to leave?"

Jon gave him a hard look. "You tell me."

Huh? "What are we talking about?"

Jon raised his eyebrows but said nothing.

Grant wasn't about to fill that silence. Let Jon think what he wanted. He gulped the rest of his water, slammed the cup down, and headed for the door. "I'll find a hotel. Tell Summer I'll be back in the morning."

"You don't have to do that." Jon followed, his voice low.

Grant turned in the middle of the living room. He was beyond frustrated, though some of that was probably due to his still grumbling stomach. He took a breath to keep from saying anything stupid. "Love what you've done with the place." He looked pointedly at the one couch, which had to be two decades older than the condo, and the cheap stand supporting the TV.

The dining area had no table or chairs, just boxes stacked in the corner beside the sliding glass door. Aside from the sofa, the only seats were cheap barstools in the kitchen.

"It's temporary. I didn't see any point in froufrouing it all up, though Denise..." Jon shook his head, and Grant figured Jon's girlfriend would have happily decorated the condo for him. "I have everything I need."

"How temporary?"

"That's between me and Denise. This"—he pointed at Grant, then himself—"is between you and me."

"I don't know what *this* is." Grant imitated Jon's motion. "Are you accusing me of something?"

"Not an accusation, dude."

Jon said nothing else, but his earlier question hung in the air. "I wanted to make sure she got here safely."

"She's asleep upstairs." Jon nodded toward the staircase. "Do you not think I'm capable of protecting her?"

Fine. He saw what his friend meant. "She's my partner."

Jon didn't respond.

"What do you want me to say?"

"It's just you and me, so the truth might be a good idea." Jon crossed his arms and gave Grant that intent, brows lowered, eyes glaring look. "She's my cousin, but so there's no confusion, for the sake of this conversation, you should think of her as my sister."

"Are you trying to intimidate me? Because you and I have known each other a long time. I think we're a little old to settle our differences with a fistfight, don't you?"

Jon's lips almost tipped up in a smile, but not quite. "All I'm saying is, sisters trump friends. What's going on?"

"Absolutely nothing."

Jon and Grant had been not just friends but brothers-in-arms for many years. The last thing he wanted was for Summer to come between them.

But she was there now, hovering in the space where nothing but friendship used to live. Grant could only make it worse by lying.

So he said, "It's possible... You can't be shocked that I find her attractive."

Based on the glare Jon sent his way, Grant figured that hadn't been the best way to start. He resisted the urge to take a step back, not that it would help. Jon wasn't asking for much, right? Just honesty. Just for Grant to bare his soul, lay his heart out there, expose it so it would be easier to crush. Jon wasn't the one who'd do the crushing, though.

"If attraction is all you feel for her," Jon said, "then you'd best move along."

"You know me better than that."

Again, Jon said nothing.

"It's possible I have feelings for her."

"Possible?"

He managed not to growl. "Fine." He kept his voice low in case she could hear. "I have feelings for her." And had for much longer than he was about to admit. Nothing like a little unrequited love to make a guy feel good about himself.

Grant wasn't sure what reaction he'd expected, but the slow smile that spread across his best friend's face surprised him. "Was that so hard? Took you long enough to admit it."

They'd been standing there for all of two minutes.

"Let's not pretend this is some new and shocking revelation," Jon said. "It's *possible* you've had feelings for her for a long time."

How long had he known? Did Summer know?

Jon chuckled. "Don't worry, she's clueless. And I would never betray you. Just understand—she'll always be my priority."

"So you'd be okay with it? If I could ever convince her...?"

Summer had no interest in dating, and even if she did, there was no reason to believe she would want to date him. She'd never even indicated she liked him all that much, though he had felt a twinge of hope when she'd chosen him for her partner.

"If anybody can do it," Jon said, "you can."

It was stupid the way Grant's heart thumped at the words. Nobody knew Summer like Jon did. Maybe he was right. Maybe Grant could open his heart to her and not get it stomped, smashed into a ball, and shoved back in his face.

Jon clasped Grant on the shoulder, giving it a squeeze before he let his arm drop. "To be honest, I've actually been... It feels weird to admit, but I've been praying about it. I think you two would be great together."

Praying? Jon was new to the faith that had meant so much to Grant over the years. Since Jon had become a Christian, Summer had mentioned attending a new church in the city. She didn't discuss deep things with him, but if she was a believer, then that meant the last obstacle to their being together was gone.

Well, except that she could barely stand him. That obstacle was still firmly in place.

"Any words of advice?"

Jon laughed, though he kept the sound low. "Tread lightly. She spooks easily. Normally, knowing what I know, I wouldn't want you staying under the same roof with her. But I figure you want to stay close." He nodded to the sofa. "You'll sleep there."

"Fair enough."

"And if she does start to return your feelings...well, all the more reason for you to tread lightly. I've always liked you. I'd hate to have to kill you."

Grant laughed at that. Jon defending her honor.

She'd *love* that.

"Do you have a plan?" Jon asked.

"We have to prove Ramón is who she thinks he is and find some way to put him behind bars. Whether he recognized her from the kidnapping or just believes she overheard his conversation today, she's made herself a target. We're going to have to take him down before he gets to her."

Jon was nodding, his obvious amusement fading to concern. "The thing is, I'm flying out tomorrow. Denise has to go on a press junket."

"This is a word you use now? Junket?"

Jon ignored him. "There's security, of course, but I don't like the idea of her traveling without me, just in case, you know?"

Grant figured it wasn't easy for Jon to let her go anywhere by herself, especially after she'd been abducted by a serial killer just a few months before.

"You know I would never leave Lake unprotected," Jon said, "but you're here. I can't think of anyone I'd trust with her safety more than you. And let's face it, my cousin is no damsel in distress. She can hold her own. But I'll come back if you need me."

"The whole team can be up here in two hours if we need help," Grant said. "The problem is whether Summer will be willing to call them."

Jon's eyebrows lifted. "You call her Summer?" Even Jon usually called her Lake.

"Not to her face, not on purpose, anyway." It was a little

ridiculous, having to refer to her by her last name. "In my head, she's always been Summer."

Jon said nothing for a long time, just watched him through slitted eyelids. Grant wasn't going to apologize for using the first name of the woman he loved. Now that Jon knew the truth, he didn't need to explain himself.

"Okay," Jon said. "I have to wrap up a case tomorrow morning, so I'll be out of here around nine, and then I'm headed to the airport. But I could fly out Tuesday."

"I don't even know what our next steps should be. If I start to think Ramón is closing in and we need your help, you'll be the first to know."

"See that I am."

The conversation made Grant feel oddly lighter. Carrying a torch for his best friend's cousin hadn't been easy, but now Jon knew—and was supportive. That was a good start. Grant just needed to get Summer on board.

But first, he needed to figure out a way to bring down Ramón, and considering he knew almost nothing about the man, that wasn't going to be an easy task.

CHAPTER FIVE

———————

S ummer woke up in the guest room at Jon's house to the sound of light rapping on the door.

"Are you awake?" She might've expected Jon to annoy her first thing in the morning, but what was Grant doing here?

"I am now."

Through the door, he said, "I was beginning to worry."

She glanced at the time on her phone and gasped. It was almost ten o'clock. She hadn't slept so late in years.

Not that she'd slept soundly. The memories of the day before and those from seven years past had collided to bring all new nightmares. Terror in technicolor.

Grant was still standing outside. He was silent, but she could sense his presence. "I'll be down soon."

"I'm leaving a few things for you."

She waited until his footsteps retreated before climbing out of bed.

Wow. Everything hurt.

She opened the door to find a plate on the carpet outside her room. On it were two pieces of buttered toast beside two round orange pills. A bottle of water was perched against the wall, and next to that, a plastic shopping bag.

She hooked the bag on her uninjured wrist, snatched the plate with the same hand, and gripped the bottle in the other, only registering her extreme hunger when she caught the scent of the toast. She closed the door with her foot, set the plate on the nightstand, and dropped the bag and water bottle on the bed.

She was curious about what was in the bag, but first, she took a bite of the toast.

Exactly what she needed.

Weird that it'd been Grant to deliver it, though. Where was Jon?

While she scarfed down the food, she dug through the bag.

Toothbrush, toothpaste, hairbrush, and deodorant.

Also, a package of black socks, two packages of underwear—in different sizes—and two tunic-style sweaters. There was also a pair of black leggings, extra long.

The clothes weren't fancy, but they should work.

After swallowing the pills, she took a long shower, cataloging her injuries. The right wrist hurt, but she could move it. The brace Grant had found helped a lot. Her shin was bruised and ached when she put weight on that leg. Her stomach hurt, but she was thankful the thug hadn't hit her ribs or it would be much worse. Her head ached, no shock with the two goose eggs that smarted to touch. She was surprised there were no bruises on her face. Somehow, it had managed to escape the carnage.

She brushed out her wet hair and left it to dry naturally, then chose the longer of the two sweaters. It was blue, fitted at the waist and flared out, the hem hitting her upper thighs.

She regarded her image in the mirror. Whoever'd gone to the store had done a decent job. The clothes fit well enough. She'd need to find some jeans and tops, but this would do for now. It wasn't her typical black-on-black business attire, but she needed a little color in her life. There were a few things about her job that she did not like. One of them was the boring clothing.

Not that she would ever admit it to anybody, but when she'd been modeling, she'd fallen in love with the fashions. High-dollar fabrics and high-class styles, some of which were so outrageous no woman in her right mind would wear them in real life. But most of the clothes had been reasonable—sweaters and blouses and tank tops, jeans and slacks and skirts. Pumps and boots and strappy sandals.

Summer had never been a girly girl, but she was still a girl. She cared about clothes, shoes, purses. She liked to look good. She liked to feel good about how she looked.

After sliding on her black sneakers, she headed downstairs and through the small living room to the kitchen. She'd come to Jon's condo the weekend he'd moved in. It hadn't changed much. Looked like the boxes they'd stacked in the corner of the dining room hadn't been touched.

Grant was seated at the bar, tapping away on his laptop. At least he had his. He turned and then stood when she walked in. "How do you feel?"

"Better. Thanks."

"Are you still hungry?" he asked. "Two pieces of toast probably isn't enough after skipping dinner."

"Where's Jon?"

"He had work this morning." Grant glanced at the time on his phone. "His flight leaves—"

"Flight?"

"He didn't tell you? He's going to California today. Denise has some press tour. He's going with her."

Hurt and irritation flashed, and she turned away from Grant before he could read them on her face.

"If you ask him to stay, I'm sure he will." Grant's voice sounded calm and logical, which didn't help.

She rounded the peninsula to the coffee maker and poured herself a cup before turning to him, lifting the pot in a silent question.

"I've had plenty."

She added some sugar and sipped. It was palatable, which told her Grant had made it. Jon's was almost too strong to drink.

"Did you talk to Bartlett? How's my apartment?"

"Bartlett said it didn't look like anybody had been there. Obviously, you'll need to check your belongings, but they didn't trash the place—or empty it."

She was glad to hear that. She didn't have much, but her things were hers. She'd worked hard for everything she owned.

Would she ever be able to go home again? Would she ever feel safe there again?

"We think they were waiting to ambush you," Grant said. "We assume they saw the cops pull up and got out of there."

"Or you were wrong and they weren't there."

"Do you generally leave your door unlatched?"

She didn't bother to answer the stupid question. Grant had been right, of course. Would she have noticed? Or would she have gone inside, then been killed or kidnapped?

Funny how death wasn't her biggest fear.

"Does it bother you that Jon isn't here?" Grant was never one to let something go.

"I'm fine." She sounded petulant. She opened the refrigerator, then shut it again. She wasn't hungry, just needed something to do with her hands. An excuse not to look at Grant. She stepped into the pantry and surveyed the options. Cereal. Bread. Crackers. Cans of soup. A gourmet, Jon wasn't. "It's just that I thought he'd want to stay and help me put Ramón behind bars." Finding nothing interesting, she returned to the kitchen.

"But I guess Denise..." How was she supposed to finish that sentence? Obviously, Denise was more important to Jon than Summer was. He was in love with Denise. Like, head-over-heels, life-altering, world-shattering love.

Summer was just his cousin.

It was only that...that Jon was her closest friend. The only person in the world she knew, hands down, she could always count on.

Had that changed? Would Jon join the long list of people in her life who'd let her down?

"I think he believes Denise needs him more than you do," Grant said. "Not that you don't need him, but I'm here. So I can—"

"It's fine." She sipped the coffee again.

"And their relationship is brand new."

"I said, it's fine. He's just like his father. If Aunt Sally needed Uncle Marshall, he'd drop everything to be there for her."

"That's a good thing, right? It's the wise man who appreciates his woman."

What did Grant know about that? He wasn't dating anybody, was he?

Fresh irritation bubbled up from Summer's middle. She knew what it was, but there was no reason for her to feel jealous. What did she care who Grant dated?

"The clothes seem to fit."

She took in his blue jeans and maroon sweater, which still had fold marks, much like the tunic she wore. "You bought them?"

"This morning, before Jon left. I needed to pick some things up myself."

"Let me know what I owe you." Not that there'd be any way to pay him back for the rest of this. Dropping everything, taking time off his job, all to make sure she was safe. "When are you returning to the city?"

"When you do."

"You don't have to hide out here with me."

"We went over this last night."

Right. The whole *I'm your partner* thing. He felt responsible for her.

"When Jon gets back, he can take over. Shouldn't be too long."

"Whether Jon's here or not," Grant said, "I'm not leaving you alone. Can we move on from that, please?"

She was trying to give him an out, but he seemed annoyed. Did he *want* to stay with her?

Why?

Rather than try to figure it out, she picked up her cell. Jon might not be there, but she still needed something from him. The phone had barely rung before he answered.

"How you feeling?"

His voice soothed her rough edges. She had no right to be angry with him. He had a life. It wasn't his fault that she didn't. "I hear you're headed to LA."

"Grant's going to stay with you. Is that all right? I can cancel—"

"I don't need another babysitter."

Grant looked up from his laptop, hurt crossing his features.

She tried to lift her lips into a smile, though she was feeling anything but happy. "He's going to help me."

At that, Grant returned his focus to the screen.

"I wanted to ask you," she continued, "do you still have the photos you took in Mexico?"

Grant straightened, eyebrows hiking.

On the phone, Jon said, "Yeah." The word was drawn out, uncertain.

Summer set the phone down and put it on speaker. "Grant's listening. Can I look through them?"

"Why?"

"In the building where we were held, there was some kind of a carving. It was stone and looked as if it'd been chiseled off a larger rock. It was leaning against a huge crate. We were told to stay away from it, that if we damaged it, we'd be in trouble. I thought maybe you got a photo of it."

"Not that I recall," Jon said.

Grant said, "I don't remember that."

"Maybe it was taken out before you got there. I don't remember. They were always moving boxes in and out. It doesn't matter, though. Maybe there'll be something else, something we can use to link yesterday's events to the kidnapping. Or just spark a memory."

Jon said nothing.

Grant stared at the phone.

"What?" she asked, glaring at the top of Grant's head.

Jon was the one who spoke. "Some of those photos are pretty graphic."

"I can handle it. I lived it, remember?"

"It would be perfectly normal if you *couldn't* handle it," Grant said. "It was traumatic. Do you really want to—?"

"Obviously, yes, since I asked." To the phone, she said, "I need to do this."

"What do you think, Grant?" Jon asked. "You remember the photos."

Grant looked from the phone to her and back. "I think she's on a mission. If there's any chance those photos will help us bring down Ramón, it'll be worth it."

"Okay." Jon exhaled loudly. "They're on an SD card somewhere."

"Here, though?" she clarified. "Not back in Boston?" Jon

had left most of his things in a storage unit in the city. He'd only brought up what would fit in the backs of the cars and pickups of the friends who'd helped him move.

"It should be in the office."

"We could just look around."

"Or you could be patient," Jon said. "When I remember where it is, I'll get back to you." With that, he ended the call.

She looked up from the phone. "Well, that was friendly."

Grant smiled. "You know your cousin. He'll remember where the card is and give us detailed instructions on how to find it. Meanwhile, we wait."

Waiting. Her least favorite activity.

CHAPTER SIX

Quiet settled between them, and Grant didn't bother to try to fill it. There were people who couldn't stand long silences, but Grant wasn't one of them, and Summer wasn't either. He didn't mind that they could be alone together without feeling the need to fill every second with conversation.

They were comfortable together.

Maybe, eventually, Summer would realize that meant something. Maybe, eventually, she'd let her guard down in his presence, feel free to be herself. Though, after seven years of acquaintance—Grant couldn't even call it friendship—he was starting to lose hope.

On the other hand, this trip to New Hampshire, their teaming up to bring down Ramón, might be the catalyst their relationship needed.

Or it could be the end of his dreams. Both seemed equally plausible.

Summer scrolled through her phone.

"Anything interesting?" he asked.

"Researching Ramón. According to this, he's a rancher and entrepreneur."

"Entrepreneur. That's pretty vague."

"Right?"

He settled beside her with his laptop. "Where's his ranch?"

She clicked the map and zoomed out so he could get context. According to Google, Ramón owned a large spread in Guanajuato, north of Mexico City.

His property was nowhere near where Summer and the other models had been when they were kidnapped, nor where they'd been found and rescued. But that didn't mean anything. Ramón wouldn't want his criminal enterprise anywhere near his legitimate one.

"That's not the state where his sister is governor," Grant said.

"Maybe they aren't that close."

It'd been two hours since Summer'd eaten the toast. "You getting hungry?"

"Yeah." She started to push to her feet, wincing as she did.

"I'll find something."

She looked about to argue, but Grant headed for the kitchen and started to forage for food. After checking out the fridge, he called from the kitchen-side of the peninsula, "Soup and sandwiches or macaroni and cheese?"

"What kind of soup?"

He returned to the pantry and called, "We have...New England clam chowder."

"Canned?" Summer said. "No thanks."

"Tomato, chicken and noodle. Let's see..." He spun the other cans to read them. "Meat and potatoes. Chicken tortilla."

"That sounds good to me."

"On it."

Grant warmed two cans of soup, choosing the meat-and-potato option for himself, while he assembled sandwiches. He and Summer had known each other long enough that he could guess what she liked, so he fixed her turkey and provolone with mustard, lettuce, and sliced tomatoes. He made himself a ham-and-cheese sandwich. If Jon had owned a coffee table, they could eat in front of the fire. But the only option was the kitchen counter.

"It's a feast." Summer smiled at him as she slid onto a barstool, and his heart did that same stupid flip it did every time she let her pleasure show.

Would he ever get accustomed to her beauty?

Would he ever get over the joy he felt when he made her smile?

Unless she changed how she felt about him, he hoped so. This unrequited love stuff sucked.

Maybe his feelings would someday be...requited. Was that a thing?

She bit into her sandwich. After she swallowed, she said, "This is perfect. How did you know?"

"I'm observant."

She watched him for a few moments, taking a spoonful of her soup.

Did she guess his feelings? Jon had, so Grant wasn't hiding them as well as he thought. Did Grant mind if she guessed? At this point, what was the worst that could happen?

She could tell him she didn't want anything to do with him and send him away. The first part of that he could live with. It would hurt. It would be agonizing, but it wouldn't be all that different from what he believed her feelings toward him to be now—indifference.

But the second part—her sending him away? That, he couldn't live with. Somebody needed to have her back, and Jon was too busy with his new job and too focused on his new girl-friend to do it. Grant needed to stay nearby to make sure Summer was safe whether she ever returned his feelings or not.

They ate in relative silence until her phone rang. She fished it from her pocket and answered, putting it on speakerphone. "I'm here with Grant," she said.

"I think I remember where it is," Jon said. "Go to the office..." He described where he thought the SD card was, and Grant and Summer went upstairs, listening to his instructions.

The room was designed to be the third bedroom in the condo, though it held no bed. Jon had furnished it with a huge desk that had two oversize monitors on it, two file cabinets, and a beige love seat that matched the nineties-era couch in the living room. One wall was covered with butcher paper, on which Jon had written notes about his current case. Now that he was no longer working for the protection agency, he was devoting himself full time to his new work as a private investigator. The space was, as Grant had expected, tidy and utilitarian.

At Jon's instruction, he crouched down in front of one of the file cabinets and pulled open the lowest drawer. There were no vertical files in this one, just a stack of thick manila envelopes.

Wincing, Summer started to crouch down beside him, but Grant waved her off. She settled into the chair behind the desk.

He shifted the envelopes out of the way and located the box. He pulled it out, stood, and set it on the desk.

When he opened it, Summer leaned forward to see.

"We've got the box," Grant said.

"In the back, there's a white envelope."

Grant pulled it out and peeked inside. Then, he shook the contents onto his hand.

He held the SD card up for her to see and aimed his words at her phone. "Found it."

"I have a slot in the desktop. You two might as well work in there so you can use the big screens. Let me know if you find anything useful."

"You got it, boss."

Summer smirked as she disconnected the call. "Boss? Funny how you never call me that."

He laughed. Summer might've been part owner of the security firm, but only because she'd accumulated more cash than her cousin and Bartlett, thanks to her modeling career. In terms of experience, she was years behind most of them.

He wasn't dumb enough to say any of that. "I can call you boss, if you want. Or would you prefer 'your highness' or maybe, 'most extreme annoying one'?"

The sound that came out of her mouth was almost a giggle. Except this was Summer, and she definitely wasn't a giggler. "I dare you to call me that."

"Not to your face. I'm not an idiot."

She shook her head. "Well, slide it in there. Let's see what we find."

His amusement faded. He knew what was on this card, and the images weren't exactly heartwarming. Lots of men had died that day. They were kidnappers and guards, but still, human beings. Their bodies hadn't been cleared when Jon took his photos, nor had that of the only victim who'd died, Tiffany Hilliard.

He didn't want to see her body covered in blood.

He didn't want to think about everything that had led up to that moment. If he'd done things differently, she might have survived.

"Why don't I go through them and pick out the ones you might want to look at."

Summer crossed her arms. "Why?"

"Your cousin records everything. Not because he's got some weird desire to see the images but because he likes to remember exactly what happened. He likes to figure out if something could've been done differently and if so, how. It's research for him. What are we looking for exactly?"

"I'll know when I see it. Which means I have to see everything."

There was no point in arguing with her. He clicked to open the images and enlarged the first one. It was a picture of the overall site, which Jon had taken before the ambush. A couple of buildings about as stable as a house of cards were surrounded by tents and tumbledown shacks with tin roofs. The Hilton, it wasn't. The whole thing was surrounded by short, scrubby evergreen trees. It had been near sunset, though in the photo they couldn't see the sun dipping behind the hills. According to the locals, some of the "ranch hands"—who were actually guards—started drinking at siesta and kept right on past dinner. Through the binoculars, Grant, Jon, and the rest of the team had witnessed enough to know the locals hadn't steered them wrong. They'd waited on a nearby hillside until the camp quieted down.

Grant could still picture the fury on Jon's face when he'd looked at that jumble of makeshift structures.

He'd understood Jon's rage, knowing two of his cousins were being held there. Grant hadn't felt anything but the nervous anticipation he always experienced before a mission. That was before he'd known any of the girls they were going to rescue. Before he'd met Summer.

Jon had been different that day. Normally the consummate professional, he'd been more intense, more nervous, than Grant had ever seen him. He'd hardly spoken except to bark commands since he'd gotten the call from Summer.

"Which building?" she asked, her voice nearly a whisper.

Grant tapped the image of one of the permanent structures, where Summer and her friends had been held.

After a minute, she said, "Okay. Go on."

Grant clicked to the next photo.

Suddenly, the scene was very different. It was dark now, but

Jon had a bright flash and a good camera. This photo had been taken from the edge of the village. In it, Grant could make out the outlines of four bodies on the ground.

"This was taken immediately before we started the cleanup effort," Grant said. "Jon must've bolted to the edge of the clearing to get the wide shot."

"Is that part of his job? To catalog what happened?"

"Higher-ups liked images, when there was time. Jon always took it further than anybody expected. He got in trouble a couple of times for dawdling. The brass worried that he was taking unnecessary risks, but it seemed important to Jon to know exactly what happened. It was one of the things that made him such a great commander. He was always looking for ways to improve."

Summer nodded toward the screen, and Grant clicked to the next one. "This was taken inside one of the structures."

"What are those?" she asked, leaning closer. It was hard to make out what they were seeing in the darkness, but he remembered.

"Bedrolls and personal items. Their quarters."

He clicked to the next, a tin-roofed shanty filled with munitions. The gang had been well-outfitted. If they'd had any inkling Jon's team was coming, Grant and his friends wouldn't have stood a chance. Fortunately, Bartlett had known just the right palms to grease in the nearest village to get the information they needed to rescue the captives without incurring any casualties. The local police had been a great source of information. As Bartlett had assumed, they had known all about Ramón's operation. They were dirty as the criminals, so they could be bought— by both sides, apparently. That was what made Señora Hidalgo special. Assuming she didn't know about her brother's illegal activities, she was one of the few political figures trying to fight crime.

Grant clicked to the next photo, and the next. More living quarters. Then they came to an image of one of the men who'd been shot and killed. Grant glanced at Summer, whose lips were flattened in a grim line.

If she recognized the man, she didn't show it.

Grant clicked quickly to the next, which was similar enough that he didn't stop to look.

How many of the captors had been killed that day? Seven or eight, he thought.

What did it say about him that he couldn't remember? As if those lives hadn't mattered?

The next photograph was of the kidnappers who'd been captured. Three guys standing shoulder to shoulder, their hands bound behind their backs. At their feet and behind them, Grant was attaching leg irons, preparing them to be returned to the US for trial. He was about to click away when Summer said, "Wait."

She leaned closer to the computer screen and stared at the men's faces.

Grant did the same, studying each one. It took him a second to see what she was seeing. "Do you think that's him?"

"It's both of them. She tapped the taller one, who was scowling at the camera. Long, black hair, heavily lidded eyes, and a beard that covered the bottom half of his face. The one next to him was shorter and stockier and had a stupid-looking beard with no mustache.

It could be them. But he hadn't gotten as good a look as Summer had.

She leaned back. "That's the proof we need that Vasco Ramón was the mastermind behind the kidnapping."

He wagged his head back and forth. "I think maybe *proof* is the wrong word. It's definitely an indicator."

She stood, her chair rolling back, and glared at him. "The

men who attacked me yesterday were two of our captors seven years ago."

"I'm just saying that a defense attorney could easily argue that those two aren't associated with Ramón at all, or if we can prove a connection, that they met him after."

"You really think that?"

"Do *I* think that's what happened? No. I'm saying it's possible, and if there's another possibility, then it's not proof. But do I think we're on the right track? No question about it." He tapped the screen. "I'm convinced. Now we just need enough evidence to convince the authorities."

"I see what you mean. Send me a copy."

He forwarded the image to Summer's email address and his own, then clicked through another few photographs—the insides of some of the tents, the grounds. And then Summer said, "Stop."

This image had been taken from within the second permanent structure. The rough walls were barely discernible in the dim light. Wooden crates were stacked against the far wall.

Still on her feet, she leaned closer to the screen. "Can you enlarge it?"

He did, but the crates had no markings on them. Which was strange. Shouldn't they be stamped with some kind of indication to let people know what was within?

"Those are like the crates that were in the building where we were held." She reached for the mouse.

He angled to give her space. As she bent closer, he resisted the urge to inhale her unique scent. She'd used Jon's shampoo, not her normal coconut-scented one—and what did it say about him that he noticed?—but the essence of Summer lingered.

She shifted the image until she found something propped against one of the crates. It was a slab of stone, a man's face carved in relief, though in the dimness, it was hard to make out details.

"That was in the building with us the first few days we were there. Or one like it, anyway."

"What is it?"

"Something very old, I'd guess. And valuable."

Here was another link between Summer's kidnapper and Vasco Ramón.

He faced Summer, who held his eye contact. Finally, after seven long years, they'd identified the mastermind behind her kidnapping.

The man responsible for Tiffany Hilliard's death.

The memory of that moment, of that poor girl dying...

Grant wanted to take this guy down as much as Summer did. Maybe, after seven years, he'd finally be able to find redemption for his mistake, which had cost that young woman her life.

CHAPTER SEVEN

S ummer's heart raced.

She'd believed Ramón was involved in her kidnapping, but to see the two thugs who'd attacked her and now another relic like the one she'd witnessed being handed to the stranger the day before...

She was going to make her kidnapper pay. Finally. Maybe, once she did, Misty would be able to find some peace. To all the world, Summer's little sister was a successful attorney who had it all together, but Summer knew the truth. The nineteen-year-old who'd accompanied Summer and the rest of the models to Mexico that spring had not come back the same. Misty had gone on that trip cheerful and optimistic—amazing qualities, considering their past. She'd returned reserved, withdrawn, nervous. After counseling and therapy, she'd become driven, as if every bad guy she put behind bars was in some way responsible for what had happened to them in Mexico.

No matter how many criminals she prosecuted, Misty never found peace.

But maybe...maybe now she could. Maybe, if Summer and

Grant took Ramón down, Misty could relax and be like she used to be, more carefree.

Summer would do anything in her power to make that happen.

And make Ramón pay for what he'd done.

"We have what we need." Grant copied the photo and pasted it into an email. "Let's leave it at—"

"We need to look at them all."

He gave her a smirk, a look she'd come to recognize over the years that meant he thought she was being stubborn. Well, she *was* stubborn—and she wouldn't apologize for it. "Click on."

He did, saying nothing.

The next few photographs showed more crates, more munitions.

And then she saw a familiar room.

As soon as the image filled the screen, memories covered her like the hood they'd cinched over her head when they took her out of the room, dark and stifling. Suddenly, she could feel the grit of dirt on the rough wooden floor, hear women crying nearby, men laughing outside. She could smell the unwashed bodies, urine, excrement. Fear.

Her sister's arm pressed against her side, unwilling to lose contact for even a moment. Other girls stayed close, all vulnerable, all terrified. Silently weeping because any noises summoned the guards.

Angry, masked men at the door, breathing threats.

"Keep those girls quiet!"

"Shut that one up!"

The commands, spoken in heavily accented English, were always directed at Summer, as if she were in charge. She hadn't been the oldest, nor the strongest, nor the smartest, but somehow, she'd become the leader.

She could still see the terror in the eyes of her friends, all looking at her as if she could rescue them. She hadn't had any idea what to do. She'd been just as afraid, terrified for her sister. She'd gotten Misty into this. She had to find a way to get her out.

When Tiffany had panicked and tried to run, a guard had come in and kicked her in the head.

The rest had shrieked and scrambled behind Summer as if she could protect them. She'd left them cowering in the corner and walked across the room, glaring at the cruel guard, to gather poor Tiffany in her arms.

Tiffany, the youngest at seventeen.

A terrified teenager who only wanted to go home.

Summer had lifted her, dragged her away from the glowering guard, and laid her among the other girls. She'd wanted to shout at the man, to demand he leave them be.

But she hadn't been stupid. Helpless, scared, and vulnerable, but never stupid.

Tiffany eventually woke up. In the light that shone through the slats of the poorly constructed building the following day, they could see the bruise that darkened her temple. She hadn't been the same after that. Not just quiet but slow and confused. She'd forgotten the kidnapping entirely.

"Where are we?"

"When do we get to go home?"

"Can I call my mom?"

They softened the truth for her, promising they'd go home soon. She'd see her mother and father again eventually. The girl had believed them every time. And then, moments later, the questions would begin again.

Summer took care of her, but all she could think was...what if it had been Misty?

What if Misty were kicked? Or raped? Or killed?

She'd spent her life protecting her little sister. She'd wrangled and begged until Misty had been invited to join the photo-shoot, not wanting to leave her alone in New York.

Summer couldn't let anything happen to her now.

She couldn't let anything happen to any of them.

"Hey, hey." The man's voice made her jump.

She blinked, tried to bring the present into focus. She wasn't in a shack in Mexico. The man wasn't a guard.

Grant clicked a button, and the photograph disappeared. He stood and wrapped an arm around her waist and urged her away from the computer. Her legs hit something soft, and she dropped back, landing on the loveseat.

Grant sat beside her and pulled her into his arms. "It's okay. You're safe here."

She knew that. She did. Yet she couldn't seem to get her bearings. She settled in, somehow curling against Grant's chest. His arms encircled her, wrapping her in warmth and safety.

"I'm not going to let anything happen to you."

It all felt so real, so raw. They could have died. They could have all died, and she couldn't have done anything to stop it. Her total lack of control was offensive. Horrifying.

"You're safe here," Grant said again. "In Jon's office, in New Hampshire. Nobody knows where you are."

But was Misty safe?

"Your sister's not in danger," Grant said.

Had he read her mind? Or had she spoken out loud?

"The other girls are safe now. Summer, you're safe here." He rubbed her shoulders, her back, warming her up.

Which was strange, not because she wasn't cold but because she was.

What was happening?

Slowly, slowly, the memories faded. She wasn't in Mexico. Her sister was alive and well, a prosecutor in Boston. The kidnappers had never known Summer and Misty were sisters.

Even if Ramón realized who Summer was, he wouldn't connect her with Misty, who'd always only been known by her first name, not wanting to be pegged as Summer's little sister.

As the memories faded, she inhaled the truth of the moment. She felt safe in Grant's arms. His musky scent replaced that from her memories. His solid chest was comforting.

"Sorry. Sorry." She started to pull away. "I don't know—"

"Don't apologize to me." He held her tighter. "That picture... I wanted to protect you from those memories."

She extricated herself, discomfited by the comfort of his arms. "I don't need to be protected."

He blinked, straightened. Said nothing.

"Seriously. I'm fine." Once on her feet, nausea rolled through her stomach. She waited until the feeling passed. "Let's go through the rest of them."

"There's nothing wrong with being human. Those images disturbed me, and I didn't live through—"

"I'm fine."

He stared at her. Glared might be a better word. Then he stood and walked out.

"I want to look at them." She spoke to his back.

"But you can't. I have the SD card in my pocket." He reached the stairs and started down.

How dare he take it? Who did he think he was?

She wanted to demand he return the card, slide it into Jon's computer, and click through the photos again. But...but the truth was, she couldn't handle any more images today.

What if she saw another one that landed her in Grant's arms? She couldn't believe she'd let him hold her.

How embarrassing.

And yet...how reassuring he'd been.

CHAPTER EIGHT

Grant refused to watch the staircase. Summer would come down when she was ready. He knew her well enough to know that her moment of weakness—of humanity—would embarrass her.

That she'd been vulnerable with him gave him hope. Even if she hadn't done it on purpose, it had to mean something that she'd trusted him enough to let her guard down.

He tried to shake off the memory of her. How well she'd fit in his arms. How his heart had raced, his body responding.

But she hadn't noticed any of that. As much as he'd love to analyze Summer's actions and reactions, try to figure out what they meant, years of doing just that had amounted to exactly nothing.

Summer had allowed him to comfort her, but that didn't mean anything—or so he needed to believe.

No big deal.

Otherwise, she'd freak out and scuttle back into her shell. Or worse, demand he leave.

So he shoved all his feelings back into their little box as he dialed his phone.

The FBI agent's voice was gruff. "Golinski here."

"This is Grant Wright from GBPA. I was with—"

"I know who you are. You have something for me?"

"Have you looked into the kidnapping Lake told you about last night?"

"Got the file here." A chair creaked. "What about it?"

"Tell me your email address. I want to send you two photographs." He'd already emailed the photos to himself, so he typed the agent's email address and forwarded them.

While Grant waited for the emails to go through, Summer descended the stairs. He put the phone on speaker while she sat on the barstool beside him.

After a minute, Golinski said, "The file contains these pictures. What about them?"

"These were taken by my team's commander right after the rescue."

"Jon Donley. He was on the call last night, right?"

"Yes." The agent's memory was impressive. "The first shows some kind of stone relief."

"I see that."

"It might have been taken from the same place as the statue Lake saw handed over last night. An archaeological dig site— Mayan, if what the guy in the parking garage said was true. Which tells us—"

"I'm keeping up, Wright."

Grant sent a wry look at Summer, but she didn't glance away from the phone.

"The next picture? The captives?" the FBI agent prompted.

"Two of them—the tall one with the thick beard and the shorter one with that stupid chin beard—were the ones who attacked Lake yesterday."

Silence. Then, "Huh."

Grant waited.

"You're sure? You recognized them?"

"Lake got a better look than I did, and she's sure."

"Under all that stress, is she reliable?"

Irritation sparking, Summer opened her mouth, but Grant shook his head. "Absolutely. There's no doubt in my mind. Can you figure out their names?"

"They're in the file. I'll find them." Golinski huffed, and his chair squeaked again. "This is good. I'll talk to the higher-ups. You two sit tight."

The call ended.

"Sit tight?" Summer was indignant. "He can't be serious."

Rather than argue, Grant pulled his half-eaten sandwich across the counter. "We might as well finish our lunches."

"How can you eat?" She was still glaring at the phone. "Is he going to call us back?"

Grant shrugged, chewing his bite.

She left the stool and paced. "I'm not going to just sit here and wait for Golinski to call. Assuming he ever will. We need to make a plan."

An idea had been simmering in the back of Grant's mind, one he was tempted to ignore. But wouldn't because…Summer. "I was thinking—"

"We've given them enough information. They should arrest Ramón."

He didn't agree but let it slide. "They probably won't, but—"

"If that's not enough to tie Ramón to the kidnapping…" Summer continued pacing, clearly thinking aloud. "I need to figure out who the stranger was in the parking garage. I wish I'd seen his face. There can't be that many collectors of Mayan antiquities in the area. How can we find him?"

"I have an—"

"Maybe we could call—"

"Summer."

She swiveled halfway across the living room. "I've asked you not to call me that."

"Do you think you could stop talking for two seconds?"

She crossed her arms.

"My brother is a history professor at Bowdoin."

She blinked.

"Maybe he could point us in the direction of somebody who could tell us more about the artifacts."

"Your brother is a history professor?" The incredulity in her voice was insulting.

Was it so shocking that he could be related to somebody smart?

But she followed up with, "I didn't know you had a brother."

"I don't have *a* brother." Her eyebrows lifted, so he clarified. "I have *five*." At least he used to. He still couldn't come to terms with what had happened to Daniel.

"You have *five* brothers? How did I not know that?"

It wasn't as if they sat around chatting about their families. Summer had always been careful to keep their relationship perfectly professional.

She settled onto the barstool beside him, curiosity brightening her gray eyes. "Where are you in the birth order?"

A personal question? Not *very* personal, but it felt like progress. "I'm fourth of six."

"Are you close to them?"

"Sure." He used to be, anyway. When he was young, he'd considered his brothers, at least the ones nearest him in age, his best friends in the world.

"The professor—older or younger?"

"He's the fifth, two years behind me."

"And you think he'll help us?"

"If he can." *Wouldn't he?*

"Let's call him, then. That seems as good a place to start as any."

Now that Grant had suggested it, he didn't have much choice. He and Bryan weren't close, not like when they were kids. That was Grant's fault, of course. The problem was, there was no coming back from some mistakes. Some mistakes were permanent. And some mistakes had lifelong consequences.

But Summer's eyes flickered with hope for the first time since he'd found her in the parking garage the day before. This wouldn't be easy, but he'd walk through fire for this woman.

Worse, he'd risk a conversation with Bryan Wright.

After sending up a silent prayer for help, he dialed Bryan's number, keeping his phone on speaker.

"Grant?" The single syllable sounded worried. "Are you okay?"

"Uh...why wouldn't I be?"

His brother took his time answering, and the long pause made Grant's stomach churn.

"It's just..." Bryan cleared his throat. "Never mind. It's good to hear from you. How've you been?"

"Fine. Listen, I need a favor."

The pause was even longer this time. "Seriously?" The one word held pounds of pent-up annoyance. "I don't hear from you for...what has it been? Two years? Three? You didn't come home for Christmas. You blew off Dad's seventy-fifth birthday party, and now you *need a favor*?"

"I was on a job at Christmas. And the party." Wincing, Grant avoided Summer's eyes. The Christmas job had ended weeks before the holiday. Grant had been on a job when they'd celebrated Dad's birthday, but with all their new hires, he could easily have gotten the time off. He hadn't bothered to ask for it.

Any excuse to avoid facing his brother.

Bryan knew that, which explained the sarcastic, "Sure you were."

Grant still didn't look at Summer, but he could feel her stare boring into his skull. If he'd wanted to impress her, he was failing miserably. He should have made this call outside.

"It's well established that I'm the lousy brother," Grant said. "Unlike you. You're the good one, always quick to help."

There. Bryan wouldn't be able to resist proving him right.

Except he said nothing.

"The favor's not for me," Grant added. "You remember Jon?"

"Of course."

"His cousin is trying to track down somebody who collects Mayan antiquities, and I thought you might be able to help. I know it's not exactly your field of study, but—"

"I could point you in the right direction. We have a Hispanic studies department on campus."

"That'd be great."

"But only if you can tear yourself away from your job for a few hours and drive up here."

Grant risked a glance in Summer's direction. Her eyes narrowed, and her lips turned down at the corners. When he met her gaze, she tipped her head to the side.

Like she was trying to figure him out.

"We really don't have time for a field trip," Grant said.

Summer mouthed, *I don't mind.*

Well, he minded.

"All right, then," Bryan said. "Nice catching up with you."

His phone beeped three times.

Grant looked at the screen to confirm what he already knew. Bryan had hung up on him.

He'd known there was bad blood there, but to flat-out refuse to help him?

No, surely not. Surely Bryan would call right back and apologize for the bad connection.

Beside him, Summer tapped her phone screen. "You said he teaches at Bowdoin? It's in Brunswick, only two-and-a-half hours from here."

"We're not going."

"Why not?" The flecks of green in her gray eyes flashed her irritation. "What else do we have to do? We need his help."

"I'll just..." He dialed his phone again.

Bryan answered with, "You on your way?"

"Listen, we don't want to bother you. We just need a name, somebody who can answer some questions for us."

"And I'll be happy to give you one. In person."

"Why are you being so stubborn?"

"It's a family characteristic."

For most of them, that was true. Grant's brothers were a bunch of bull-heads. He'd been the exception, always trying to make sure everybody got along. One moment of selfishness...

Bryan's voice broke into his thoughts. "Don't call me back until you're in town." Again, the line went dead.

Summer rarely smiled, but when she did, it transformed her entire face. Now, her grin almost counteracted the chilly response he'd gotten from his younger brother. "This should be fun."

For her, maybe.

For him, it would mean revisiting the worst memory of his life.

CHAPTER NINE

Summer clicked on the seatbelt in her cousin's Land Rover and watched Grant type into the keypad by Jon's front door. Jon might not have fully settled into the condo, but he'd had an alarm system installed straightaway. Grant closed the door, jogged to the SUV, and climbed into the driver's seat.

"Where's your truck?"

"Jon took it. We figured if Ramón and his thugs had gotten my license plate number, and if they had the resources to track my pickup down, they'd find it in the airport parking lot and assume you'd flown somewhere safe."

"Huh. Smart."

He chuckled, the sound deep and rich in the small space, and backed out of the parking spot. "I'll try not to be insulted by the tone of surprise."

"I didn't mean it that way." Though, honestly, she was impressed. It hadn't occurred to her that Ramón might be looking for Grant's truck. In her defense, her brain had been a bit scrambled the night before. "But then Jon was in danger while he drove it. If those guys—"

"He wasn't exactly worried."

Jon wasn't the type to shrink from a fight.

She was shocked he hadn't stayed, hadn't insisted on being there for her. Before he'd met Denise, he wouldn't have let anything get in the way of keeping Summer safe. But now he had higher priorities.

That was Summer's life, always slipping lower on people's contact lists.

She'd called Misty that morning to warn her that their captor was in town. He shouldn't be able to find her and wouldn't know they were sisters, but Misty needed to know.

Misty had offered a brusque "I'll keep alert" and hung up.

Summer's call to Krystal had gone straight to voicemail. Summer was less worried about her older sister, who'd been married for years and thus didn't share their last name.

There was a time when the three sisters were the most important people in each other's lives, especially after cancer took Mom. Dad was a useless, abusive drunk—even if he did pull it together for a while to help Summer and Misty regroup after the kidnapping—but the sisters had always had each other.

And then Krystal married, and suddenly her most important person was her husband, a dull accountant who worked in the city and bought her a big house and gave her three kids. With each of those kids, Summer and Misty slipped a little farther down on Krystal's *important people* list. It wasn't that Krystal didn't love her anymore. But she didn't need her, and she sure didn't make an effort to keep in touch.

Summer imagined the contact list on Krystal's phone. Husband, kids, in-laws, friends. Did she make the short list of favorites?

Probably not.

It was ridiculous how much that bothered her. But then, when you only have a handful of people in the world you consider family and you lose one of them, it's kind of a big deal.

But Summer and Misty had been the best of friends. Summer had spent much of her life trying to protect her little sister from their abusive dad. When Summer had been offered a modeling contract, she'd refused to go unless they would take her sister as well. Fortunately, Misty was tall and willowy. Add to that her symmetrical, pixie-like features, and Misty was the perfect candidate for glossy photos. Summer's agent had signed her, and the two sisters had moved out of Dad's house to an apartment in Boston, then to New York. They'd cooked together, played together, gone on photoshoots together. They'd only grown closer over the years.

And then the kidnapping.

Summer's dream to get herself and her sister away from their father had morphed into a nightmare that had almost gotten them both killed. She had never forgiven herself. And it seemed Misty had never forgiven her either. Their relationship had never been the same. It wasn't that they'd had words or argued. But Misty had moved on, just like Krystal had, leaving Summer behind.

Fine. That was fine. Because Summer had always had Jon.

Except now she could feel herself slipping down on her cousin's contact list too. Denise had the top spot. And Ella, Denise's daughter, would be on there. And the new friends Jon was making in Coventry.

Summer would be lucky to stay in the top ten.

"You all right?"

Grant's voice snapped her out of the melancholy. They were stopped at one of the few lights in Coventry, though she had paid no attention as they'd made their way down the mountain.

"Did you want to drive?" He squinted at her as if trying to read her face.

"Not unless you want me to."

Summer knew how to drive, of course. But after years of living in the city, she didn't own a car and rarely needed to get behind the wheel. It was the one area in which she was perfectly content to let somebody else be in control.

"You were awfully quiet. I thought maybe..." He made a left turn. "I prefer driving to being a passenger."

In the distance, the mountains were snow-capped, but along the road, the trees were budding, some sporting pale green leaves. It wasn't the prettiest she'd ever seen the lakes region in New Hampshire, but she couldn't imagine the area would ever be ugly.

Eventually, the mountains faded in the rearview mirror, giving way to rolling hills covered in tall pines and white-barked birches and a hundred other kinds of trees she couldn't identify as they whizzed past. She'd been a city-dweller for years, and she liked it. But there was something both grand and humble about the New England landscape with its winding roads and acres of forest, the mom-and-pop businesses scattered along the two-lane highway.

They stopped at an ATM in a little town about an hour east of Coventry and withdrew as much cash from each of their accounts as was allowed. Hopefully, it would tide them over for a while.

Back in the car, Grant adjusted the fan blowing warm air on their feet, then lowered the volume of the music.

She recognized the song as one from an artist Jon had suggested and enjoyed the folksy, acoustic sound. More than that, she liked the message of hope in the lyrics.

Did Grant like those things too? She knew he was a Christian—had been as long as she'd known him. Maybe she'd tell him about her own...conversion. Was that the right word? She was new to this and didn't know all the lingo. Faith wasn't exactly the kind of thing that came up in normal conversation.

Especially where they barely spoke about anything beyond their current assignment.

Being alone with him in the middle of nowhere...definitely nothing normal about this.

His fingers tapped the beat on the steering wheel. Nervousness tightened the skin around his eyes, though she suspected that had to do with the impending visit with his brother.

Which begged the question... "What happened between you and...what's your brother's name?"

A wrinkle formed between his brows. "Bryan."

She waited, but he didn't elaborate.

"You and Bryan had a falling out?"

One corner of his mouth ticked up. "Something like that."

"Was that funny?" She waited for an explanation, but none came.

"I'd rather not talk about Bryan."

His answer only made her more curious.

She tried again. "Must have been fun growing up with five brothers."

"Yup." His dark eyes darted her way. "We lived in a big farmhouse surrounded by apple orchards."

"Where exactly?"

He nodded forward. "Maine. Little town near Sanford."

"On a working orchard?"

"Used to be. My grandparents sold most of the land years ago. Granddad was a doctor and had no time to tend the trees. When Mom and Dad married, my grandparents gave them the house and moved to town."

"I bet that was a great place to grow up."

Grant's slight smile told her it had been. But there was more to the story, as evidenced by the stormy look in his eyes—not to mention the strange conversation with Bryan.

"Tell me about your brothers."

He turned the music down a little. "What do you want to know?"

"What do you want to tell me?"

His eyebrows rose. Was he surprised she'd asked?

"Derrick's the youngest," Grant said. "He'll be thirty-one this week. Then Bryan, who's two years younger than I am."

"So, thirty-three?"

"Yeah. Sam's thirty-eight, Michael's forty-two, and Daniel..."

Grant took a breath and blew it out. "He would have been forty-eight."

Would have been? "Oh, Grant, I'm sorry. What happened?"

His mouth got tight at the corners. He swallowed again. "He was living in St. Louis. He followed in Dad's footsteps, became a physician. But where Dad prefers a slow, small-town pace, Daniel thrived on busy-ness and adventure. He worked at an ER in a pretty rough area. We didn't realize that about his job—that it might be dangerous. I didn't realize, anyway. Maybe my brothers knew."

Why wouldn't they have told Grant about Daniel's job, if they'd known? Was the rift not just between him and Bryan but between him and all of them?

Why?

"Anyway," he continued, "at the hospital, Daniel witnessed a murder—one gang member taking out a rival, who happened to be Dan's patient. He could have kept his mouth shut, but my brother..." Grant's lips pressed together. A moment later, he said, "Anyway, he disappeared a few years ago. They've never found a body, but everybody knows what happened."

Pain tightened her insides. "I can't imagine how difficult that must be for all of you. Not just losing him, but the uncertainty." If Misty or Krystal went missing, never to be heard from again, would Summer be able to find peace? "You must have tried to find him."

"There wasn't much we could do. We don't know St. Louis, and the FBI and local cops were investigating. They warned us away, and my parents were so worried one of us would become targets that we just...we had to trust the authorities."

"Your poor parents. All of you."

"He was married, two kids. They're the ones who suffered the most. Are still suffering. Camilla's raising two teenagers by herself. We tried to get her to move home, but..."

Grant's words trailed. He kept his focus on the narrow, winding road.

"When did it happen?"

"Almost four years ago."

Grant and Summer had been working together then. She'd *known* him then. How had she not heard this story? She thought back, vaguely remembering that Grant had taken some time off for family reasons. He'd been gone a few weeks. Back then, the business had still been brand new, struggling to gain a foothold in the market, but that was no excuse. Had she ever asked him what the emergency was? Had she cared?

One of the people she considered like family had lost someone close to him, and she hadn't even known.

What was wrong with her?

"I'm sorry." The words came out before she had a moment to consider them. "I didn't know. And if you told me, I didn't—"

"You were dealing with your own stuff."

She hated that he knew that. Even though, at the time, three years had passed since the kidnapping, she'd still been in a haze of grief and PTSD. She hated to admit how long it had taken her to overcome it.

But still. How incredibly self-absorbed. "It's not okay. Don't let me off the hook so easily."

A smile tugged his lips up. "I have a feeling you never let yourself off the hook for anything. I hope the people in your life are easier on you than you are on yourself."

That was...insightful. It seemed Grant knew her a whole lot better than she knew him.

Except for the *people in your life* comment. She didn't have many of those.

They drove in silence for a long time, eventually crossing from New Hampshire into Maine.

According to Grant's GPS, they were forty-five minutes from Brunswick before he spoke again. "Do me a favor?"

"Sure."

He lifted his phone from the mount on the dash and handed it to her. "Text Bryan. Tell him our ETA and ask him where we can meet."

She did. A moment later, the phone dinged, and she read the response. "He says he'll meet us at a place called Molly May's."

"How far is it from campus?"

A strange question, but she found the address for the pub and searched the directions from Bowdoin. "Depends where he is, I guess. Looks to be about half a mile, maybe three-quarters."

"Ask him if we can pick him up."

"He said he'll meet us—"

"Just ask. Please."

She texted the question and got an immediate response. "He says he has legs."

Grant mumbled under his breath. She couldn't make out the words, but it was clear he was annoyed—at what, she couldn't fathom.

She plugged in the address and stuck Grant's phone back into the holder. "You think your brother will be able to point us in the right direction?"

"If nothing else, he can point us to someone who can. I hate that we're wasting time driving to Maine."

"If your brother steers us in the right direction, this won't be a waste of time. Besides, we don't have any other leads."

"True."

Obviously, Grant hated that they were going to see his brother. Which made her very curious. What had happened between Grant and the brother who was closest to him in age?

Had it happened—whatever *it* was—after their oldest brother had gone missing? Was it related to that? Or was this an old wound that had never healed?

Whatever it was, it was significant, and neither brother was over it. What ghosts haunted him, and why?

CHAPTER TEN

Grant drove along the pretty tree-lined road, scanning the sidewalks for his stubborn brother. Bryan would walk just to spite him.

Or... Bryan probably walked around campus all the time. And would Grant handle it any differently? Forget the pain, forget the embarrassment—not that Bryan had anything to be embarrassed about. It wasn't as if the accident had been his fault.

But nobody wanted to admit weakness, especially the Wright brothers. They might not be inventors of air flight like the more famous men of that moniker, but they were stubborn and determined in their own ways. And none of them relished the idea of needing help.

From anyone.

Maybe, if Daniel had been honest about the danger he was in, Grant and his team could have flown to St. Louis to protect him. The guards who'd been assigned to keep him alive had failed. Was Grant crazy to think he would've done better?

He didn't think so. Because he'd never have let Daniel leave by himself that night. He'd have known something was wrong.

He'd have gone with him. Nobody on his team would have been that sloppy.

If Daniel had asked for help, he might still be alive.

Grant should have asked more questions, found out what was really going on. He should have been there for his brother.

He was trying to learn the lesson Daniel hadn't—that asking for help doesn't make a man weak. Asking for help proved a man's strength.

Even if the opposite felt true.

Not that his attitude would matter. Whether he arrived at the restaurant feeling humble or proud, nothing would change how Bryan saw him.

Or how Grant saw himself.

"Cute town," Summer said.

He shook off the depressing thoughts and took in his surroundings—rows of brick or white-sided buildings, pretty little storefronts, window boxes filled with spring blooms.

"There it is," she said, "up ahead."

Following her gaze, he saw the sign and parked in a spot along the street. He considered hurrying around the SUV to open her door for her and help her out, but she wouldn't want that.

If their relationship ever progressed past friendship, maybe she'd learn to let him pamper her. Maybe she'd even get comfortable with it.

She paused on the sidewalk and seemed to take a minute to get her bearings. With her bruises, after almost three hours in the car, she probably needed to stretch a little. He gazed at the restaurant while he waited—the dark green sign, the gilded words, and the four-leaf clover that acted as an apostrophe. It was barely dinnertime—only five o'clock—but the sandwich and cup of soup hadn't exactly filled him. He could eat.

They walked toward the door, and he stepped forward to

open it for her, waiting for her signature glare. It didn't come. Instead, she said, "Thanks."

Interesting. Maybe their conversation in the car had bridged a gap between them. Maybe he should tell her more about his life, his family. Maybe she was starting to see him not just as a partner and her cousin's best friend, but as a man.

That would be one good thing to come from this situation.

They paused in the entry to let their eyes adjust to the dimly lit interior. The place was all wood paneling and green-shaded lights. Signs advertising Guinness, Smithwick, and Murphy's hung over the long bar alongside aged kegs and liquor bottles of various shapes and colors. The walls were decorated with images of rolling hills and signs that had either come off actual pubs in Ireland or had been painted to look that way. Names like O'Shanahan's and McCluskey's. All they needed to complete the picture was the overhead speakers to pipe in "Danny Boy." But the rock-and-roll he heard was decidedly not Irish.

The host—no doubt a coed from Bowdoin—said, "Two for dinner?"

Grant answered, "We're meeting somebody."

"Oh." She looked him up and down. "I'm guessing Professor Wright. You two could be twins."

Was his brother that well known? Or maybe this was one of his students. "Good guess."

She nodded toward the back of the pub, where Bryan sat at a small round table.

"Thanks." He settled a hand on Summer's back, only realizing after the fact what he'd done. She didn't jerk away, though.

She'd probably dress him down for it later, but at least she wasn't going to tell him off in front of his brother. They reached the table, and Bryan pushed his chair back.

"Don't get up," Grant said quickly.

Bryan stood, sent Grant a frown, and then smiled at Summer, holding out his hand. "Bryan Wright." Bryan was a shade shorter than Grant and wore his brown hair longer than Grant's high-and-tight. He had the same dark brown eyes and the same square chin.

"Summer." She shook his hand. "Nice to meet you."

She was *Summer* for Bryan, a virtual stranger, but Grant was supposed to call her Lake?

Irritation prickled, but he ignored it, pulling out a chair for her. After she settled into it, he stuck his hand out to his brother.

Bryan regarded it, then him, before he finally gripped it. "How was the drive?"

"Uneventful. Thanks for seeing us."

Grant caught Bryan's smile as he looked down, settling into his chair again. He seemed pleased with himself, which only ratcheted up Grant's nerves. What was this about, forcing them to drive all the way to Maine?

Before he could think how to start, a server approached, and they gave her their drink orders.

When she walked away, Bryan focused on Summer. "You're Jon's cousin."

"You've met him?"

"Of course. He's been at the house a couple of times. There's a resemblance."

Grant gave Summer an appraising gaze. He'd heard people say she looked like Jon, but he didn't see it. Summer was beautiful, with those high cheekbones, those striking gray eyes, that shiny blond hair. She was tall and lean and curvy in all the right places.

Whereas Jon was just...Jon.

"Tell me about yourself, Summer." Bryan shifted to face her as if Grant weren't there.

"Not much to tell, I guess. Grant and I work together."

"So you're a bodyguard as well?"

"I am."

Grant said, "She's one of the owners of the company."

Bryan didn't even glance his way. He'd always been good at fully focusing on whatever had his attention. When he was a kid, Bryan roughhoused as much as the rest of them, but eventually, he'd get bored with it, and they'd find him curled up in the corner of the sofa with a book, utterly unconcerned about his brothers wresting or arguing or laughing around him. He seemed that engrossed with Summer. "How did you get into the business?"

While Summer answered the question, relaxed and smiling, Grant's pulse kicked up. Was this something different? Was Bryan *flirting*?

Worse, was Summer flirting back?

She told him about how Jon had asked her for a loan to start his business, how she'd agreed to invest only if he'd let her work there too. How she'd spent months training for the job so she'd be as competent as anyone else they hired.

Grant had directed that training, but Summer didn't bother to mention that. In fact, she seemed to have forgotten he was there.

The server returned with their sodas. "You ready to order?"

"We haven't even looked." To Summer, Bryan said, "What kind of food do you like? I've tried just about everything on the menu."

"I'm not that hungry. We could share an appetizer."

He turned back to the server. "Bring potato skins, nachos, the pretzel with both cheese and mustard, and..." He gave Grant an innocent look. "And you?"

"Are you planning to share?"

"There's enough for the two of us." He shot a look at

Summer before meeting Grant's eyes again. "But you might want to order something."

Grant barely stifled a growl of frustration. Unlike Summer, he'd had plenty of time to study the menu. "Fried pickles and the stack of onion rings."

"Two of my favorites." Summer smiled in Grant's direction, and he managed to stop the smug look he wanted to give his brother.

Your move, dude.

Except...except Bryan wasn't a flirter or a womanizer. As far as Grant knew, he wasn't seeing anybody and had very little time for romance. If he was truly attracted to Summer, not just flirting to annoy Grant, then Grant would step away.

He owed his little brother that. Maybe, if he sacrificed the woman he loved for Bryan, they could finally be even.

Never mind that the thought of it made his empty stomach clench.

"Your cousin must be busy if you're stuck with this guy." Bryan dipped his head toward Grant.

"See, there's this woman..." Summer rolled her eyes, and Bryan chuckled.

She was enjoying Bryan's attention. She was bantering.

She *liked* him.

It was Grant's worst nightmare.

Bryan met Grant's eyes. "Amazing the things we do when we meet someone who matters."

Summer and Bryan continued to chat, continued to virtually ignore him while they waited for their food. Summer told Bryan about the agency and how much work they'd had recently. She might have played that up a little, and maybe she'd done so because Grant had claimed to be busy when he should have gone home. Was Summer trying to help him? Or just trying to make nice to get the information she needed?

He assumed the second. Couldn't help but hope the first.

Their food was delivered, and they dug into the appetizers. Grant didn't like fried pickles and didn't bother pretending to. Summer wasn't paying enough attention to realize he'd ordered them solely for her.

They were halfway through the finger food when Bryan finally turned his attention to him. By the way his expression closed, Grant figured the small talk portion of the dinner was over. "Why the sudden interest in pre-Columbian antiquities?"

"It's sort of a long story." He nodded to Summer.

She explained what she'd overheard in the parking garage the previous day, neglecting to share that she'd been attacked.

Bryan's head dipped to one side. "Sounds like those guys are up to no good."

"There's that Ivy League intellect," Grant said, instantly regretting the sarcasm.

But Bryan chuckled. "Bowdoin isn't Ivy League."

Maybe not, but Princeton was. That Bryan didn't mention his alma mater when Grant had served it up for him said a lot about his character. Despite all his achievements, Bryan remained humble.

Maybe he and Summer could be happy together.

Grant sipped his Coke, wishing he'd ordered a beer. Or a nice Irish whiskey. Maybe a little alcohol would take the edge off his frustration.

More likely, it would just loosen his tongue and make him say things he shouldn't. Which was why he so rarely indulged.

"We're trying to figure out who that guy was," Summer said. "Grant thought you might be able to steer us to somebody who knows about local collectors."

"Local as in Boston, I assume."

"Probably," Grant said. "But I figured it would be a small group."

Bryan was quiet as he ate a potato skin.

Summer glanced Grant's way, hope evident in her eyes.

Rather than give them any ideas, Bryan snatched his phone from the table and tapped a text. "I might know somebody who can help. If she's not too busy."

"I thought you said you'd get a name for us." Grant couldn't keep the frustration out of his voice. "That's why we came. You haven't even started the process? What was the point of us driving up here?"

"The point was to see you, you idiot." Bryan softened the words with a slight smile.

His brother had *wanted* to see him?

Why?

Bryan's phone dinged, and he snatched it and read the text. "She thinks she can help. It'll be faster if I explain over the phone." He pushed back from the table, grabbed the cane he'd propped in the corner, and headed toward the front door.

Summer watched him leave. "Why is he limping? Does he always use a cane?"

"Yup."

"What happened?"

"Bad fall when he was a kid."

She turned back to where Bryan had disappeared out the front door. "That's why you wanted to pick him up. Doesn't seem to slow him down, though."

"He's stubborn."

She grinned, the look transforming her normally serious expression and adding fuel to the flame he'd been trying to extinguish for years. "A family characteristic."

He returned her smile. "You're not wrong about that."

She took an onion ring from the dwindling pile and dipped it in honey mustard. An odd combination, but Summer was anything but normal. "He seems nice. And you two...I don't know what happened between you, but obviously, he wants to move past it."

"Not all rifts can be repaired."

She tilted her head to one side, blond hair falling over her shoulder. She hadn't put it up today, and the soft locks only heightened her beauty. "Is that...? I thought... I mean, I don't know as much about this stuff as you do. And maybe he's not..." Her words faded.

"It'd be really helpful if you'd finish at least one of your sentences."

"I don't know if Jon told you that he became a Christian a few months back."

The change in subjects piqued his interest. "We've talked a lot about it."

"Oh. Well." Her shoulders squared as if she were preparing for an attack. "I did the same. Converted or...however you say it."

Joy blew through him, fanning that ever-present flame. Summer was a Christian.

Finally.

He'd been praying for years that God would work on her heart, draw her to Himself. That He'd used a Hollywood actor, working through Jon, to do it reminded Grant how big, how powerful, his God was.

Now nothing stood in the way of their being together... except that she saw him as a partner and nothing else. But maybe this was a good sign. Maybe God was doing something amazing.

"You know more about this than I do," Summer said. "But are there really rifts that can't be mended? Or is Bryan not a Christian? So maybe that makes a difference? I don't under-stand, but I want to."

Whoa. He needed to watch his words. "You're right. Of

course. God can mend it. And maybe He will. I shouldn't be so..." He couldn't think of an appropriate word.

Yes, he could.

Faithless. He shouldn't be so faithless where his brother was concerned. Especially considering Bryan had lured him to Maine because he wanted to see him.

"Maybe you should forgive him," Summer said. "I mean, that's the Christian thing, right? To forgive?"

"I'm not the one who needs to forgive." If only he were, this would be so much easier. "I'm the one who needs forgiveness."

Her head tilted to the side. "Oh. Bryan doesn't seem..." She paused, probably to get her thoughts together.

Bryan returned before she finished her sentence. He leaned his cane against the wall and sat. "She's compiling a list of names. She'll email it to me."

Summer sent Bryan a generous smile, and Grant clenched his fists. She was a Christian now. Maybe God was preparing her to meet the man who'd become her spouse.

Maybe that man was Bryan.

That would leave Grant to deal with the stupid torch he couldn't seem to put out—only then he'd be carrying it for his brother's girl.

As if Bryan didn't already have reason enough to hate him.

CHAPTER ELEVEN

———————————

S ummer couldn't imagine what Grant had done to cause a rift with his brother. Something he deemed unforgivable. Which was weird because wasn't everything forgivable with God?

"It's a long way." Grant sounded annoyed as the words left his mouth.

She'd been musing about the brothers, not listening to them.

"I have room at my place," Bryan said. "You'll stay with me."

Wait. What?

"We don't want to impose," she said. Not that she'd mind. She didn't relish the long drive back to Coventry. But she didn't have any of her things.

"We can just talk to your friend on the phone." Grant waved the server over and asked for the check. When the kid set it down, Grant snatched it and handed over his credit card.

"You don't have to buy my dinner." Bryan seemed offended.

"I can split that with you," Summer said.

"I got it." By the growled words, Grant was offended too.

There was way too much going on under the surface that she didn't understand. She hated that. Hated having to read subtext and facial expressions. Why couldn't people just say what they meant?

Life would be so much simpler.

Not that she was exactly forthright.

The brothers glared at each other, so she wasn't sorry when her phone rang. She checked the screen, said, "It's Jon," and stood to head outside. "Hey."

"Where are you? Are you safe?"

The concern in his voice had her heart thumping as she stepped into the chilly May evening. She should have grabbed her jacket. "Yeah."

His exhale was audible. "Thank God. You guys didn't set the alarm off accidentally, did you?"

"Not that I'm aware of. What happened?"

"I got a call from the Coventry PD. It looks like somebody broke into my condo. Where are you?"

"Maine. We left your place hours ago."

"Thank God."

"Did the police catch anybody?"

"No. The front door was open when they got there, so they let themselves in. They said nothing seemed out of place, but I'll need to look around, see if anything's missing or...amiss."

Summer scanned the street, the sidewalk, the people walking past the storefronts. People were gathering outside of Molly May's and another restaurant on the opposite side of the road. She saw nothing concerning and wandered to the restaurant's window. Past all the diners, she caught sight of the brothers talking. They were both pressed against their chair backs. Grant's arms were crossed.

Had she ever seen him use such guarded body language?

She leaned against the brick beside the window. "You think it was a burglar?"

"Uh, no," Jon said. "I assume your friend tracked you down."

Oh. *Oh.* Summer looked around again. Surely Ramón wasn't close. If he was, she didn't want to be outside. Alone. She hurried back inside the restaurant. She scooted into the corner in the entry, blocked one ear so she could hear, and said, "How could he have found me at your place?"

Jon was quiet for a beat. "He's smart. Maybe he put together that we're cousins."

But how could he have? They didn't exactly advertise their family relationship. They owned a security company, both very paranoid about personal security. Thank God Jon was out of town. And they'd left before the thugs got there. "Grant and I are nowhere near there now."

"Don't assume that means you're safe. I'm careful not to put my home address anywhere public. This guy's resourceful, Summer."

Jon almost never called her by her first name. His use of it now showed his worry, his affection.

"He's probably employing a lot of people," Jon added. "Meaning—"

"He could find me."

Jon's words were low and gruff. "I should be there. I shouldn't have left. But I promised Denise, and I didn't want... I'll get a flight back. There's probably a red-eye."

"No, don't do that." Summer hated the idea of Jon disappointing his girlfriend. Denise's security mattered too. It meant a lot that he wanted to be with Summer, to protect her. "Grant's with me. If we need help, we can call on the team. Grant's brother's going to help us figure out who that collector was."

"Which brother?"

"Bryan. He's a professor."

"That makes sense, but... Huh."

When Jon didn't elaborate, Summer said, "*Huh* what?"

"They don't get along very well."

She saw the brothers across the dining room, sitting at the table but no longer talking. "Do you know why?"

"Not my story to tell. The point is, you can't go back to my place. I'd send you to Denise's, but I'm afraid if they tracked me down, they could figure out my connection to her and track her down too. I'm not sure you'd be safer there. Obviously, you can't go home. You'll need to find somewhere else to stay—preferably somewhere you don't need to use your credit card."

"I can't stay hidden forever."

"So you'll have to find a way to take him down."

Denise's voice carried through the phone, though Summer couldn't make out what she said.

"One sec, sweetheart. I'll be right there." Then to Summer, Jon said, "Let me know what I can do from here."

"Sure," Summer said. But he didn't need to be distracted by Summer's worries.

"I'm serious," he said, guessing her thoughts. "I have my laptop. I can do research. We have a lot of downtime. I'd welcome the distraction."

Across the dining room, Grant caught her eye, then pushed away from the table and stood. He waited for Bryan to grab his cane and then followed him toward the entry.

"I have to go," Summer said. "I'll tell Grant about your condo. We might have a place to stay near here."

"Good. Keep in touch." Jon ended the call.

They could stay at Bryan's, but would Ramón think to look for them at Grant's brother's house?

Ramón had gotten too close already.

Surely he didn't have the resources to watch all of Grant's family.

But what about her own?

Krystal. Krystal's children.

Misty.

If Ramón knew who Summer was, if he could figure out who her cousin was, then how hard would it be for him to figure out who her sisters were? And if he did that, would he put it together—that she and Misty had once been his captives?

Fear raised goose bumps on her skin.

Bryan and Grant approached. Over his brother's shoulder, Grant said, "We're going back to Jon's."

Bryan huffed his frustration.

She shook her head.

He must've seen something in her expression because he stepped around his brother. "What happened?"

In a low voice, she told him about the break-in at Jon's condo. Bryan leaned in to hear.

Grant's brows lowered over his dark eyes. "Thank God you weren't there."

"Both of us." She doubted he heard her whisper over the music and the gathering crowd. It seemed Molly May's was a popular spot with the college crowd.

"That settles it," Bryan said.

Grant ignored him. "I'm not bringing this to his doorstep."

Before she could agree, Bryan said, "Whatever *this* is, my doorstep can handle it." He stepped forward and squared up with his brother.

Though their voices were low, the students nearby must've sensed what she did—that these two who looked so much alike—both tall, dark, and barrel-chested—were about to go toe-to-toe.

The murmurs in the waiting area died down.

"Why don't we take this outside?" Summer suggested.

It was Bryan who broke away. Nodded at a couple of co-eds who stared back, wide-eyed. He limped past the crowd and outside.

Grant held out her small purse and the jacket, which she'd left draped across her chair. "Sorry about that."

"No need to apologize." She shrugged into her jacket. "This is all my doing."

"The stuff between Bryan and me has nothing to do with you."

Outside, Bryan stood in front of the dark windows of the neighboring storefront. Summer walked toward him, pasting on a smile.

Behind her, Grant said, "Thanks for meeting us. We'll start going through the information as soon as we get it."

Ignoring him, Bryan focused on Summer. "Just because he's as stubborn as a mule doesn't mean you can't stay with me. There's a spare bedroom with its own bath. I'll be holed up in my office all evening, and I have an early class. You wouldn't even have to see me."

"That's very kind," Summer said. "I'll stick with Grant, though."

Bryan glared at his brother. "So where are you going to go if you can't go back to Jon's? You'd really rather get a hotel or sleep in a shelter than spend time with me?"

"Don't be stupid," Grant snapped.

Before Bryan could respond, she explained. "The guy in the parking garage—he saw me. He knows who I am. Grant was there too. We're worried he'll look for us at your place. It'll be better if we're nowhere near there." She paused. "In fact, you should think about staying at your office for a few days. Just to be safe"

Bryan's eyes narrowed as he looked from her to his brother and back. "You're in danger?"

"We'll be fine," Summer said.

"They broke into Jon's place," Grant added, "which tells us

they're smart. If they can find Summer's cousin, they can probably figure out who I am, which means—"

"I'm subletting from a professor on sabbatical. The utility bills aren't even in my name."

"Oh." Grant shifted beside her. "I didn't know that."

"If you came home every once in a while..." He let the rebuke drop, turning to Summer. "You'd be safe at my house. Both of you."

This was Grant's decision, but she couldn't see the harm in accepting his offer, at least for one night.

Grant seemed to wrestle with his answer. Finally, he said, "Yeah, okay. Tonight only. We'll figure out where to go from there tomorrow."

That settled where they'd stay tonight. But Summer needed to contact her sisters immediately. She and Grant might be safe for now, but if Ramón got to Krystal or Misty...

She'd never forgive herself.

CHAPTER TWELVE

G rant was still trying to make sense of this trip to Maine. Bryan had forced him to come here because he'd wanted to see him. Not to argue with him. Not to challenge him. Not for any other reason. And he'd seemed offended when Grant hadn't immediately agreed to stay at his place.

Maybe Grant wasn't the only one who hated the distance between them. Was there a chance for real reconciliation?

He needed to focus on keeping Summer safe, but if Bryan wanted to repair their relationship, Grant would do his part. He'd do anything to get back to the easy friendship they'd had as kids.

But first, he and Summer had to deal with the fact that, once again, they found themselves bereft of basic personal items. As they drove toward the department store, he said, "From now on, we pack all our stuff in the SUV every time we get in it."

"Agreed. Right now, I have to call my sisters." A minute later, she said, "Krystal. I need to tell you something."

Summer explained what was going on, assured her older sister that she was being cautious, and offered her personal security. After a few minutes of conversation, Summer said, "Good.

I'll dispatch a team to your house tonight." She hung up and called Bentley, asked him to send a team, and rattled off an address west of Boston.

Then she dialed Misty. She'd already told her sister that Ramón was in town, so this conversation was shorter. Though Grant could only hear Summer's end of the conversation, it was clear Misty declined protection. He assumed Misty was either not taking the danger seriously or was angry with Summer for getting herself—and by extension Misty and Krystal—involved. But then, Summer put the phone on speaker, and the woman sounded neither angry nor flippant.

"We get threats sometimes." Misty was a prosecutor in Boston, so Grant figured that was probably true. Her tone was perfectly calm, almost clipped. "I'll talk to my boss about providing me protection. If he refuses—and I don't think he will—I'll let you know."

"Our team is better than whatever you'll get from the county." Summer looked at him. "Tell her, Grant."

"Hey, Misty." The only time he'd met Misty was when he'd found her, Summer, and the other models in that rundown building in Mexico. "It's Grant Wright. I don't know if you remember—"

"I know who you are." Her tone shifted to something softer, and he pictured the scared teenager she'd been seven years earlier.

"If you let us protect you," he said, "you'll be getting the best."

Misty's response was measured. "I have no doubt you guys are excellent. But I've trusted our office's security before. They've never let me down."

"If they do," Summer said, "it could mean your life."

"That's my risk to take."

"I'm just trying to keep you safe." Frustration oozed from Summer's words.

"I'm all grown up." Misty didn't sound amused. "I don't need you protecting me anymore."

"Obviously you do, if you're too pigheaded—"

"Wow, really? You're calling *me* pigheaded?"

Whoa, that had gone south fast.

"If you'd just—" Summer cut her own words off and took a breath. Though anger wafted off her, her voice was calm when she next spoke. "Promise you'll let me know if your boss refuses."

"If you promise to quit treating me like I'm seven years old."

"Right." Summer took a breath. "Old habits and all that."

"*Bad* habits need to be broken."

"I don't want anything to happen to you because I love you. Is that so awful?"

"You're the one who followed that creep," Misty snapped. "You're the one who put yourself in danger. Focus on your own protection because I love you too."

Grant had never heard those words traded in such an angry tone of voice.

Sisters. Definitely different than brothers. Sisters traded I-love-yous, even when they were furious.

Brothers called each other names.

Like Bryan had earlier. *"Because I wanted to see you, idiot."*

Before he could analyze that to death, Summer hung up and huffed. "If anything happens to her..."

"I'm sure her protection will be adequate."

"I'd prefer better than adequate for my baby sister. We had *adequate* protection in Mexico."

Obviously, they hadn't, but he saw no point in parsing words.

He wished he could offer to pray with Summer about her

sisters' safety, but their relationship wasn't there yet. He'd do his praying for them silently—for now.

After parking in the nearly empty lot, they entered the discount department store.

Under the too-bright overhead lights, Summer said, "Let's meet back here when we're finished."

Let her go by herself? Fat chance. "We stay together."

She rolled her eyes but didn't argue.

With some of the cash they'd withdrawn in Coventry, they bought the clothes and toiletries they'd need for a few days and headed to the address Bryan had given him, which led to a little blue house just a couple of blocks from campus. Lights shone through the windows and over the welcoming front door.

Grant parked beside his brother's old Subaru, grabbed the sacks from the store along with his laptop bag—thank heavens he'd brought it with him—and followed Summer to the front door, which swung open as they approached.

"You made it." Bryan waved them in.

The place was bigger inside than it had seemed outside, with gleaming hardwood floors in a large living area that opened to a kitchen in the back. In the entry, a staircase led to the second floor. On the left, an office was filled with a desk and shelves lined with books. The space was too sparse to be cozy, but the beige sectional looked comfortable enough.

"Nice," Grant said.

"I like it." Bryan looked around. "It's only temporary. If I ever get tenure, I'll buy something."

Did that mean Bryan's job wasn't secure? Grant hated that he didn't know more about his brother's life.

"You two find everything you need?" Bryan asked.

"I think so." Summer stopped in the living area and turned. "We really appreciate this."

"Happy to do it. There're two empty rooms upstairs.

They're kids' rooms, so nothing fancy, and twin beds." He glanced from Grant to Summer and back. "Too short for both of you."

"They'll be fine." To Grant, she said, "Mind if I grab my stuff?"

"Sure." He set the sacks on the sofa, and she dug through them, separating her things from his. "I'll just pick a room, I guess." To Bryan, she said, "That okay?"

"Make yourself at home."

After she disappeared up the stairs, Bryan said, "You need a drink?"

Grant followed his brother and stood at the edge of the eat-in kitchen. "Not right now."

"If you change your mind, help yourself. You're welcome to anything you can find. And Summer is, too, of course."

"Thanks for doing this. We'll be out of your hair in the morning."

Bryan leaned against the black granite countertop. "You can stay as long as you like."

"Oh. Well..." He didn't know what to say to that, or what to do with the silence that stretched between them. He'd spent almost zero time alone with his brother in years. Probably since before he'd joined the Army at eighteen. He'd gone home for holidays and celebrations, but only when the whole family was gathered. Between his folks and his brothers and girlfriends and friends, there had rarely been an opportunity for Grant and Bryan to talk privately.

And Grant could admit that whenever such an opportunity presented itself, he made himself scarce.

He loved his brother dearly. He just didn't know what to say to him, how to bridge the distance between them. How to make up for the horrible thing he'd done.

"How dangerous is this guy?" Bryan asked.

"Dangerous." There was no point sugarcoating it. "But we'll stay one step ahead of him. He won't get to her."

"Or you?"

"That's the plan."

"Because Mom and Dad have already lost Daniel. I don't know if they could take losing you. If any of us could."

The grief had nearly done them in. "I'm not going to do anything stupid."

Bryan's eyebrows hiked, and that tiny movement felt like a punch to the gut. He'd fought terrorists and protected dignitaries and rescued hostages, but in his family, he'd always be the reckless one.

He swiveled and returned to the living room.

"What?" Bryan followed him, the distinctive thump of his cane echoing in the quiet.

"There a washer and dryer we can use?"

"In the basement. Help yourself."

Grant gathered the bags Summer had left and turned to find his brother watching from the entry, wearing a pained expression.

They were never going to get past it. There was no *past it.* Bryan would always have that limp, that cane. And it would always be Grant's fault.

"Thanks," Grant said. "Again. For this."

"You're welcome. Again. Stay as long as you need."

"We'll be out of here tomorrow." If not for Summer, Grant would leave now. He'd rather sleep in his car than have to face Bryan and the mess Grant had made of his brother's life.

"Let me know if you need anything. I've got papers to grade." Bryan limped past him and into the office, closing the door behind him.

Grant was about to head up when Summer descended and stepped into the living room. She'd stuck her hair in a ponytail, the shorter strands escaping and framing her face, much softer than the harsh style she wore at work.

"I waffled on which room to take, the blue one decorated with sports paraphernalia or the pink one with the princess bed."

Grant groaned. "Please tell me—"

"I'm not *that* cruel." Though she didn't smile, he saw amusement in her eyes. She nodded toward the bags in his hand. "You going up?"

He had been, only to get away from his brother. He dropped them back on the couch. "Let's see if Bryan's friend sent that information."

Grant booted his laptop at the table while Summer made herself at home in the kitchen, fixing them both glasses of ice water.

She sat beside him. "Well?"

He hadn't thought to get the Wi-Fi passwords, so he connected to his phone's hotspot and scanned his email.

Sure enough, there was one from a university address. After a quick note from Bryan's friend promising to keep thinking about it, there was a list of names and universities they worked for.

"Long list."

Summer leaned close as he scanned it. "How did she come up with so many so fast?"

The woman was obviously a quick thinker.

"What do we do with all those names?" By her tone, Summer felt overwhelmed. He couldn't blame her. She was a good bodyguard, but she'd never done any investigating. Not that Grant had a lot of experience, but he'd done a little in the previous couple of years, and he'd had occasion to do some investigating with the Army. He and Jon had both taken criminal justice classes at night with the dream of ultimately expanding the company into private investigation. Though Summer was on board with the idea, she'd had little interest in joining them.

"We take it one name at a time." Grant copied the information and pasted it into a spreadsheet, then scanned to the bottom.

There were fifty-seven lines.

Grant pasted the first name into his browser, along with the name of the university she worked for. He found an image of the woman on the university's website. "Not her, I guess."

"It was definitely a man."

In the field next to the woman's name on his spreadsheet, Grant typed an F for female. They might want to sort the list by gender later.

Then, he copied the second line, found the professor, clicked on an image, and looked at Summer.

She studied it, then shook her head. "I have no idea. I didn't see the guy's face."

"Okay, but—"

"Is this the plan? Because I don't know what he looked like. I'm not going to recognize him." She sat back with a huff. "We're never going to figure this out."

"We'll narrow the list, at least figure out which ones we know aren't the guy."

"And he probably wasn't a professor. He could've been an accountant or a lawyer or...whatever."

"This is just a starting point." Grant kept his voice level. No need to rise to the level of her frustration. "If we don't find him, we'll find somebody who knows him."

Summer's attention was still on his screen. "But how am I supposed to know?" She gestured to the image of the forty-something guy. "That could be him. Or not. I have no idea." She pushed back in her chair and stood. "There's got to be a better way. Something else we can do besides... This feels like a rabbit trail."

"Investigators follow trails. Some end up being rabbit trails. In this case, this is the only trail we have."

"We could be looking into Ramón himself. Maybe—"

"Golinski is working that angle. We've given him all the information we dug up. He's FBI. He knows what he's doing, and he has a lot better resources than we do." Grant took her hand and squeezed gently. The connection probably did nothing to her, but his heart thumped, and he let go. "I know you didn't see the guy's face, but you can learn a lot from a man by other things about him. Remember your training. What can you tell me about him?"

She pulled out her phone and consulted the notes she'd made in the garage. There was nothing here she hadn't already told Grant. "I don't know anything else."

"Close your eyes and think." She might be the boss at work, but when she'd still been learning the job, he'd been in charge. He put on his trainer glare and waited, half expecting her to lash out at him.

But she didn't.

She sat again, closed her eyes, and leaned back in her chair. "He was Caucasian. Average height."

"Taller or shorter than Ramón?"

"A couple inches shorter."

Ramón was five-ten or five-eleven, so that put their unknown man at five-eight or five-nine.

Grant typed the information.

"He had brown hair."

"Dark brown or light?"

"Light. Graying, I think."

"Long or short?"

She touched her shoulder, though Grant doubted she realized it. "It brushed his jacket collar. It was thinning. He had a bald spot on top."

"In front or on the crown."

"Crown. Maybe both, but I didn't see him from the front."

"Good. You heard his voice, right?" At her nod, he said, "What did you hear?"

"It was higher than Ramón's."

"Accent?"

"Local, but high-brow."

"If you had to guess an age...?"

"Forties or fifties."

"Based on what?"

She considered the question a long moment. "His clothes seemed older. His shoes—black, kind of ugly. Sensible. His pants were baggier than most young people wear them. The trench coat was the kind that's coming back in fashion, but this one looked like it'd been worn since the last time it was in style."

"Excellent. What else did you notice?"

Though her eyes remained closed, they squeezed, wrinkling the skin at the corners. Then, they softened. Her lips, which had been pinched, opened the slightest bit. She took a deep breath and blew it out. Relaxed.

She was, quite simply, the most beautiful creature who'd ever lived. He'd thought so the first moment he'd laid eyes on her, and nothing had changed since. He could stare at her for the rest of his life.

"Oh." Her eyes popped open, and her open expression shuttered.

Uh-oh. She'd caught him staring.

He shifted his attention to the screen. "Yeah?"

"Probably nothing. He seemed completely confident until

Ramón started to tell him when the drop was going to take place. He told Ramón he didn't want the details, that he didn't need to know, only a window so he could make sure his family wasn't there. I'm guessing it's a vacation home."

Grant tapped that final bit. The man had a family and feared for them. Also, wealthy enough for a vacation home—on the coast somewhere.

"This is a great start." He highlighted the names on his spreadsheet. "I'm going to send you this list. I want you to look up all the ones with women's names, just to be sure. And I'll go through the men and eliminate the ones who don't fit. Then, we'll go through what's left together, okay?"

She agreed, and they settled in to work. Summer focused on her phone while he tapped on his laptop.

He wasn't sure how long they'd worked when Bryan called, "I'm going up, you two." He waved from the bottom of the stairs. "Make yourselves at home."

"Thanks," Summer said.

Grant watched as his brother disappeared, still trying to figure out why he was being so nice to him.

Summer was able to get through her list quickly, confirming all but one—a man named Leslie—were women. When she was done, she scooted closer to him and watched over his shoulder.

Distracting him with her closeness, her warmth, her distinct scent—something sweet and floral. More than once in those few minutes, Grant had to remind himself to focus.

It was amazing how many men on the list fit Summer's vague description. He couldn't rule anybody out just because his hair was too short or wasn't exactly the right color. Hair color and style were easy enough to change. He couldn't tell height from most of the photos he found. The only people he was able to immediately cross off the list were non-Caucasians, a couple of elderly men, and a guy who stood a head taller than others in a group picture.

That left him with...a lot.

He looked at Summer and smiled. "Twenty-two is better than fifty-seven."

She scooted her chair away. "Still, a lot of people to track down. Assuming our guy is even on that list. Maybe this Professor"—she checked the email address—"Cissy? What kind of a name is that? Maybe she doesn't know as much as your brother thinks."

"We have to start somewhere." He rubbed his eyes and glanced at his watch. It was after ten. Not that late, but he yawned anyway.

Summer stood and stretched her long, lithe body.

Grant forced himself to look away.

"My eyes are crossing," she said. "I hate that we didn't get more accomplished, but—"

"Every hour of work tonight is one we don't have to do tomorrow. We'll start in the morning with a shorter list."

"And do what?"

"Well, we know the guy we're looking for owns property on the coast, so we can check the names with real estate records."

"Maybe Jon can help. He said he has time on his hands."

Grant sat back down. "Excellent idea. He's got more resources than I do." Because, unlike Grant, Jon was actually using his detective skills in his work, whereas Grant was still working protection, which rarely afforded him the opportunity. "I'll send him the list. It's only seven on the West Coast. Maybe he can get started tonight."

"I don't want him to feel obligated, though. He's got Denise and—"

"He wants to help. I'm sure it's killing him that he's not

here." Grant tapped a quick email, attached the list, and sent it. He stood, and she stepped back to give him room.

"Well, then." She glanced awkwardly from him to the staircase. "I guess I'll go up."

"Thought I'd turn on the TV for a little while. Want to watch something?"

"No, thanks. I'll see you in the morning."

"Bryan said to help yourself to anything you want, tonight or tomorrow. And we can do laundry if we need to."

"Okay. Good. We'll figure out what's next..." Her words trailed as she yawned again.

"Tomorrow. Sleep tight."

She walked to the staircase, then turned. "I...uh...I just wanted to say how much I appreciate that you're here with me. I don't know what I'd do if I were by myself. I mean, I'd still be at Jon's, and they'd have..."

Ramón would have tracked her down. Grant didn't want to think about that.

She took a breath. "I'm sorry I dragged you into this."

"You didn't drag me. I insisted."

"Still, I'm sorry. I've pulled you away from home. I have no idea how we're ever going to figure this out. And now they know who you are, which means you're in as much danger as I am. I'm just...I'm sorry."

He approached, only stopping when he was a couple of feet away. He wanted more than anything to take her in his arms and tell her how very *not sorry* he was to be there with her. How it would have killed him to not be with her now.

"There's no place I'd rather be."

"Okay. Well, when that changes, don't feel like you have to stay. You can leave—"

"I'm not leaving you alone." He hadn't meant the harsh

tone, but seriously? Did she think he was just going to get bored and abandon her? What kind of man did she think he was?

Her gray eyes widened. "Okay. I get it. Thanks."

She didn't get it. She definitely *didn't* get it.

Grant watched as she walked up the stairs.

Ridiculous woman. Gorgeous, ridiculous woman.

Apparently, she still had no idea how he felt about her. Not that he could blame her. He'd done his best to hide it. He'd been in love with her for so many years that the longing for her seemed like a part of him now, as constant as the faith that never felt strong enough and the guilt that always hummed below the surface.

He checked the doors to make sure they were all locked.

After brushing his teeth and changing into the sleep pants and T-shirt he'd bought, he grabbed a throw blanket from the back of a chair and stretched out on the lumpy sofa, not bothering to turn on the TV. He'd only offered to watch something because he'd wanted to extend his time with Summer. They'd spent the entire day together, and all evening the night before. But he was pretty sure he'd never get enough.

There was a bed awaiting him at the top of the stairs—probably a too-short bed, though at least it would have a decent mattress. But he wanted to stay near the doors, the first line of defense in case Ramón somehow tracked them down.

CHAPTER THIRTEEN

Summer slept harder than she had in ages. She'd spent some time researching an idea she had while Grant had been looking up names the night before, one she hadn't wanted to mention yet. So far, he'd been leading their...investigation, if they could call it that. She wanted to contribute. Maybe that was silly, but she didn't like having to depend on Grant—on anybody. Ever since he'd rescued her in that parking garage, she felt like he'd been doing the bulk of the work, protecting her, coming up with the good ideas. She'd just been swept along in his plans. Not that she didn't appreciate him, she did. She just hated playing the role of damsel in distress. She hated having to depend on him, on anybody.

She'd had enough experience with people to know it was only a matter of time before they got bored or distracted or...drunk.

After an hour of research and a couple of quick emails, she went to bed thinking her idea might turn into something worth following up on.

She'd conked out within seconds of lying down, not stirring

again until nearly six thirty. She flipped on the overhead light to start her day, shocked anew at the explosion of pink.

She might as well have spent her night inside a package of bubble gum.

The little girl who lived here was very lucky to grow up surrounded by whimsical images of princesses and castles and unicorns. What flights of fancy must this girl enjoy? What happily-ever-afters did she envision for herself? Summer hoped the child could hang onto those dreams. Life was hard. She saw zero downside to believing in fairy tales for as long as possible.

Her own childhood fantasies had been ripped from her at eight years old. From that moment on, she'd known there'd be no knight coming to her rescue, that the only person who could be counted on to take care of Summer was Summer. And if she wanted her little sister safe, she certainly couldn't look to her parents or anybody else.

Misty found Summer's protectiveness annoying now, but she certainly hadn't when their father's drunken rages had sent Misty scurrying to hide behind her big sister. Summer'd perfected her tough-as-nails demeanor at an age when most girls were playing with Barbies and learning to braid their hair.

Rather than dwell on unwelcome memories, Summer changed into the cheap yoga pants and sweatshirt she'd bought the night before, laced up her sneakers, and tiptoed down the stairs in the quiet house. As she descended, the sound of light snoring got louder.

Silently, she crept across the dark living room and peeked over the back of the sofa. Grant was sound asleep, one arm bent over his eyes, the other hanging off the cushions. Didn't look comfortable but, by the rhythmic breathing, he wasn't complaining.

She hovered to study him, barely visible in the darkness, surprised by the affection that rose inside her. She'd always appreciated Grant's professionalism. Considering his wealth of experience compared to her lack thereof, it was ridiculous that he technically worked for her. He'd always been loyal, not just to Jon but to the whole team.

In the last thirty-six hours, he'd proved a dedication to her that she'd never anticipated. He'd gone far beyond what anybody would expect of a work partner, putting his entire life on hold to ensure she was safe.

Why?

Did he stay by Summer's side out of allegiance to Jon? Because she and Grant had never been friends, not really. She figured if it came down to it, he'd risk his life to protect her—like she would him—but that didn't make them buddies so much as brother-and-sister-in-arms.

Would she have put her entire life on hold for Grant's sake? She had to admit that, before this week, it wouldn't have occurred to her. If he'd had a problem, she'd have wished him luck in solving it and then stepped away. Not because she didn't care but because she figured he had people in his life who mattered more than she did. Surely, he had a whole gang of people who could be counted on in a pinch.

Five brothers, for instance. Well, four now. And parents who loved him. And a best friend in Jon. And the guys at work, and probably other friends. It wouldn't have crossed her mind that Grant might want or need her help.

But when she'd been in trouble, he hadn't waited for someone else to step in. He'd stuck by her side without being asked, and when she'd offered him an out the night before, he'd acted insulted.

There was something very attractive about a man who willingly made himself into a woman's protector.

She hadn't expected rescue from a handsome knight since she was eight years old. And yet...yet maybe that was exactly who Grant was—some kind of modern-day knight, willing to take up arms in defense of someone weaker.

Did that make her the damsel? Ha. Nobody'd ever confused her with a princess, and she hadn't been defenseless in a long, long time. No, Grant didn't see her as somebody who needed rescuing. They were partners.

Partners who...cared.

Like she and Jon had been. Except Grant wasn't her cousin. He was a strong, handsome, kind man who'd chosen to stand by her side.

He shifted and stretched, and she stepped back, not willing to get caught staring. When his breathing settled again, she hurried to the door and urged it open quietly. She slipped into the chilly morning.

She walked, stretched, and then jogged as the sun turned the gray-and-black world to color. Some of the trees that lined the street were still bare, others sported new leaves.

The pale blue sky brightened as the sun climbed higher, a backdrop to the little houses that lined the college town's narrow roads.

Like the world around her, Grant was coming more into focus as well. She'd thought, working as his partner for months, that she had a pretty good handle on him. But he was much deeper, more complex, than she'd imagined.

Of course, weren't all people? It was easy to shove strangers into neatly labeled boxes—"smart," "kind," "competent," "cruel." But the longer Summer lived, the more she realized that nobody was quite so easily categorized.

Take Jon's girlfriend, for instance. At first glance, Denise had seemed privileged, beautiful, and talented. And she was those things, no doubt. But she was also sweet, gentle, and generous. She adored her daughter and would do anything for her. She might have been privileged—though she'd earned everything she had. She was also courageous—proved not only when she'd been kidnapped but before that, when she'd faced her ex-husband and told him all her secrets.

Summer couldn't imagine being that transparent.

Denise had refused to stay in the box Summer had labeled for her.

And Grant wouldn't stay in his either.

The more she knew about him—the more she knew *him*—the more she liked him.

She froze, barely seeing the stately brick university buildings all around, as the truth of that burrowed into her.

She didn't just like Grant, she *liked* Grant.

In a way she hadn't liked any man...ever.

With her family the way it was, she hadn't had the emotional energy for boys in junior high or high school. After that, she'd been signed by the modeling agency, and suddenly men had fallen over themselves to get close to her. But she'd seen through their flattery. She had a good body and a decent face, but so what? Those didn't encapsulate who she was, and the men who were attracted to just those things didn't know her. She'd managed years of modeling without any romantic entanglements.

After the kidnapping, she'd fought for her sister's emotional recovery—and her own. And then she'd started the business with Jon and Bartlett, poured herself into getting physically fit and training for the job so she'd be able to defend herself and others.

Sure, there'd been men around her all along, but none had ever stood out. She'd always had a tender place in her heart for Grant, but that was only because he'd been one of her rescuers.

She'd never forget the first moment she saw his face, half-hidden behind the helmet, giant rifle aimed and ready. In her travels during her modeling career, she'd seen some beautiful sights, but nothing would ever compare to the image of a man in camouflage, holding out his hand and saying, "Come on. Let's get you out of here."

But even then, aside from gratitude and eventually camaraderie, she'd had no *feelings* for Grant.

Until now.

What was wrong with her? She was falling for her partner. How ridiculous. How...cliché.

She started jogging back toward Bryan's house, trying to figure out what to do with her inappropriate emotions. In years past, she'd have berated herself, called herself all kinds of idiot. When she felt her mind going that direction, she shook off the unhelpful thoughts and decided to pray instead.

She was getting accustomed to praying, but she was certainly no expert on hearing God's voice or sensing His presence. She got no quick answers, so she tucked her inappropriate feelings away and walked up Bryan's driveway. She'd left the door locked, unwilling to risk the two sleeping men inside, and she didn't have a key. If nobody answered her knock, she'd be stuck on the front porch until someone came out.

But as she climbed the three concrete steps, the door swung open. Grant's oversize body filled the entry, and her heart did a strange little flip that had nothing to do with her workout.

By his glower, he was far less happy to see her than she was to see him.

"What?"

He took her by the upper arm, pulled her inside, and slammed the door. "Are you out of your mind?"

"I just went for a—"

"What if Ramón's men had found you? You could have been taken, or..." He balled his hands into fists. "I didn't even know you weren't here until I saw you outside. He could have shoved you in a trunk and been halfway to Canada before I even realized you were gone."

"He doesn't know where we are."

"How do you know?" The words were loud enough to shake the foundation, and she fought an urge to retreat. She'd seen anger like that, and it rarely ended well. But she'd never cowered in front of her father, and she sure as heck wasn't going to cower now.

She stepped forward, kept her voice level. "Don't. Yell. At. Me."

He blinked and swallowed. Ran a hand over his messy hair. He was breathing heavily as if he'd been the one to return from a jog, not her. He eased away, inhaled a deep breath, and blew it out. "I'm sorry. The thought of you out there, alone, unprotected... It scared me."

"As you can see, I'm fine."

"You might not have been. You got lucky."

"I considered the chances that Ramón could have tracked us to your brother's house. Remember Bryan said this place isn't in his name? Not even the utilities? I felt pretty strongly that I was safe."

"Here, maybe. But out there"—he gestured to the windows as if to encompass the entire city of Brunswick, maybe the whole state of Maine—"he could have seen you."

Summer brushed past Grant and headed for the kitchen.

She stopped short at the door frame. Bryan was leaning against the countertop, a steaming mug in his hand. "Good morning."

"Oh. Hi."

"Sorry for my brother's—"

"Don't apologize for me," Grant snapped.

Bryan half shrugged and sipped his coffee.

Okay, then. "Mind if I get a drink?"

"Help yourself."

She grabbed a glass and pressed it against the dispenser on the refrigerator. The sound of clinking cubes was deafening in the otherwise silent kitchen. She added cold water and sipped.

"It's good to get the most awkward moments out of the way early, I always say."

Summer chuckled at Bryan's attempt to lighten the mood.

Grant growled. "I'm just saying, it was stupid."

She didn't think so, but she heard the concern behind his anger. "I'm sorry I scared you."

"You want to go for a run in the morning, wake me and I'll go with you."

She could picture that, the two of them falling into step together. He could beat her in any race, any day of the year, but he'd never let her know it. That was the kind of man he was.

"If you think you can keep up," she said. "I wouldn't want to make you look bad."

His glower morphed to a wry smile. "I'll do my best."

Something about his words, the look on his face, had her skin overheating. She took another long sip of her water.

Bryan looked from his brother to Summer and back. What was he seeing? More than she'd probably intended to show.

She had no idea how to behave in front of a guy she liked. It felt weird and...squishy or something. Good, but also scary and potentially painful. And...

And she needed out of that kitchen before Bryan and Grant figured out what she was thinking. Grant was too much of a gentleman to call her on her utterly inappropriate reaction, but that didn't mean she wanted him to know. And who could guess what Bryan might say if he got wind?

"Okay if I take a shower?"

"Help yourself," Bryan said. "There're towels in the linen closet in the upstairs hallway."

"Great." She downed the rest of her water and fled upstairs before she let anything slip.

Summer's hair was still wet when she descended the stairs wearing the stiff new clothes she'd bought the night before. The jeans fit well, but the pale green sweater was snugger than she'd thought it would be, hugging her curves. She'd only bought a couple of tops, so she was going to have to wear it eventually.

She'd checked her email and was eager to tell Grant what she'd learned. She'd expected to hear the brothers chatting, but it was quiet when she reached the landing. Bryan's office was empty. A glance through the window showed his Subaru wasn't there.

When she stepped into the kitchen, Grant was seated at the table, attention on his laptop. His hair was wet, combed back the way he always wore it. He must've used Bryan's shower. He looked up when she stepped in. "Good morning. Pretty, uh..." He waved vaguely toward her, and his cheeks turned pink.

He'd nearly complimented her. On her looks. Rather than react to that, she said, "Trying for civil this time?"

"Sorry about..." He huffed a deep breath. "I wasn't just mad at you. I slept on the couch so I'd hear if anybody came in. I guess I was mad at myself when I realized you'd gone out without me hearing. Some watchman."

Summer leaned against the wide doorjamb that separated the kitchen from the living area. "If you'd needed to wake up, you would have."

"What makes you say that?"

"Don't you think there's some instinct that warns us when danger is near?"

His eyes squinted as he studied her. "Has that been your experience?"

She thought of the way she used to wake up when her father was on a tear. It wasn't that he was loud, only that there was something unique about the sounds he made when he was drunk and angry—the low growl of his voice, the seething hatred in his words.

She'd pop out of a deep sleep, wide awake and ready. Nobody could predict who would receive his vitriol—Mom or Krystal. Rarely Summer, because she was the only one willing to stand up to him. And she made a point to protect Misty.

She wasn't about to explain that.

She made her way into the kitchen, where Bryan, she assumed, had left a package of bagels on the counter. "You eat?"

"I was waiting for you." Grant stood and opened the fridge. "He has eggs. I could make omelets."

"I'm not a huge breakfast eater. Any fruit?"

He opened one of the crisper drawers, slammed it shut, and opened another. "Apples okay?"

"Sure."

He handed her one, then pulled out the egg carton. "Not that apples aren't a perfectly nice breakfast, but I'm having eggs."

While she sliced her apple into bite-sized pieces, Grant fried himself two eggs and toasted a bagel. He settled at the kitchen table with his feast, eyeing her tiny breakfast. "Is that seriously all you're going to eat?"

"I might have a bagel in a bit. I'm not that hungry right now."

He swallowed a bite of his eggs. "You never struck me as the type to worry about your weight." He watched her over the top of his mug as he sipped.

She paused, a piece of apple halfway to her mouth. "Are you calling me fat?"

He nearly spit out his coffee. "What? No. I just meant..."

She laughed, the easy sound sending heat to her cheeks. What was she doing, teasing him? That wasn't her style. But it was fun with Grant.

He glowered at her. "Not funny."

"Very funny." She popped the apple in her mouth.

"And who cuts an apple into tiny pieces?" he asked. "Why not just bite into the thing?"

She swallowed the small bite. "I prefer not to attack my food like a wild animal."

He growled and shoved the bagel in his mouth, tearing off a hunk.

Eliciting another laugh from her.

He chewed and smiled and looked away, his cheeks turning red for the second time in ten minutes.

Not that the conversation was personal or flirty or... anything. Yet she tried to imagine it taking place in the break room at work but couldn't conjure the image.

They ate in silence for a few beats, the only sounds coming from his fork scraping against the plate.

"I had an idea last night." She'd been so distracted by him, she'd forgotten.

He swallowed a bite. "What was that?"

"We're looking for collectors of pre-Columbian antiquities. The guy in the garage obviously knew his stuff. That he might be a professor makes sense. But maybe this isn't about someone who wants to collect the pieces so much as sell them."

"Okay...?" He drew out the word.

"We could look at antique dealers. And not just that, but... Did you know that a lot of antiquities that are found in museums and private collections could have been stolen?"

"From other dealers, or—?"

"No. More like... Many nations have made it a crime to remove antiquities, or to sell them, in an effort to preserve their cultural heritage."

"So you're saying Ramón is stealing these antiquities from... wherever he's getting them?" Grant's dark eyes glimmered with amusement. "Because I think that was pretty obvious by the way he's bringing them in."

"Yeah, I know that. And maybe this is irrelevant, but think about that little gold statue. Because it was stolen, probably straight from a dig site or even a grave—"

"No, really?"

"I guess it's pretty common for locals to dig up grave sites looking for valuables and then sell them."

"That's"—he set his bagel down—"distasteful."

"Sorry to ruin your appetite."

"Oh, don't worry about me." He forked the remainder of his eggs into his mouth and nodded for her to continue.

"Because it's illegal, pieces like the one I saw Sunday would need provenance before they could go up for sale."

"Provenance is...?"

"Details about where the items came from, who owned them when, and how they got on the market. Without paper-work showing that stuff, dealers would assume they were stolen. From what I can tell, it's a federal crime to buy and sell items that are considered cultural heritage."

"Okay. But maybe Ramón's things are destined for the black market."

"But people who buy items like that want to display them, right? I mean, how many people are out there spending that kind of money on something they can't show off? And if it does end up on the black market, it gets sold for a fraction of what it would get at auction or in a shop."

"Really? I always assumed things were more expensive on the black market."

She shrugged. "Maybe other stuff, but not antiquities, not according to my research. For all those reasons I mentioned."

"So all of this led you to conclude...what?"

"That we need to be looking for somebody who not only knows all about antiquities but who would have connections with dealers and forgers."

"To create the...provenance."

"Exactly."

Grant wiped his mouth and set his napkin aside. "So, where do we start?"

"I found someone last night. She wrote an in-depth article about this for the *Boston Herald*. She seems to really know her stuff."

"A reporter?" By his tone, he wasn't eager to talk to someone in the media.

"She's a curator at the Museum of Fine Arts. She lives in Newburyport, and she's available today."

He sat back. "You already reached out?"

"Last night. She responded this morning."

"What'd you tell her?"

"I might have led her to believe I was working for a private investigator."

His eyebrows hiked. "There are rules about that, Summer. You can't just—"

"You have a license. Call me your assistant."

He regarded her through narrowed eyes. For a moment, she feared he'd be angry, but then he smiled. "Good thinking. What time do we have to be there?"

CHAPTER FOURTEEN

Grant cleaned Bryan's kitchen while Summer nibbled half of a bagel with cream cheese. He'd starve to death if he ate like she did. Of course, with that body, she was obviously doing something right.

And that was a train of thought he needed to climb off of straightaway. Though her words echoed in his brain. *Are you calling me fat?*

She'd been teasing him. *Teasing.*

That was a first. And he was pretty sure he'd even seen her blush.

Not that he'd come with her to pursue her romantically, but it seemed like, it *felt* like, maybe their relationship had at least progressed past coworkers and partners. Maybe she was starting to see him as a friend. Maybe even as more than a friend.

He needed to be careful. He couldn't let on about his feelings until he knew she was open to the idea. Otherwise, he'd scare her away.

"What?"

He blinked, realized he'd been watching her, and returned his focus to wiping down the countertops. "Just thinking about

Jon. He looked up all those names last night. Only one of them owns property near the coast. Maybe we could drive by today, see if there's a cove or a dock or something."

"Sure. Where is it?"

"Ogunquit. It's about an hour down the coast, right on the way."

She nodded, her lips tipping up in a smile.

Oh, man. When she smiled at him, his stupid heart flipped like a pancake. And she was smiling at him more lately.

He sent what was probably his millionth prayer heavenward that she would eventually *see* him. "Bryan found a couple of duffel bags he wasn't using. They're on the sofa. Grab one and pack up your things."

She carried her empty plate to the dishwasher and slid it in. "I know you and your brother have some history, but this seems like a safe place. Why don't we come back?"

"I'd rather not."

She was quiet for a long moment, studying him through narrowed eyes. "Is it so awful, whatever happened, that you can't get past it?"

"We'll find somewhere safe, I promise." Though where, he had no idea.

"We don't have a lot of options. And he obviously wants us to stay."

Before Bryan had left for his class, he'd practically begged Grant to reconsider staying there. But...

Being with Bryan made the guilt that always hummed beneath his skin crawl its way to the surface like a rash.

Which wasn't Bryan's fault, or Summer's, for that matter.

He was being selfish.

"Maybe." It was the best he could do. If they couldn't find somewhere as safe as this, they could come back. "Bring your stuff anyway, just in case."

She smiled at him, a real smile this time, wide and open, and a whole griddle-full of pancakes flipped inside him.

"What time should we leave?"

He cleared his throat and forced his gaze away. "Whenever you're ready."

Fifteen minutes later, they locked Bryan's house and pulled out of the driveway. Grant had a new key on his keyring. Before he'd left that morning, Bryan had insisted he take it.

His brother was being exceptionally nice to him. Grant didn't know what to do with all that kindness.

The drive was uneventful. Grant didn't bother forcing conversation, knowing Summer was as comfortable with silence as he was. They listened to music, chatted occasionally, but mostly kept to their own thoughts until they neared the address.

"It's coming up now," Grant said.

They gazed at the little cabins tucked into the forest on both sides of the road. Through the trees on the left, he caught glimpses of the Atlantic not a hundred yards away.

These homes were mostly cedar shake, weathered and gray. The places were small, but he figured this close to the shore, they were probably valued at a million or more.

"There it is." Summer pointed to a two-story white house with a wraparound porch.

He whistled. "Nice digs."

"No kidding. Where does a professor get the money to buy something like that?"

"Could be a family home, an inheritance," he said. "Or maybe he does business with smugglers." He passed the house and pulled over on the narrow road. "Come on. Let's have a look around."

He climbed from the car and inhaled the fresh, briny scent of the ocean. A cool breeze rippled through the trees as he started up the gravel drive as if he owned the place. One thing he'd learned—act like you belong and people rarely question you.

At his side, Summer walked with her back straight, all swagger and confidence. He loved that. He caught her eye and winked, and she smiled.

Oh, man.

They reached the house, but rather than approach the front door, they skirted around the side. As he'd guessed, it had a great view of the Atlantic, so close that the sound of waves crashing against rocks carried over the whisper of the wind, the roar growing louder as they approached. But was there access to the water? The Maine coastline, because of all its inlets and islands, was longer than the coast of California. But unlike California, it was rocky and, in many places, treacherous. Beautiful, but not exactly inviting.

Grant and Summer kept to the edge of the property, where the wide lawn met the thick woods that separated this house from the next. The backyard was covered with grass, which ended at a waist-high stone wall. They climbed atop the wall and looked down at a rocky cliff that dropped a good thirty yards, nearly straight down, to the water below.

"Look." Summer pointed at giant boulders that stuck a couple of feet out of the water. At high tide, they might be hidden, which would make this area treacherous for anybody foolish enough to try to get a boat close. "Not exactly a hospitable port in the storm."

"Nope." Grant leaned forward to get a better view of the shore below.

Summer stood beside him, her gaze flicking all around, looking for threats. Just like he'd taught her.

"No staircase. No access at all."

"This is not our guy."

"Just a name to cross off the list."

They were headed back toward the road when the squeak of a door warned him an instant before a woman stepped onto the wraparound porch. She shielded her eyes with her hand and squinted their direction. "What are you doing here?"

Grant grabbed Summer's hand as if it were the most natural thing in the world. "My girlfriend and I are trying to find an old friend of hers. She swears she lived around here." Grant walked toward the woman, swinging Summer's hand as if this were all perfectly normal. "She said they used to jump off the rocks into the ocean."

"We did," Summer said. "It was the most magical summer." Her voice took on an airy tone as she pressed her hand against her chest. "Her house was so much like yours, though, come to think of it..." She tilted her head to the side and surveyed the structure. "Smaller, I think. You know how everything seems huge when you're a kid."

As they got closer, the woman's pinched expression became clearer. She was on the heavy side, wearing a purple sweatshirt over blue jeans. She did not look happy.

"Obviously, this isn't it," Grant said. "You'd have to be an idiot to jump off that into the ocean. And how would you get back up?"

"Can't," the woman said. "We wouldn't let our kids anywhere near the edge. Course, they're grown now."

"I'm so sorry we bothered you." Summer tugged on his hand, and they started toward the side of the house. "You have a nice day."

"You'd better stay off private property," she yelled. "Not everyone's as hospitable as I am."

When they neared the side of the house, Summer whispered, "You're a quick thinker."

"You're a good actor." He glanced over his shoulder to see the woman watching them. He picked up his pace, urging

Summer to hurry. He led her to the passenger side and opened the door—keeping up the pretense and all that—before rushing around to the driver's side.

He made a U-turn. When they were out of sight of the house, Summer burst out laughing.

"I know it's not funny, but…"

"She looked like she wanted to rip our heads off." Grant joined in the laughter.

"She called herself 'hospitable.'"

"About as hospitable as that cliff." He navigated back to the main road. "I'd hate to see her version of *in*hospitable."

Summer chuckled one more time. "Too bad, though. A dead end."

"It's good to eliminate suspects. Eventually, we'll find our guy."

"I appreciate your confidence."

"One thing I've learned." Grant turned back toward the highway. "There's nothing more important than confidence, especially when you have no idea what you're doing."

CHAPTER FIFTEEN

This feeling, this joyful, fluttery feeling... Was this what all her silly friends in high school had been going on about? It'd started the instant Grant had taken her hand, and it hadn't abated.

If Summer didn't know better, she'd think she needed a couple of Tylenol and a nap. But she wasn't sick. She felt light and optimistic and bubbly.

Happy.

All because she had a crush.

It was ridiculous. But also...

Sort of nice.

Except, beside her in the Land Rover, Grant's hands were gripping the steering wheel as if it'd offended him.

"What's wrong?"

"Nothing."

But he was practically scowling. "Are you sure?"

"Just thinking... We got lucky with that woman. What if we'd been at the right house? What if the collector had seen us there?"

"We'd have made up a story and gotten out of there, just like we did. Only now we'd know where Ramón would be off-loading his goods."

"Maybe. Or maybe he'd have recognized you, pulled a gun—"

"We have guns, too, Grant. Besides, the stranger in the garage didn't see me."

"You didn't think Ramón knew you'd followed him."

"Ramón must've sensed I was behind him. But I was well hidden when his contact arrived. There's no way he would have seen me."

"But Ramón could have told him—"

"Do you think he would tell the guy whose house he's using that somebody might be on to them?" She considered the idea, then said, "No, I don't think so. He wouldn't want to spook the guy."

Grant's hands loosened the tiniest bit. "You're probably right."

"Is that what you were worried about? That we could have bumped into the nasally-voiced collector? Because he wasn't exactly intimidating. I think you could take him."

"Not worried about me," Grant mumbled under his breath.

Oh. He was worried about her. The words did nothing to cool her growing crush.

"I saw the guy," Summer said. "I'm pretty sure *I* could take him too."

That elicited a quick smile. "Probably."

Back in the day, Newburyport, Massachusetts, just south of the New Hampshire border, had been a fishing village. Summer had never been there, and as Grant navigated to the restaurant where they would meet the museum curator, she gazed at the charming little town. Maybe it was the most charming place she'd ever seen. Or maybe her newfound—and utterly inappropriate—feelings for Grant were affecting how she saw the world because she'd been pretty charmed by Ogunquit. And the Bowdoin campus.

She wasn't generally the type of person to be charmed by anything. Or to use the word *charmed*, for that matter.

He found the restaurant and parked. They walked in the chilly breeze along brick-paved sidewalks to the bar and grill. The sun peeked through the growing clouds but barely made a dent in the temperature, which would probably peak in the midsixties. The summer season was just six weeks away, but nobody had told the temperature that.

When they stepped inside, the scents of grilling meat and fresh seafood hit her.

At the stand, Grant said, "We're meeting someone. A woman."

"I just sat a lady." The host pointed toward a woman gazing out the back windows. "That her?"

Summer shrugged. "I guess we'll find out." She led the way and stopped near the table. "Kathleen Hopkins?"

The woman stood and held out her hand. "Summer Lake. It's nice to meet you. I love your name."

For once, a remark about her silly name didn't bring irritation. She smiled. "Thanks. This is my partner, Grant Wright."

The woman shook his hand. She looked to be in her late fifties, maybe early sixties, with short brown hair and matching eyes that sparkled over makeup-free cheeks. She was short—maybe five-two—and on the chubby side, but she had a pretty face and a warm smile. "So you're the detective," she said to Grant, then turned to Summer. "And you're the assistant?"

"Sort of." Summer took the chair across from Kathleen at the small square table, leaving the one between them for Grant.

He settled his overlarge frame into it, giving the woman a kind smile. Before he could correct Summer's less-than-forthright remarks from that morning, she said, "Grant and I work for a personal security company. We're trying to assess a threat."

"I see. I hope I can help."

Before they could ask their questions, a server stopped and took drink orders.

"I hope you two will eat with me," Kathleen said after he walked away. "They make a Cajun shrimp pasta to die for. I don't usually splurge on lunch, but as long as we're here—"

"Lunch is on me." Grant raised a hand. "It's the least we can do, taking your time away from your busy day."

"Oh, it's my pleasure. Ever since the divorce, I find myself alone far too often. It's gotten to where I dread days off."

"I know what you mean," Summer said. "I live alone myself." Living alone, her sisters busy with their own lives, and now Jon living in Coventry, days off felt like time served in purgatory. She knew her life was pathetic when she longed to return to work. But she didn't say all that. "It's nice to break up the day."

Grant gave her a long, appraising look that Summer had no time to analyze.

"Exactly," Kathleen said. "You're doing me a favor."

Summer gave the menu a quick look and decided on a salad,. "The article you wrote for the *Herald*—that must've taken some extensive research."

"It did. There's nothing that gets my goat more than rich people stealing from poor people. There's a special place in hell for the likes of them."

Grant set his menu aside. "What do you mean?"

"Well, that's what happens. Some wealthy sort shows up in a poor village in Peru or Bolivia or wherever, offers the locals money for whatever they can find. The locals are dirt poor, barely scraping by. So what do they do? They dig up ancient burial sites, dig around in their own ancestors' bones—risking arrest or worse—in hopes of finding something valuable. They turn it over to the thief, who pays them pennies compared to what it's worth. But they need those pennies—those pennies feed and clothe their families.

"And then the antiquities are smuggled away from their cultural homeland and into the US or Europe or wherever, and sold to museums or auctioned off to the highest bidder. It's despicable."

"From my research," Summer said, "there's been a backlash against that kind of thing."

The server delivered their drinks and took their orders.

After he left, Kathleen said, "A lot of museums have had to return items they'd purchased to their countries of origin."

"Including the Museum of Fine Arts?" Grant asked.

"Sure. The MFA isn't immune. We returned eight pieces of Nigerian origin. Those were different, though. They were a gift from a collector who'd bought them in good faith. How was he to know they'd been stolen?"

"How do they figure it out?" Summer asked.

"Oh, depends on the piece. Someone'll recognize it and notify the country or the person from whom it was stolen. Or just demand to see the provenance." Kathleen sipped her drink. "At the museum, we want to display art from all over the world, from various time periods. It's a desire to share the beauty of those cultures with the public that drives us. Still, if the items belong to Nigeria..." She shrugged as if to say, *what can you do?*

She went on to tell stories of other museums dealing with similar situations. And auction houses having to either cancel shows or remove certain items.

Summer sipped her Coke, Grant his iced tea, giving the woman ample opportunity to talk. Minutes passed without either of them interrupting. The woman was a wealth of information.

"Of course there are lawyers involved, and negotiations with heads of state and the like," Kathleen said. "Some of the items are quite valuable."

Their meals were delivered. Grant's burger smelled divine, and the scents of garlic and shrimp wafted off Kathleen's pasta dish. Summer was almost regretting the salad—until she bit into it.

Spicy walnuts paired with tart green apples and warm salty chicken, all mixed together with a sweet vinaigrette. Delicious.

They quieted as they dug into their meals.

Setting her fork aside, Summer said, "The museums have good motives for collecting those things, of course."

"Well, sure," Kathleen said. "But not everybody does. You wouldn't believe the kinds of people who get into this business because they want to make a profit or display their conquests like peacocks do their feathers. They don't care who their little 'hobby' hurts."

"Anybody come to mind?" Grant asked.

"You mean names?"

He dipped his head.

"Well, gosh. I don't know." Kathleen shifted in her chair and sipped her drink. "I can think of a few. Well, two were arrested. I think they're in jail. You really need names?"

"The thing is," Summer said, "I think I got wind of someone trading stolen pre-Columbian antiquities." She had to be careful she didn't say too much. This woman didn't need the details. "We believe this person is planning to smuggle them into the country. We wondered if you had any idea who might be interested in such a thing."

Kathleen wiped her mouth and leaned forward, lowering her voice. "When I was researching that article, one name kept floating to the top."

Summer and Grant shared a look. Grant said, "Go on."

"Now, I'm not one for pointing fingers, and I have no proof, but this guy... I wouldn't put it past him." She huffed, shaking her head. "He's as greedy as they come. Married himself some sort of heiress, as I hear it."

Summer managed to keep her mouth shut. She didn't want to say or do anything that might stop Kathleen from sharing.

"You didn't hear it from me." She looked around as if spies lurked everywhere. "Owns a little antique shop, procures things for rich people with more cash than morals, if you know what I mean."

Grant's glance flicked to Summer. "What's his name?"

"Bannister. Richard Bannister."

He sat back. Met Summer's eyes, and based on what she saw in his expression, the name meant something to him.

"Does that help?" Kathleen looked eager and hopeful.

"Very much," Summer said, though she wasn't sure how. But Grant's knee was jiggling beside her. Seemed he was ready to get out of there, get moving on the tip.

A tip she'd led them to.

She tried not to congratulate herself too much. All they had was a name. They were a long way from proving Richard Bannister and the stranger in the parking garage were one and the same.

CHAPTER SIXTEEN

As soon as Summer's seatbelt clicked, Grant asked the question that'd been humming in the back of his mind ever since Kathleen had given them a name.

"You looked up the female professors last night. Wasn't one of them a Bannister?"

Summer pressed her lips together, looked up toward the Land Rover's ceiling, and then nodded. "I think, maybe."

On his cell phone, Grant navigated to the email Bryan's friend had sent and tapped on the list. "Right here. Beverly Bannister."

"An heiress," Summer said. "Could explain how they can afford a house on the coast."

Grant dialed and pulled into traffic.

"What's up?" Jon asked in lieu of *hello*.

"I'm here with Summer," Grant said. "Can you research someone for us?"

"Sure. Did any of those other leads pan out?"

"None of the ones we sent you yesterday, but I have a good feeling about this one. Two names. Richard and Beverly Bannister. We think they're married."

"Any idea where they live?"

"According to this," Grant said, "Beverly's a professor at UNH."

"I'll get right on it. Summer, you all right?"

"I'm good."

"Grant's on his best behavior?"

He scowled at the speaker, and Summer smiled. "As good as he gets, I suppose."

"Hmm." Jon didn't sound amused. "Grant, remember what I told you."

"Thanks for your help, man." He disconnected the phone.

"Told you about what?" Summer asked.

"He's just worried about your safety." Which was true, but in this case, Jon was thinking about a different kind of safety than what Summer probably assumed. Not that Grant needed the reminder. Summer wasn't the type of woman to let a guy take advantage, and Grant certainly wasn't the type to try. The fact that his best friend didn't know him better...

"Where are we headed now?" she asked.

"Hopefully, Jon'll find that address, and we can either cross it off the list or, if it's on the coast, swing by."

"And then?"

That was the question. He was driving toward the interstate but had no definite destination in mind.

They could rent a couple of rooms in Portsmouth, but figuring Ramón had his name, he didn't want to run his credit card—or Summer's. How did one go about finding hotels that accepted cash? That didn't need to run a credit card for incidentals? Did such a place exist? If it did, would it be the kind of place he'd want to take Summer?

What other options were there? He could reach out to a couple of former clients from that summer, Thomas and Josie. He didn't know them well, but Jon had introduced them the weekend he'd moved into his apartment. Thomas had an apartment over his business. Maybe they could stay there.

He handed his phone to Summer. "Text Jon and ask him for Thomas Windham's phone number."

"He lives in Coventry."

"Yeah. I'm going to call—"

"That's way out of the way."

"You have a better idea?"

"Um, yeah. Your brother—"

"I don't want to go back to Bryan's."

When she said nothing, he glanced her way and found her staring at him. "What?"

"What happened between you two?"

The last thing he wanted was to tell her the most horrible thing in his life. But...but she had asked. She cared enough to want to know. And by the way she was looking at him, she was genuinely curious.

So maybe...

He was angling onto I-95 when his phone rang, too loud in the quiet car. He pressed the button on the steering wheel to answer. "This is Grant."

"Hey, sweetie." His mother's voice was more cheerful than usual. "I'm glad I caught you. Bryan said you were in the area."

"I was last night," Grant said.

"Oh." The single syllable had lost some of its cheer. "I was hoping... Camilla and the kids are here for the weekend. Everyone's meeting at the camp."

"I didn't know they were coming."

"We didn't either until yesterday. She doesn't like to broadcast their plans. You know, with the...the people who..." Her voice faded.

"That makes sense," Grant said quickly. "I'm glad she's being cautious."

"So?" Mom sounded so hopeful. "Can you come?"

He glanced at Summer, who was watching him closely. "I'm not alone."

"Bryan said you're traveling with your partner. Jon's cousin, right? He's talked about her before. I'm sure she's a lovely woman."

Summer smiled at the compliment.

"Yes, she's something. She's right here, actually."

"Oh. Hello, dear. I'm Peggy."

"Hi. Nice to sort of meet you."

"Hopefully, we'll meet in person. If you two are going to be around, that is."

"I'd love that." Summer sounded genuinely eager, meaning Grant would get no help from her.

He could think of no good excuse to avoid his family, and he couldn't imagine a safer place for the two of them to hole up.

Plus, he wouldn't mind seeing Daniel's widow and kids.

"We're not prepared for the ride," Grant said.

"Dad can bring blankets. We're already here. Well, obviously, Dad and I have come back for supplies. We've already got the stoves going."

He caught Summer's confusion out of the corner of his eye. Ha. If she thought this conversation was weird, wait until she saw the place and met the rest of his family.

"Bryan'll be there?"

"Already is," Mom said. "He's gathering wood. It would mean so much to your father and me. To all of us."

Grant couldn't think of a single excuse not to go, aside from the long, long drive. But what else did they have to do? "Fine."

"Great!" Her enthusiasm started his heart pounding. Nerves. Anxiety. And maybe a little bit of anticipation bubbling up. He loved his family, every one of them. It wasn't their fault that he'd wrecked his place with them.

"I'll let Dad know," Mom said. "Call when you know your ETA. And try to get here before sundown."

"I remember. See you soon." He ended the call, shaking his head. "I'm not sure if you're going to thank me or curse me for this."

"She seems nice."

"Mom? Yeah, she's the best. Dad too. But between them and my brothers, and my sister-in-law and her kids...and my grand-parents will probably be there. It'll be total chaos."

"Really?" She seemed not put off but excited by the prospect. "I think I can handle it."

He had no doubt she could. The question was—could he?

"Do me a favor?" he said. "Call Jon and find out if he's close to getting an address."

She used Grant's phone, so Jon's abrupt, "I'm working on it," came through the speakers.

"Wow," Summer said. "Annoyed much?"

"Sorry. Thought you were Grant. Richard and Beverly Bannister own a house in Durham. But she comes from money. Couple of trust funds, a non-profit. It'll take some work to track down all the properties they own. I'm going to need more time."

"No problem," Summer said. "Grant and I are headed to his family's...camp?" She looked at him for confirmation, and he nodded.

"Mom called," Grant said. "Camilla and the kids are in town, so—"

"That's great," Jon said. "I can't think of a safer place. Is the whole family going?"

"Yup."

"So you'll be off the grid for a while?"

"Sam got a satellite or something. No cell service, but we should have Wi-Fi."

"I'll let you know if I learn anything," Jon said. "We have until...when?"

Summer fielded that. "Ramón just said it would be some-time next week."

"A few days then," Jon said.

"We need eyes on the property well in advance." Grant's tone was serious.

"One step at a time. I'm working as fast as I can."

"Yeah. I know." Grant ended the call.

Traffic was stacking up all around him. Along with typical commuters, there'd be vacationers headed north. It was the first weekend in May, and though it was forecasted to be cloudy, the people were ready for springtime. And, like Grant's family, plenty of folks would want to get away to vacation homes, regardless of the weather.

He slowed to well below the speed limit and inched along with the crowd.

Beside him, Summer sighed. "There's something to be said for living in the city. At least I don't have to deal with this." She waved toward the cars all around. "Should I put the address in the GPS so we can give your mother an idea what time we'll be there?"

"Aren't you going to ask?"

"What?"

He'd expected her to grill him about the camp. *What kind of a place has no cell service? Why will we need blankets for the ride? Are the stoves the only form of heat?*

He just lifted his eyebrows, waiting for her to voice the questions.

But she said, "I trust you not to take me anyplace too rustic."

He chuckled. "You're giving me—and my family—more credit than we deserve."

"I am a little concerned with your brother out looking for firewood."

"Oh, there's plenty of firewood for the stoves. That's not what he's doing."

"So...?"

"Nope. You said you trusted me. I'm not giving anything away."

They were stopped in traffic now. He tapped the town into his phone, made note of the arrival time, and texted his mom. "Might as well settle in." He gestured to the cars all around. "We've got about three hours of this ahead of us."

Summer groaned, and Grant smiled. One thing he could say about his family's camp—no chance Ramón would stumble across them out there.

CHAPTER SEVENTEEN

Summer spoke with Krystal and was cautiously appeased that her older sibling was not in imminent danger.

But Misty? The call to her younger sister brought Summer only angst. The DA had assigned someone to guard her, and Misty seemed satisfied she was protected.

Summer wasn't sure she agreed, but her sister wouldn't be talked into accepting protection from their agency. There was nothing she could do but pray.

Grant parked, and Summer gripped the handle of a bag containing fresh-baked cookies. She'd insisted he stop along the way. Maybe he didn't feel the need to take a gift to his parents, but she was about to intrude on a family gathering. The least she could do was bring something.

She'd suggested they pull into the liquor store off the interstate in New Hampshire, but he'd nixed that idea. "We're not really drinkers. We'll open a bottle of champagne on special occasions, but half the time we end up dumping most of it out. That stuff's disgusting."

Not drinkers? She knew Grant didn't drink, but the whole family? She liked the Wrights already. Considering her father's battle with alcoholism, she hardly touched the stuff and didn't like being around people who did.

Knowing she wouldn't have to deal with that tonight made her even more eager to get to this so-called camp.

But when she climbed from Jon's SUV and looked around, she figured this couldn't be their final destination.

Where in the world were they?

Grant hadn't been kidding about the three-hour drive. They'd passed the exit they'd taken to Bryan's house in Brunswick, then ambled their way along a two-lane highway for an hour and a half. She'd had no idea they were even near the coast until a couple of moments before when she'd caught sight of the gunmetal gray waters of the Atlantic.

"Where are we going?"

"You'll see." Hefting both their duffel bags, Grant slammed the tailgate closed. "Ready?"

"I guess."

"This way." He walked through the parking lot, passed a small brick building, and turned down an alley.

The wind kicked up, bringing a chill and the scents of fish and brine.

At the end, the Atlantic spread out before them.

"Come on." Grant looked back at her, and she realized she'd stopped to take in the scene. So unlike Newburyport, this town was a true fishing village. The few people she saw were men, some bearded, most rough-looking, though one smiled when she caught his gaze.

She followed Grant onto a boardwalk, and they walked down a long pier lined with boats in their slips. A sense of unease churned in her stomach.

What were they doing at a marina?

These weren't fancy yachts or sporting boats. They were mostly fishing boats, or maybe...lobstering?

"There's our ride." Grant lifted his hand in a wave, and up ahead a man hopped off a speedboat onto the pier and started toward them. He was tall like Grant, though slimmer. He wore a knit cap, a thick parka, jeans, and hiking boots. His smile was wide, crinkling the skin around his eyes and mouth.

He looked just like she figured Grant would in thirty years. Handsome, fit, and distinguished.

Grant had barely dropped the duffels when he was enveloped in a big back-slapping hug.

"How are you, son? I'm so glad you made it."

"Me, too." Grant stepped back, his own smile wide. "Dad, this is Summer Lake. Summer, my dad."

She held out her hand. "Mr. Wright. Pleasure to meet you."

He took her hand in both of his, his palms almost as warm as his welcome. "Call me Roger. It's a pleasure to meet you." He stepped back, gave her a head-to-toe appraisal, and said, "Yup, you're Jon's cousin, all right. You got his eyes. And height, obviously. 'Course, you're better looking than he is." He winked at her. "And you can tell him I said that."

"Thanks for the invite." She liked Roger already.

"The more the merrier." He turned to Grant. "We're just waiting on Derrick and Maria."

"She's coming?" Grant asked.

"Been working as Nana and Pop's nurse. They were going to make the trip without her—to prove they didn't need her, I think. But then they forgot their meds." Roger rolled his eyes. "She's gonna stay the weekend. You two make yourselves at home. Your mom stuffed a bunch of blankets in there." He waved vaguely to the boat, then wandered toward shore.

Grant gave Summer a look that could only be seen as challenging. "You ready for this?"

That sense of unease expanded to full-blown anxiety. "What are we doing? I don't know what *this* is."

He laughed and hopped onto the boat, dropped the duffels, and then turned back and held out his hand. "Come on. Let's find those blankets."

She looked from Grant to the tiny motorboat. Unlike the others in the harbor, this one looked more designed for sport than work. It had a small roof that covered only the front half. Lined with benches on the back and both sides, it was low to the water. Probably fast.

Definitely terrifying.

Dad had rented a speed boat once for the family. She'd loved the feeling of the wind in her hair as he'd sped across the lake. But he'd brought a cooler of beer. As the day wore on, as the cooler emptied of cans, he'd gotten reckless, taking more and more chances.

After a sharp turn that'd nearly resulted in a crash with a jet ski, Mom had tried to get him to slow down or relinquish the wheel. They'd argued.

Dad pushed her away, and Mom flew over the edge.

Summer could still see her, reaching for the railing, missing, flying, flying. Splashing into the water, and disappearing beneath.

Dad just...drove on. Maybe only for a minute or two, but to Summer, it had seemed like hours. Finally, he spun around to pick her up. Laughing, as if it'd all been a big game.

Dripping but no longer arguing, Mom climbed into the boat. She'd been fine. But Summer would never get that image out of her head of her mother's body hurling through the air.

The only other time she'd been on a boat was for a photoshoot back in her modeling days, and it'd been a sixty-foot yacht rented for the occasion. They'd motored a couple of hundred yards from shore, spent a couple of hours posing, and then gone back.

Even then, surrounded by the warm waters of the Caribbean, she'd been afraid.

She'd lived in New York for years, but she'd never taken the ferry out to see the Statue of Liberty. And not because she wasn't curious.

They were going to ride this tiny little speed boat on the ocean? She was already cold. They'd freeze before they got... wherever they were going.

And that was assuming they made it. What if the boat stalled? Or...flipped?

"Hey." Grant shifted into her view. "It's okay."

"I don't like boats."

"I didn't know that." His lips twitched at the corners like he thought she was amusing.

"It's not funny."

"No, of course not." He pressed his lips together, swallowed. "It's just, the irony that a woman named Summer Lake—"

"Yeah, I get it." She sounded annoyed. Well, she *was* annoyed. He should have told her.

Her own fault. She should have asked. It had never occurred to her...

"Is there another way to get there?"

"The camp's on an island. It's this or we find a hotel. Or drive to Coventry. Maybe Thomas could still put us up." But, as much as he'd balked at the idea of seeing his family, the closer they'd gotten, the more eager he'd seemed. He'd been humming along with the music on the radio for the last hour.

She didn't want to disappoint him.

And really, was she going to let a little thing like this boat stand in her way?

Yes.

No.

"I promise," Grant said, "you'll be perfectly safe. I won't let anything happen to you."

Right. Like he could singlehandedly ensure the boat wouldn't sink. But the look he gave her, all confidence and kindness, settled her nerves. A little.

"Come on. It's freezing. Let's find a blanket." His hand still hovered in the space between the boat and the dock.

She stuck her arm through the handles of the sack and reached out. He gripped her firmly. She took a deep breath and stepped through the little opening in the flimsy railing.

The boat moved. Or maybe she pushed too hard. Or maybe both. She stumbled forward, nearly losing her footing.

But Grant pulled her into his chest, wrapping her tightly. "You're okay." His words rumbled in her ear. "I've got you."

She stayed there, in the safety of his arms, while the boat settled beneath her. Finally, she pushed back and looked up. The humor was missing from his expression. His warm brown eyes searched her face. "Are you... Is it all right?"

She nodded. Tried to speak, but her throat was thick with fear or tension or...something. She averted her gaze. She'd already confessed her fear. The last thing she needed was to let him see it in her expression.

He still held her hand. "Don't trip over the duffels. I'll stow them in a minute." He walked her to a bench along the side and beneath the small roof.

She sat and wrapped her arms around herself. The wind was frigid.

Grant lifted the bench seat in the back and pulled out a couple of blankets. "Here we go."

A loud thump, and the boat swayed in the water.

Summer gasped.

Once again, Grant seemed to be fighting a smile. He looked toward the front of the boat. "You made it."

A man a little shorter than Grant hugged him as his father

had. "Hey, bro. It's been too long."

"I know, I know." Grant stepped back. "Derrick, this is my partner, Summer."

Summer waved but didn't dare stand.

A pretty dark-haired beauty headed for the opposite bench. "Hi. I'm Maria. No relation to these guys." She sent the men an affectionate look. "Just the next-door neighbor. And nurse to their grandparents."

"You guys can chat when we get there." The boat swayed again as Roger climbed aboard. "It's getting dark."

Grant tossed his brother a blanket, tossed another to Maria, and draped a third over Summer. It was amazing how warm the scratchy wool felt.

"Right back." While his father started the engine and backed out of the slip—the movement only adding to her anxiety—Grant lifted the bench seats to stow their two duffel bags, Derrick's backpack, and Maria's small wheeled luggage. He walked to the front, said something to his father—who laughed and nodded—and returned to sit beside her.

"You want a life jacket?" he asked.

"Do I need one?" She hadn't meant the terror to bleed into her words, but there it was, audible enough for even Derrick to hear.

He was kind enough to avert his gaze, though not so fast that she missed his smile.

"Dad could do this with his eyes closed," Grant said. "You're safe. I promise."

"Then, no, I guess."

Grant settled beside her. "Mind if I share?"

She lifted the blanket, and he draped it over himself with one hand while the other slid across her shoulders. "We might as well keep each other warm. If you don't mind, that is."

Mind? The only thing holding her panic at bay was Grant's

proximity. She nestled into his side, forcing a breath to calm her chattering teeth. When they were away from the dock, Roger pushed the lever forward, and they took off across the choppy waters.

Summer squeezed her eyes closed and prayed.

The ride was terrifying, but less than fifteen minutes after they left the marina the boat slowed, and Summer risked opening her eyes.

They approached a tree-covered island that led to rocky slopes angling—in some places, very steeply—to the coast. She couldn't figure out where they were going to land until they rounded a bend. The cliff was no less steep, but it wasn't as high here, and a dock with a little boathouse jutted into the water.

Grant nudged Summer and pointed.

She had to lean out from under the boat's small roof to see.

When the house on the top of the cliff came into view, Summer gasped. It was three stories, mostly stone, with windows everywhere. She wasn't sure what she'd expected, but not this.

"I thought you said it was a camp."

Grant shoved the blanket off himself. "I gotta help. You'll be okay for a sec?"

"Sure." She sounded confident, but when he stood and hopped onto the dock, her pulse raced.

Sitting across from her, Maria smiled. "They know what they're doing."

"You've been here before?"

She shook her head. "But they've been doing this for years. I have every confidence."

Grant and Derrick tied up the boat, then unloaded the bags.

Summer should probably move, but she'd be more of a hindrance than a help. She stayed where she was, ashamed of her fear. Had she really *hugged* Grant when she'd first gotten onto this floating deathtrap?

Had she really let herself nestle into him during the ride?

Horrifying. No, she wouldn't show any more weakness, not now, not while she was here, and not when they were on their way back. She could conquer this.

But after Maria hopped ashore like an old pro, Summer couldn't wait any longer. She stood, lifting the bag with the cookies in it. But the boat rocked, and she gripped a support pole as if it were her only link to safety.

Grant hopped back on like it was nothing and held out his hand. "I got you."

"I can do it." She ignored his hand and made her way to the opening in the railing that led to the dock. Only a few inches separated the boat from the solid wood.

Derrick stood on the far side, reaching toward her. "Grab my hand."

She didn't want to be rude. But she didn't want his help, either. Everybody else had gotten off without aid. She hopped the few inches, managed to keep her feet, and straightened. "Thanks, anyway."

Derrick shifted his focus to Grant behind her. "Go on up. Maria's already halfway there. I guess Pop needs his medication. Dad and I can take care of this."

"I don't mind helping," Grant said.

Summer grabbed her duffel bag in her free hand and moved out of the way. Roger was still on the boat, digging into one of the storage compartments.

"She's a guest," Derrick said. "And for as often as you come—"

"Yeah, I got it." Annoyance infused his words. He bent and

grabbed his duffel, then reached for hers. "Let me take that."

"I can carry it."

His eyebrows lifted, but he just shrugged. "At least give me the sack."

She was going to argue, but by the look in his eyes, she figured it wasn't worth it. She handed the cookies over, and he turned and marched toward the end of the dock.

He was definitely annoyed. With his brother? She didn't know as she followed him. All she could see ahead in the gathering darkness was what looked like a solid wall, but lights placed every ten feet or so snaked up the side of it. Oh, and there was Maria, nearly to the top already.

As they approached, she realized a metal staircase had been attached to the stone cliff.

Grant paused at the bottom. "Ladies first. Hang onto the railing. Thanks to the ocean spray, the steps can be slick."

She shifted her bag into her left hand and gripped the cold metal railing with her right.

"You sure you won't let me carry that for you?" Grant asked.

"I can manage." But she understood now why he'd offered. The steps were steep and slippery, and her small bag kept bouncing into them, getting in her way. She paused, slipped her arms through the handles of the duffel so it acted like a backpack, and climbed what seemed the equivalent of three flights until she reached the top and stepped past a low stone wall onto a beautiful grass-covered lawn.

She took in the giant house in front of her. Light spilled from nearly every window. Smoke from chimneys filled the air with its homey scent, which always reminded her of Jon's house in the wintertime. Unlike her family, they used to gather around the fireplace on snowy days, roast marshmallows, and tell stories.

Those were some of her favorite memories.

"It's gorgeous."

Beside her, Grant said, "I forget sometimes. Will you please let me carry your bag? Otherwise, my mother'll lecture me about how to treat a lady. I'm begging you."

She shimmied her bag off her back. "Only if you let me take that." She nodded to the sack, and they traded. "I wouldn't want to get you in trouble."

"You think I'm kidding? You have no idea."

He nodded toward the first floor, and she peered through the sliding doors at a ping pong table and...was that an air hockey game?

"That's the game room," he said. "The family will be gathered in the kitchen and living room, up here." They took a gravel walkway to an outdoor staircase that led to a wide, covered deck, where outdoor furniture was stored beneath canvas.

Through the floor-to-ceiling windows, she counted six...no, eight people, all standing around a huge island, cooking, eating. Smiling and laughing. All talking...at the same time, or so it seemed. The low murmur of conversation carried through the glass.

"The gang's all here," Grant said. "You ready?"

"I guess."

"You look almost as scared as you were when you realized we'd be traveling by boat."

"I'm not scared. Just...my family's not that big. Or talkative."

"I warned you," Grant said.

She straightened her shoulders, plastered on a smile. "It's fine. Let's go."

His smile was genuine. "Don't worry. They're going to love you." He crossed the deck and slid open a door. "Go on."

She stepped inside, Grant right behind her.

Immediately, everybody turned their direction.

"You made it!" a man called.

"Told you," another voice said. "You owe me ten bucks."

"You two." That came from a woman who smacked one of the oversize males as she walked by. She approached Grant, and he enveloped her in his arms. "I'm so glad to see you."

"Me too." Grant hugged his mother tightly.

The murmur of conversation died. Everybody in the room stared.

Finally, Grant stepped away. "Mom, everybody. This is Summer." He gave her a quick, nervous look. "That okay?" he said low. "Or should I tell them to call you Lake?"

"It's fine." She stuck out her hand to his mother. "Nice to meet you."

"I'm Peggy. We're huggers around here." The older woman wrapped her in her arms. Summer had to lean down to return her embrace, enjoying the moment of comfort.

Peggy stepped back, holding Summer by the shoulders. Unlike just about everybody else in the room, Peggy wasn't tall, maybe five-four, and just the other side of plump. She had short blond hair and a cheerful smile. "Well, aren't you lovely? You look a little like your cousin, but he didn't get that pretty blond hair."

"Thank you." She held out the bag, hoping it hadn't been jostled too much on the ride. "For you."

Peggy opened it, pulled out the gift, and lifted it high like a prize. "Cookies!"

A small cheer rose from the crowd, and Summer blushed.

Three oversize men—she recognized Bryan—all with dark brown hair and eyes, regarded her, the other two smirking as if they didn't quite buy that *partner* bit. There was also an older couple standing beside Maria, a woman, and two teenagers.

Bryan lifted his hand. "Glad you're here."

"Hi." She felt her cheeks burning. She wasn't used to being

the center of attention. She didn't love it.

Grant said, "First, these are my grandparents, Tom and Susie Wright."

She stepped forward and shook their hands. "Pleasure." Though Tom was very thin and a little stooped, he was still nearly as tall as Summer. Like the rest of the crowd, he had a warm smile.

Susie's hands were freezing when she gripped Summer's. "So, you and my grandson, then?"

"Oh, no. We're just partners. And friends."

The woman frowned, her blue eyes flitting from Summer to Grant. "Mmm-hmm. You could do worse."

"I'm sure. I just—"

Grant cleared his throat, saving her having to finish the sentence. "Okay, oldest to youngest brothers. That's Michael."

The only one as tall as Grant stepped forward and shook her hand. "Glad to meet you."

"And Sam. He's next up from me."

This was the one who'd bet against Grant showing up. "You play ping pong like your cousin?"

"Used to," she said.

"Let's have a game later. Just for fun."

Grant leaned down and stage-whispered, "If you knock him off his high horse, I'll owe you for life."

"Challenge accepted."

Grant grinned, and Sam laughed. "I'll feel bad about beating a woman, but..."

Grant shoved him, knocking him backward, but Sam righted himself. "Watch yourself, kid."

Kid?

Approaching the only other woman in the room, a brunette with bright blue eyes, Grant held out his arms. When she stepped into them, he gave her a hug. "It's so good to see you."

She stayed enveloped in his arms a long time before stepping away. She wiped her eyes quickly, then turned to Summer. "I'm Camilla. Nice to meet you."

They shook hands. "It's a pleasure."

Camilla gestured to the two teens, who'd hung back. "Jeremy and Zoë."

The kids waved, and then Peggy said, "Grant, she'll stay in the blue room. We're eating in an hour."

"Okay." Grant scooped up the two bags and lowered his voice. "The worst is over. Come on."

They skirted the crowd to an open staircase and climbed to the second floor.

It was quieter up there, though the murmur of voices carried on the hardwood floors.

"I feel bad taking up a bedroom. I can sleep on a sofa or—"

"There's plenty of room." Grant walked down a hallway lined on both sides with doors, most of which were closed. At the second on the right, he stepped in and dropped his bag on a twin bed. The other bed already had somebody's bag on it.

"Michael's," Grant said. "We usually share."

Back in the hall, he continued to the end and pushed open a door on his left. "Here you go."

She stepped into a room painted a soft blue with a white bureau, two twin beds—the extra-long kind, she was happy to see—both covered with blue-and-white quilts. The back wall was all windows.

Grant set her duffel on the closer of the two beds. "You can close those curtains if you want."

She crossed and looked out at the expanse of ocean. "Wow. This is..." She turned to face him. "Why do you call it a camp?"

"It *was* when Dad first bought the property. The first time we came, we slept in tents. He started building the house when I was about six. It wasn't like this, though. It was nothing but a cold basement at first. Then, we built the main floor. It took us ten, fifteen years to get it from the camp to this."

"Us?" Summer sat on the bed. "You guys did the work?"

"We all did. When I was ten, I helped tile that bath." He nodded toward a doorway on one side of the room. "That's shared, by the way. I assume Camilla and Zoë are in the adjoining room."

"You laid tile when you were ten?"

"Daniel did most of the laying. Dad worked the wet saw in the basement. My job was to run up and down the steps. But I laid a couple of the tiles. Daniel taught me how. We finished the basement when I was in high school, and by then I was the one laying the tile."

"I didn't know you were so handy."

"Not that we had a choice. We painted, installed light fixtures, laid hardwood." He tapped the floor beneath his feet. "We all did our part."

"It's amazing."

"Mom and Dad's vision. They have a plan to build cabins around the place. I think they figured we'd all have wives and kids by now."

"But only Daniel...?"

"Yeah. He married pretty young. Right out of college. But the first time we met Camilla, we knew she was the woman for him. They were..." His words faded, and he cleared his throat. "Anyway, hang out here or come down. Whatever. I'll be downstairs with the guys." He closed her door, leaving her alone.

She dug into her bag, pulled out her toiletries, and stepped into the bathroom. Thanks to the wild ride out there, her hair was a mess. She was yanking a brush through it when she heard rustling from the room next door. There was a knock on the adjoining bathroom door.

Summer swung it open to find Zoë on the opposite side.

"Oh, sorry," the girl said.

"No problem. I'll get out of your way."

"I was just going to plug this in." She lifted a curling iron and shoved the plug into the outlet. "I thought I'd try curling my hair, give me something to do. The Wi-Fi is terrible, and there's nobody to talk to. I mean, don't get me wrong. They're my family, and they're nice and everything..." Her cheeks turned pink.

"What do you have in common with a bunch of unmarried men?"

Zoë seemed relieved. "Exactly. And everybody looks at us with these pitying... Anyway, no rush."

It was a big bathroom with double sinks. "You can come in. I'm almost done." Summer felt for the girl. At least Jeremy had his gender in common with his uncles. This girl seemed as out of place as...Summer.

"How old are you?"

"Twenty."

"Oh. I didn't realize..." She wasn't a kid at all. "You go to college?"

"In Oklahoma, near home. I didn't want to leave Mom and Jeremy."

"I'm sorry about your father."

"Thanks." She grabbed her own hairbrush from a drawer and started brushing. She had long, straight brown hair, the same color as her uncles', but aside from the brown eyes, she looked like her mother. Pale skin, high cheekbones.

Summer finished brushing, and they chatted about nothing while Zoë curled her hair. After ten minutes, the long locks were wavy and beautiful.

"Impressive."

"Thanks." Zoë ran her fingers through the curls, then gave Summer a sidelong glance. "Your hair is gorgeous."

"Not as pretty as yours. It's so shiny."

"You wouldn't let me"—Zoë lifted the iron—"practice, would you?"

"Oh. Uh..."

The girl's expression fell. "It's fine. I'm just—"

"Sure." She didn't know where the word came from, but it popped out of her mouth. And what did Summer care? It gave her a good excuse to hang out upstairs and avoid the chaos for a few more minutes. She loved the idea of a big family, but she wasn't sure of her place or how she fit in.

Zoë disappeared into the bedroom and came back with a chair. "You'll need to sit or I won't be able to reach it."

Unlike the rest of the Wright clan, Zoë wasn't that tall, maybe five-five. Summer sat, and Zoë started expertly wrapping Summer's hair around the wand.

It'd been a long time since anybody had done Summer's hair. Most girls would probably remember times with their sisters, but she, Krystal, and Misty had never had the do-each-other's-hair kind of relationship. Instead, Summer remembered photo shoots and models she used to know. Women who were comfortable in their own skin, comfortable with their feminin-ity. Summer missed those days, back when she thought the scariest man in the world was her father.

Since then, she'd met worse.

But while Zoë chatted and curled her hair, and then applied some of her own makeup to Summer's face—"Because, come on, you might as well look fabulous as long as you have to endure this family"—Summer remembered how much she used to love being female.

Before Ramón and his henchmen had scared the girl right out of her.

CHAPTER EIGHTEEN

"Whoa."

Grant and Sam had been catching up by the fireplace. At Sam's tone, Grant followed his gaze.

Zoë was coming downstairs, but as pretty as their niece was, Sam wasn't staring at her.

Summer was two steps behind Zoë. Her hair was wavy, framing her face. And if he wasn't mistaken, she'd applied makeup.

He'd never seen Summer in makeup.

As if she hadn't already been gorgeous.

Sam leaned close to Grant. "So, are you and her, uh...?"

It would be one thing to lose his shot with Summer because Bryan wanted to pursue her. Bryan was a good guy, steady and trustworthy. And Grant owed him, big time. But Sam? Grant loved his older brother, but he'd never been impressed with how he treated women—like they were disposable.

"I will literally kill you." Grant didn't bother to soften his words with a smile. "Unlike when we were kids, I can take you without breaking a sweat."

Sam tore his gaze away from Summer, who'd reached the

landing and was talking to Camilla. He gave Grant an amused, appraising look. "I see."

"She's my partner and my best friend's cousin. Not that she'd give you a second glance. She's got a top-notch BS detector."

Sam's smile faded. "You don't know me, Grant. Keep your thoughts to yourself." He turned and headed back toward the kitchen.

Grant felt a twinge of guilt but tamped it down and approached Summer, who glanced his way.

"You clean up nice."

She ran a hand over her curled hair. "Zoë did it." If he wasn't mistaken, he would swear Summer's cheeks turned pink. "We had some girl time."

He forced his gaze to his niece. "Nicely done. How's school?"

While Zoë told him about her classes, Summer headed for the kitchen, where Mom promptly put her to work arranging steaming dishes on the granite countertop.

Grant forced himself to focus on his niece and sister-in-law, though he found his gaze straying toward Summer often.

The meal was a typical Wright affair, all of them gathered around the long dining room table, talking over each other, the brothers telling stories—mostly about Grant, since he'd been dumb enough to bring a guest.

Though he caught his mother giving Maria looks often enough. She'd lived in the house closest to their property when they were kids, the veritable girl next door. Grant hardly knew her, but she and Bryan had been in the same grade.

Now, they sat beside each other, talking, though neither seemed pleased. If Mom was hoping to spark romance on that front, she'd missed the mark.

He'd wanted to sit beside Summer, but he'd been intercepted before he could make his way to her, and the chairs around her were taken—Sam on one side, Zoë on the other.

Bryan sat across from her, leaving Grant to watch from the other end of the table.

He'd always known Summer would get along with his family. He'd always known she'd fit in with this crew as if she were one of them.

He caught her eye, and she smiled at him.

And his heart did that pancake-flipping thing again.

"You got it bad."

He turned to Derrick, seated across from him.

Rather than lie, he twirled some spaghetti and forked a meatball, then shoved the bite into his mouth.

Derrick laughed. "Does she know?"

He swallowed the food, shook his head, and lowered his voice. "She spooks easily."

After a long look in Summer's direction, Derrick leaned in. "She looks pretty tough to me."

Usually, he'd agree, but tonight Summer reminded him of the model she'd been for years. Gorgeous, and all girl. He loved the woman he'd trained to be a bodyguard, the tough-as-nails woman he worked with. But the pretty, smiling woman at the other end of the table made his heart swell.

While most of the crew cleared the table, Dad roped Grant and Jeremy into helping outside.

Grant cast one last gaze at Summer, who'd planted herself at the sink and was happily washing dishes, and followed his dad and his nephew out the back door into the pitch-black night.

The sounds of the party faded as they made their way down the steps from the covered deck. Following the bouncing beams of flashlights, they crossed to the far edge of the lawn, where a pile of sticks waited.

"He get enough kindling?" Grant asked.

Dad nodded. "And replenished the supply, so we'll be ready next time." He held out a long lighter to Jeremy. "You want to do the honors?"

Sixteen-year-old Jeremy took it, eyes wide. "Sure." He walked toward the pile. "Uh, where do I...?"

Dad showed Jeremy where to light the bonfire, teaching him —like he'd taught all the boys—not just how to get it going but also how to keep it safe. As much rain as they'd gotten lately, with the sodden grass that had probably still had snow on it a month earlier, there was little chance of starting a forest fire, but Dad never missed an opportunity to pass on knowledge to his sons—and now his grandson.

Grant watched the teen, so like his father, feeling the sting of grief that hit whenever he thought of Daniel. How could his oldest brother be gone?

Daniel would have loved Summer. Grant could imagine that crooked smile, his big, warm hand on Grant's shoulder. He'd say, *"Good choice, bro."* And he'd tell him to be brave. Be honest.

Grant needed to heed that advice. There'd never be a better time than now to confess his feelings to Summer. If she rejected him, then he'd move on. Or fight for her. But he couldn't continue this limbo-living anymore.

The fire caught.

Jeremy and Dad stepped back, and the three of them watched as the flames rose first from the smallest pieces, then to the dry kindling until the big branches lit.

"Wow." Jeremy stared. "Awesome."

Dad backed up to stand beside Grant. "Glad you're with us, son."

"Yeah. Me too."

They watched the flames grow for a few minutes in silence.

Using a big stick, Jeremy poked the fire, trying to get more of it to light.

"You need to stop avoiding us," Dad said. "It's not necessary."

Grant's overfull stomach churned. "Bryan has every right to hold a grudge against me."

"Does he?"

"You know what happened, what I—"

"Hold a grudge, I mean." Dad didn't look away from the flickering light. "I think it's time you two had a real conversation, stopped dancing around it."

"There's nothing to say."

Dad gripped his shoulder. "The only person who's still angry with you is you. It's time to move on, son. It's time to be a part of this family again."

The door opened, and the rest of his family spilled outside, their chattering voices saving Grant from responding.

Dad squeezed his shoulder and leaned in. "By the way, I like her."

"Oh, we're just... She's...uh..." Still reeling from Dad's last words, Grant couldn't think of what to say.

"I get it. Trust me, I get it." Dad patted him on the back, then moved to join the crowd as they reached the lawn.

Grant stood there, staring after him stupidly until Summer approached and held out a cookie. "Chocolate macadamia nut."

"My favorite." He took it, and she smiled.

"Your family is amazing. I love them all."

He watched as they gathered around the bonfire, munching cookies. He was sure his mother'd had a different dessert planned for tonight, but she'd served the cookies to make Summer feel special.

That was the kind of person Mom was. The kind of people they all were.

This bonfire...this was the kind of people they were. Every time they gathered at camp, unless it was pouring rain, they had a bonfire. After this, they'd go inside and play games and tell stories and laugh. This house didn't even have a TV—nobody cared to watch anything, not when they were together.

He loved that. He loved being here.

And sharing it with Summer.

"This is my dream, to have a family like this." Her tone was wistful. The breeze kicked up, blowing her pretty curled hair into her face. She shook it away, crossing her arms.

He wandered to the far side of the bonfire, and she followed him, away from the crowd. Their voices were muffled by the crackling fire, the breeze, and the surf below. "What's your family like?"

She held her gloved hands out toward the flickering flames. Their light danced on her skin, in her eyes, and he found himself mesmerized.

"My mom was sweet and gentle. She was no match for my father." Her voice took on a hard quality.

"Was he... Did he hurt you?"

"Once. I was just a kid, and he was drunk, and he grabbed me, hard. Shook me. But I didn't know the rules. I was supposed to cower, apparently. I was supposed to cry and do what he told me. I didn't. I kicked him in the knee."

He could picture the woman in front of him standing up to an angry man, but she'd been a little girl. A little girl whose father should have protected her, not hurt her. "Served him right."

Her head dipped, lifted again. "I ran to my mom. She and Krystal were in the kitchen. Misty was there, sitting at the table, looking up at me with those wide eyes. I told Mom what happened. I thought she'd defend me or protect me or...something. But she looked more afraid than I was. I tried to get her and Krystal to run away with me. We could go to Jon's house. I thought we'd be safe there. I thought...I never knew he did that, you know? I'd never seen him or... I'd heard fighting, of course. But I'd never realized..."

Grant waited a few beats, giving her time to finish her story, but she just stared into the bonfire. "What happened?"

Summer shrugged. "Mom looked at my arm and said it seemed fine. Dad was yelling for her in the other room, and she started for the door. I grabbed her, begged her not to go. But she patted my head and told me it would be better, that she could calm him down. And then, she walked in there. He was yelling, she was whimpering.

"And Krystal...she went back to setting the table, as if it were all normal. But I knew it wasn't normal. I knew it wasn't okay. I tried to get Krystal to come with me, but she said no, we had to stay. We'd get in trouble if we left. Well, I didn't care. I wasn't going to let my father treat me that way. So I picked Misty up, and I marched out. I carried my sister down to Jon's house—they lived a couple of streets over. I told Uncle Marshall and Aunt Sally what happened. Uncle Marshall called the police."

"Good." At least somebody had half a brain. "Did your father get arrested?"

Summer shook her head. "Dad told the police it was an accident, and Mom backed him up."

Oh, man. What kind of mother...? "I'm sorry."

She shrugged. "Dad never laid a hand on me again. And I kept a close watch on my little sister. I wasn't going to let him hurt her. But Mom and Krystal..." Her voice faded, and she said nothing for a long time. When she spoke again, her voice was hard. "They shouldn't have put up with it. Mom shouldn't have made excuses for him. Krystal walked on eggshells all the time, trying to keep the peace. Why? Why did he deserve that? Not me, though. I spent half my childhood at Jon's house, and I took Misty with me whenever Mom would let me. If she and Krystal were stupid enough to put up with him, that was their problem."

A pretty callous attitude for a little girl. "I hate that you had to deal with that."

"I learned pretty early on that nobody was going to protect me but me. And if I wanted my little sister to be safe, that was up to me too."

She'd learned more than that. She'd learned that the only way to be safe was to be tough, to never back down. It explained a lot.

"Your mother should have protected you," Grant said. "One might argue that Jon and his family did what she couldn't."

Summer's eyes narrowed, though she didn't look away from the bonfire. "I guess."

"You were wise to seek their protection."

"I just needed to get away. They weren't protecting me."

"Weren't they?"

She blinked. "I never thought of it that way. I just thought of their house as a safe place."

"They did protect you, though. And you were smart to seek it—from your mother, and when she didn't step up, from Jon's family. There's nothing wrong with admitting you're not strong enough to take on the world. We all need help sometimes."

"I'm not very good at that."

"No kidding." He infused his sarcasm with humor.

Her lips tipped up at the corners.

He turned to look at the flames, heart pounding. Because he wanted...he needed to tell her how he felt. Would she accept it? Or would she push him away? He took a deep breath and turned to her again. "I need to tell you...you're amazing." He faltered. "Incredibly courageous. I don't know any other woman

who'd have the nerve to stand up to an abusive man—her father
—like that."

"Sometimes I think I was just stupid. I mean, not to stand
up to him, but to expect my mother to have my back. She was a
good woman, but she didn't have it in her. Over the years, she
seemed to shrink. It almost felt like...like a foregone conclusion
when she got cancer. She'd been wasting away. It's probably
wrong of me to blame my father for her death, but I do. I think,
if she'd been happy, if she'd been able to thrive, maybe she could
have fought it. As it was, it was almost as if, when she got diag-
nosed, she felt relieved. Like she looked forward to being free of
him."

"I'm sorry, Summer. I'm sorry you had to deal with that. But
look what an amazing woman you turned out to be. Strong and
brave and...beautiful."

She dipped her face as if she were suddenly bashful. Oh,
man, that look...

Laughter carried from the other side of the bonfire. Bryan
punched Michael lightly, and Mike stumbled back, exaggerating
the movement.

Maria stood with his grandparents, but her eyes were on the
brothers.

More laughter erupted.

"What happened between you and Bryan?" Summer faced
him, her head tilting to one side.

She'd told him her story. If he wanted to tell her how he felt,
if he hoped she might return his feelings, she needed to know
him, even the ugliest thing about him.

"Come on." He took her gloved hand in his, only realizing
after he did it what he'd done. But Summer didn't yank it away
as they walked.

"Where we going?"

He didn't answer until they reached the stone wall that

surrounded the property. He nodded out toward the ocean. They were only twenty yards or so from the bonfire, but the wind blew off the Atlantic, stealing the fire's warmth and swallowing up the laughter.

"You remember the cliff wall as we approached?"

She nodded, looking down at the waves that crashed below.

"Dad, Sam, and Michael were laying hardwood upstairs. I was nine. I was supposed to be keeping an eye on Bryan. We weren't allowed to go down to the water by ourselves, but I'd been itching to show off. See, I'd been secretly climbing up the cliff."

"You *climbed* that?"

"It's not as steep as it looks. There're plenty of handholds. It wasn't that hard."

By her wide eyes, Summer disagreed. She'd always seemed so tough, but as he was getting to know her better, he realized she had fears, just like everybody else. Here was a woman who'd followed a terrorist alone into a parking garage, but she was afraid of boats and didn't seem inclined to climb a rocky slope.

"Bryan didn't want to get in trouble, but I talked him into going down the steps with me. I told him to stay on the dock and watch. I wanted to show off."

It was hard to see Summer's face in the darkness. He was glad he didn't have to watch her reaction. Glad, too, that she couldn't see his face.

"I was a lot shorter then, and the climb was hard. I had to really focus. But I did it. When I got to the top, I lifted my arms in triumph, figuring Bryan would be impressed. But he wasn't there."

"Oh, no."

"I was sure he'd fallen into the water and was drowning. I screamed his name." He shook his head to clear the memories. "I bolted down the steps, got to the bottom. That's when I saw him. He'd decided to follow me. He was halfway up the cliff. Stuck. I tried to help him, but..." Grant could still see his little brother, his tiny body pressing against the rocks. Calling for help. Afraid to go farther up, unable to go down.

"I ran back up the stairs and got my dad. He grabbed a rope, but by the time we got back..." He took a breath, blew it out. "He'd fallen. Landed on the jagged rocks below. Dad had one of those old radios, and he managed to call for help. A helicopter came and took Bryan away. Both legs were broken. One of them never healed right."

"The limp," Summer said.

"My fault. I never should've left him. I should have called my dad before I ran down there. I should've stayed with Bryan, not run away. If I hadn't left him, he wouldn't have fallen."

"You don't know that."

"I know he was scared." Grant could still see his little brother's body, crumpled on the rocks. He'd been sure he was dead.

Dad had barreled past him, screaming Bryan's name as he descended the steep metal staircase.

When Grant closed his eyes, he could still hear the anguish in his father's voice.

"He was all alone, in pain."

"Because you'd gone for help," Summer said.

Grant should have been with him. He should never have left him.

"You've never forgiven yourself." Her voice held certainty.

"Should I? Bryan used to dream of playing football. He was good too."

"He was, what? Seven?"

"I'm just saying, he might have had a future. He was a fast runner. He was quick. There're lots of things he never got to do because of me. And he never let me forget it, either. As he recovered, and then over the years, he'd mention it often, how he followed me. How he should never have been there, wouldn't have been if not for me. That's why I left. The rest of my brothers went off to college, but that wasn't far enough away for me. I joined the Army. I figured they were all happy to have me gone."

Summer watched him a long moment. "It doesn't seem that way. Your family couldn't be more welcoming. And Bryan obviously doesn't hold a grudge against you. I mean, if I had to guess, I'd say he wants to make things right."

"You think so?" Grant had hoped the same thing.

Summer squeezed his hand, then reached out and took the other one. "Maybe you two should try to find a minute to talk about it—away from the crowd. Because...I don't know. I think maybe this is the time to put it behind you."

Exactly what Dad had said.

Would it be possible to move past it? Could Bryan really forgive him?

Summer still held both his hands, and all thoughts of his brother blew away on the breeze. "Summer, I...I have a confession to make."

He blocked what little light came from the bonfire, shrouding her in darkness.

"What's that?" Her words were a little breathless.

"I...I don't always only think of you as a partner." Way to wimp out. But was she really ready to hear he was in love with her?

"Oh. I don't always...only think of you as a partner, either."

Which seemed obvious, come to think of it. They were holding hands, after all.

He didn't want to ruin their working relationship. But he didn't want a working relationship with her anymore. He wanted so much more. He wanted to give her so much more. More than his protection. More than his friendship.

"That wasn't a very honest confession on my part." She said nothing. He thought maybe her eyebrows lifted, but it was too dark to know for sure. "The truth is..." Though he'd like to see her face, maybe this would be better said in the dark. Maybe, if she responded with horror or revulsion, he didn't want to know. "I have feelings for you. I have had for...some time."

"Oh."

"And I'm sorry if that makes you uncomfortable, and maybe this wasn't the time to tell you, but I can't imagine there'll ever be a better time, and I just told you the worst thing I ever did, and you didn't toss me over the cliff, so maybe..."

She chuckled, the sound low and amused. "Do you always babble when you're nervous?"

"Probably."

A long moment of silence passed.

And then, she squeezed his hands. "I don't know if you noticed, but I'm still standing here."

"I noticed." His voice was rough. He was afraid to let go of her hands, afraid she'd bolt. But she didn't seem inclined to run away. He let go, placed one hand on her hip.

Her palm slid against his jacket, and he wished he'd gone without it. He'd be freezing, but he'd take the cold wind if it meant feeling her warmth against his skin.

He wrapped his other arm around her back, closing the distance between them. Lowered his head. His lips found hers, and he kissed her. Softly, gently. Giving her the opportunity to push him away. But she didn't.

She pressed closer. Her hand slid around his neck, her fingers warm through the gloves, and though he warned himself to go slowly, he couldn't help the way he deepened the kiss.

When she opened up to him, he nearly exploded with desire.

The sound of the surf, his family's distant laughter, the cold wind...everything faded away except the feel of Summer in his arms, her lips moving against his own.

For the first time since they'd arrived at his family's camp... maybe for the first time since the day his brother had fallen from that cliff, Grant felt like he'd come home.

CHAPTER NINETEEN

What in the world had Summer been thinking?

She hugged the borrowed bathrobe closer as she paced to the window overlooking the sea the next morning, calling herself all sorts of idiot.

She'd let Grant *kiss* her. Worse than that, she'd kissed him back.

She hadn't been kissed since a neighbor had invited her to a New Year's Eve party back in New York, "just as friends." But by midnight, he'd decided he wasn't content with the *friends* part of the deal.

When his lips had touched hers, she'd felt nothing but frustrated at the guy for not being honest—and at herself for worrying about hurting his feelings. As if she owed him something.

Between her father, male models who thought they were all that and a piece of cake, and fawning, pawing men she'd met in New York—and since—she'd decided years before that she wasn't ever going to fall in love.

But somehow, Grant had slipped past all her defenses. Not

that she loved him. Just that...she could see her feelings going there if she let her guard down.

The memory of the moment the night before made her face burn as if she were standing too close to the bonfire, not in her bedroom staring out at the rough water of the Atlantic.

Water she'd have to cross again—with Grant.

This was a nightmare.

Made worse by the fact that, along with her typical bad dreams, she'd had a good one. About Grant. About his lips moving against hers. About being wrapped in his arms, feeling safe and secure.

The thought brought a shiver of pleasure, which she shook off.

She'd spent an hour with the Lord that morning, trying to figure out what she should do. But she'd gotten no good answer, certainly not from reading her Bible on her phone app. She'd been slowly working through the New Testament, and today's reading happened to be in the book of 1 John.

Perfect love casts out fear.

Bad timing, that. Maybe God's perfect love did cast out fear. In Summer's life, love was scarier than all the boat rides and smugglers and kidnappers in the world.

Not that she was in love with Grant. No way. As far as she could tell, Grant was good and kind and noble. If she ever was going to fall in love, he'd be a decent choice. Maybe. But that was the problem, wasn't it? Who knew what a person was really like? Dad had probably seemed like a good, kind, noble guy, too, when Mom had met him.

Loving someone meant opening up to him, being vulnerable. And she wasn't climbing on that crazy train.

She turned away from the view and dressed in jeans and a sweatshirt. Her hair was still wet from her shower, but she yanked it back in a bun. She certainly wouldn't be curling it.

And there'd be no makeup. All that dressing up had put her in the wrong frame of mind. Made her feel feminine and pretty. It made her lower her guard.

She needed to get off this island. She needed to focus on the job at hand. It was nine o'clock, only six in LA. Too early to call Jon. She hoped, prayed, he'd have a lead for them. They needed to bring Ramón down so she could return to her job and her boring, predictable life.

She'd been awake for hours but hadn't ventured out of her room, too embarrassed to face Grant and his family. They'd teased Grant about the kiss when they thought she wasn't looking. She had no idea how anybody had seen it, but someone had been watching. Spying, more like. She'd played it like it didn't matter. Running to her room would have made the already awkward situation worse. So she'd held his hand and rejoined the party, smiling and laughing as if her nerves weren't trembling, as if she weren't burning with shame. When the fire had died down, she'd gone inside with the rest of them and played ping pong, besting Sam two out of three.

Maybe she'd been a little aggressive. Maybe she'd been eager to show herself superior to the brother who'd bet against Grant. Maybe she'd wanted to prove she wasn't some weak-kneed damsel just because she'd let a guy kiss her.

Just because she'd enjoyed it. A lot.

A knock sounded at her door, and she spun as if preparing to face an enemy.

"Summer?" Grant's voice was low. "You awake?"

She took a deep breath for courage, plastered on a smile, and opened the door.

He was standing on the far side, dressed just like her—jeans and a sweatshirt—looking gorgeous as a smile spread across his face. "Good morning."

"Hey." Her cheeks heated. She turned away and started shoving clothes in her duffel bag.

"You sleep okay?"

"Uh-huh." She stalked into the bathroom and gathered her toiletries. "We leaving soon?" She returned to the bedroom to find him leaning against her doorjamb.

His smile faded. "In a hurry?"

"Jon'll have an address for us today."

"Yup."

"We're a long way from civilization. I figured we should get moving."

"Huh."

She zipped the bag and looked up.

He stood there like he hadn't a care in the world.

"What?"

"You don't have anything to be embarrassed about."

"Why would I be embarrassed?"

"I'm the one who confessed my feelings. All you did was kiss me back."

"I don't want to talk about that."

"Well, I do. I very much want to talk about it. Because I confessed my feelings to you. And I'd like to know where I stand."

"Right now, you're standing in my bedroom, and I don't like it."

His expression hardened. He took a purposeful step back. Then another. "Better?" he asked from the opposite side of the hallway.

Not at all. Because there could be people out there, listening.

"Let's just..." She walked to the door and grabbed the knob. "We'll talk later." She started to close it, but he stepped across the hall again and shoved his foot in the space.

"Mom wanted me to invite you down for breakfast. I'll keep my distance." He swiveled and walked away, then disappeared down the stairs at the end of the hall.

Well, that couldn't have gone worse.

Summer didn't want to socialize, but she also didn't want to be rude to Grant's family. She definitely didn't want anybody thinking she was embarrassed or...whatever. She needed to prove she hadn't been affected by that stupid kiss.

She slipped on her sneakers. As she descended the stairs, the scents of a wood fire mingled with those of bacon and toast. It smelled like morning should.

Grant sat at the dining room table with Derrick, Bryan, Roger, and Jeremy. He didn't even glance up.

In the kitchen, Summer took a spoonful of breakfast casserole and a buttered English muffin and joined Peggy, Camilla, and Zoë at the round table. The grandparents and Maria weren't around.

Within a couple of minutes, Summer had forgotten her embarrassment and joined their conversation, feeling at home and comfortable despite the circumstances.

She'd give anything to have a family like this.

Except...except that obviously wasn't true. Because maybe, if she opened herself up to Grant, she could have not just a family *like* this one, but this actual one.

What would that be like? She could imagine them decorating a Christmas tree, ripping open packages.

She could imagine them setting off fireworks on the Fourth of July, the bonfire flickering in the background.

And, God help her, she could imagine herself snuggled up at Grant's side, feeling at home, feeling safe.

But to get there, she'd have to get past a whole lot of baggage. It was one thing to count on Grant as a work partner, to count on him to have her back, but to open herself up to him, to trust him with her emotions?

No. She couldn't do it. She wouldn't weaken herself with Grant the way her mother had weakened herself with her dad. When they'd first fallen in love, Mom had trusted Dad. She'd believed in him. And he'd betrayed her in the worst way. He'd gone from being her protector to being the man she'd needed protection from.

Summer would never take that risk. Never.

And Grant deserved a woman who could love him back. She was too damaged to be that woman.

"What are you two up to today?" Peggy asked.

"We've got some business."

The older woman's eyes lit. "A client? Someone famous? Grant told me you guarded Denise Masters a few months back."

Zoë's eyes lit. "No kidding? What's she like?"

"She's down to earth. Kind and generous and humble." Summer leaned in and lowered her voice. "Jon, my cousin... He's dating her."

"Whoa!" Zoë's jaw dropped. "That's so cool. Is it like...a big secret?"

"Not at all. They're very serious. Jon's traveling with her now. I'll be surprised...and this *is* a secret. But I'll be surprised if he doesn't propose in the next couple of months."

Peggy smiled wide. "That's great news. I hope they'll be very happy together." Her gaze scanned the men gathered at the table on the opposite side of the great room. "I wish my boys would settle down. Ridiculous they're all still single." She reached across the table and squeezed Camilla's hand. "Daniel was the wisest of them, snatching you up before you got away."

Camilla gave her a fond smile. "I'm so glad we came. I've missed you." She shifted her gaze to Summer. "And I'm glad we got to meet you."

"It's been nice to get to know you. All of you." Summer braced herself for some comment about her and Grant, but Camilla returned her attention to her breakfast, and Peggy turned to Zoë, asking about her part-time job.

Summer's phone buzzed in her pocket. A message from Jon. *Got an address. This could be it.*

"Thank you for breakfast. It was delicious." She stood and cleared her dishes. Then she got Grant's attention across the room, lifting her phone.

He gave her a nod and returned his focus to his family.

Fine, then. He'd be ready when he was ready.

She climbed the stairs to her room and, using an internet service, dialed Jon.

"What'd you learn?" she asked.

"Where's Grant?"

"Busy."

"You're at camp?"

"Why does everybody call it that?" she snapped. "There's nothing camp-like about it."

"Wake up on the wrong side of the sleeping bag?"

She scowled. "Could you give me the information, please?"

Jon chuckled, which just annoyed her further. "Beverly Bannister owns a house in York. According to satellite images, it's got a private dock."

"Is it pretty secluded?"

"Seems like it. You'll have to check it out to know for sure."

"Address?"

He told her. She tapped it into her phone, then clicked on it to see where it was.

And groaned. "It's over two hours from here."

"You're in the middle of nowhere," Jon said. "Whatever Ramón is smuggling, York would be a good place to off-load. It's not far from I-95. It's only an hour from Boston, less than an hour from Manchester. Not far from Portland. I don't know where they're distributing them, but—"

"I'll let Grant know."

"Keep me informed. And don't hesitate to call in the team if you need backup. There's no shame asking for help."

"Got it." She ended the call, not in the mood for one of Jon's lectures.

A knock sounded on the door. "Can I come in?"

Grant, again.

"Sure."

He pushed open the door and stood in the opening. "Jon?"

"He has an address for us."

"Okay. I'll tell Dad. You're ready?"

She nodded, words clogging her throat. Because, as much as she'd acted like she wanted off that island, she didn't really want to leave.

"Fine." Grant pulled the door closed without a word.

The day before, they'd had an easy working relationship. They'd talked and laughed and shared stories. Now, all that was gone.

That stupid kiss had ruined everything.

CHAPTER TWENTY

Grant couldn't decide who he was angrier with, Summer or himself.

He should have kept his stupid mouth shut. And his hands —and lips—to himself.

When they'd left the house under cloudy skies, Summer had offered thanks and hugs to his family, nice as could be. But when he'd sat beside her on the boat, she'd shifted as far from him as she could get without moving to a different bench. He figured the only reason she hadn't was because his dad was there. Never mind that her fists were clenched, her skin pale with fear. He could've offered her a blanket but didn't.

If she'd rather suffer alone than let him offer his warmth and comfort, so be it.

At the marina, she'd hugged Grant's father goodbye while remaining politely distant from Grant. The wind had freed her hair from the bun, and she yanked it out, let it fall around her face, but the soft look didn't reach her eyes.

Her politeness faded as they'd walked to the car.

He hadn't turned on music, hoping they could talk. But

considering he'd already tried to discuss what happened once, the ball was in her court.

Apparently, she had no plan to hit it back.

An hour and a half along a narrow highway and she'd said not a single word.

They hit Brunswick and angled onto the interstate in silence.

By the time they were passing the exit leading to Kennebunk, he was fuming. "This is ridiculous." He hadn't meant to speak, but he couldn't stand it anymore. "Are we seriously not going to talk about what happened?"

"There's nothing to talk about." Her voice was cold, detached. "We got caught up in the moment. The meal, the fire... It was...unprofessional."

He'd confessed his feelings, and she was calling him *unprofessional?*

"We weren't at work, Summer."

"Call me Lake."

"No."

He could feel her glare but didn't bother looking her direction.

He wasn't going to pretend nothing had happened.

That kiss...it had been more than a meeting of lips. It had proved to him—as if he hadn't already known to the depth of his being—that they were meant to be together. She was the woman for him.

He was the man for her.

And there was no chance he was letting her off the hook. She'd need to face it, deal with it. If she wanted to end their friendship, fine.

This was going to be the beginning of *them* or, once Ramón was behind bars, it was going to be the end.

"Just...no?" Her calm demeanor cracked.

"I'm not going backward, *Summer*. I'm no longer going to pretend that I don't know you. That I don't have feelings for you. If that makes you uncomfortable, then that's your problem." He angled off the highway toward York, eager to get where they were going.

"You have no right—"

"This isn't about rights." It was about the fact that he loved her. And she obviously didn't love him back.

Even if she had returned his kiss, fervently. Even if she had held his hand and looked at him with an expression he'd never seen on her face before. Not just a smile, but pure pleasure. As if she'd loved being there as much as he'd loved having her. As if the kiss meant something to her.

Or maybe the flickering firelight had made him see things that weren't there.

He followed the directions on his cell's screen. It was Saturday morning, which meant light traffic. He turned down a road that led through the center of town, passing churches with tall white steeples and shops with cedar-shake siding. Parking lots packed with cars beside little mom-and-pop restaurants. Overflowing window boxes and freshly planted flower beds bursting with color.

But cold spring air was blowing. Like Summer, it looked pretty until you got up close. Then you felt the chill.

Except, in his arms the night before, she'd been plenty warm.

"Stop the car." Her words were abrupt. She took a deep breath and started again. "Please, pull over for a second."

It was pure stubbornness on his part that tempted him to keep driving. But if she wanted to say something, then he wanted to hear it. He angled into the lot of a small office park and stopped. "What?"

"I'm being...unreasonable."

"No kidding."

Her eyebrows lifted over those stormy gray eyes. "You're usually more gracious."

"Yeah, well…" He was annoyed.

No, furious. Furious was the word.

"I'm sorry." For a second, he thought that would be the end of it, but then she continued. "I just don't know how I'm supposed to act now. I shouldn't have kissed you back. I got caught—"

"Why?"

"Why…what?"

"Why shouldn't you have kissed me back?"

"Because I don't… You said you had feelings for me, and I just, I didn't know how to—"

"How to what? Say no? I've witnessed men hitting on you for years." Clients, friends of clients, even coworkers, and he'd always watched, horrified at first, then amused as she'd shut them down. "You've never had any trouble telling them no."

"This was different." She tipped her head down, her hair falling in front of her face, blocking his view. But a second later, she lifted her gaze. "It was you."

"So?"

"So, I didn't want to…I was trying not to…"

He faced forward, closed his eyes. "If you say you didn't want to hurt my feelings—"

"Well, I didn't."

He took a breath. *Lord, what am I supposed to do with that?*

She was lying. He knew she was lying.

He faced her again. "You kissed me back because you wanted to."

Her eyes widened, but she masked the expression fast.

"You kissed me back because you liked it. And you admitted to me that I'm more than just a partner to you."

"I thought we were friends."

"Jon's my friend, but I've never been tempted to kiss him."

"That's not... So what if I'm attracted to you? I'm not interested in a relationship."

Grant watched her for a long time, trying to discern truth—or fiction—in her words. But nothing showed in her hard expression. Her lips, usually pretty and naturally pink, were pressed closed and tight at the corners. Her eyes held a challenge, daring him to disagree.

"When this is over, you can request a different partner." He shifted into drive and headed out of the parking lot.

"And if I don't want a different partner?"

"You're out of luck. Because I'll be looking for a new job."

"What?" She sounded genuinely shocked. "You're going to quit?"

"Yup." He watched the map, taking a left on a country road lined with restaurants and hotels. He followed it a half a mile or so, thankful for the quiet he'd cursed for hours.

He turned on a road barely wide enough for two cars. Tall, spindly trees rose on both sides. He caught sight of the ocean through the woods on his left.

"Why?" Summer's voice was soft, barely audible over the sound of the tires on the gravelly pavement.

He could honestly tell her that he hated the job, that he found the work dull and was desperate for something that stimulated his mind. He could honestly tell her about the different companies that'd tried to recruit him over the years. He could honestly share his dreams.

He didn't have to tell her the real reason.

But he did. "The only reason I took the job was to be near you."

"Wait...what? How long...why would you—?"

"Shh. We're almost there. I need to focus."

To her credit, she quieted, her gaze skimming their surroundings.

They passed the driveway, and he peered through the woods toward the house. Checking for security cameras. He didn't see any, but that didn't mean they weren't there.

He continued about a quarter mile to the end of the road and parked.

"What's the plan?"

"This isn't like the last place." He grabbed his phone and climbed out. "Stay here."

"I'm not some underling—"

He slammed the door. He guessed she'd follow, but he wanted to check it out first, make sure it was safe. After tucking his sweatshirt so his holstered gun would be easier to grab, he cut through the woods toward the little inlet. If the map was to be believed, they could get a look at the back of the house from here.

There was no path, but there was a break in the trees not far ahead. He skirted trunks and climbed over fallen branches and around bushes. The forest ended abruptly at a rocky drop-off that created one wall of a cove. The other wall, maybe fifty yards from him, was steeper and rocky on the top and had no trees for cover. A strong, briny breeze whipped against his jacket.

He leaned forward and looked down, guessing he was forty or fifty feet above the water. But this was a gentler slope than the cliff at his folks' camp. It would be easy to navigate.

He couldn't see the property from where he stood, so he climbed down the boulders, careful to check each one before putting his weight on it, heading toward the outer edge of the cove. Though the inlet was calm, the crash of waves breaking on the rocky shore carried from his right. If he followed the land around the bend, he'd get a view of the open ocean. But that wasn't his goal.

Sure enough, as he moved to the end of the jut of land, the property came into view. He found a good-sized boulder and crouched behind it.

The house had looked big in the satellite image, and from his vantage point, it was impressive. At least twice as big as his folks' camp, six or seven thousand square feet. It had two wings that stretched from either side of the grand center, the back wall of which was mostly windows. It looked more like a hotel than a personal dwelling. The landscaped yard led to stone steps that descended to a small rocky beach and a long dock.

There were no other properties in view.

"Good place to off-load contraband."

Summer's voice didn't surprise him. He'd heard her coming. For all her training, she didn't have the stealth he did. He turned to find her standing on a rock above him. "Get down. We don't want to be seen."

She crouched beside him. "You think there's somebody looking?"

"I don't know. Maybe. Could be cameras."

Summer was a great bodyguard, but stealth and surveillance were definitely out of her wheelhouse.

"I want you to stay here, alert me if you see anything." Staying low, he moved out of sight of the property.

"What are you going to do?"

"Check out the house."

She turned as if to follow. "I'm coming with you."

"I need you to keep an eye out. From here."

"Why?" Her look—eyes squinted, brows lowered—told him she suspected his true motives.

Because he needed to protect her. But he didn't say that. "Because if somebody comes, I need to know."

"But if someone drives in—"

"Then I'll see. I need eyes on both sides of the house. Can you do that?"

She seemed like she wanted to argue. But after a brief moment, she nodded.

"Stay there, out of sight." He nodded to where they'd been hiding. "Keep your eyes on the dock, the back of the property. You should hear if a boat comes."

Without waiting for a reply, he climbed back up the slope, passed the Land Rover—Summer'd turned it off and pocketed the keys—and jogged through the forest, keeping close to the road. If there were cameras, they'd surely be angled to catch people driving by. Hopefully, nobody would give the black SUV a second glance.

Grant was banking on the belief that Ramón wouldn't tell Bannister that their conversation in the parking garage had been overheard. He wouldn't want to spook the guy. So even if Ramón had guessed they were in Jon's vehicle, and even if someone were monitoring the house's security—both of which he highly doubted—that someone wouldn't know to look for a Land Rover.

There were no guarantees, though. Sometimes, you just had to take a chance.

Approach the house.

Kiss the girl.

What was life without chances? Maybe this venture would prove less risky—and more fruitful—than last night's.

He slowed as he neared the property, moving through the woods carefully so as not to alert anybody to his presence. He caught sight of the driveway and walked parallel to it, picking his way among the skinny trunks. The ground was damp and marshy, muffling his footsteps.

When he had a good view—circle drive, four-car garage on

one end, oversize front doors—he crouched behind a tree and watched.

A light shone through the narrow windows in the center of the structure, but there were no other lights on in the house.

No movement anywhere.

If he had to guess, the place was empty. He waited fifteen minutes, twenty.

Nothing changed.

Slowly, he made his way to the garage. A door on the side was locked, but he peered through a small window, saw a boat on a trailer, two jet skis on another trailer, and a four-wheeler.

He returned to the forest and picked his way around to the back of the house to get a closer look at the dock. Staying in the cover of the forest, he snapped some photos. Then he went back to the front, all the way to the road, and dashed across the driveway before checking out the opposite side of the property. When he reached a spot that had a good view of the dock and the rocky hill where he'd left Summer, he took cover behind one of the bushes that lined the yard and looked for her. Even knowing exactly where she was, he couldn't see her.

He sent her a quick text. *You see the house?*

Yes.

You see me?

He inched out from behind the tree. A moment passed, and then she replied. *Yes.*

Excellent. Her view should be perfect.

He was about to jog back to the road when a branch snapped nearby.

He crouched, scanned the forest, the yard.

It was quiet now, but that noise hadn't been made by a woodland creature. Something big was out here. And he highly doubted it was a bear.

Silently, he shifted around the tree so it was between him and where he thought the sound had come from. Waited.

There was movement deeper in the woods. Not far, maybe ten, fifteen feet away, if his guess was right. Footsteps.

Grant inched his handgun out of its holster. Prepared to defend himself, shoot if necessary.

Had to be a guard. If the guard knew Grant was here, then catching Ramón in the act had just become much, much harder.

If Grant ended up showing himself...he didn't want to think about the ramifications. He could be in serious legal trouble—he was trespassing, after all. But more importantly, Ramón would know that they'd found the property. It would blow their one opportunity to catch him in the act, to bring him down.

Summer would never be safe.

The guy was still moving. He wasn't trying to be quiet. Which meant he probably had no idea Grant was there.

He was getting closer. Five feet away. Four.

Grant could hear him breathing.

He stopped on the opposite side of the tree Grant was hiding behind. Stayed there a long time.

Then, he moved along, his footsteps gaining speed. Grant shifted silently around the tree to keep it between them. As the footsteps faded, he chanced a glance.

Medium height, dark blond hair that grew past the collar of his black jacket. Wore black jeans, black boots.

The long end of a rifle swung out to the side.

Definitely a guard. Maybe he'd seen movement in the forest. Maybe he patrolled the grounds often.

Either way, Grant needed to get out of there. Silently, he backtracked to the road and dashed across. Only when he was off the property did he text Summer to meet him at the SUV.

"Well?" She was standing beside it, arms crossed, when he emerged from the woods.

"Get in." His words were harsh, and her eyes flashed. But she did as he asked.

He did the same, shifted into gear, but he didn't start driving. "The place is being watched."

"What? Did you see somebody? Were you seen?"

"I saw a guard. It's possible he saw movement in the woods and went to check it out. It's possible I tripped a wire. It's possible there are cameras, though I didn't see any."

"So maybe you were seen."

"I don't think so."

"But if you tripped a wire—"

"Could have been a deer, a bear, some other large animal. The guy didn't seem nervous. Wasn't making much effort to be quiet. I don't think he thought he was in danger."

Summer's gaze skimmed the area. "Why are we sitting here?"

"I want that guy to get comfortable again before we move. I don't want him to see us driving away. And there's no other way out."

They were a good quarter mile past the house. Grant doubted that guard would patrol this far. They should be safe here for the time being.

"A guard tells us—"

"This is the place. I have no doubt."

"Okay. So, now what?"

After what Ramón's men had done to Summer the previous week, after kidnapping her and all those models...everything in him wanted to take Ramón down himself. Not just take him into custody but *take him out*. But this wasn't a mission. Ramón wasn't a terrorist, an enemy of his country. At least the powers-that-be in America didn't know he was. Grant couldn't exactly lead a team in, guns blazing.

This was Maine, not Afghanistan.

And he didn't have a highly trained team of special opera-tives. He had Summer, and his number one job was to keep her safe. All of which meant he was going to have to put his personal desire on the back burner.

He started the Land Rover and shifted into drive. "We call Golinski."

CHAPTER TWENTY-ONE

"You've got to be kidding me."

Summer winced at the fury in Grant's words. Until today, she'd never heard him speak to anybody with such anger. At least this time it wasn't directed at her.

They were parked in front of the same office building where they'd stopped earlier. The clouds had broken, revealing a sliver of pale blue sky.

Grant had already explained to Agent Golinski what they'd seen at the Bannister property.

"You might be onto something." The FBI agent's voice sounded just as tired as it had the last time they'd spoken. "But I need evidence."

By Grant's expression, he was about to let the guy have it.

She slipped her hand over his wrist. It was probably the shock that she'd touched him that stifled his words. "I told you what I overheard," she said. "Now, we've found somebody who owns a house on the coast that has a private dock and an armed guard on the premises. The owner's husband has been suspected of dealing in stolen antiquities."

"Suspected by who?" the FBI agent asked. "Not us. The guy's not on our radar."

"He should be." Grant shifted his arm, and Summer let it go.

She adopted a friendly tone. No need to irritate their only law enforcement ally. "We were given his name by Kathleen Hopkins, a woman who works for the Museum of Fine Arts. She wrote an article about this, did a lot of research."

Golinski grumbled. She picked up the sound of typing through the phone. "Yeah. Okay, I see who you're talking about. What's her evidence against Bannister?"

"She's not a cop." Grant's dark eyes glowered at the dashboard screen as if Golinski were standing right there. "She doesn't have evidence."

Summer added, "She said his name kept floating to the top when she was researching the article."

"Rumors?" Golinski infused his voice with scorn. "Innuendo? Maybe whispered accusations by competitors? You really expect me to act on that?"

"We expect you to act on the information Summer overheard," Grant snapped. "We expect you—"

"Look," Golinski said. "If I take this to my boss, he's gonna laugh in my face. We can't just stake out the home of a private citizen on a hunch. We need solid evidence."

Grant's hands clenched the steering wheel.

Summer resisted the urge to touch him again, just to calm him. "What do you recommend we do?"

"You think Ramón threatened you," Golinski said. "We've got him under surveillance, but so far he's not gone anywhere but back and forth from his hotel to the hospital."

"Governor Hidalgo made it through the surgery all right?"

"That's what I hear. Our guys haven't seen Ramón meet with anybody but family. Because of who his sister is, it was virtually impossible for us to get permission to tail him in the first place. Fact is, there's not a whole lot we *can* do."

"So—what?" Grant asked. "Should Lake just change her name, move away, hope he never finds her?"

"I wish there were more we could do, Ms. Lake. We can't arrest the guy. He didn't threaten you himself. He didn't harm you in any way."

Grant said, "Those men—"

"Might or might not have been working under his orders."

Before Summer could react, Grant did. "They beat her up." His volume was rising. "They tried to kidnap her. They broke into her home."

"If we find the guys who did that, we'll take them into custody. But there's no proof they're associated with Ramón."

"They mentioned him by name." Summer was trying to be the reasonable one—since Grant had clearly adopted the opposite role. But her frustration was mounting.

Golinski said, "It could have been a co—"

"You think it was a coincidence?" Grant's shout bounced off the windows and reverberated in her brain.

"It doesn't matter what I think," Golinski yelled back. "Don't you get it? I work for the FBI. I'm not..." He paused, breathed, lowered his voice. "If it were up to me—"

"You think we're right?" Summer asked. "Off the record, or...whatever?"

"Me, personally? Maybe. But my opinion doesn't matter."

"What if we bring you evidence?"

Grant's question was met with a long stretch of silence. Finally, Golinski said, "What do you mean?"

"What if we...?" He shifted, not just positions, she guessed, but what he was about to say. "Got photos of him, or...or his men. What if we got proof?"

"I recommend you don't go anywhere near that house."

"Noted," Grant said. "But if we did get evidence...?"

"I'd want to see it, yeah. But even photos... Without the actual smuggled goods, without stolen artifacts and whatever else—"

"Drugs is my guess," Grant said.

Summer still assumed Ramón was transporting people, but she didn't say so because it didn't matter.

"If that's what this is, then... Look, I'll pass the information along to the DEA. Maybe they'll want to follow up. But you two need to step away, let the professionals handle it."

"The professionals, like you? Who can't be bothered?"

"I told you—"

"We'll be in touch."

Grant mashed the button on the steering wheel, ending the call and muttering under his breath words she'd never heard him use. Before she could think of anything to say, he was dialing his phone again. A moment later, it rang through the speakers.

A woman answered, "York Police Department."

Grant asked to be put through to a detective. When a different woman took the call, he explained what they suspected was going to happen at that house.

The woman actually laughed. Apparently, Beverly Bannister's family was well known in York, had lived there for generations. Gave a lot of money to charity.

They'd be getting no help from the local police.

A conversation with the state police garnered a similar response. It wasn't that they didn't care or didn't believe him. There simply wasn't enough evidence.

Beside her, Grant looked ready to chew his way through a steel door. "I wonder if Jon knows anybody at the Coast Guard. Maybe they'd be interested."

"I think we should get something to eat."

He shot her a look that could leave a bruise. Opened his mouth to argue, then snapped it shut. "Yeah. Okay."

She'd worked with him long enough to see the signs of hunger. Though she'd never seen him as angry as he was right now, he was always more short-tempered before lunch.

She pointed to a restaurant down the street. "That place has had a steady stream of customers. Usually a good sign."

He headed that way and found a parking spot quickly.

They were seated at a table near the window overlooking the dreary day. The place smelled of greasy hamburgers and fried potatoes, and her stomach growled as she read her menu.

She decided what she wanted, then sent Jon a quick text. When her phone dinged with a response, Grant looked up from his menu, question in his eyes.

She read the message. "Jon doesn't have any contacts with the Coast Guard."

"Figures." Grant returned his attention to the menu.

Summer found a phone number for the Coast Guard online and dialed. She told the person who answered that she had a tip and was directed to another person. She was still on hold when she gave the server her order.

Finally, someone came on the line. She related all the information they had, answered questions for a few minutes, and then was thanked for the information. "We'll keep our eyes open," the man said.

She hung up and told Grant what they'd said.

"Another dead end."

"Probably."

All around them, diners chatted, most seemingly having a good time. Smiling, laughing.

Overhead, oldies piped through speakers.

Across the aisle, a young couple wrestled toddlers in their booth while a baby in a high chair shoved dry cereal into his mouth. He was adorable, all squishy and messy, focus intent on the little bits of food as he worked to get his chubby little fingers to pick them up.

Despite the chaos of their three children, the parents never lost their tempers. They seemed...happy.

A rush of longing had her turning her eyes forward, but Grant was watching the family too. And his expression mirrored all the things she was trying to pretend she didn't feel.

He looked at her, then out the window.

She hated the tension between them. She hadn't realized how much she'd counted on Grant's friendship until it was gone.

Not just his friendship. His kindness. His warmth.

All the time she'd worked with him, she'd taken those things for granted. She missed them. She missed him. The real Grant. She'd had enough of this furious impostor.

"Look," she said.

His gaze snapped to hers.

"First, I'm sorry. I'm sorry I can't be who you want me to be."

"You're exactly who I want you to be."

"I'm..." She lost her train of thought, trying to make sense of what he'd said. "You know what I mean."

He sipped his water and stared outside again.

"Maybe Golinski's right. Maybe we should just forget the whole thing."

Very slowly, he turned back to face her. "Ramón already kidnapped you once. He tried again the other day." His words were measured and calm, but they hummed with fury like electricity in a power line. "He knows who you are and where you live. He knows you overheard his plans. You think *he's* going to 'forget the whole thing'?"

"I can just..." What? What could she do?

Leave her job? Sell her stake in the business? Move away? Spend the rest of her life in hiding?

No, she couldn't do any of those things.

"The point is, it's not your problem." She unwrapped the silverware from the paper napkin to give herself an excuse to look away. "If you're going to find another job, there's no reason why you shouldn't do that now." The words felt like sand in her mouth. The idea of Grant quitting, of never seeing him again... Her eyes tingled as if she might cry. In front of a man.

Over a man.

She looked up and saw, for the second time in an hour, Grant's face turn bright red. "You really think I'm going to...to leave you to deal with this by yourself?" His voice was low and vehement as he leaned toward her. "Just because you don't have feelings for me doesn't mean mine just...just blew away on the wind. Even if I didn't love you—"

"Whoa. What?" Surprise skimmed over her skin. Or was it pleasure?

"Pretend I didn't say that," he snapped. "It doesn't matter. The point is, I'm sticking by your side until you're safe. I didn't rescue you seven years ago, watch your back ever since, to see you get kidnapped or killed by that guy. So...stop talking."

Summer stared at him, trying to rearrange all the words he'd said so they made some sort of sense.

Had he had feelings for her since he met her?

Did he *love* her?

Their meals were delivered, and though she'd been hungry, now she could barely force down a couple of bites of her sandwich.

Grant, undeterred by the bomb he'd just dropped, shoveled food into his mouth. Or maybe he just didn't want to talk.

If only she could get Jon's advice. He'd always been smart and insightful—so much more than herself. Since he'd become a

Christian, he'd become even wiser. She needed his counsel. She needed to tell somebody what was going on.

Except Jon was Grant's best friend. Grant probably wouldn't appreciate her spilling all this to him. Unless...

"Does Jon know? About"—she gestured between—"what you said?"

"He guessed. Some of it." Grant swallowed some of his Coke. "I think he suspected for a while."

Huh. And obviously, he wasn't against the idea, if he'd left them together. Of course, his priority was Denise now.

Even if Jon were on board, that didn't change how Summer felt. "I can't..." she started. "I just... I don't..."

"Know how to finish a sentence?"

"Apparently."

He set down his oversize burger and wiped his hands on his napkin. "I didn't mean to tell you that...other thing. And I know I'm acting like a jerk. I'm not mad at you. I'm mad at myself, and I'm sorry I'm taking it out on you."

When his gaze met and held hers, something inside her leapt, replacing the fear that had pulsed since she'd woken up. Yesterday, she'd felt attracted to him. Nestled against his side on that tiny boat ride, she'd felt warm and safe, so different from the stark terror she'd experienced as they'd bounced over the waves this morning.

She'd liked holding his hand. Laughing with him. Sharing stories.

She'd admitted to herself that she had a crush on him.

But it was more than a crush, wasn't it? Maybe she didn't feel the depth of feelings he felt, but there was something there. When he looked at her like he was now, the *something* flickered like a candle flame. Or a fire in a fireplace.

Not a bonfire, but...there might be bonfire potential.

The mom and dad across the aisle were packing up their

things and their children. They looked happy enough, but her parents had looked happy in public. Nobody had known the truth.

"None of this is your fault," Grant said, pulling her out of her thoughts. "I should've told you a long time ago. It's on me that I kept my feelings to myself for seven years."

"Surely not seven years, though."

Grant leaned toward her. "Do you remember when I found you?"

Remember?

Was he kidding?

It was the most memorable event of her life.

She, her sister, and the other models had been trapped for days, only let out of that cramped building one at a time, and only after black canvas bags had been dropped over their heads and cinched around their necks. And only to call their families and beg them through the thick fabric to send ransom money.

Their captors hadn't known Summer and Misty were sisters. Misty had called Dad, but Summer had no confidence that Dad would pay to get them back, even if he'd had the money—which he didn't.

She had even less confidence that their kidnappers planned to let them go. She figured the families would send their life savings, and then the women would be sold as slaves—or murdered.

When it was her turn to make a phone call, she'd dialed Jon's cell. If anybody could find them and rescue them, he could.

She hadn't told Misty, or anybody, what she'd done, afraid one of the women would let it slip.

Days passed, and her hope had faltered. Tiffany was beaten so badly that her memory couldn't hang onto information for more than a few minutes. It seemed only a matter of time before the rest of the women suffered a similar fate—or worse.

But then, their sixth night in captivity, gunshots pierced the air.

A couple of the girls screamed.

"Quiet!" She silenced them, gathered them together, and told them to be ready to move. "Misty, Cheryl, get Tiffany up. Stay with her."

Her sister and their friend stared, shocked.

"Now!"

All of them scrambled to their feet while Summer put herself between her friends and the door. Maybe rescuers would burst in.

Maybe kidnappers.

Either way, she would be ready. She had nothing to use as a weapon, no way to defend herself or the others. But she would fight if she had to.

Shouts in Spanish, more gunfire.

Then, a few words of English.

The door flew open. A soldier stood on the threshold. Camo-clad, he wore a helmet and black boots and held an automatic weapon, which he aimed at every corner of their room, looking for enemies.

A few of the women gasped, but not Summer. She'd hoped it would be Jon, but she'd take this guy. She'd take anybody who could rescue them.

"Come on," the man said. "Let's get you out of here."

"You have another weapon?"

He gave her a long, appraising look. "You know how to shoot?"

She was formulating a reply, but he must've seen something in her expression. He pulled a handgun from a holster and handed it over. "As far as we can tell, they're all either dead or surrendered, but we're still clearing the buildings. You'll bring up the rear. You see anybody not dressed like me, you shoot. Got it?"

"Got it."

He held her eye contact another moment. "You see anybody who *is* dressed like me, please don't get spooked. Those are my friends out there."

"I understand." She turned to the women. "Stay close. Keep up."

For the first time since they'd been taken at gunpoint, she saw hope in their eyes as they passed her, following the soldier out the door.

Now, that soldier stared at her from across the table, watching her remember.

"I'll never forget it." To her shame, emotion wavered in her voice, and her stupid eyes tingled again.

"I walked through that door and saw the bravest woman I've ever seen in my life." Grant's lips tipped up at the corners, though his eyes held none of the smile. "Thirteen terrified models—and one warrior, itching to fight. Demanding a gun so you could do just that."

"I was tired of being helpless."

"I don't think you've ever been helpless."

Ha. He had no idea.

"At that moment..." Grant's voice lowered. He shook his head. "Sheesh. You already know everything anyway. I might as well tell it all."

Her heart thumped, though from anticipation or fear, she couldn't have said.

"When I asked you if you knew how to shoot, and you gave me that look, that *don't ask stupid questions* look... I fell a little bit in love with you right then."

Her breath caught.

"I haven't stopped falling since."

"Oh, Grant—"

"I don't need your pity." He pushed back against his chair, sipped his Coke, set it down. "Like I said, it's not your fault. You didn't know. It's my problem. I'll deal with it."

He dove back into his meal.

But she was too overwhelmed to eat.

Grant had been in love with her for seven years, and she'd had no idea. And now that she knew, she couldn't figure out how she felt. Because she was terrified of trusting anybody, terrified that, when push came to shove, she'd be left alone.

Her mother hadn't stood between her and danger.

Her older sister had escaped their household the second she was old enough, hardly ever bothering to check on her and Misty.

The so-called guards who'd been hired to protect the models in Mexico had turned tail and run when Ramón's men closed in.

And then, the second Misty had felt strong enough, she'd moved on with her life, leaving Summer behind.

It was easier to stay alone than to discover that yet one more person she counted on had let her down. If she gave in to her feelings for Grant, he'd abandon her like everybody else had.

But he'd just handed his heart over like an offering, fully expecting her to crush it.

And he'd called *her* brave.

CHAPTER TWENTY-TWO

Seven years, Grant had kept secret his love for Summer. Now, in the space of about eighteen hours, he'd spilled everything. He'd always hoped that, when he finally told Summer how he felt, she'd admit to similar feelings. He'd hoped she'd at least be open to the idea of dating him.

But his worst fears had come to pass. She'd shut him down.

He chanced a glance up from his lunch, catching her as she looked away. Was that indecision in those stormy gray eyes? Or maybe he just saw what he wanted to see. Because her jaw was tight, her mouth firmly closed. Though most of her meal remained on the plate, she hadn't taken a bite in minutes.

"You done?" he asked.

She got the server's attention and asked for the bill. "I'm buying."

Normally, he'd argue, but he didn't bother as she handed over the cash. If she felt she owed him something, if spending fifteen bucks on him would make her feel better, then so be it.

As they walked out, he couldn't bring himself to regret his honesty. Now he could move on—assuming they brought Ramón down and secured her safety. Maybe, if he didn't see her five days a week, his feelings would fade. He was thirty-five years old. If he wanted to get married and have a family, he needed to get started.

He did want that. The family he'd been watching in the restaurant—the squirming kids, the little baby in the high chair —he wanted all of it.

Was recovering from crushing heartbreak akin to recovering from the flu? Would it take a few months to find normalcy again?

Or was it more like cancer? Would the cure, like chemotherapy, leave him weaker than ever?

Either way, he was done hoping Summer would be his wife, the mother of his children. If she never planned to marry, then any attraction she might have felt toward him didn't matter. Her feelings—if she had any at all—were irrelevant. Seemed the wounds from her childhood cut deeper than he'd understood.

They climbed into the SUV, and he pulled into traffic.

"Where are we going?"

"I need to stop at the store, if that's all right with you."

"That's fine."

They were being overly polite. The easy camaraderie they'd once shared was gone.

"And then we need to come up with a plan," he said. "You and I can't stake out the house twenty-four seven. We're going to need to bring in the team."

"And get supplies. Weapons, binoculars, comms."

His phone rang, the trill too loud in the quiet car. He recognized the number and hit the button to answer. "This is Grant. I'm with Lake."

"I got some information for you." Agent Golinski's voice was monotone, not that he ever showed much emotion. It seemed his only emotions were bored and angry.

Grant signaled to change lanes, headed for the mostly empty parking lot of a little white church.

Summer pulled her cell from her bag and turned on a recording app. "Go ahead."

"Vasco Ramón owns a ranch in Central Mexico."

"We know," Grant said. "Discovered that days ago."

"I've been looking into the ranch's holdings. Property, equipment, that kind of thing. Nothing unusual, except I've been following a rabbit trail that paid off today. It took some serious digging, but Ramón's business is in partnership with another business—in the Cayman Islands."

Golinski said the words as if they were significant.

"That's important?" Grant asked.

"The Caymans are a popular place to register pleasure boats —for tax reasons and because a boat registered in the Caymans is considered a British vessel, which means it flies under the British flag and is protected by the British Royal Navy. I guess that's a big deal."

"And you're saying...?"

"The company Ramón's ranch is partnered with owns a yacht registered in the Caymans."

"Shocking," Grant deadpanned. "Who would have guessed he had access to a yacht?"

"Do you have any idea where it is?" Like before, Summer's voice was far more reasonable than Grant's.

"It checked in with US Customs in Miami four days ago."

Summer's eyes widened. "Was the vessel searched?"

"They hardly ever search pleasure boats unless they have some reason to believe—"

"I'd think what I overheard the other day—"

"You overheard that conversation on Wednesday. The boat hit the US on Tuesday."

"Oh. Right," she said.

"And anyway, it's not like it's in Ramón's name. I'm just lucky I found the connection."

"Ramón's not on the boat, I guess," Summer said.

They might be able to stop whatever he was planning, but unless he was present, they probably wouldn't be able to link him to the operation. She'd still be in danger.

"He's in Boston. Maybe he'll meet up with the boat eventually. Or maybe his crew will be doing the off-loading."

Grant navigated to his map program, but that wouldn't be helpful. "How long does it take to get from Miami to here by sea?"

"I researched the type of yacht he has. From what I can tell, it's fast. I've got a call in to someone who should be able to look up their location—assuming they have an AIS tracking system and it's on. All we know now is that they left on Thursday. They could be headed anywhere. Back to Mexico, to Cayman—"

"They're headed to Maine," Grant said.

"Wait," Summer said. "How do you know when they left?"

"Talked to the guy who runs the marina where they docked in Miami."

"What's your guess, then?" Grant asked. "How soon can he be here?"

"Obviously depends on their speed. My research tells me most yachts don't go much more than twenty knots. At that rate, three days, give or take."

"So he could be here as soon as tomorrow?" Grant clarified.

"Afternoon, maybe. Assuming they're going fast. Assuming they haven't stopped somewhere."

Summer's eyes were scrunched at the corners. Her head tilted to the side. "But...what are the chances he'll have that... tracking system engaged? Don't you think it'll be turned off?"

"I know about as much about yachts as I do about private

jets and polo," Golinski said, "which is to say, nothing. Maybe they need the system to navigate, in which case, would he turn it off?"

"Most fishing boats and even a lot of small crafts have GPS units for navigation," Grant said. "I agree with Summer. I'm guessing, if there is an AIS system on the boat, it'll be turned off."

"Which might be a red flag, but not illegal." Golinski muttered a curse word. "I don't know what to tell you, then."

"We're going to have to watch the house." Summer shot a glance at Grant, and he nodded for her to continue. "Maybe we can get the evidence you need."

"You see something going down, you call 911 and get out of there. No sense putting yourselves in danger."

"This isn't evidence enough to get the FBI involved?"

"Not even close."

Frustrating, but there was no point arguing. "Call us if you get any more information."

"You do the same."

Grant ended the call. "Our window just got smaller."

"That's a good thing. The sooner this is over, the better."

Was she so eager to be rid of him? Even as he hid the jolt of pain, he agreed—for a different reason.

He'd do anything to get Summer out of danger. His job at this point was to figure out how to do what needed to be done—and keep her safe at the same time.

CHAPTER TWENTY-THREE

Summer wouldn't have minded heading back to the Wright's camp for one more night. She'd brave the horrible boat ride to be surrounded by people who'd made her feel at home. But it would be awkward, considering how courteous—as opposed to friendly—she and Grant were acting toward each other.

She checked in with her sisters. Both assured her they were safe. Otherwise, the drive was silent. She wasn't sorry when, less than an hour after they'd left York, they arrived at Bryan's house, the empty driveway confirming what Grant had told her —that Bryan had stayed with the family.

Grant should have, too, but instead, he was stuck with Summer.

At least there was a light at the end of this nightmarish tunnel. When the yacht arrived at the Bannister house, maybe Ramón would be on it, and they could take the guy down.

Otherwise...well, she didn't want to think about the alternatives. One way or another, she had to prove Ramón was a criminal, and she had to do it before he found her.

She hadn't exactly mastered the art of praying, but she asked God to please work out all the details.

She and Grant very politely made their way inside, and she carried her duffel bag to the room where she'd slept two nights before. She'd called Bartlett on the drive, but until he called her back, there was nothing to do but wait.

Which she intended to do in the privacy of that Pepto-Bismol pink bedroom. No need to endure any more awkward silences with Grant. Downstairs, the TV blared the shouts from some sporting event.

Not much time passed, though, before a door slammed. Voices. Was that...?

She crept down the hall to the top of the stairs.

"I thought you were staying at camp." Grant's voice came from around the corner. He didn't sound happy.

Bryan was standing on the landing, a rolling suitcase at his side. "Changed my mind."

"If I'd known you were going to be here—"

"That's why I didn't tell you. No need for you to go to a hotel."

Grant mumbled, "Didn't want to inconvenience—"

"You're my brother, idiot. You're not an inconvenience." Bryan looked up and smiled. "Hey, Summer. How you doing?"

"Thanks for letting us come back here."

"I'm happy to do it." He glowered at his brother. "Seriously."

She didn't catch Grant's answer because her cell rang. She hurried back to the bedroom to grab it. "This is Lake."

"I'm trying to figure it out." Bartlett, abrupt as always. "We picked up a new client yesterday."

"That's great." She hated the thought of all those people on the payroll with no work to keep them busy—or cover their salaries. "From where?"

"I've been trying to get this company's business for a while. Haven't got a long-term contract yet, but there's some big convention in town this week, and they decided they needed extra security. They wanted to hire everybody we could spare, but I kept a few back, just in case."

"Thanks for doing that." She hated that her trouble was costing her business money.

"I sent them seven."

She did the math in her head. "You're saying we only have six people available?"

"Ian, Jones, Greta, Hughes, Marcus, and Smitty. I could shuffle some around."

Jones and Hughes were very experienced. Ian was new but competent. The rest had been with the company long enough to prove their abilities. With her and Grant, that meant eight guards. She would have preferred four six-hour shifts, but they'd need three per group. Eight-hour shifts would work.

Unfortunately, one of the teams would be down a man.

"We could hire contractors."

She didn't miss the tentative tone in Bartlett's voice. Contractors would cost money the company didn't have.

She considered her bank account. Yeah, she had what she'd earned as a model, but most of it was tied up in the business and her apartment. She wasn't exactly cash-rich.

"Let me talk to Grant and see what he wants to do."

Summer descended the stairs and found Grant sprawled out on the couch. As soon as he saw her, he swung his feet to the floor and sat up.

She settled in the chair. "Just got off the phone with Bartlett. He only has six people to spare."

His cheeks, shaved that morning, were now covered in stubble. His lips turned down at the corners. "How did that happen?"

She told him about the new client.

"He should have held more back," Grant said. "He knew we might need help."

"It's his job to keep the business afloat."

Grant's expression shifted. He squinted those dark eyes. "Is it in trouble?"

"Every day we pay people who aren't working—"

"I get that. You hired all those new guys for the Masters job. But are you saying—?"

"Bartlett had a lot of irons in the fire this winter. He was sure the work would come in. Otherwise, he'd have contracted the new hires short-term. But the business hasn't come in like he'd hoped, not yet anyway. That means..." Grant didn't need the ins and outs of the company. He wasn't an owner. Soon enough, he wouldn't even be an employee. "The point is, he can send six starting tomorrow."

"I don't want to leave a team down a man."

"Our team." She wasn't about to put anybody else at greater risk to protect herself. And nobody was better at this than Grant, except maybe Jon. He'd be back in three days.

"We need one more," Grant said. "Doesn't have to be anybody super experienced. One person staked out in the woods near the road to get a visual on cars going in and out. One on the rocks where you were today, watching the water. I'll be in the woods at the side, watching the dock and driveway. Soon as we get confirmation, we do what Golinski said and call 911. With any luck, the cops'll be there before they get away, but even if they aren't, if we can get license plates, the cops should be able to track the cars. With luck, they'll get there in time to intercept the boat too."

Summer nodded as he talked. It was a good plan. As long as Ramón's men didn't know they were there, it should work.

"Let's call Bartlett, ask him to hire a subcontractor for the job. I can pay for it out of—"

"I'll do it." Bryan stepped into the living room. He must've been in his office.

Grant stood. "This has nothing to do with you."

"You just said it doesn't have to be someone experienced."

"I said it doesn't have to be someone *super* experienced. You have zero."

"I know how to take pictures and write down license plate numbers and make phone calls. How hard can it be?"

"That's what you think I do for a living?" Grant failed to keep the frustration out of his voice. To Summer, he said, "Call Bartlett. Tell him—"

"Seriously? You're not going to let me help?"

"It could be dangerous."

"I can defend myself, Grant. And I'm as good a shot as you."

"I doubt that very much."

"There's a gun range down the street. Let's go."

"Shooting paper targets isn't the same as shooting human beings."

"You're planning on shooting somebody?" Bryan asked.

Summer stood, unsure of her place in this conversation, feeling like she shouldn't be hearing it at all. But she couldn't exactly walk away.

"You just assume, because I have this stupid thing"—Bryan lifted his cane, thumped it against the hardwood—"I'm helpless. But I'm *not* helpless. I can't run very fast, but anything else you need me to do—"

"You experienced in hand-to-hand combat?"

"I can hold my own."

Summer said, "There shouldn't be any hand-to—"

"No." Grant's single word seemed to echo against the walls. "Absolutely not."

The brothers glared at each other.

Summer lifted her cell. "I'll make that call."

"Don't." Bryan didn't take his eyes off his brother. "I'm tired of you treating me like an invalid because of a stupid limp. I can climb. I can fight. I can shoot. And I sure as heck can read a license plate. All you need is somebody to watch, right? You're not planning on bringing these guys down."

"Things don't always go according to plan," Grant said. "People get hurt."

"No kidding." Sarcasm dripped from the words. "What would I know about that?"

Grant flinched as if wounded.

Summer would rather hire a professional, but Bryan wasn't wrong. They didn't need a pro. They needed someone to hide in the woods, act as lookout, and take pictures of any cars that drove to or from the property.

She'd be watching the cove. She'd be more exposed. The lookout in the woods should be hidden. "We're talking about eight-hour shifts," she said. "Can you—?"

"—He's not—"

"I can handle that," Bryan said.

Grant plopped down on the sofa. "Forget it."

She ignored Grant. "Can you sit in the same position for long periods of time? I'm talking hours, not minutes."

"As long as I stretch occasionally."

"We'll make sure you're in a position to do that. Shouldn't be a problem."

From his seat on the couch, Grant said, "No."

"Let me think about it." Because at the end of the day, she was the boss.

Yes, she'd prefer a pro, but Bryan wanted to do it. Just like he'd wanted her and Grant to be there. Just like he seemed to want very much to repair his relationship with his brother. If she could help with that, it would be one small thing she could do for Grant.

She hoped he wouldn't hate her for it.

CHAPTER TWENTY-FOUR

G rant left Bryan's before dawn the next morning. The house was silent.

The night before, he'd called Bartlett, requesting (though Bartlett might have called it *demanding*) that he hire another bodyguard.

"Apparently, there've been threats against a big conference in town," Bartlett had explained. "Any company with personnel to spare has been asked to send help. I could have gotten work for all of us, you and Summer included, but—"

"We're not coming back until she's safe, and we need—"

"I know the situation. I'm just saying, there's nobody. You're going to have to make do with who I send."

He'd been frustrated, to say the least. Was Summer's security less important than the business's bottom line? She was a part owner, after all. "Fine. I'll take care of it. I'll hire—"

"I've checked every agency from here to the Canadian border. I'm telling you, there's nobody."

After he finished the call, Grant had stretched out on the sofa, furious, barely sleeping a wink.

Either he and Summer would work alone or he'd have to pull Bryan in.

He'd almost gotten his brother killed once. He didn't relish the idea of doing it again. He'd fought with himself all night long.

Now, considering the situation as he drove, he pounded the steering wheel. He shouldn't have to decide between protecting his brother and protecting the woman he loved. If it were up to him, he'd send them both straight back to the family's island and leave them there until Ramón was in custody or dead.

No chance Summer would hide out, and Bryan seemed determined to put himself in harm's way.

Frustrating as it was, Summer wasn't wrong. If they placed Bryan in the woods and made sure he was well hidden, he shouldn't be in any danger.

Which was why Grant was heading to York now. He wanted Summer far away while he staked out places to hide—and ways to get there without alerting Ramón's men at the Bannister place.

He reached York and found a narrow road not far from the property. It was lined with vacation homes, which all looked abandoned at the moment. Once Memorial Day hit, people would flock to the area, but for now, during the week, if the teams parked their SUVs off the road, they shouldn't raise suspicion.

He parked and cut a trail through the woods toward the Bannister place, careful to emerge beyond the driveway. He found a path Bryan would be able to navigate with his cane. It wouldn't be easy, but he could do it.

It took hours, but Grant marked the trail by tying red twine around tree trunks close enough together that the team would easily see from one marker to the next. That way, he wouldn't have to guide anybody in. The twine wouldn't be visible from the road or the Bannister property, so it shouldn't raise any flags.

He finished and waited in the SUV until the first team arrived. Even though chances were good Ramón's yacht was still making its way north, Grant wanted eyes on the place now. He met them and stowed the supplies they'd brought for himself, Summer, and Bryan—rifles, scopes, binoculars, night-vision equipment, and comm units. Then he trailed them through the woods, making sure the markers were clear enough for them to follow. Once they'd reached the woods across the street from the property, he told them where to set up. "There's a guard patrolling the grounds. Take proper precautions."

A few minutes later, Jones spoke through the comms. "It's a good plan." He, Greta, and Ian were all in position. "As long as this is the place—"

"This is the place," Grant said. "Be sure to make note of every car and every boat that goes anywhere near the house, no matter how innocent they might seem. If you see anything suspicious—"

"Call 911." Jones's words had an *I-heard-you-the-first-ten-times* tone.

"Right." Grant needed to calm down. Jones knew what he was doing.

Grant usually wasn't so nervous. Of course usually, they were on protection duty, not find-and-expose missions against smugglers.

And usually, it wasn't Summer's life on the line.

Jones's team would be on duty until four p.m. Grant, Summer, and Bryan would take over from then until midnight, and Hughes and his team would take the midnight-to-eight shift. They'd keep up that schedule until Ramón and his men made their move.

Satisfied everybody was in position, Grant drove back to

York. If not for Bryan, they'd stay in the hotel rooms Bartlett had reserved in town. But Bryan had classes to teach when they weren't staking out the Bannister estate. So, the three of them would be trekking the hour back and forth every day.

Of course, Grant could let Bryan make the drive alone. He and Summer could stay in York if they wanted. But, as awkward as it felt sometimes, hanging out with his younger brother was giving him hope. Maybe Bryan wasn't lying when he said he wanted Grant around. Maybe, through this situation, they could improve their strained relationship.

Assuming he didn't finish what he'd started twenty-six years ago and get his little brother killed.

With that in mind, he used his key and stepped into Bryan's house. Following the sound of voices, he crossed the living room into the kitchen, where Summer and Bryan were cozied up at the table. The dirty plates pushed to the side told him they'd eaten lunch together. Looked like they'd been sitting there quite a while.

By the guilt on their faces, they'd had a nice little chat. About him?

Or about *them*?

Either way, the sight ticked him off. "We're all set. Be ready to go at two thirty." He focused on his brother. "Wear dark clothing and dress warmly."

"Got it," Bryan said.

"We were just..."

Summer's words faded as Grant swiveled and marched back out the door, slamming it behind him.

He didn't know what he'd interrupted, but his imagination offered all sorts of suggestions.

No, there'd be no fixing his relationship with his brother. If Bryan wanted Summer, if Summer wanted him back, so be it.

But Grant wasn't going to hang around and watch.

CHAPTER TWENTY-FIVE

When Summer woke, pale dawn light filtered around the curtains. She told herself to go back to sleep, but her mind had other plans.

Their first night on lookout at the Bannister place had gone according to plan. They'd gotten into position, and then they'd watched for eight hours.

Nothing had happened. No cars had driven to or past the driveway. No boats had come anywhere near the cove.

Which meant she'd had hours to contemplate Grant's attitude. Obviously, he'd been angry to find her and Bryan together when he'd returned from York.

Did Grant really think she'd dive into a relationship with his brother? After everything Grant had confessed to her?

The man didn't know her at all. Or maybe, after everything, he wasn't thinking clearly. Because Grant was a good guy. A *great* guy, if his brother was to be believed.

While Summer had eaten lunch the day before, Bryan had extolled Grant's finer qualities and told her more about their history. "I blamed him for my fall," Bryan had said. "Treated him like dirt for years. But he never once lost his temper with me. Never got angry. Never defended himself. Always just... took it." Bryan had shaken his head. "You couldn't ask for a more patient man. I don't know what's going on between you two—"

"Nothing." Even as Summer said the word, she'd felt like a liar. There was something between them. Something she couldn't name yet. But it was definitely *not* nothing.

Bryan's wry smile told her he wasn't convinced. "I'm just saying, you could do worse."

Exactly what their grandmother had said.

If Summer were to marry, Grant would be a good choice. Her problem was that she didn't know if she could trust him to have her back when things got hard.

After all, when his relationship with Bryan had been strained, he'd joined the Army.

Would he leave Summer if they ran into a rough patch? Or would he stay and fight for her?

She, Grant, and Bryan had gotten back to Bryan's place around one thirty in the morning, and she'd collapsed into bed.

Now, lying on that too-short twin, staring at the ceiling, she recalled their conversation in the restaurant the day before.

He'd told her he loved her. That he'd worked at GBPS to be near her.

But he'd also said he worked there to keep her safe.

To watch her back.

Her mother hadn't watched her back.

Her older sister hadn't.

Even the hired bodyguards in Mexico hadn't.

But Grant had stayed with Summer for years to make sure she was safe.

Maybe...maybe Grant could be counted on. But there was still something she needed to understand.

It was too early, but she felt wide awake. She threw on a

sweatshirt, headed for the stairs, and made her way to the first floor, where Grant was sleeping on the couch.

That was another thing. There was a perfectly comfortable bedroom upstairs. He'd chosen to sleep on the couch, and it wasn't because that lumpy sofa was more comfortable than a bed.

He was willing to stand—or in this case, sleep—between her and the evil man who was after her.

It embarrassed her what a big deal that was. She'd spent most of her life being the person who stood between people she cared about—or clients—and danger. She was a protector, not someone who needed to be protected. But it wasn't about that. It wasn't about being weak, something she'd sworn she'd never be. It was about knowing that another person loved her enough to risk everything for her. That had been the problem with Mom—she'd loved her daughters, but not enough to protect them from their dad. She'd let them be vulnerable to his drunken rages because she didn't have the strength to fight him, to leave him.

Mom had been an amazing person, and in a lot of ways Summer wished she were more like her. She wished she possessed her mother's kindness and compassion, her ability to forgive, even her penchant for making people feel comfortable.

But Mom had been weak. Not just physically, but emotionally. She hadn't had the strength to walk away from Dad.

Nobody had ever called Summer weak.

Summer was physically and emotionally stronger, sure. But on the other hand, she had never proved she had the capacity to love that Mom had. What if she could love like Mom but also be strong? What if she could love like Mom and be married to a man who loved her back in the same way?

Grant could be that kind of man.

The living room was dark, a little light slipping in between the blinds. Summer rounded the sofa, crouched beside him, and tapped him on the shoulder.

His eyes popped open. He sat up. "What happened? What's wrong?"

"Nothing. I'm sorry." What was she thinking, waking him up after such a long night? "I shouldn't have... This was stupid." Summer started to stand.

His fingers slid gently around her wrist. "You might as well tell me. I won't go back to sleep until you do."

Summer sat on the coffee table across from him. "I'm sorry I woke you. I wanted to ask you a question."

Grant stretched his arms over his head, which lifted his loose T-shirt above his flat abs. As soon as she noticed, she looked up at his face again, but that wasn't better. His hair was sleep-tossed. His cheeks were unshaven and stubbly.

Sexy.

A wave of desire skimmed over her.

He tossed his blankets aside. "I'm listening." His voice was low and sleep-roughened, which didn't help at all.

She cleared her throat, hoping she could sound normal. "Yesterday, you said something about how you worked for the company to be with me. And then, you said you hadn't been watching my back for years just to let me run off and get myself killed."

"Okay?"

"Did you really work at GBPS to keep me safe?"

He stared at her. Or glared, maybe. "Of all the things I said, that's what needs clarification?" He sat back and ran his hand over his head, smoothing down the messy hair.

She itched to run her fingers through it, to mess it up again.

"I worked there for both reasons—to be near you and to protect you." He seemed frustrated. "It's a mind-numbingly boring job ninety-nine percent of the time, but that other one percent can be dangerous. I couldn't stand the thought of some-thing happening to you. Whenever you worked on a job without me, I'd pray extra hard for your safety. When Jon left and you chose me to be your partner, it was...I was relieved."

Oh.

She felt overwhelmed. Utterly unworthy. And...cruel for what she was about to say. But she needed to understand. "Now you're going to quit, though." At his narrowed eyes, she hurried to say, "Not that you shouldn't. Not that you owe me anything, obviously." She paused to get her thoughts together, trying not to notice the way he held her eye contact, waiting for her to explain. "Why are you leaving now?"

"Do you really expect me to hang around you for the rest of my life when you want nothing to do with me? I'll keep praying for your safety. But I have to trust you into God's hands. I mean... I can't..." He shifted like he was ready to be done with this conversation. "What are you asking me?"

"You're not leaving because you don't care."

"Don't care?" He huffed a breath. The more he talked, the angrier he grew.

She was feeling something very different.

"I've been in love with you for seven years. I hoped you'd feel the same way someday. Or at least feel *something*. I'm leaving because it hurts too much to be with you. And it's got to be weird for you. Don't you want me to leave? When I first told you, you were surprised. But now that you've had time to think it over, with all the awkwardness between us, I figured you'd be ready for my resignation. Right?"

No, not *right*. Not at all.

She wasn't sure how to say what she wanted to say. She'd never had feelings, real feelings, for any man. The thought of being honest now, being vulnerable, terrified her. But this was

Grant. Grant, who'd bravely confessed his feelings for her not once but multiple times.

Who'd worked a job he considered mind-numbingly boring for years to keep her safe.

She needed to be brave. Was she emotionally strong, like she wanted to believe? Or had she been eschewing men for her entire life because she was a coward?

Courage, Summer. "I'm just saying maybe it's possible I don't want you to quit."

She thought she might see hope in his eyes, but they hardened. His lips pressed into a tight line.

She hurried to continue. "If you want to, if you want to find another job, then do it. I want you to be happy. But I don't...I don't want you to not be in my life."

"I can't do the friends thing." He scooted down the sofa and started to stand. "I know that's what you want—"

"It's not." She grabbed his hand and tugged him back. Only when he'd sat in front of her again, his face awash in confusion, did she continue. "That's not what I want. I mean, I don't think that's what I want. The truth is"—she took a breath and prayed for help—"I have feelings for you too. I'm not very good at this, obviously. And I'm not even sure what I feel, except I feel something, and that something—"

He pressed his lips against hers, mercifully silencing her flow of words.

His fingers weaved into her hair, sending tingles across her scalp, down her body to her very core.

Everything faded away except the warmth of his body pressed against hers, the feel of his lips, the scent of his skin—like forest and sea breeze and musk.

All she wanted was to be closer to him. Her desire burned, hotter than a flicker. Hotter than fireplace flames. This was bonfire, house-fire, forest-fire desire.

Abruptly, he ended their kiss, then held her against his chest, his arms wrapped around her back. Her ear pressed into his thin T-shirt, his racing heart. She fought to catch her breath. Grant's kiss two nights before had been sweet and tender, filled with promise. It'd raised desire in her she hadn't known she possessed, but it had been nothing like this.

This...this was dangerous.

After a few moments, Grant's breathing returned to normal. He gripped her shoulders and held her away from himself, studying her face. "Do I need to apologize?"

"Technically, I'm the boss. Maybe I should apologize."

"Do I look like I'm complaining?" His lips stretched, his teeth shining in the dim light.

That smile... She'd seen Grant smile a thousand times. But this one...this one was just for her. It was open, honest, and pure. It had her itching to press her lips to his once again, to absorb some of that joy.

Somehow, she'd put that smile on his face.

The thought sobered her. If he truly loved her, then she had a unique ability to make him happy.

And a unique ability to hurt him.

Which was the last thing she wanted to do.

CHAPTER TWENTY-SIX

G rant and Summer sat at the kitchen table, drank coffee, and ate breakfast. All he could think was, *I could do this every day for the rest of my life.*

They sat there for an hour, two hours, and talked. He told her about the companies that had tried to recruit him, the jobs he'd never allowed himself to get excited about.

And he admitted he was afraid to leave GBPS, afraid she wouldn't be safe.

Summer squeezed his hand and leaned in. "I love that you want to protect me. But if you stay just for me, then I'll feel like I have to resign. And I don't want to do that."

"You wouldn't quit your job for me." He hadn't meant to allow the disbelief into his words, but it was there, floating between them.

"I think I would."

That was the last thing he wanted.

Well, maybe not the *last* thing. He'd love it if she took a nice, safe job. A boring office job or a checker at a grocery store.

He couldn't picture her in either of those roles.

"When this is all over," she said, "I want you to find something you love. Let's trust the team and...and God with my protection, okay?"

"I'll try." Though he couldn't imagine going off to work for some government contractor every day while she strapped on a handgun and put herself in danger.

"Have you ever wanted to do anything besides protection work?"

By the smile she tried to hide, the way her eyes flicked away, he guessed there was.

"Tell me."

"I've always thought it would be fun to own a high-end boutique."

"Seriously?" He'd never have guessed.

"I like clothes. Always have. That was the best thing about modeling, getting to enjoy the fashions."

Before Grant could ask a follow-up question, Bryan stepped into the kitchen, hair wet from the shower, wearing sweatpants and a sweatshirt. When he saw them, he stopped short, leaning on his cane. His eyebrows hiked to his hairline. "Good morning."

"Hey." Summer's voice was casual, almost...breezy.

He'd never heard that tone. He loved it.

Bryan's expression showed surprise, maybe pleasure. And no jealousy. Grant had obviously misread what he'd seen the day before.

"Thought you had classes this morning," Grant said.

"My TA can handle them." Bryan poured himself a cup of coffee. "Considering we did nothing but keep our eyes open for eight hours last night, I'm exhausted."

Summer pushed back in her chair. "I'm going to take a shower." And then she did something Grant would never have expected.

She leaned down and kissed his cheek.

Bryan and Grant both watched her walk out. When her footsteps faded, Bryan said, "Feel free to thank me with gifts."

"What do you mean?"

Bryan leaned his cane against the wall and limped to the coffee pot. He took his time pouring himself a cup. "Your feelings for her might as well have been tattooed on your face."

Grant didn't respond.

Bryan took a sip. Irritatingly quiet.

"Obviously, I'm asking about the other part," Grant finally said. "Why do I owe you a thank-you?"

"Gifts," he repeated. "I said thank-you *gifts* because I spent the better part of an hour yesterday telling her what a great guy you are."

Oh.

"Which you are, except you thought I was trying to steal her from you. That makes you kind of a jerk." Bryan stuck a bagel in the toaster and grabbed cream cheese from the fridge.

Grant didn't disagree. "Jealousy makes you do stupid things."

"True. Go ahead then." Bryan pulled a plate from the cabinet. When no reply came, he set the plate on the counter and crossed his arms. "Well?"

"I'm sorry I was a jerk. And thank you."

Bryan squeezed his earlobe and jiggled it. "Sorry. Come again?" Based on his grin, he'd enjoyed that.

"Stop gloating. You need someone to take your place tonight?" Not that Grant had any idea who he'd hire. "Jon'll be back tomorrow, but I can probably—"

"Don't be an idiot."

"Staying hidden, being on alert—it's harder than it looks."

Bryan's bagel popped, and he took his time smearing on the cream cheese.

Grant shoved the chair opposite out with his foot. "I bet you're sorry you insisted on helping us now."

"I like seeing what you do." Bryan set his plate and coffee on the table and sat.

"You enjoy your job?" Grant asked.

"I'm good at it. I had all these ideas of what I wanted to be when I grew up. Just dreams, really."

"It's my fault you couldn't—"

"Not your fault, bro."

Grant stood and grabbed a bottle of water from the fridge, mostly to hide his rush of frustration. They both knew Grant was the reason Bryan had fallen. Hadn't he reminded him a thousand times during their youth? But, as he usually did with his brother, he tamped down his reaction. Bryan deserved his lifelong devotion and anything else he ever asked for. He certainly didn't deserve Grant's annoyance.

Bryan bit his bagel and swallowed. "I think it's time for you and me to have a real talk about this. As adults, not stupid kids."

Grant leaned against the wall, twisting the top off his water. Then he took a sip and another. He was thirsty. More than that, he was unsure where this was going. He tossed the cap into the recycle bin. "I'm not sure what there is to say."

"That's because you're not the one who has to say it." Bryan knocked on the table in front of Grant's chair.

He seemed...was he nervous?

Though Grant preferred his spot near the door—easy escape—he took his seat again.

"You've apologized to me for that day more times than I can remember," Bryan said. "Not just apologized, but gone out of your way to try to make it up to me. Like with Summer, for instance. At camp, when Sam hinted that he might hit on her, you shut him down. By the way, he wasn't serious, just trying to figure out what was going on between you two. But when I flirted with her at dinner the other night, and then when you walked in on us yesterday, you said nothing. Not because you didn't care but because you think you owe me something."

"I *do* owe you something." He gestured to the cane. "I'm not sure if that fall scrambled your brains—"

"It wouldn't have happened if you hadn't talked me into going down to the dock that day and climbed up the cliff yourself. No question about that. It wouldn't have occurred to me to do it." His eyebrows hiked. "It wouldn't have occurred to me *yet*. I've since learned that every Wright brother eventually climbed that cliff. I'm the only one who fell."

Grant hadn't known that.

Bryan must've read his surprise. "You think that daredevil streak is unique to you?" He chuckled, the sound too light-hearted for the serious moment. "Even after my accident, Derrick tried it when he was about twelve. He's such a dope, though. Mom caught him and lost her ever-loving mind."

Grant couldn't help but laugh. "Slow learner, that one. All those years watching us, and he never figured out how to get away with anything."

Bryan smiled, but the expression didn't hold. "You told me to stay on the dock and watch. It's not your fault that I didn't. And then, when you saw me on the cliff, you told me in no uncertain terms not to try to climb down. You said to stay where I was. I had good footholds and handholds. I could have stayed there a long time. If I had, Dad would have gotten me down safely. But I wanted to prove I could do it on my own. That's why I fell."

"Yeah, but—"

"And then," Bryan said, talking over him, "I spent the next twenty-plus years blaming you. I made my feelings about you so obvious that you left the family, joined the Army, and hardly ever came home again." Bryan shifted in his chair to face Grant full-on. "I need you to understand something, Grant. My fall was not your fault. I'm the one who decided to climb that cliff. I'm the one who decided to ignore your advice and try to get down on my own."

Grant's heart was pounding as if he were climbing that cliff right now. "But you would never have been in that position if not for me."

"Right. And I was only seven."

Grant gestured toward him. "Exactly. You made my point."

"And you were nine."

"Older. I should have been smarter. I was supposed to be watching out for you."

"You were a kid. A little kid, just like me. You didn't think about what could happen. Just like me, you didn't look forward and see all the possible consequences of your actions. You weren't trying to hurt me. You were trying to impress me."

True. Which made him a first-class jerk.

"I spent all those years making you feel like you weren't welcome in our family." Bryan's tone was serious. "Do you have any idea how many times Mom and Dad told me to knock it off? That last fight you and I had..."

Grant would never forget it. He'd been thinking about joining the Army, not because he wanted to but because that had been Bryan's dream. He was trying to honor his brother. He wasn't ready for college. He was sick of school, sick of sitting in classrooms, sick of being compared to brilliant Daniel, studious Michael, quick-witted Sam—and his younger brothers too. The rest of them were off-the-charts smart. Grant had thought he was stupid. Since then, he'd learned he had smarts his brothers didn't possess. Maybe it hadn't translated to good grades, but it did translate in other areas of his life. He could strategize, plan, anticipate others' movements. He'd become a Green Beret, something most soldiers could never do. And he'd been good at it. And when he finally had gone back to college, he'd graduated from his night classes with high honors.

The Army had been a good route for him. It'd been a place where he could excel, by himself, without being compared to his book-smart brothers.

He'd told his parents his plan to enlist. They'd been supportive, if disappointed he wasn't planning to go to college.

Bryan had overheard. Grant would never forget the look of utter betrayal on his brother's face. "You stole my future, and now you're stealing my dream. What kind of a brother are you?"

The very worst kind. He'd known that for years.

"Obviously, you remember," Bryan said.

Grant dipped his chin.

"I was a world-class jerk. I mean, seriously. Can you see me as a soldier? Sure, I can shoot. I can defend myself. But my idea of roughing it is having to read paperbacks over hardbacks. If I'm forced to read an e-book..." He mock-shuddered.

"Not a lot of time for reading on missions."

"Exactly. Remember when we went to that parade and saw those soldiers? I thought they were so cool. I wanted to carry one of those big guns." He laughed as if the idea were hilarious, though the night before he had carried one of those big guns— and he'd seemed rather comfortable with it. Though Grant hadn't seen him shoot, he'd certainly handled the rifle well.

"I went to college," Bryan said, "went on to get a master's degree and a doctorate. That was where I belonged. No seven-year-old boy thinks he wants to be a teacher. I'm living the future I was meant to live. If anything, this"—he tapped the leg that had never healed properly—"shifted my focus to some-thing I could do and do well. I know it's going to take you some time to believe this, but in a weird way, that accident was a gift."

Grant couldn't help the short bark of laughter, though there was no amusement in it. He could have gotten Bryan killed, and Bryan called it a *gift*?

Bryan stood, limped to his cane, and turned to face Grant. "I hate to break it to you, bro, but you don't have the power to destroy God's plan for my life. He was in it all along. And if I was miserable for years, that wasn't your fault either. I was miserable because I refused to forgive you for something you didn't do on purpose and would never, ever have wanted for me. I let myself be steeped in anger and resentment and blame, and they ate at me like cancer."

"I'm sorry. I wish—"

"I'm not finished." He banged his cane on the floor, shutting Grant up. Bryan took a deep breath and blew it out. "Last year, I was on the highway. About a hundred feet ahead of me, a deer ran into the road, right in front of a little car. A Mustang. The driver swerved into the next lane and got hit by a pickup truck. The pickup spun out. The Mustang skidded across the highway, hit the opposite shoulder, and flipped."

Grant winced at the image. "Was everybody okay?"

"It was two young men, early twenties. Brothers. The passenger was killed instantly. They'd had barbells in the back, and one of them hit him in the head. The driver..." Bryan swallowed, his Adam's apple bobbing. "He had broken bones, I don't know what other injuries, but all he cared about was making sure his brother was all right. He kept screaming his name, telling me to check on him." Bryan looked away, blinked. Swallowed again. "I told the guy, 'It wasn't your fault. It was just an accident. It's going to be okay.'" Bryan's voice cracked. "All the while, looking at that driver, the terror in his eyes, covered in blood. All I could see...was you."

As Grant imagined the scene, his own eyes prickled. Because all he could see was his brother, lying at the bottom of a cliff, body crumpled.

He'd been sure Bryan was dead. As Bryan was airlifted to the hospital, Grant had been certain he was going to die. He hadn't, but in a lot of ways, both of their lives had ended that day. The lives they would have led. The men they would have become.

Bryan sat in the chair again, angling to face him. "I need to say this to you now, something I should have said a long, long time ago. It wasn't your fault." He swallowed hard. "It was just an accident. And I'm okay. I'm better than okay. I'm happy. The only thing, the *only* thing, I need right now is your forgiveness."

"Mine?" Grant's voice was too high. He cleared it. "You didn't do anything—"

"I blamed you for that accident for years. I'm sorry about that. I'm sorry I made you feel unwelcome in our family. I'm sorry that my selfishness kept you away from us for so long. From Daniel..." He looked up and shook his head. Trying to make the tears go back.

Grant swiped his away.

He would give anything to have time with his oldest brother again. The last time Daniel and the family had come home, Grant had only stopped by the farm for a couple of minutes to see them. He'd been full of excuses, but mostly, he'd just been avoiding Bryan.

He could never get that time back with Daniel. But maybe, with the rest of them...

"I've already apologized to Mom and Dad and the guys," Bryan said. "I've been trying to figure out a way to...to say this. Which is...I should've just said it. I should've said it a while ago. I'm sorry for that, too, that it took me so long. I just...I'm asking you to forgive me."

Rather than try to find words that wouldn't come, Grant stood, pulled his brother up, and hugged him.

He'd hoped for, longed for, Bryan's forgiveness. This...this he'd never imagined.

CHAPTER TWENTY-SEVEN

By the time they arrived at the meeting spot about a mile from the Bannister property that afternoon, the overcast skies had blown off, leaving chillier temperatures to go along with the blue skies and puffy cotton-ball clouds. The dirt road Grant had found, surrounded by budding trees and thick bushes, was only wide enough for one car. Despite the cold weather, spring was nudging winter aside. The area smelled of bracken and new growth with a hint of the sea carried on the breeze.

In a different circumstance, Grant would appreciate the beauty.

According to Jones, there had been no movement at the house all day long except for the lone guard, who patrolled regularly.

As far as Jones could tell, the guy was unaware that they were there, seemed mostly bored, and had made little attempt to protect himself. "I could have taken him out without breaking a sweat," Jones told Grant.

Grant, Bryan, and Summer gathered their weapons and equipment from the back of the Land Rover.

Grant stuck the comm unit in his ear, and Bryan and Summer did the same. He walked away, said, "Check."

"Check."

"Check."

"Just like yesterday," Grant said, "stay where I put you and relate what you see quietly. Keep talking to a minimum. Be safe and don't engage with anybody unless you have no choice." Since Summer knew all this, he was talking mostly to Bryan. "We're just here to observe."

"I'm not going to go all Dirty Harry on you," Bryan said.

Grant was careful not to smile at the reference, though the Dirty Harry movies had been among their favorites when they were kids. "Remember the drill. We all stay in our positions. We see something, we tell each other. As soon as we see anything being off-loaded, Bryan calls 911." Grant swung his focus from his brother to Summer.

Her eyebrows rose. "I know what I'm doing, Grant."

"Not exactly rocket science," Bryan said.

Grant resisted the urge to scowl. This was dangerous. Very dangerous. Their enemies would be well-armed and well-equipped. But he'd told them that more than once. "On channel six. Backup channel four. Anyone gets into a pickle and can't say it, hit your comm unit four times. Dat-dat-dat-dat. E-mer-gen-cy."

Bryan grinned.

"What."

To his credit, Bryan attempted to stifle the expression. "Sorry. It's just funny seeing you all serious and soldiery."

It was bad enough taking two of the people he loved the most in the world into danger, but one of them had just used the word *soldiery*.

"Don't worry," Bryan said. "I can walk and chew gum at the same time."

"Always throwing that Ivy League education in my face," Grant said. "One of us is compromised, the other two switch to channel four. You see anything illegal, say it, and Bryan calls 911."

Summer slid her fingers over Grant's wrist. "We're ready."

He was going to review everything anyway, for Bryan's sake. "Tap three times on the comm unit if you see something illegal and can't say it out loud. Dat-dat-dat, nine-one-one. You hear that, Bryan, you announce that you heard and then make the call. We don't hear you announce it, we'll assume you can't talk, and one of us will make the call. Got it?"

Bryan nodded.

"Got it," Summer said.

They trekked through the woods until they reached Ian, who was crouched about thirty feet off the road, where he had eyes on the driveway. Ian heard them coming and hopped up as they approached. "All's quiet."

"Good." Grant's voice sounded normal, but it made him ill to think of leaving his brother here, where he could fall into danger. It had been just as hard the day before, but he'd been angry then. The anger had kept his fear at bay.

Not so today.

Ian headed out, and Bryan dropped his cane, laid down on the all-weather mat where Ian had been, and settled his rifle where he could lift and aim it fast.

"You good?" Grant asked.

"Snug as a bug in a rug."

Grant wanted to tell him to be careful. To watch his back. To not take any risks. He kept all those useless words to himself and started out again.

They'd walked about fifty yards when, behind him, Summer spoke in a low voice. "I know where I'm going."

It was going to be hard enough to leave her on that rocky

hillside alone. He wasn't about to abandon her sooner than he had to.

Even though he'd walked this route a couple of times, and others on his team had as well, it still couldn't be called a path. He held aside branches, stepped over fallen limbs, and skirted thick brambles that reached out to snag jackets and jeans.

Summer moved behind him, louder than he was but relatively quiet, until they were close enough to see where Greta was lying on the ridge overlooking the water and the back of the property. He turned suddenly, and Summer stopped abruptly to avoid bumping into him.

He pulled her into his arms, inhaling her scent, feeling her healthy and whole. "I hate that you're here."

"Gosh, you know how to make a girl feel special." Her voice was tinged with amusement.

It was so unlike Summer to be lighthearted, to joke, and a little part of him lightened at her tone. But most of him was terrified.

"I don't want you to do this."

"I did it yesterday. It was fine." Her words were muffled against his jacket.

"For me, it was torture. But this is worse." Like with his brother, he'd been angry with her yesterday. Suspicious of her and Bryan. Hurt because she'd shut him down. Today, those ugly feelings had been ripped away like a scab, leaving his fears exposed and raw. "If anything happens to you—"

"It won't."

Grant had expected Summer to sound confident, maybe even irritated. But he caught a twinge of concern in her voice.

And why not? She'd been kidnapped by Ramón and his men once already. The previous week they'd almost taken her again.

This was personal for Summer.

Speaking of... "Did you ever get in touch with Misty?" She'd called her sisters on the ride down, something she did often.

"She finally answered. Too busy to talk, as always."

"You've made sure she's safe," Grant said. "Promise me you'll keep yourself safe as well. If anybody comes close, tap the comm. If they see you, just call for help. Don't be brave. Or stupid." He held her eye contact. "Promise me."

"I know the procedures."

"I'm not talking about procedures right now. I'm talking about you." He pressed his lips to hers, and all the emotions he'd been trying to tamp down for hours rose to the surface. Joy that she had feelings for him, desire like he'd never known. Overwhelming terror that he was leaving her exposed.

He needed her, more of her.

He walked her backward until she bumped into a tree. Held her closer and deepened the kiss.

Kissed her like he'd never kissed her before. Maybe like he never would again.

The thought had him coming up for air.

Her eyes were wide. "Whoa. That was..." Her words trailed.

It was a moment before he caught his breath enough to speak. "Yeah." He studied her face—eyes sparkling. "Maybe I shouldn't have..." He wasn't going to apologize. It would be a lie if he did. "I'm afraid to leave you."

Because bad things always happened when he left.

When Grant left, Bryan had fallen from a cliff.

In Mexico, Grant had been directed to stay with the rescued models in the van, but one of his men was injured. When he'd gotten the women settled, he went to his friend to get him to safety. But while he'd been gone, Tiffany, the model who'd been beaten, had panicked.

She'd opened the back door.

Jumped from the safety of the vehicle.

He'd never forget the shock he'd felt at the sight of that young, beautiful woman, running across the compound. He'd let his buddy fall to the ground.

Shouted at Summer, who was about to jump out and follow her friend.

"Get back inside. Shut the doors." And he'd taken off running.

The gunshots had probably been meant for him. Or maybe for Jon, who was also running to intercept the panicked model.

But they'd hit her. Killed her instantly.

Bad things always happened when Grant left.

He lowered his forehead to Summer's. "I don't know if I can do this."

"We have to do this."

She was right. Of course she was right. "If anyone finds you—"

"You'll come, right?" she said. "If I need you, you'll be here."

Again, he heard fear in her voice.

He was afraid to leave her.

She was afraid for him to leave.

He took her face in his hands. "I promise you, nothing is more important to me than your life. Nothing."

"Okay, then." She breathed him in. "Let's do it."

Reluctantly, Grant stepped back and walked Summer to the edge of the woods.

Greta turned, saw them, and then crawled up the hill. When she was within the cover of trees, she stood. "Boring shift. I hope you guys get more action than we did."

Grant definitely didn't hope that, but he didn't say so. Tomorrow, Jon would be back. Jon would take this position, and Summer would be in Bryan's, where she'd be much safer.

They just had to get through one more day.

After Greta gathered her things and left, Grant pulled Summer close. "Take very good care of yourself."

"You too."

He kissed her forehead and forced himself to walk away.

Darkness descended over him as if the sun had decided to set a few hours early. *Please, Father. We have to do this, but I hate it. I leave them in Your hands.*

He repeated the prayer all the way to the nest where he'd keep an eye on the dock, but the darkness didn't lift.

Because two of the people he loved most in the world were putting their lives on the line. If anything happened to either one of them, Grant didn't think he'd survive.

CHAPTER TWENTY-EIGHT

Summer swung her gaze from the water to the dock to the woods beside the Bannister property where she knew Grant was hiding. Everything looked different through night-vision binoculars, but nothing had changed in the five hours she'd been there.

Three more, and they'd be done for the night.

She'd eaten a protein bar around eight. That had been her big activity for the shift. She yawned, and through the comm, one of her partners did the same. And then the other. And then a quiet chuckle.

Definitely Bryan.

When Grant had left her, he'd been far too keyed up to laugh about anything, and she doubted that had changed in the hours since. The last time she'd caught his expression before he walked away, he looked as if he was in physical pain. As if leaving her was killing him.

The memory of that, of their kiss, and of everything he said to her had her heart fluttering.

Nothing said *tough-as-nails bodyguard* like a fluttery heart. But she couldn't help it. And anyway, Grant was tough as nails.

The last time she'd seen him, he'd worn all black. Even had black smeared on his face. He'd looked dangerous.

And he'd been in love with her for seven years.

Being in love didn't make Grant less tough, even if it did make him more vulnerable.

Maybe she didn't have the depth of feelings he had yet, but she could. Now that she'd admitted—to him and to herself— her attraction, her feelings were growing. His obvious concern for her helped, and that amazing kiss certainly hadn't hurt.

Another hour passed, an hour of Summer's thoughts and prayers flitting between Grant and her sisters. And catching Ramón and his thugs.

Maybe they suspected that Grant and Summer had located this house. Maybe Ramón had made other arrangements. Maybe the guard they had patrolling the grounds was only there to throw them off.

The problem was, she and Grant had no other leads. If this wasn't the place, or if Ramón had found a different dock to unload his goods, then Summer would never get her life back.

She'd never be safe again.

"Car approaching."

Bryan's words had her heart pumping.

A moment later, he said, "Utility van. I see two men."

"Got it," Summer said. "Grant?"

He tapped his comm, which told her the guard who'd been patrolling was close.

"Turned in the driveway." Bryan had been joking and laughing earlier, but his voice was all business now.

Across the water, Summer heard the engine cut off.

"Grant, you have eyes on it?" she asked.

One tap.

"How many?"

A moment passed, and then he tapped his comm four times.

"Four men?" she confirmed. Because he could have been signaling emergency.

One tap. Yes.

They walked into her view, across the yard, and down the steps that led to the water. Three huddled on the rocky beach against the cliff wall, probably trying to avoid the cold breeze. The fourth walked to the end of the dock and stared out at the Atlantic.

She swung her binoculars that direction. Saw nothing for seconds that turned into minutes.

And then, lights. Coming their way. "Boat coming in."

"It's happening." To his credit, Bryan didn't sound excited. His voice was calm and steady, so like his brother's.

One tap from Grant. Either the guard was nearby or Grant was being extra careful.

She hoped, prayed, for the second.

As the craft made its way into the mouth of the cove, she got a better look. Forty-five or fifty feet from stem to stern. At its highest, it looked almost as tall as it was long. Even in the dark, it was obvious this was no fishing boat but a fancy yacht.

Either owning a ranch in Central Mexico was extremely lucrative or Ramón was making money on the side. The question was, from what?

As the boat approached the dock, the guys who'd been waiting on the shore made their way to the end. Voices carried over the water, though she couldn't make out the words. She watched as ropes were tossed and tied to the pier.

Through her night-vision binoculars, she searched the faces of the men on the boat. Three, four, five so far, not including those who'd come in the van.

No Ramón, not yet. But he could be in the cockpit or belowdecks.

Or he could be back in Boston, sitting at his sister's bedside.

According to Golinski, he was still being followed, but she guessed he knew that. If he wanted to lose a tail, how hard could it be?

Please, God. We need to catch him.

The back of the boat was dark, but bright lights shone onto the dock in the front. Grant must have an excellent view from where he hid.

He'd be taking photographs.

So far, this was all going according to plan.

A person walked up from belowdecks. Smaller than the rest, he or she wore a thick parka, but this one had long blond hair. A woman? Ramón's girlfriend or wife?

Just like Summer guessed, it was people Ramón was smuggling. Another figure climbed up and grabbed her arm, then hauled her toward the front of the boat.

Another man lifted part of the boat's floor. A trap door.

The perfect place to hide contraband. "Grant, there's a—"

"Well, look what we found."

Summer looked up.

Two men stood over her. Both aiming weapons. Both smiling.

CHAPTER TWENTY-NINE

G rant was crouched in the woods where he had a good view of the dock. Nothing happened for hours and hours. And then two things happened at once.

Moments before, a woman had come around the side of the yacht. She wore a puffy, shapeless coat. She could've been a girl-friend or wife or financier of the operation. But he caught sight of her face, and his heart lurched.

In that same instant, Summer's words were cut-off by a gasp.

"Summer!" Bryan's voice was low but vehement.

Grant wanted to shout into the phone. *Say something!*

But the guard was nearby. Grant couldn't give away his position. If he did, he'd blow the whole operation.

He lifted his binoculars to the cliff at the end of the cove, where he'd been keeping an eye on her. She was there now.

And so were two more people.

They'd found her. They *had* her.

God, please...please—

"Switching channels," Bryan said.

Grant did the same. A moment later, Bryan's voice carried again. "You think she's okay?"

Two taps.

"That's a no?" Bryan asked.

One tap. Grant paused a couple of beats, then tapped three times. *Nine-one-one.* Waited a beat. Tapped four times. *E-mer-gen-cy.*

"Calling now." Bryan's voice carried through the comm as he spoke to the 911 operator, telling them everything they needed to know. And then he sounded furious. "What do you mean?" A beat. "No, this is happening now. That's already—" Another pause. "A woman's life is at stake."

Two women's, but Bryan didn't know that, and Grant couldn't risk speaking.

"Fine. Hurry!" Then, to Grant, Bryan said, "There was a shooting in town. A cop was killed."

Grant kept his howl of frustration inside. He had a good idea who was behind the shooting.

Ramón knew they were there. He knew their plan, and he'd figured out how to thwart it.

"They'll send someone out," Bryan said, "but not soon, and just one car. You're going to Summer's aid, right?"

He wanted to. With everything in him, he was desperate to run to Summer, to protect her. But...

But that woman on the boat.

Two taps.

"No?" Bryan said. "You're not? You can't?"

Grant didn't respond. The questions were too nebulous.

"Are you all right?" Worry infused Bryan's words.

One tap.

A pause. "Okay," Bryan said. "Obviously, you can't explain. I'll go after her."

Did Grant want Bryan to rush into danger to save Summer?

On a cane. In the dark. In the woods. With zero combat training?

Absolutely not.

But it was Summer, so...

Yes.

No.

How could he make that decision?

"I'm going," Bryan said. "I'll keep you informed." He waited a beat, then added, "Okay?"

Bryan didn't sound apprehensive. He was waiting for permission. Respecting Grant's authority.

Grant cursed his authority.

Please, let him be as good with a rifle as he claimed. Keep them both safe, Lord.

He tapped the comm unit once.

"On my way."

The comm went silent.

Grant squeezed his eyes closed, cursing himself. What had he done?

He'd promised Summer that if she needed him, he would be there. He'd *promised* her.

But if she knew what he knew, she'd understand.

He prayed that someday she would. Someday, maybe she'd forgive him for abandoning her.

Grant had to put Bryan and Summer out of his mind. He had to focus on the woman on the yacht. She was standing on the deck, peering toward the land. A man stood beside her, holding her in place with a hand on her upper arm. He had a gun in his other hand.

Through the night-vision binoculars, Grant had a good look at the woman's face. Which was obviously the point of them stationing her there.

It was Misty.

Summer's little sister.

The girl she'd spent more than half her life trying to protect.

Misty, who'd told Summer that evening that she was safe. Either she'd been taken after that or she'd been forced to lie when Summer called.

He studied the expression on the woman's face. He saw fear, no doubt. But also defiance.

Good. That was good. Maybe she'd be a fighter. Because they'd definitely need to fight their way out of this.

"Mister soldier man!" The voice carried over a speaker on the boat. It hadn't come from the thug holding Misty in place, and Grant scanned the other men in view.

They were busy off-loading goods, boxes, and bags.

He swung his binoculars back to the boat and saw the outline of a man in the cockpit, barely visible through the glass.

"As you have no doubt been informed, your companion is in our custody now." The voice was Ramón's, spoken with a Spanish accent as he had at the hospital, though his voice wasn't smooth and charming. It was mocking. "And we have her sister as well, as you can see."

Grant shifted the binoculars to Misty. She was peering into the darkness now, probably looking for him.

"Do not call the police," Ramón said. "If they show up, we will be forced to shoot more police officers tonight. And this pretty little blonde as well. That would be a terrible waste."

The police weren't planning on showing up anytime soon. But if they did, would they come prepared, bringing backup, or just get themselves shot?

Grant didn't need police. He needed...

He yanked his phone from his pocket and tapped out a quick text. He should have done this before. He prayed the three minutes it'd taken him to think of it wouldn't matter.

"You will show yourself now," Ramón said, "or the girl will die."

He hit send as the man at Misty's side aimed his firearm at her head.

"I will count down. Ten, nine, eight..."

Grant scrambled to his feet. He left his phone, rifle, and binoculars on the ground and pushed forward.

"Seven, six, five..."

He ran, hurtling roots and stumps and bushes.

"Four, three—"

"Don't shoot!" he shouted.

"Two..."

"Don't shoot," he screamed. "I'm here. I'm right here."

He burst out of the woods onto the back lawn.

Within seconds, he was tackled. Searched. Disarmed. His comm unit taken.

"Got him," the man who'd tackled him said in Spanish. "Got his gun. Got his backup gun." Grant translated in his head.

His face was pressed into the ground. A foot on his back.

"Sanchez, put the girl belowdecks," Ramón said, also in Spanish. "Gael, bring him up here."

The one called Gael hauled Grant to his feet and propelled him forward. He reached the staircase that would take him down to the dock. Looked for a way of escape. But the walls of the cove were steep and exposed. Unless he managed to kill or disable every thug who'd come to this party, any effort to climb out would fail.

Could Misty swim? Despite Summer's fear of boats, she could. He prayed Misty had learned as well. Because their only hope for escape would be found in those cold, dark waters.

Goons all around, their weapons trained on him, he descended the stairs, hit the long pier, and walked toward the yacht.

Away from Summer and Bryan and whatever they were dealing with.

Toward Misty and almost certain death.

CHAPTER THIRTY

The half-moon sent just enough light through the heavy cover of trees for Summer to see her next step. The men used no flashlights as they walked beside her, each with a firm grip on her arm, picking their way through the thick forest.

She was still alive. Ramón's men hadn't already put a bullet in her head. But why? What did he want with her?

More importantly, where was Grant?

She'd heard a loud voice—had to have been projected on a speaker—but the words had been lost in the wind. Something was going on back there. She prayed Grant and Bryan were all right.

Summer had resisted her captors, trying to keep them from dragging her away. She'd known she wouldn't be able to overpower them, but she'd hoped to slow her captors down, to give Grant an opportunity to get into place. They'd subdued her and dragged her to her feet, but it had taken a few minutes.

One eye was already swelling, and blood trickled from her nose into her mouth, which she couldn't wipe away thanks to the vice-like grip they had on her.

Her arm ached where one of the men had twisted it. She was thankful she wasn't more seriously injured.

She faked an injured ankle, limping. One more excuse to move slowly.

If Ramón were here, she figured he'd tell his men to carry her. Fortunately, he wasn't, and his men were lazy.

She'd counted on them moving toward the Bannister property, toward Grant. But they went in the opposite direction.

When they stepped out of the woods, there was no road or property ahead, just another little cove like those that wound all the way up the coast of Maine.

Come on, Grant. She'd given him plenty of time to get there. He'd find her, wouldn't he? He'd follow their tracks.

He'd promised to rescue her. He'd promised.

She was propelled forward toward the land's end. Would they shove her off? Kill her? Hope her body was washed out to sea? The fall would be painless, cold briny wind whipping through her hair. Would she land in the frigid water, have a chance to swim to safety?

Or would she hit rocks?

Would she feel the pain, or would she be killed instantly?

This was the end, and all she could think was...*Grant.*

Where was he?

Like her mother, like those Mexican guards, when Summer most needed someone to have her back...she was alone.

She looked down at the rocky cliff, waiting for a shove that didn't come.

Her captors were speaking to one another in Spanish. She didn't bother to try to translate as she stared out at the black sea, at nothingness. All alone.

Beside her, Ramón's man said, "Go down now."

So they didn't plan to push her. Her rush of relief faded as she looked over the cliff, this time searching for a manageable route. Moonlight glinted off something at the bottom. Something bright in the darkness.

No.

The cliff she could manage. Even the armed thugs she could manage.

But a boat? She was expected to climb onto a floating death-trap with two armed enemies?

Lord...

No longer picturing a fall off the cliff, now she imagined drowning, drowning in the frigid Atlantic, limbs too frozen to move. Eyes closing, drifting to sleep, then sinking, sinking—

A gunshot rang in the silent night.

The man to her right fell.

She angled away from the other and ducked to give Grant a good shot. But no second shot came.

Her captor was off-balance.

She reached for his gun and tried to wrench it away.

But he was strong, much stronger than she was. Pushing her toward the edge of the cliff.

He punched her in the side with his free hand.

She kneed him in the groin.

"Oomph." He doubled over.

She kneed him again, but he blocked her with his thigh, pushing her back. Back. Behind her, open air, a long fall. Certain death. She worked to keep her hand on the gun and propel herself toward him and away from the cliff.

He stumbled back. But he held fast, yanked the weapon from her hands.

Any second, any second Grant would burst out of the trees and help her.

Come on!

She couldn't do this by herself. All her training, all her

strength-building, but she'd always be at a disadvantage against a strong man.

Hurry, Grant. Hurry. Please!

But Grant wasn't coming.

And then, a loud *thunk*.

The guy collapsed.

Behind him, Bryan held his rifle like a club. Eyes wide with terror. "Sorry. I was afraid I'd hit you. We have to go." He grabbed her hand and pulled her toward the cliff.

"What? Where's—"

"They're coming."

Who was *they*?

He reached the edge of the cliff. "You first."

The sound of an engine carried over the breeze. Not a car but...a four-wheeler, she guessed. Getting closer.

"Down," he said. "It's our only option." He looked over the cliff. "We'll take the dinghy."

The dinghy?

Willingly float away in something called a *dinghy*?

"Go!"

With no choice, she lowered to her belly and scrambled over the cliff, then made her way down. It wasn't that high, maybe twenty feet. But it would hurt like the dickens if she fell.

Bryan had a bad leg. How could he...?

She looked up, afraid she'd find him still standing at the top. But he was hopping down mostly on his good foot, his rifle slung by its strap over his back. "Keep going."

For a college professor, he was surprisingly adept. She should be the one giving him orders.

She needed to get it together if she was going to keep them both alive.

She reached the bottom, staying close to help Bryan if he

needed it. He landed beside her. When he looked her way, she caught pain in his eyes.

"How did you—?"

"You do what you have to do. Come on." He took her hand, pulling her to the boat. It was an inflatable, but it had an engine. An engine could get them out of there.

But the sound of the engine above them cut-off suddenly.

Bryan had reached the small watercraft when she grabbed his hand to pull him back. "We have to take cover. Against the rocks!"

Bryan pressed himself against the cliff wall beside her seconds before a gunshot came from above.

Thanks to the rocks that jutted out, the shooters didn't have an angle. If she and Bryan could stay there, right there, maybe they could survive.

How many men were up there? Two, three? One could find another way down, come at them from the side. "Give me your gun."

Bryan handed it over, and Summer aimed up. She leaned out a few inches, hoping to get one of them in her sights.

Another gunshot. The bullet hit the rocks a few feet in front of her. She pressed herself against the rock wall.

This wasn't good.

Ramón's men knew exactly where they were. From where they stood, they couldn't shoot her or Bryan, probably. But she couldn't shoot them, either. And if she tried to move...

She jabbed a hand out, yanked it back. A bullet hit the rocks just a foot away.

"We're pinned down." Bryan sounded furious. "I got you out of the frying pan and dragged you right into—"

"If not for you, I'd be on that boat, floating off to...who knows where. Or dead."

"We're not dead yet." His words were tight.

"You're in pain."

"Least of my worries."

Silence settled between them. The surf hit the rocks just a few feet away, the spray from the larger swells occasionally reaching her. Her jeans were damp, her feet wet. The chilly wind sent violent shivers through her.

She listened for the sound of falling rocks, of someone clambering down. Listened for boats. For more engines. Even voices. But aside from the waves against the rocks, all was quiet.

"How did you do it?" she asked. "You must've moved fast. With your limp—"

"I'll pay for it tomorrow. Assuming we get a tomorrow."

She wanted to assure him they'd escape, but how? How could she make that promise? How could she keep them safe?

"You're still on comm? They took mine."

Her question elicited a tortured expression. "I think Grant surrendered."

"What? Why would he do that?"

"I have no idea."

"Try him."

Bryan pressed the button on his comm unit. "Grant, you there?" After a minute, he shook his head.

"No tap? No...nothing?"

"I'm sorry."

"But he was fine. When I was taken..." A horrifying thought occurred to her. "He must've been captured when he tried to rescue me."

This was her fault. She should have told him to hold his position no matter what happened. Instead, she'd sought his promise to rescue her.

He'd been captured trying to come to her aid.

"That's not what happened," Bryan said. "He told me to come after you."

What? He hadn't even *tried*? Betrayal covered her like chain mail. "Why?" She couldn't keep the hurt from her voice.

"I don't know. He couldn't say. Just...tapped."

Maybe he'd been too close to a guard. But the guard was always patrolling. Couldn't Grant have come after he'd moved off? Nobody could move as quietly as Grant. He could've rescued her if he'd tried.

"I'm sure it killed him to send me," Bryan said.

Yes, of course it had. She thought back to their final kiss. His tortured words. *I don't know if I can do this...nothing is more important to me than your life.*

And second to that would be Bryan's.

Yes, it must've killed Grant to send his brother.

"I think it says a lot about how much he trusts you that he did."

"And didn't I do a stellar job?" Bryan's words were infused with sarcasm. "I got us trapped."

"Better trapped than dead."

Voices drifted down from above occasionally, barely audible over the surf. The words were lost.

Summer continually surveyed the surroundings. Above, to the right, to the left. "You called the police?"

"Right after you were taken. But there was a shooting in town—a cop was killed. They told us they'd get here when they could, but—"

"You have your cell, though?" Why hadn't she thought of it before?

Bryan pulled it out and unlocked it.

She handed Bryan the gun. "Keep your eyes open." She took the phone and dialed Hughes.

He answered immediately. "What's going on?"

"I was ambushed. Bryan and I are taking cover at the water's edge in a cove just south of the property. There're men on the

ridge above us, at least two. We think Grant surrendered. Probably on the boat, but I don't know for sure. We need both
teams—"

"We're close. Grant texted a few minutes ago. But the traffic
getting through town—"

"Traffic?" She couldn't help the frustration. They were
being held up by traffic? On a freezing cold weeknight in a
beach town?

Beside her, Bryan said, "Caused by the shooting, probably."

Ramón. Of course.

Hughes said, "Tell us what you know."

With Bryan's help, she related everything that had
happened so far. When she was finished, Hughes said, "Sit
tight. We'll contact the police again. We'll get you out of there.
Keep yourselves alive."

CHAPTER THIRTY-ONE

Grant tried to ignore the distant sound of gunshots. *Keep them safe, Lord. Please.* He scanned the area as he descended the stairs at the back of the property and walked the long pier toward the yacht. No sign of Misty, which meant she had been taken belowdecks.

No sign of Summer either. Hopefully, she and Bryan were safe somewhere. It killed him that he didn't know.

He'd been keeping up a constant stream of prayers for their safety. In a million years, he'd never have envisioned leaving his brother and the woman he loved to fight their enemies alone.

He'd never envisioned Misty being sucked into this mess.

The man Summer had shot in the parking garage was helping off-load goods from the boat, one-handed. Grant recognized him by his height and weight—and the cast on his arm, courtesy of Summer's bullet. By the glare the guy aimed his way, he was holding a grudge.

Grant passed close enough that, if he'd had a mind to, he could've shoved him and his duffel bag, which Grant had no doubt was filled with drugs, into the frigid water.

But now wasn't the time to fight. He needed to get on that boat.

The goon manhandling him down the pier was the other one who'd attacked Summer. Short and stocky. Both his eyes black. Grant was pretty sure he'd broken the thug's nose, but he wore no bandage.

Grant would hit him harder next time.

"What's the matter?" Grant gave his stupid chin-curtain beard a long look. "Not enough testosterone to grow a proper beard?"

A meaty fist connected with Grant's skull so fast, he barely saw it coming. His head snapped to the side. He stumbled, contemplated stumbling right off the wooden dock. He could take his guy with him and probably defeat him in the water. He could escape.

But that wouldn't help him save Misty.

He knew what it was to lose a sibling. He'd do everything in his power to protect Summer from that pain, and from living with the belief that her sister had died because of her choices.

He'd seen his share of boats in his life. His family weren't exactly yacht people, but a boat was a boat. This one was fancy, probably fifty, fifty-five feet long. The deck gleamed in the lights strung all over it. From afar, it might've looked like they were hosting a casual get-together with friends. Except for the armed thugs all around. And the contraband being hauled to shore.

Grant jumped from the pier to the deck, hoping he'd come face-to-face with Ramón. At least the guy was here. If the authorities arrived and made arrests, Ramón could be stopped tonight.

Assuming they were ready for a shootout, because Ramón and his men wouldn't go down easily. But Hughes and the teams would be there to help.

No sign of the mastermind as Gael pushed Grant through

an opening so narrow that Grant had to angle his shoulders side-
ways in order to fit. They went down a short flight of stairs and
into a living area. As soon as they were alone, he'd disable Gael
and search for Misty.

But there were men down here too. Had another vehicle
arrived, or had all these guys been on the boat? This made...
eight, ten? More than were needed to unload. And all of them
carried weapons.

Ramón had come prepared for a fight.

One of them tossed a plastic-wrapped package about the
size of a box of crackers to the other, who dropped it into a card-
board box, then looked up just in time to catch another package.
Grant peered into the box and saw stacks of similar packages.

Drugs, just like he'd suspected. White powder—heroin or
cocaine or fentanyl.

The sight contrasted strangely with the gleaming wood and
leather furniture, empty cans, and a couple of plates on the
table. This was a pleasure boat for the rich and famous. Probably purchased with the income from the sale of its illegal
freight.

The goons barely paused in their work as Grant was
propelled across the room to a louvered door.

"Open it," Gael said.

Grant did and was shoved inside.

No Misty. He'd counted on being held with her.

"You try to come out," Gael said, "I shoot you. Got it?"

Grant turned in the space barely wider than the staircase
had been, set his feet, and crossed his arms. "So, you're saying, if
I open the door, you're going to shoot me? But if I don't open the
door, you won't shoot?"

The thug's eyes narrowed as if he couldn't figure out if
Grant was serious.

Not the sharpest hook in the tackle box.

The door slammed shut, and the room was thrust into darkness.

Beneath his feet, the boat swayed, thanks to the light tide and the men moving around. The area smelled of brine and old food.

He waited a few seconds, just in case Gael came back. Then, by the little light coming through the slats in the door, he turned his focus to the space.

The closet was so small it was a job to turn around. A couple of plastic storage containers were stacked against the back wall. He opened them and felt around inside. Clothes. He lifted the items to the light. Women's bathing suits, cover-ups, sandals. Men's trunks. Flip-flops.

He grabbed a bikini, a skimpy thing in bright pink. The straps might come in handy.

Digging deeper, he found plastic buckets and shovels for building sandcastles, imagining Maritza Hidalgo and her two kids on board. Were they as ignorant of Ramón's business as they seemed?

Even if Ramón's sister and brother-in-law were guilty, their children were innocent. Yet they or other equally innocent kids had been on this drug-smuggling vessel.

The thought infuriated him.

He dug deeper. Pulled out something large and coated in plastic...a bag. There wasn't much light to see it, but he recognized the design. A waterproof backpack.

That could come in handy.

But the real treasure was in the second bin.

Beneath neatly folded beach towels, he found wetsuits.

He remembered the conversation he'd overheard in the hospital, a suggestion that they go surfing. Maritza Hidalgo had humored her brother, though it was obvious it would be some time before she'd be healthy enough to surf. She'd complained about the cold water.

Ramón had reminded her of his wetsuits.

Breathing "thank You," Grant stripped to his skivvies and forced his oversize body into the biggest one he could find. It was tight, but he managed to zip it.

Not only would it keep him warmer, but it was black and sleek. It would hide him in the darkness. There was a smaller one, but there wouldn't be time for Misty to change. He'd have to get her out of the water fast.

He shoved the bikini and a couple of beach towels into the waterproof backpack and returned everything else to the boxes. He slipped the bag onto his back.

Why hadn't Ramón killed him yet? If he were in Ramón's position, he would have killed him straightaway. Grant would make sure the man regretted that error in judgment.

He needed to find Misty and get her out of here.

And make sure Summer and Bryan were safe.

He couldn't do anything stuck in that closet. He kept his eyes wide open and trained on the door, waiting, waiting.

And prayed God would make a way.

CHAPTER THIRTY-TWO

Grant watched the time tick by on his watch. Ten long minutes passed. Ten minutes of praying for help. Praying for Summer and Bryan and the rest of the team. He couldn't figure out where they were. Shouldn't they be there by now? Where were the gunshots? Where was the chaos he'd been sure would erupt any minute?

He didn't know. Just prayed for help. For guidance on what to do next.

The voices beyond the louvered doors had faded. Gael surely hadn't left him alone, and maybe another of Ramón's men was out there as well. Grant peered through the slats to gauge where they were. He could see nothing but bare carpet.

He waited another five torturous minutes, listening for anything that would tell him how many waited outside his door. Above deck and on the shore, men called to each other, some with orders, others quick to obey. But the room on the other side of the door was quiet.

Time to move.

Grant crouched low, kicked open the door, and dove across

the space toward Gael, who was reclining on the white leather sofa. The man's raised his gun, but not fast enough.

Grant barreled into him, disarming Gael before he had the chance to fire and jabbing a fist into his throat.

Gael's eyes went wide. Choking sounds issued from his mouth, but he couldn't get any volume. Couldn't call for help.

The whole thing took about five seconds.

Grant hit him in the head with the weapon, then wrapped his arm around Gael's neck and squeezed. Not enough to kill, just enough to turn his lights out.

When Gael went limp, Grant dragged him into the storage room, contemplating tying him up. Decided against it. Gael wasn't moving. It would be some time before he could sound the alarm, and they'd be gone by then.

One down. Countless to go.

He dug through Gael's pockets and found a phone and a switchblade. He took those, made sure Gael's gun was loaded, and headed through the living area and into a small galley.

Dishes were piled in the sink. A half-full bag of chips lay open on the counter.

But the room was empty.

Grant stopped every few feet to listen.

A short staircase took him down to a landing where a bathroom door stood open, two other doors were closed. He peered down the half-staircase to another closed door at the bottom. Probably the master suite.

Misty had to be in one of these rooms. But it was possible a guard was as well.

He waited. Ten seconds, twenty. Listening.

Which door?

Then the barest sound came from the room beside where he waited, almost a sigh. He prayed it was her.

Tried to slide the pocket door aside. It didn't open. He

searched for the reason and discovered a vertical lock near the top edge. He disengaged it.

Keeping his voice very low, he said, "Misty?"

He heard a gasp, then an equally quiet, "I'm here."

Grant slid the door away silently.

She stared at him with wide eyes. Wearing a pair of slacks, a blouse, a blazer, and ridiculous spiky heels, she seemed ready for court, not a swim in the Atlantic.

He'd forgotten how similar she looked to her sister. She was a little shorter—maybe five-ten. Her hair was paler, and her features smaller, almost pixie-like. But there was no pixie in the fierce look in her eyes.

"Leave the shoes and follow me."

To her credit, she didn't argue or ask questions, just did as he told her. "You have an extra gun?"

So like her sister. A fighter.

"Not yet."

By her quick smile, she liked that answer. He handed her the knife he'd taken off Gael. "Aim for the neck or chest."

Shouts, then footsteps pounded above.

Crap. They knew.

Grant and Misty were going to have to fight their way out.

He crept up the stairs. "Stick close."

"Call me Elmer's."

They crossed through the galley and living area and started up the stairs toward the deck. A figure moved into view at the top. Grant scrambled up, gut-punched him, and yanked him down. The thug came head-first, landing on the stairs, gasping but unable to get a breath. Grant grabbed his gun, shoved him against the wall of the stairwell, and punched him hard in the face. Then again, just to be sure.

Behind him, Misty was making herself as small as possible

in the narrow space. Grant shoved the guy past her. He fell, unconscious, half on the stairway, half on the floor.

Grant ensured the second gun was loaded, then held it out. "Trade ya."

Misty took it, handing him the knife. "Good form."

He folded the blade away and shoved it into the neck of his wetsuit. "Walk up backward. Anybody you don't know comes toward you, fire."

"Got it."

Shouts came from overhead. Grant was surprised more men hadn't arrived after the first. What were they doing? What could be more important than...?

The yacht's engines roared to life.

Misty uttered a word he heartily agreed with.

"We have to hurry." He bounded up the last few steps, sensing her behind him. "Can you swim?"

"If I say no, will you come up with a better solution? One of us isn't wearing a wetsuit."

He took that as a yes, wishing she had time to put one on. At the top of the steps, he poked his hand out.

The bang of a gun, and a bullet whizzed over him.

Now he knew where the guard was.

But how to stop him?

Misty fired, and Grant shoved her out of the way, prepared to finish where she'd left off.

But the man who'd come up behind them lay at the bottom on top of the one Grant had immobilized.

"Nice."

She didn't respond, her face white with fear.

"Go down. Grab his gun. Stay alert."

She did as she was told.

"Shove it in the bag." He spun the waterproof backpack so it hung from his front. No need to have a bright yellow beacon showing people where they were. "We might need it later."

While she did that, Grant considered his options. He needed a diversion, something to get the goons to look away from the stairwell. He gazed up, afraid to pop his head out. From this position, there weren't many targets. Just an all-weather padded sunbathing area, but firing at that wouldn't create the diversion he needed.

He turned, leaned back as far as he could, and glimpsed the glass that surrounded the cockpit.

That should do it.

To Misty, he said, "Be ready. We're gonna—"

From above, a man swung into view, aimed.

Grant fired. The man stumbled out of sight.

More gunshots flew just over his head.

Misty screamed, fired.

Grant wanted to turn that way, but another man came at him. He pulled the trigger, hitting a chest before the man fell out of view.

"Stick your gun in the bag," he said.

"Are you nuts?"

Now that he had a plan, they needed to move. He grabbed her weapon, shoved it inside, and zipped it shut. He held her eye contact. "We're going. Stay with me. Ready?"

At her nod, he turned and fired at the cockpit window.

It crashed, sending glass skittering across the deck.

He grabbed her hand and scrambled up the last couple of steps, Misty stumbling behind him. They bolted for the side. There was no time to pause.

He flung her over and followed her in, bullets whizzing over them.

They plunged into the frigid water.

CHAPTER THIRTY-THREE

The sound of gunshots carried over the water.

"Oh, God, please..." Pressed up against the rocky cliff, Summer breathed the prayer.

Bryan finished with, "Keep him safe. Keep us safe. Get us out of this."

But he'd barely finished the words when a figure appeared from behind a rock.

She swung her weapon that direction.

But the man fired, the bullet hitting above her head, raining stone fragments and dust onto them.

"Drop it," he said. "The next one won't be a warning."

She dropped the rifle.

He yelled, "Got 'em!" Then to Summer and Bryan, "Empty your pockets."

She'd already been disarmed. Bryan slipped his phone from his pocket and dropped it in the sand.

"To the boat."

The boat.

The thought of stepping out from the cover of their cliff was terrifying, but that was nothing compared to the fear that gripped her at the thought of that little floating deathtrap.

"Now!" The man moved closer. He was not quite as tall as she but thick and stocky with the look of someone who spent a lot of time at the gym. No way she could take him. She wasn't sure that she and Bryan together could overpower him, even if he didn't have a gun.

And he looked murderous.

At the top of the cliff lay two men, one likely dead and one injured. If those had been her friends, she'd feel murderous too.

Bryan limped across the uneven ground. Summer hooked her arm in his, supporting him, thankful for the contact, the warmth.

"Thanks." His word was clipped, filled with fear or anger or both.

She lowered her voice. "Help is on the way."

"I'm sorry I couldn't rescue you. I'm sorry for—"

"Push it into the water," their captor said. "And then climb in. Don't get any ideas. I'm not alone." He gestured to the top of the cliff.

She followed his gaze to two men above, both with rifles trained on them.

"I can do it," Bryan said.

"Together." She took one side, Bryan took the other, and they dragged the boat into the cold, cold water. It soaked her sneakers and seeped through her jeans to her knees.

Her teeth chattered as she held it steady while Bryan climbed over and settled on the opposite side.

A tiny inflatable boat in the ocean? Were they all insane?

"Now!" their captor shouted.

She stepped in. There was barely room for their feet on the floor of the thing, so she sat on the fat edge, gripping the ropes beside her thighs. She wouldn't think about the thin bit of material separating her from the ocean.

She wouldn't think about the way the boat swayed in the waves.

She wouldn't think about the added weight of the thug when he climbed aboard and started the engine, how easily he could shove them over.

They were near the shore. If she and Bryan went in, they could swim for it. Maybe they could make it before hypothermia set in. As long as the boat didn't go too far out.

She was tempted to fall backward. If she were swimming, at least she'd be in control. Until the thug shot her, anyway.

And where would that leave Bryan?

The boat motored toward the open ocean, and her hope of swimming shrunk as small as the men watching from the cliff.

Untethered. The foundation beneath her feet was no thicker than a lasagna noodle.

There'd been times she'd believed she lived on a solid foundation. When she was young, she'd thought her home was safe. Until her father's drunken rages had disabused her of that fantasy.

Later, she'd built a career as a model, socking away as much cash as she could manage as if money could insulate her. And then she'd been kidnapped.

One week prior, she'd believed her team—and her own toughness—could protect her. And yet, here she was.

All of it...no more substantial than the thin material beneath her feet.

Maybe that was the lesson of life, that there was no true security. That nobody was safe, ever. That the world was one dangerous threat after another. All humankind existed on noodle-thin floors that could tear at any time.

That was true.

No matter how tough she became, she'd always been and would always be vulnerable. And no human being had ever cared enough to save her, to protect her.

Not true. Bryan was there. And if Grant could be...

She didn't want to think about what must have happened to him.

Even if someone had wanted to protect her, none had ever been strong enough.

Not for long, anyway.

But...but God.

God offered a true foundation. Not sand or water—or noodle-thin rubber—but stone. God was a strong tower. *Her* strong tower. Not Grant and his promises. Not weapons. Not her own strength.

Only God.

Did she believe that?

Knowing she was about to face Ramón again, the man who'd kidnapped her once and tried to snatch her a second time. A man who was no doubt enraged at how she'd thwarted his plans.

Did she believe God was stronger than Ramón? Capable of seeing her through this?

It was a simple question. But trusting God now, when her life was in danger... when Bryan's life, Grant's life...when they were all in grave danger...?

It might've been simple, but it wasn't easy.

What were her choices? Believe God, or descend into despair.

She did believe. She *would* believe. She *chose* to believe.

She knew very little about this new faith of hers, but she knew God was her defender. He was with her. Now that everything else had been stripped away, she would learn how strong her faith was.

It's weak, Lord. It's so weak. But You're strong. Help me.

Like a warm breeze, barely noticeable in the bitter air, His presence wafted over her. He was there. He saw her. He cared.

Maybe He would deliver her from Ramón. Maybe He wouldn't. But no matter what, she'd be with Him.

God wasn't a consolation prize. He was the only prize worth living for.

The little boat reached the end of the jut of land that separated them from the Bannister's property. What she saw then terrified her.

The yacht was no longer docked near the shore. It was headed toward the open ocean.

Their captor shifted to intercept it.

They were going to be forced onto it. And then sail away.

Even if Hughes and the team arrived, they had no boats.

Once again, Summer would be Ramón's captive. So would Bryan. And this time, there'd be no chance for rescue.

Please, God. You're our only hope.

CHAPTER THIRTY-FOUR

Grant dragged Misty across the bitterly cold water toward the jut of land where Summer had been perched earlier. "Kick," he commanded.

He thought she tried, but her efforts weren't helping.

Not that he needed her help. He just wanted her to stay alive. She needed to get her blood pumping to stave off hypothermia. But she wasn't a trained soldier. She was a barefoot attorney wearing nothing but a business suit.

At least she hadn't gasped when she'd hit the water and inhaled a lungful of ocean.

Thank God for the wetsuit. He wished they'd had time to get her into one.

They'd swum underwater a long distance, so that by the time they surfaced for air, Ramón's men couldn't locate them in the dark waters. They'd given up trying, the yacht motoring away. Slowly...very slowly.

That was good. The red and blue lights flashing off the trees near the house confirmed that the police had finally arrived. Someone would have called the Coast Guard or Marine Patrol or both. If their boats were nearby, Ramón wouldn't get far.

Big *if*, though.

Hughes and the rest of the team must be on shore as well. He hoped, prayed, that Summer and Bryan were safe and warm somewhere.

Finally, his feet touched the ground, and he lifted Misty out of the water and carried her onto the rocky shore. Her chattering teeth were as loud as the crashing surf. He set her on her feet between a couple of large boulders, then yanked open the bag at his chest. He slipped her jacket off her, took out the two beach towels, and wrapped them around her before pulling her in close. He rubbed his hands down her arms and her back, trying to warm her. "You with me?"

"Y-y-y-y..."

She didn't quite get the word out, but he got the point. "Good. Sit down while I figure out—"

"W-w-what's that?"

He followed her gaze.

A dinghy was motoring past, coming from the far side of the land. Its path would intersect with the yacht's any minute.

He yanked Misty down and stared through the darkness. He didn't miss the blond hair blowing in the wind.

"S-s-s-s—"

"I see her." And if Grant wasn't mistaken, the man sitting across from Summer was Bryan.

Both of them, captured. Soon, they'd be with Ramón.

"Stay here." He handed her one of the guns and zipped the bag up again. "Stay warm. Stay out of sight. The police are here, and the rest of my team, so know who you're firing at."

Her answer was lost in the wind as he dove into the freezing water and started swimming.

Because yes, the Coast Guard or Marine Patrol would intercept Ramón's yacht. Probably. But Grant wasn't about to stake the lives of two people he loved on a *probably*.

And he didn't want to think about what Ramón would do with them.

Grant ignored the chill, the pain. Ignored the salt on his lips, the burning in his lungs. He swam below the surface, coming up when he was desperate for air.

The yacht was only a couple hundred yards from shore. Not close, but he wasn't in uniform like he'd been back in training. And back then, only his pride and future had been on the line.

Not lives. Lives of people who mattered to him.

He closed the distance in less than four minutes, slowing as he approached, quiet as could be. He reached the side of the yacht, treading water in the shadow of the starboard side. The boat's engine idled, masking the sound of his heavy breathing.

The dinghy was tied up to the back, where a light shone down on it. Summer had already climbed a short ladder to the deck, and Bryan was making his way up. By the looks of it, his leg was hurting badly.

Their captor, a formidable-looking man, was still on the dinghy. "Move faster!"

Bryan responded, but Grant didn't pick up the words.

From above, someone yelled in Spanish, "Ramón says to cut it loose. There's no time to stow it. Hurry!"

"*Sí, sí.*"

Staying close to the yacht, Grant floated toward the man, praying the one on deck had moved away. Bryan reached the top and disappeared from view.

The dinghy driver pulled a knife from his pocket and started working on the rope.

Grant grabbed the guy's wrist and yanked him into the water. He squeezed his neck, cutting off his oxygen. Precious seconds passed before the man went limp.

Now what?

He couldn't exactly let him go to sink to the bottom of the Atlantic.

With one hand on the unconscious man's wrist, Grant climbed into the dinghy and then hauled him in behind him.

He didn't have a lot of options. If he cut the rope, he'd have more time to rescue Summer and Bryan. But no way of escape.

If he didn't cut the rope, anybody could glance out the back and see that the dinghy was still there, the thug unconscious on the floor. They'd know Grant was on board.

And the guy could wake up and sound the alarm.

He hated to do it. Hated to. But he hopped to the small platform on the back of the yacht and cut the tie, then kicked the dinghy toward shore.

Somehow, he'd have to get control of the yacht or, at the very least, place himself between harm and the people he loved.

The yacht's engines kicked up, propelling the boat forward and leaving a trail of white in its wake.

Rather than climb the short stairway to the main deck—which he figured would get him killed—Grant stowed the knife, hopped up, and grabbed the lower chrome rail surrounding the higher deck. His hands were wet, but he held on tight and slid toward the front. He dangled above the water as the boat bounced over the waves, sending cold spray to his bare feet. He kept moving, praying his grip would hold.

Finally, he reached the forward deck about the same time that the boat got past the worst of the waves. He paused to listen and get his breath.

No voices, no unexpected sounds. He swung himself over the side, landing on his stomach on the gleaming wood. He flipped over, yanked open his waterproof bag, and pulled out a handgun.

Prepared to fire.

No alarm was raised. Nobody had seen.

He took a moment to get his breathing under control and bring his heart rate down. He needed to think.

When his body was calm and ready, he peeked up to the cockpit. His bullet from earlier had shattered the rear glass but hadn't reached the other panes that surrounded the area. A man stood there, gaze on the open ocean ahead.

Grant knew there was a way to get to the lower deck from the bow because men had come at him and Misty from behind when they'd been in the stairwell, men who hadn't been belowdecks before. There wasn't a second set of stairs, and he'd seen no ladder. So...

A trapdoor?

That would make sense—a way of escape if there were an emergency on board.

Where would it be? Staying low, he crawled across the deck, hands and eyes searching for some opening in the floor. Nothing.

Think.

Where would...?

The answer was embarrassingly obvious. It wouldn't be out here, exposed to the elements. The trap door would be in the cockpit.

Crap.

He had no choice. He remembered what he'd seen when he'd first come aboard. The cockpit entrance was near the opening to the stairwell leading to the living area. Probably, dressed in a black wetsuit, nobody would see him if he went up that way. He didn't care for probablys.

Was there a way to access the cockpit from the side?

He crawled that direction, reached a small entrance not a foot from the railing he'd just slid across.

Through the window, he saw the driver seated in a swivel chair, staring forward. The cockpit was lined on two sides with bench seats that started just behind the entry where Grant crouched. The back of the room held narrow windows flanking the door. The front had the controls, steering wheel, and windows.

Glass was still scattered on the floor. This was going to hurt.

The driver's hands weren't on the wheel. Did yachts have auto-pilot?

That would be very helpful.

Staying low, Grant took a breath, prayed for help, and turned the knob. Not locked. He pushed open the door and stepped into the room. He was quiet, but the cold air must've alerted the driver that somebody was there.

He turned with a benign expression, clearly unprepared for a threat. His eyes widened, and he launched himself to his feet and scrambled to grab a handgun from a holster at his waist.

Grant throat-punched him, then followed up with a punch to the gut.

Doubling over, the guy didn't even put up a fight.

Grant whacked him with the gun, hard, and he collapsed at his feet.

Unfortunate, because the trap door was right below him.

With a grunt, Grant lifted the dead weight and settled the guy back in the chair where he'd been seated. Then he angled him to look like he was staring out to sea. Okay, his head was tilted oddly, but from behind...

Maybe the ruse would buy Grant a few minutes.

After taking the man's shoes—too small, but better than bloody feet—he looked for a radio like the one on his father's boat. Saw a phone attached to the dash with an old-fashioned coiled cord. He grabbed it and dialed 911.

It felt miraculous when a man said, "Nine-one-one. What's your emergency."

"I'm on a yacht that just off-loaded drugs at the Bannister property in York, Maine. We're headed"—he glanced at the compass—"southeast. There are two hostages on board. I'm guessing four hostiles at least, plus one disabled. And me."

"What's your name?"

"Grant Wright. Also, a woman had been taken hostage, Misty Lake. She's on the land that borders the south end of the cove at the Bannister property. She's not injured, but she's cold and scared and armed. Have the police approach with caution."

"Got it."

"The owner of the yacht is Vasco Ramón. I'm going to protect the hostages."

"Sir, stay put. We might need—"

"I'm going for the hostages. The yacht will be moving on auto-pilot."

"Shut the engines down or put someone else in charge."

"The hostiles can't know I'm on board."

The man must've heard the determination in his voice. "Slow the boat as much as you can. Keep the line open so we can find you."

It took Grant a few moments to figure out how to adjust the speed. He didn't want to make too drastic a change and alert anybody that he was there. "Done. Hurry." He set the receiver on the floor and glanced at all the lights on the dashboard, then forward at the open ocean. *Please don't let us crash into rocks. Or an island. Or another boat.*

What was that expression? *Jesus is my co-pilot?*

Nope. Jesus was the Skipper on this cruise.

Silently, Grant lifted the trap door. Below, an empty bed. This must be the master bedroom. Gun aimed, Grant took in as much as he could from where he knelt. Then, he dropped his head into the space.

The room was empty.

He swung down, landed on the mattress, and aimed toward the open door.

Nobody there.

After a glance into the bathroom—also empty—he made his way to the exit, which opened to the short stairway that led to the landing where he'd found Misty earlier. As he climbed, voices drifted toward him. Men, speaking Spanish, coming from another half-flight up. At least two in the living area.

Another voice intruded, this one lower—and closer.

Speaking English with a Spanish accent.

Ramón.

It was coming from behind the door where Misty had been held.

Grant could only make out a few of the words. *...trouble... killed you when I had the chance...get something...*

He had to be talking to Summer. His tone was matter-of-fact, almost casual. But Grant wasn't buying it.

He pictured the room he'd seen when he'd rescued Misty. Twin beds separated by barely enough room to walk. Ramón would be facing Summer and Bryan, if he was there too. Meaning Ramón's back should be to the door.

Hoping to find Bryan, Grant silently slid open the other door on the same level. Empty bedroom scattered with backpacks and clothes.

So, either Bryan was with Summer, or he'd been shoved in a closet. Or killed and thrown overboard.

But why go to the trouble to bring him to the yacht if that was the plan? No, Bryan was still alive, somewhere.

With the rumble of the engine, Grant should be able to slide the door open without being heard. He'd rather not shoot

Ramón if he could avoid it. It would be better to silence him the way he'd silenced the others.

But he would kill him if he had to.

And then he'd have to kill every man on board.

He really didn't want to do that. He readied himself to slide the door open.

CHAPTER THIRTY-FIVE

S ummer had prayed, prayed hard, for rescue.

As she and Bryan had been forced onto the yacht, down the first set of stairs, then the second, she'd prayed for rescue.

When they'd been shoved into this tiny room, the only window a small circular thing barely larger than her head, she'd prayed for rescue.

She'd pulled the navy bedspread up to cover the unmade sheets—no sense risking getting tangled in the mess—then helped Bryan onto the bed, lifting his injured leg and pretending not to hear his grunts of pain. Then she'd straightened the blankets on the second bed and settled on top. She was freezing, but she'd refused to get under the blankets. She needed to be ready.

Because someone would come.

Right?

The top half of the walls were papered in navy-and-white stripes. The bottom was shiplap painted white, and between the siding and the paper was a thin rope border. The walls had kitschy sailboat pictures and a white lifesaver barely large enough for a toddler.

She and Bryan had kept up a steady stream of conversation filled with hope and sprinkled with ideas for escape, none of which felt viable as the boat motored out to sea.

And then Ramón came in.

He wasn't particularly tall or broad. Beside Grant and Bryan, he would look scrawny. Except, somehow, he seemed larger than life.

Powerful. Obviously much more powerful than she was, considering that, once again, he held her captive. And he had a gun in his hand.

He closed the door behind him and looked from her to Bryan and back. "Here you are again."

Oh, God. Please help.

But God didn't intervene.

There was no help coming, no rescue.

Keeping his gun aimed at Bryan, Ramón crawled onto the bed beside Summer and slid his arm around her shoulders as if they were old and dear friends.

Chilly as she was, his body heat felt confining, a boa constrictor warming up its next meal.

Ramón's aim shifted from Bryan to her.

The gun barrel pressed against her temple.

She couldn't help it. She shrank away, closing her eyes. Praying, praying.

"Well, isn't this cozy?"

Neither she nor Bryan answered.

She forced her eyes open and saw the hard look in Bryan's expression.

Ramón jutted his chin toward him. "Who are you?"

"A friend."

"A bodyguard, like this one?" He squeezed her shoulders, and she fought a fresh round of panic. "You look much like the other one, the one who surrendered to me earlier. I think your body will sink as fast as his did."

Summer gasped. It couldn't be true. It couldn't.

The little color left in Bryan's face drained away. His eyes reddened around the edges.

"Ah, yes," Ramón said. "More than a friend. I think he was your brother, yes?"

Bryan swallowed. Nodded.

"I'd like to say I'm sorry for your loss, but it would be a lie."

Despite her efforts to stop them, tears dripped down her cheeks.

It was too late to save Grant, but she'd do everything in her power to keep Bryan alive. It was the least she could do, the very least, for Grant, the man she loved.

But how could she save Bryan now?

Ramón had been one step ahead of them from the very beginning. Though the drugs might've been confiscated, his men on shore arrested, he was still free.

Just like when the compound had been raided in Mexico, other men had gone to prison for him, some had died for him, and Ramón had escaped punishment.

She'd always attributed it to bad luck—good luck, from his perspective—that he hadn't been there the night Jon and Grant and the rest of the team had shown up to rescue them.

But this...this wasn't luck. This was strategy. Quick thinking.

And the willingness to let others stand between him and capture.

Which made Ramón not only dangerous but...unstoppable.

What had made her think she could take on this man? She'd

been a fool, all the more because she'd dragged Grant and Bryan into her nightmare.

She tried to catch Bryan's attention, but he was looking down. His shoulders shaking. Grieving his brother. She wanted to do the same. She wanted to collapse in a puddle of tears.

Grant was gone. Ramón was in control.

Her hope seeped out like air from that stupid inflatable dinghy.

"Can I ask you a question?" Summer figured she might as well satisfy her curiosity.

"I don't think there are any secrets between us now."

"Does your sister know how you make your money?"

"Maritza is completely innocent and fully dedicated to fighting the cartels. She is beautifully naive."

"And her husband?"

"Equally without a clue, I'm afraid. The man has the brains of a bowl of beans."

Summer wasn't sorry to hear it. In all the time she'd spent with the family, she'd never gotten any sense that Maritza or her husband were criminals. She hated to think she could be so easily deceived. "You can't escape." As she said the words, she prayed they were true. "You must know that."

"It is a big ocean," Ramón said. "Perhaps we'll slip by the authorities. If not, I believe two hostages might secure our freedom."

Hostages.

As hopeless as she'd felt trapped in that windowless building in Mexico, that was nothing, nothing compared to this.

Headed for the open ocean. In the hands of a murderer.

"The real question is," Ramón said, "how shall we pass the time? Perhaps you and I could—"

Bryan's head snapped up, his red-rimmed eyes hard, furious. "Don't touch her."

"How noble of you." Though she was too close to see Ramón's face, she could hear the smile in his voice. "And if I do?"

"You'll answer to me."

Ramón laughed. "You can hardly stand on your own two feet. What are you going to do against me?" He jabbed the gun into Summer's head, the cold steel pressing painfully into her skin. And then the gun was aimed at Bryan. "I think one hostage would do the trick, though. Maybe I'll just send you off to meet your brother."

Bryan swallowed, but he didn't speak, didn't look away.

Just glared.

Don't antagonize him. She shook her head quickly, trying to send the message with her eyes. The only thing keeping her going was Bryan's presence, her desire to get them both out of this.

If Ramón killed him...

She feared she'd shut down. Surrender.

Give up.

But Bryan didn't look her way, just continued with his *don't even try it* stare.

Ramón laughed and pressed the gun barrel to her temple again. He settled into the space, pulling Summer against him like one might a girlfriend, and spoke into her ear. "As long as we're chatting...how did you find the property?"

She shrugged under his heavy arm. "A little investigation. It wasn't that hard."

He tsked. "Frustrating. It would have been the perfect plan if you hadn't overheard. I figured it out, why you followed me. You were one of the models. Yes?"

She saw no point in lying. "Yes."

"Are you the one who called in the soldiers?"

Little though she'd wanted to chat with Ramón, she thought her best bet was to keep him talking.

She was in the middle of explaining how she'd contacted her cousin when the door slid open.

To the most beautiful, most terrifying sight she'd ever seen. Because Ramón had lied.

Grant wasn't dead. Wasn't lying on the ocean floor.

He was alive. Alive and well. He'd come for her, just like he'd promised.

With everything in her, she wished he hadn't. Because now Ramón would make his lie true. He'd kill him, no question.

Grant's eyes connected with hers. He saw the pistol pressed against her head.

Dropped his weapon.

Lifted his hands.

"Don't shoot," he said. "Please, don't shoot."

Ramón jabbed the gun harder against her skull, and she flinched, squeezing her eyes shut.

Certain the gunshot was coming. The last sound she'd hear before she stepped into the arms of Jesus.

"Please." Grant's voice was pleading. "Please, don't hurt her."

"Well, well, well. You've made a liar out of me. I was told you were dead."

She couldn't see his face, but Ramón's words seemed sincere. Perhaps one of his men had lied to him.

"Come on in." Ramón pulled the gun back the slightest bit. "Sit beside your brother."

Grant did as he was told, settling on the end of the twin bed, back to the wall.

Bryan was looking at Grant with an expression that probably mirrored hers. Relief that he wasn't dead.

Regret that he was there.

Grant was looking at Summer. "You okay?"

"Good as can be expected." She was proud that her voice didn't betray her fear.

Grant's gaze flicked from her to Ramón. "What do you want?"

"Is that my wetsuit?"

Grant looked down at the black neoprene, the bright yellow bag strapped across his front. "Found it in the closet where Gael put me. Very convenient. Thanks."

"Sure, sure. Why don't you toss me that bag."

Grant slipped it off his shoulders and threw it on the bed beside Summer.

Ramón made no move to grab it. "And the blonde? Did she survive too?"

Blonde? Who did Ramón mean?

Grant met Summer's eyes. "Misty's alive and well."

She gasped.

Misty?

Misty!

That was why Grant hadn't come to her rescue. Why he'd surrendered.

Fresh tears dripped down her cheeks. Her voice was tremulous when she asked, "She's all right?"

"Was when I saw her last. Cold. Worried about you." Again, his gaze bore into hers. "I'm sorry I broke my promise."

"You didn't break it. You're here." Her voice cracked. She hated, *hated* that he was here.

But she loved him for it.

"And you saved my sister."

His head dipped and rose.

She couldn't speak for the emotions crashing over her. Gratitude. Overwhelming regret that, in trying to keep his promise, Grant had probably surrendered his life.

How she loved this man. How she wished she'd have the opportunity to tell him.

"What's in the bag?" Ramón asked.

"Couple of handguns I took off your men. They're not very well trained."

"And you are, I assume."

Grant smiled, shrugged. "By comparison." He jutted his chin toward Ramón. "You never answered the question. What do you want?"

"What everybody wants," he said. "To be free."

"Huh. You probably shouldn't have smuggled drugs into the US, then. We don't take kindly to that."

"Who do you think buys them?" he snapped. "We'll be in international waters soon enough. Then I'll be safe. At which point, I'll do away with the two of you"—he nodded to the men on the bed—"and get what I can out of this one." He tapped her head with his gun. "Not as much as she would've fetched seven years ago, but there's a market for women of all shapes and sizes...and ages. It won't be enough to recoup my losses, but it'll be a start."

Grant's eyes hardened, fury and threat in his gaze. But he held his tongue.

"How did you get down here without alerting my men."

"It's a long story," Grant said. "Suffice it to say, the unconscious man at the helm isn't doing the steering."

Ramón jerked back from her. "Nobody is in the cockpit?"

"Nobody awake." Grant shrugged again as if it didn't matter. "If we ram into something...well, you've already told us we're going to die"—he tipped his head toward Bryan—"and I suspect Summer would prefer swimming for it to whatever you have planned."

"You're right about that," she said.

"So if we crash? Not my boat, not my problem."

Ramón pushed her away. "Get over there. Sit with them."

Gladly. She launched herself across the very narrow space and settled between Grant and Bryan.

Grant grabbed her hand, and she held his tightly.

With her other, she held Bryan's.

The bright yellow bag still sat on the opposite bed. She did her very best not to look at it. Better Ramón forgot it was there.

He slid toward the doorway and stood, keeping his weapon aimed at them. He backed to the doorway. "Bruno! Get down here!" The sound of footsteps came close, and Ramón spoke to a man in the hallway. "You will stand there"—he nodded to the corner opposite where they sat—"and keep watch. If any of them tries anything, shoot. Start with the one in my wetsuit. I'd prefer the woman stay alive, but if she dies..." He shrugged. "I'll send someone down to tie them up."

Tie them up?

Grant squeezed her hand, a gentle encouragement.

How had it taken her so long to acknowledge her feelings for this man? Hadn't she known he was trustworthy? Good? Kind?

All those years she'd wasted pretending she didn't need anybody. Pretending she didn't care that she spent every night alone. Pretending to love days off the way everybody else did, not dread the solitude. All that time, she could have been with Grant.

She leaned into him, desperate for more connection. She didn't care if Ramón saw and guessed her feelings. She didn't care if the whole world knew.

All she wanted, all she wanted was for Grant and Bryan to survive.

And herself, if God was feeling generous.

Bruno stepped in and took his position. It was the taller man who'd attacked her in the parking garage. One of his arms was in a cast. He glared at her a long moment, then put on an expressionless mask. As if being ordered to kill were an everyday occurrence.

As if ending their lives would cost him nothing.

CHAPTER THIRTY-SIX

They were still alive.

Grant had no idea what would happen next, but for now, they were still alive. A little worse for the wear, as Summer's swollen eye and the blood on her jacket attested to.

He'd almost asked Ramón why he hadn't killed him when he'd had the chance, but he didn't want to give the guy any ideas. Although, if Ramón had counted all the men Grant had killed or incapacitated when he rescued Misty, he should have known he had no choice.

Because Grant would do what he had to do, kill whom he had to kill, to save Summer and Bryan. Grant had led them both into danger and then left them to manage alone. This was what happened.

He should never have allowed them to be part of this operation. He should have hired mercenaries. Would have if any had been available.

He should have left Bryan in Brunswick and shipped Summer somewhere far away until Ramón was out of the picture. Bad things always happened when Grant left people alone in dangerous situations.

Except...he wasn't their last line of defense. As much as he loved them, God was their protector, and He was a lot better at it than Grant would ever be. That had to be why they'd made it this far.

Wasn't that what Bryan had been trying to tell him? That the fall hadn't been his fault? That God had been there, had kept him alive, had kept him from being more injured? That God had used it for good?

Grant was trying to believe that He would show up.

But it wasn't easy.

We need Your help!

The bright yellow bag was lying on top of the messy bed across from them, just a couple of feet away. But the goon was watching.

Summer was cuddled up beside him. As much as he hated to move, he had to be ready. He stuck his elbow out, hoping Bruno didn't see.

She sat up and let go of his hand. "It's getting warm. Can you scoot down?"

Wow, she was good. Knew exactly what they needed.

"Sure." He put distance between them. Summer shifted away from Bryan a little.

Because they'd all need room to maneuver, assuming they would get the opportunity to fight.

"Hey!" Bruno's arm had slipped a little, but now he raised the weapon and aimed it at Grant's head. "Don't move!"

Grant lifted his hands, all surrender and supplication. "Just trying to get comfortable." He switched to Spanish. "You're not our enemy."

Bruno acted as if he hadn't heard.

"To be honest," Grant said, still in the man's native tongue, "your real enemy here is Ramón. He's using you to save himself."

"He is my friend."

"Sure, sure. But how many years did you spend in prison for him? How many of his so-called friends will land there today? How many men did he leave on shore?"

Bruno's eyes narrowed the slightest bit.

"The authorities were there. You saw that, right? Your friends are all going to prison. If they're not dead, that is."

"That's your fault, not Ramón's."

"Ramón knew we'd be there," Grant said. "He knew, yet he risked all those men anyway. Not to mention your payoff. I assume you were going to make a cut? The drugs are in the hands of authorities now."

"Ramón always pays us."

"Enough to kill innocent people? What's the going rate for murder?"

"You ask me this? Where is my friend? Where is Juan?"

"Which one is he?"

"On the dinghy. Now probably at the bottom of the sea."

Grant shook his head. "I prefer not to kill people. Last I saw him, he was floating away. Unconscious but alive. How long he'll stay that way"—Grant lifted his shoulders and let them drop—"that's up to God. Maybe you should say a prayer for him."

Bruno flinched.

Was prayer a sore spot? Or maybe a soft spot?

"The police are coming, you know. The Maine Marine Patrol, the Coast Guard. Everybody's looking for you. Eventually, they're going to find you. But if you help us—"

"I will never—"

"—I'll tell them what you did, and they'll go easy on you. We can make it look like I overpowered you so Ramón will never know."

At that, Bruno grinned. "You? Overpower me? Nobody would believe that."

The man was tall and looked strong, no question about it. But Grant was trained.

He could take him.

But that wasn't how this would go.

Grant forced a smile he didn't feel. "Worth a try." He deliberately turned his back to the guy, facing his brother and Summer. He spoke low and fast. "There're weapons in the waterproof bag. If something happens to me, fight your way out. If you have to, kill every man on this boat."

Fresh tears dripped down Summer's face. "Nothing's going to happen to you. We need you."

Grant couldn't let himself be affected by her tears. He shifted his gaze to Bryan. "I notified the authorities, but who knows when they'll get here."

"Stop talking!" A threat hummed in Bruno's voice.

Bryan held Grant's eye contact a long time. Understanding what Grant wanted. What Grant was saying.

That he wanted them to stay alive. That he'd give anything, including his own life, to make sure that happened.

Grant waited for an argument. Even a shaking head.

But Bryan dipped his chin, face grim.

Grant turned forward again, hoping to see contemplation on Bruno's face, some inkling that he was considering what Grant had said. But it'd been a long shot, and the thug's face had slipped back into that expressionless mask.

He would kill without thinking twice about it.

Grant wouldn't lose his life so easily.

He closed his eyes, prayed, prayed that the God he'd loved for so many years, the One who'd given His glorious life for Grant's unworthy one, would give him the power, the courage, to do what he had to do.

Waited for the Lord to show him another way, but no other ideas came.

He pulled in a lungful of air and blew it out.

Turned again to the two people beside him. Met Bryan's eyes and said very low, "I love you."

Bryan nodded, his eyes filling. He said nothing.

"Stop talking." Bruno's voice was filled with wrath. "You look forward."

Grant focused on Summer. "I love you."

"I love you too."

Those words, those four words, made what he was about to do so much harder. Because for an instant, the future they should have had stretched out before him. A wedding. A home. Children running and laughing and playing.

The future he'd dreamed of for seven years was so close.

Tears pricked his eyes. He didn't bother to hide them, just leaned toward her and kissed her forehead.

"What are you doing?" she asked, her voice barely a whisper.

"I promised to protect you."

She leaned back, eyes wide. "Don't. Please."

He held her gaze a long time, wishing he could see another way. But the authorities hadn't found them yet. Even if they did, Ramón wouldn't turn them over. He'd use them to ensure the police didn't try to stop him.

Escaping punishment seemed to be the man's superpower.

When he got away, he'd kill Grant and Bryan.

And sell Summer into a future Grant wouldn't let himself consider.

He turned away from her. Put his feelings for her behind him. Because he had no choice. Because looking at Summer was only making what he had to do harder.

His heart was racing. His lungs screaming for air as they had beneath the cold water.

He braced himself, prepared to move.

And just then...

The boat lurched.

Bruno's gun dipped as his gaze flicked upward, toward the cockpit.

Grant propelled himself off the bed and into the big man, unsurprised when he heard the gunshot that would steal his life.

CHAPTER THIRTY-SEVEN

A scream tore from Summer's throat.

But Grant had trained her well.

As the boat slowed into a turn, she propelled herself off the bed and into the murderer who'd killed the man she loved. She tackled him, her grip on his gun arm to keep from getting shot. He hit her with his cast, but she kept pummeling him. Who cared that he was stronger than she was? Who cared how much it hurt?

He punched her in the side, in the back, muttering a stream of Spanish words she assumed wouldn't be fit for his abuela's ears.

She managed to wrench away and put some distance between them, thinking her legs would be more effective than her fists. He reared up as if to tackle her.

Then, a second gunshot split the silence.

She flinched, waiting for the pain. But it didn't come.

A hand gripped her shoulder and yanked her back. "It's okay. It's okay. I think he's dead."

"He killed him, he killed him." She wanted to attack the

man again, but there was blood on his chest. His eyes were open and lifeless.

"Not Grant." Bryan's words were clipped. "The other guy's dead. Grab that bag. We need another gun."

"Where did you get—?"

"It's the one Grant dropped when he first stepped in."

"We need...two guns."

The words, practically grunted out, had her swiveling.

Grant was sitting up, bedding pressed to his thigh, his face twisted in pain.

It was the most beautiful sight she'd ever seen.

Bryan crouched beside him. "What should I do?"

"The bag, Summer," Grant said. "Quick."

She heard footsteps closing in.

She grabbed the bag, shoved her hand inside, and pulled out a gun just as a figure stepped into the opening.

She fired, hitting the newcomer in the chest.

He crumpled, and she tossed the bag behind her, not taking her eyes off the doorway.

"Got it," Bryan said.

"There should be some string in there."

She heard scuffling, and then Bryan's incredulous voice. "Is this a bikini?"

"Straps." Grant's voice was pinched. "And a little fabric. Hurry."

She shifted backward, stepping over the dead man, never taking her eyes off the opening. She heard no footsteps, but that only meant they were being more careful.

The sound of tearing fabric.

A grunt.

"Is he okay?" Summer asked.

"The bullet went through his thigh."

"Whisper. They're out there." Grant inhaled and exhaled. "I'll be fine." His words came through clenched teeth. "Just don't let anybody through that door."

Right.

She could do that. But her hands trembled. Her gaze kept straying to the lifeless man in the doorway.

"I've got your back." Grant's words were calmer this time. And quieter. "Breathe, Summer. You can do this."

She did as he said, pulling deep breaths in and blowing them out slowly. Trying to calm her racing heart. He'd trained her well, but she'd never called on the skills she needed today. She'd been a protector, keeping evil at bay. She'd never fired her weapon outside of training.

She'd never killed a man.

The body lying in a pool of blood proved that statement was no longer true.

"Good," Grant said. "That should staunch the bleeding."

"What are you doing?" Bryan's whisper sounded indignant.

"Help me up. I'm not fighting on my butt."

Grant grunted as Bryan helped him to his feet. "Stupid, stubborn bonehead."

"Love you, too, bro." Grant moved to stand in front of her.

She shifted so he couldn't get by. "You're already injured. It's my turn."

"No." He held her right arm and pulled her behind him. "You can call me a sexist pig later, but even with a bullet hole in my thigh, I'm better."

He was right.

And having somebody willingly step between her and danger... This was the kind of man she'd always hoped to find. Except now that Grant was there, she wished more than anything he weren't.

She stayed where she was, between the two beds, slightly behind Grant but still facing the doorway.

Bryan climbed over the twin and stood in the corner where Bruno had been a few minutes before.

"Move those bodies out of the way," Grant said.

"I can help." Summer started to lean that direction, but Grant grabbed her arm and kept her behind him.

"He's got it. I need your gun focused on that door."

Despite Bryan's lame leg, the man was strong. The room was tiny, so Bryan hefted both bodies onto one of the beds.

When he finished, he stood in the corner again, breathing heavily.

"Thanks," Grant said.

"No problem."

They stood like that for another minute, two minutes.

"Where are they?" Summer kept her voice low.

Grant suddenly looked at the ceiling. She did as well. Nothing there. "Hoping for angels?"

His smile was more like a grimace. "There's a trapdoor in the master. Just making sure."

She'd have taken a trap door, another way off this deathtrap.

"We're going to have to move." Grant kept his voice low enough that she could barely hear him. "Until we have control of this ship, we're still Ramón's captives."

He snatched a pillow off the bed and tossed it through the door.

A gunshot rent the silence.

"That came from the top of the stairs."

Bryan said. "Thanks. It helps to know what angle we'll be murdered from."

Grant actually chuckled. "We need to create a diversion."

"Hold on," Bryan said. "I'll grab my grenades."

"Always with the sarcasm," Grant whispered. "Check the closet."

Bryan did, but Summer couldn't see past Grant to what he found.

"Yes," Grant whispered. "Grab that other one too."

What were they doing?

"Like that," Grant said. "A pillow..."

The blankets on the bed beside her slid forward, along with the pillow. She had no idea what was going on.

The sound of wheels moving across the hardwood had her glancing that way. Bryan had found a tall rolling suitcase, shoved a duffel on top of it, and tied it to the extended handle of the luggage with a pillowcase. He'd draped the whole thing with one of the comforters.

The invention was nearly as tall as she was.

"I'll push it out, go low, and fire up the stairs." Grant's voice was barely discernible above the engine noise. "Summer, stay behind me, aim down the stairs to the right. Bryan, there's a door beside this one on the left. Both of you, get as low as you can and don't stand up. Stay in this room except to aim and fire. When you've taken out all the bad guys in your line of vision, say 'Clear.' Got it?"

"Stay low, shoot bad guys." Bryan's words were flippant, but his tone was anything but. "Clear."

"Ready?" Grant asked.

"Ready," Bryan said.

She squeezed Grant's arm and breathed a prayer for their safety. "Ready."

They crept forward. Grant took a long, slow breath, and Summer did the same, blowing out as he did. Remembering everything he'd taught her.

Remembering what she'd learned about God. Worst case

scenario, they'd go home to be with Him. Not what she wanted —yet—but if this was the end...

She really didn't want it to be the end. She prayed hard.

Grant pushed the rolling suitcase-turned-decoy into the hallway and dove behind it.

Bullets rained all around.

Summer crouched, aimed to her right and down. Nobody there.

"Clear!" Bryan shouted.

"Clear!" Grant said.

Thank God, thank God they were both all right.

"Be ready!" Grant barked the command. "Eyes open."

Summer's gaze flicked from the empty staircase leading down to the one leading up.

But nobody else came into view.

She, Bryan, and Grant had killed...she counted four men so far. How many had Grant taken out in his bid to rescue them?

Suddenly, the engine cut off.

She'd become accustomed to its low hum.

Now, there was only silence. Silence like she'd never experienced before.

No trees swaying in the breeze. No birds chirping. No cars passing. Just the sounds of their breathing and the distant splash of water against the hull.

The yacht slowed and swayed in the waves.

Creaked like an old house in a storm.

She was afraid to move. Afraid of the oppressive silence.

Maybe there were more men on board.

Maybe only Ramón was left, having allowed his men, once again, to die for him.

Which would make it three against one.

She should have been encouraged by the odds. But blood

dripped past the wrappings on Grant's leg, glimmering red against the black wetsuit.

Bryan was struggling to stand, much less walk.

And they were about to face Ramón.

A man who'd proved he'd sink to any low to save himself.

And he knew they were coming.

CHAPTER THIRTY-EIGHT

"**P**ush this down."

The strain and pain in Grant's voice sent Summer's already pounding heart zooming as she shoved the luggage-turned-decoy down the stairs. It clattered through the door and into the master bedroom. If someone came through the trap-door, he'd have to contend with that before he could creep up behind them.

She turned back to Grant, who looked up at the short flight of stairs as if he faced Everest.

Bryan was crouched beside him, messing with the wrappings on his makeshift bandage. "We need to wrap that wound—"

"After." The single word came through clenched teeth.

Grant was not okay.

And by the way Bryan stood—slowly, testing his weight on his bad leg—he wasn't okay either.

Summer had dragged them both into this, and only she remained uninjured.

Grant tried to take a step up, stumbled and fell on the stairs. "Bryan, help me."

"No, wait," Summer said. "Let me..."

But Bryan, ignoring them both, crept up the stairs. A body was lying at the top—shot by Grant, she thought. Bryan peeked over it into the galley kitchen.

"Wait!" Summer said.

A gunshot sounded an instant after Bryan ducked again. "One guy," he whispered to his brother. "On the couch straight ahead."

"Don't do that again!" Grant's words hummed with fury. "Stay here with her." He gripped the railing as if to haul himself to the first step.

Summer stopped him with a hand on his free arm. "Please," she whispered. "It's my turn."

"I got it." But his face was white. He was losing blood fast.

She looked past Grant to Bryan. "We'll climb together. You stay in the stairwell. When I say 'now,' provide cover. I want you out of his sight, but make a lot of noise."

"No."

Ignoring Grant's protest, she pictured the kitchen as she'd seen it when she walked through earlier. Long and skinny, but there was a small peninsula of cabinets that jutted out from the side. She'd need to get behind it. "I'm going to take the shooter out."

"Got it."

"Summer." Grant gripped her arm, tight. "Do not go up there."

"I'm not going to let you die for me today, Grant. Not if I can help it."

At his wide eyes, she added, "I'm not dying either." She kissed his forehead, ignoring the terror that bubbled up inside her, and twisted out of his grip. "Bryan, help me out?"

She aimed up the stairs, hoping the thug would be dumb enough to approach.

Behind her, Bryan said, "We got this."

When she heard nothing, she glanced back. Grant looked as if he wanted to fight.

"Wait."

At the agony in his voice, she looked his way again.

He rested his hand on her arm and closed his eyes. "Please, please. Keep them safe."

"Amen. Come on." Bryan situated Grant at the bottom of the stairs, where he could defend himself if necessary.

"Get me a pillow," Grant said.

After Bryan delivered the items, he crept up beside Summer, and they took cover behind the body. She decided not to think about that.

"Ready?" she asked.

At his grim nod, she took a deep breath, blew it out, and said, "Now."

Bryan fired up and straight ahead.

She launched herself over the dead man and into the kitchen, where she dove behind the short counter. She peeked, praying the guy on the couch hadn't seen her.

He was lying on a sofa perpendicular to the stairs, taking cover behind its arm. Hidden from the stairwell but not from her.

She fired through the end of the sofa. Heard a yelp of pain.

Her gaze and aim swiveled around the space, not that there were many hiding places. Nobody jumped out at her. Nobody fired.

She grabbed a bottle from the dirty countertop and came at the love seat from behind. Aiming at the bit of skull she could see, she said, "Drop your gun. Now."

The gun fell on the floor at his side.

"Hands up."

One came up, supported by the other. Both were bloody.

She crept closer and leaned over.

Her bullet had gone through the fleshy part of his right shoulder. He was injured but still alive. Still a threat.

She didn't want to kill him. Or take the time to tie him up. Or worry about him.

"Who else is here?"

He responded with a string of slurred Spanish words. She picked up none of them. Rather than waste more time, she whacked him in the head with the bottle.

He slumped. His eyes closed.

Praying he'd stay unconscious, she grabbed his weapon and wiped the blood off of it with her shirt. Five bullets in his. Seven in hers. Should be enough.

Behind her, Bryan limped forward.

"Okay, same thing," she said. "Fire to give me cover." One weapon shoved in the waist at her back, the other prepared to shoot, she dashed up the stairs to the deck. She was itching to move, adrenaline coursing through her veins. But Bryan was slower to get into position.

He said, "Now!"

At the sound of his gunshots, she hopped over the half-wall that lined the stairwell.

No return fire came.

The yacht was dead in the water, tossed by the ocean's waves. More stars than Summer had ever seen dotted the midnight sky. She gazed out to sea, praying she'd catch sight of something. Approaching boats. A lighthouse. But there was nothing, nothing but blackness for as far as she could see.

The sight was terrifying.

She looked away quickly.

Lord, I need courage.

Because the only thing scarier than that big, cold ocean was the man who'd brought her here.

Ignoring the bitter wind, she peeked up toward the cockpit. No sign of Ramón.

Maybe he was hiding. But where?

Creeping toward the edge of the boat, squelching anxiety that urged her away from danger, she leaned out and looked toward the bow.

Nothing in her line of sight, but that didn't mean he wasn't there.

"Coming up," Bryan said.

She prepared to lay down cover fire, but there was no movement.

The deck seemed deserted.

Bryan made it up and around the half-wall, and she crouched beside him.

"Any sign of him?" His words were nearly lost in the wind.

"None. I'm going up. Watch my back."

"Let me go—"

"I'm faster and better trained. You stay here and cover me." She didn't wait for an answer, just dashed toward the staircase that led up one more flight, grabbing a cushion off the outside sofa.

She tossed it up the stairs.

A bullet shot clean through it.

Ramón was waiting for her.

What should I do?

What would Grant do?

She didn't have any idea. What she knew was that if they didn't get into that cockpit, they wouldn't be able to turn this boat back toward Maine. Grant was right. As long as Ramón had control of the helm, they were still his captives. Maybe somebody would come to rescue them.

Or maybe someone would come to rescue Ramón. That couldn't happen or she'd never be free.

Meanwhile, Grant was bleeding. If that wound wasn't tended soon, he'd bleed to death.

They were in the middle of a great big ocean. Nobody was going to find them.

She had no choice. No choice. She had to go up there. Maybe she could take Ramón out and keep herself alive. Maybe not, but if she could incapacitate him, then Grant and Bryan could make it back to shore. They could be saved, even if she couldn't.

She really, really didn't want to die.

But if she didn't act, Grant definitely would.

Lord, help me. Tell me what to do.

And then, the pop-pop-pop of gunshots.

But they weren't coming toward her.

Taking the risk, she scrambled up the stairs.

Ramón was firing toward his own feet. What in the...?

The trapdoor.

Ramón saw her coming and shifted his aim.

She fired at him, diving toward the outside half-wall of the cockpit as bullets flew over her head. Beneath her, glass littered the space.

From below, Bryan stomped his feet and yelled, "Cockpit!"

She had no idea why and didn't bother to figure it out as she heard the distinctive *click* of an empty chamber.

Ramón's gun was empty?

Inexplicably, he laughed. "Where are your protectors?"

Was he reloading?

Or out of bullets?

Was it a trick?

Summer crouched, dashed across the doorway to the opposite side to get a look at him, waiting for gunshots.

But none came.

He was unarmed.

She thought so, anyway. But she wasn't stupid. She stayed crouched behind the wall but aimed toward Ramón, making herself as small a target as possible. "Put down your gun."

He was seated in the swivel captain's chair, the picture of relaxation, the gun in his hand. "I don't think I will."

"Drop your weapon and lie down on your belly."

Another laugh. "You will have to shoot me. I don't believe you have it in you."

She could shoot him. Maybe she should, for Grant's sake. He must've gone into the bedroom and fired up at the trapdoor. How much blood had he lost doing that?

Ramón planned to murder Grant and Bryan and sell her.

She wanted to shoot him.

But shooting somebody who was actively trying to kill her was one thing. Firing on a man who wasn't firing back, no matter what he'd done, was something else entirely.

So...

She couldn't do it.

"Don't tempt me. I've already killed one of your men tonight, maybe more."

"Sure you did." His voice was laced with sarcasm. "You think, when you were in my sister's hospital room, that I didn't notice you? I noticed you. A beautiful woman—what man wouldn't? But I dismissed you as irrelevant because you are no threat to me. You've gotten lucky, getting this close, thanks to all the help you've been given. But you're just a model. You're not going to kill me. You're just a pretty girl. A pretty girl who isn't capable of protecting herself, much less anybody else. You're only capable when there are men around to do the hard work. Like now. The only reason you've gotten as close as you have is because your friend created a diversion. You are no match for me."

She was reminded of what her father used to shout at her when she was a child. *Useless, disobedient brat.*

She hadn't cared about her father's opinion of her, and she didn't care about this man's. She knew who she was, always had.

"Drop your gun and get down on the floor."

He tossed the gun away. "It's empty anyway."

He leaned forward to push himself to his feet. An instant before he looked away, she saw a gleam in his eyes.

One hand slipped behind him.

And came back with something shiny and black.

She fired.

He collapsed like a stone, crumpled on the cockpit floor.

The sound of the wind, the gentle splashing of the waves against the hull. It all faded.

The whole world went quiet.

She stood from behind the protective wall, stepped into the cockpit, crunching over broken glass, and stared down at her enemy, waiting for him to get up, to fight.

But he didn't move.

CHAPTER THIRTY-NINE

G rant had stopped Bryan an instant before he'd followed Summer upstairs. "You let me know when she goes into the cockpit. I think I can help."

"I'll stomp hard when she's on her way. Or just yell really loud."

"That should do it." Everything was so quiet, he could easily hear Summer's footsteps. "Stay alive. And keep her alive."

After Bryan followed Summer, Grant had wrapped his wounds again, more tightly than before, trying to stanch the bleeding. He'd felt weak and woozy, but as long as there was still blood in his veins, he had to try to help. He'd made his way down the short stairway to the master, pushing the decoy suitcases out of the way. He'd climbed onto the bed and pushed himself against the headboard.

And then, he'd waited.

There'd been more gunshots from the deck.

After that, the silence seemed to stretch forever.

Then, another gunshot. It had come from a different place. Summer and Bryan nearing the cockpit.

Grant had heard nothing from Bryan.

He trusted that his brother would warn him if either of them had breached the little room right above him. Unless Bryan couldn't warn him.

This would be risky, but if Ramón was at the helm, then Grant could help.

Had to help.

The quiet was disconcerting.

Nobody was moving.

Finally, he'd thought it was time.

Wasn't it?

He'd prayed it would help. And then, he'd fired up through the trapdoor toward where he thought the man should be standing, then rolled off the bed.

Ramón returned fire.

Grant crawled to the doorway as bullets buried themselves in the mattress.

And then stopped.

In the silence, he'd heard stomping, then "Cockpit!" from his brother.

Thank God.

Had Grant injured or killed Ramón? Or at least slowed him down?

Were Summer and Bryan safe?

It was torture not knowing.

The bleeding was under control for now. He'd made it up the first flight of stairs and seen the unconscious man on the couch. It was Gael, the one Grant had attacked after he'd escaped the closet.

Summer must've clocked him good. The man's head was going to pound, but at least he was alive. Maybe he'd appreciate that when he went back to prison.

Grant was halfway up the stairs leading to the deck when he heard another gunshot.

He hurried up the last couple of steps, looking for shooters. But it seemed everybody was down.

"Over here!" Bryan was near the steps to the cockpit but stopped as Grant hobbled that way. Together, they made it to the top.

Where Summer still held the gun, aimed at Ramón as if waiting for him to come around.

Blood spread beneath him. The man wouldn't be threatening her or anybody, ever again.

Bryan scooted past them and went to the helm.

The man who'd been driving the boat earlier, the man whom Grant had found and rendered unconscious, was lying on one of the benches. Dead.

Had Ramón shot him? Payback for having been bested by Grant, he guessed.

Grant touched Summer's shoulder. "You all right?"

She looked up at him, blinking. "I shot him."

Ramón still held a gun in one hand. Another rested a few feet away. Grant kicked them both away.

But Ramón was dead.

"It's okay, sweetheart." He took the gun from her hand and pulled her close. She wrapped her arms around him and held on tightly.

They stood like that a long moment, and then, she seemed to shake herself out of shock. "You need to sit."

His leg was throbbing. The world felt wobbly, and not just because they were bobbing in the ocean waves. "I wouldn't turn down a comfortable recliner."

She urged him onto a bench. "This'll have to do. Lie down."

He did, though it wasn't the most comfortable seat in the house. She lifted his leg, and he clenched his teeth against the groan that wanted to escape.

She disappeared for a second, then returned and shoved a pillow beneath his knee. "It's still bleeding. Lie still."

As his adrenaline drained, nausea rolled over him. He managed a nod.

Summer disappeared from his view, and Grant closed his eyes and listened while Bryan contacted the authorities, then started the engine and gunned it.

"They're coming," Bryan said. "I'm moving to intercept."

"Great." He couldn't get any volume and doubted Bryan heard him.

A moment later, a blanket was draped over him. He tried to pry his eyes open but couldn't seem to manage it.

"It's okay." Summer's soft voice spoke in his ear as she wrapped his hand in her own. "Just rest. We'll get you to the hospital."

He wanted to answer, to thank her for the blanket. To tell her he loved her. But he couldn't do anything but lie there and enjoy the feel of her skin against his.

And thank God they'd survived.

CHAPTER FORTY

After Grant was taken by ambulance to the hospital, Summer and Bryan were separated and interviewed by local authorities and state police. Now Summer was enduring round three, this with a couple of irritated feds from the Drug Enforcement Agency.

Summer, Grant, and Bryan had survived being kidnapped and held on a yacht filled with armed men, and everybody wanted to know how. The answer was lying in a hospital with a bullet hole in his thigh.

Gael of the chin-curtain beard was recovering from his wounds in the same hospital.

Ramón and most of the other men on the yacht were dead. Summer had killed two, Bryan, one, and Grant, one.

The driver of the boat had been fatally shot, probably by Ramón in a fit of anger, though the police were convinced Grant had done it. They'd run ballistics and figure it out.

One thug had been found, alive, floating in the dinghy.

Other bodies had washed up on shore. She couldn't account for them but figured Grant probably could. He'd rescued Misty

—that couldn't have been easy. There was so much Summer still didn't know.

The police had assured her that Misty was all right, but Summer needed to see her. To hug her.

She needed to check on Grant.

And she needed to make sure Hughes and the rest of the team were all right.

But she hadn't been able to do any of those things. She'd done nothing but endure questioning in the hours since she'd planted her feet on solid ground.

"Tell me again how you knew the drugs would be off-loaded at that property." The female DEA agent was skinny and had a stark bun so tight it made her squint.

Her partner, a younger blond man with eager eyes, reminded Summer of a puppy eyeing a treat just out of reach. She'd already forgotten both of their names. In her defense, it had been a very long day.

"I already told you that." Summer stifled a yawn. They were seated in an interrogation room at the local police station. It wasn't the kind you saw on TV—no two-way mirror and old scuffed table. It was small and windowless and cold. A camera was mounted in the corner.

"Are we boring you?" the woman asked.

"I've told you everything I know."

"It's a simple question, Ms. Lake. How did you know—?"

The door banged open, and an overweight gray-haired man stormed in carrying a black briefcase. "Golinski, FBI." He announced himself to the room, then approached the table. "Summer Lake?"

The DEA agent shot to her feet. "You can't just barge in here—"

"Sit down, Agent Perry. Or take it up with your boss." Golinski barely spared the woman a glance as she clamped her lips shut and sat. To Summer, he said, "Sorry for the delay. I've spent most of the night piecing things together."

She stood and shook his hand. "I'm glad you're here." She'd called him from a cell phone they'd found on the yacht, and he'd promised to do what he could. Summer had expected him to make some phone calls on their behalf, not drive to Portland.

Bryan followed Golinski inside. She hadn't seen him since they'd both been checked out by paramedics and then ushered into separate police cruisers. He looked ragged as he limped inside, but he brightened when he saw her. "You okay?"

She smiled at him. "Happy to see you." She shifted her focus to Golinski. "We couldn't have done any of this without Bryan."

Bryan grunted as if he disagreed as he sat beside her.

"Have you heard anything about Grant?" Summer asked. "They won't tell me—"

"Hospital says he's fine." Golinski lowered his substantial girth into a chair at the end of the table. "They cleaned and closed the wounds. They're hoping to avoid a transfusion. I called his room, and his brother answered." Golinski's gaze slid to Bryan. "Sam."

"I bet they're all there," Bryan said. "I'm glad he's not alone."

"Apparently," Golinski said, "every time his eyes open, he asks after you two."

"We'll go over as soon as we're done here," Summer said. "My sister?"

"Ms. Lake is at the hospital."

Summer sucked in a breath, but Golinski hurried to add, "Waiting for you. She was examined and released."

"You talked to her?"

"Briefly. Physically, she's fine, just frantic to make sure

you're all right. She was going to come here, but I told her I'd take you over there as soon as I could."

Agent Perry cleared her throat. "If you three are finished catching up, we're trying to get some answers."

"That's why I'm here." Golinski plopped his briefcase on the table. "I'm sure Ms. Lake has told you everything already, and I can corroborate." Golinski explained that the DEA had been informed of the possible drug-smuggling operation and had decided not to intervene. While he talked, he opened his briefcase and pulled out page after page of records, explaining everything that had happened from the attack in the parking garage almost a week before to that moment—and every effort on his part and theirs to get them involved.

The interview became much less contentious at that point.

By the time Summer and Bryan followed Agent Golinski outside, the sun was brightening the eastern sky. A light breeze held the scent of springtime and hope. For such a large man, Golinski moved fast, much faster than Bryan could. He probably had no idea they trailed so far behind.

It felt like a month had passed since she'd told Grant she had feelings for him, not twenty-four hours. Amazing what could change in a day.

One thing that hadn't changed was her affection for him. Or, if it had changed, it had only grown. Because her fears were based on the false belief that depending on others would only lead to abandonment and disappointment. She'd been protecting those beliefs like a cherished pet. But now she knew they were nothing but lies that had kept her alone and lonely.

She'd tried to pretend she didn't need anybody. How foolish. How ridiculous. She didn't just *need* people in her life, she *wanted* people in her life.

Not just any people, either.

Bryan limped beside her. At some point in the last few

hours, somebody had found him a cane. Even with it to lean on, he was moving more slowly than he had before.

"Does it hurt?"

He shrugged. "It'll be all right."

Bryan would never replace Jon, the closest thing she'd ever had to a brother, but she could imagine a bond building between them.

Between her and all of Grant's family.

The thought of it made her heart thump with anticipation. Family. How she'd always secretly longed for a real family, a happy family. Like Jon's.

And Grant's.

She wanted that. Needed it.

Wished she had it with her own sisters.

Summer grabbed Bryan's free hand. "This is probably a lousy thing to say, but I'm glad you were there last night. I'm sorry about your leg, and about all the...horror of it." She didn't know how to sum up what they'd endured, the terror, the trauma of shooting people, killing people. "It was awful, but I couldn't have survived it without you."

"I wish I'd done more. I wish I'd kept us from getting captured."

"You helped get all three of us free. But it was more than that. If I'd been alone, if you hadn't come... I can't think how I would have handled it. Having you there made me want to fight."

Bryan halted and turned to face her, yanking his hand away. "Are you in love with my brother?"

The sudden shift took her by surprise. She stopped and was formulating a reply when he continued.

"You told him you loved him. But emotions were running high. I thought...I mean, he thought it, too, right? He was planning to sacrifice himself to protect us."

If the boat hadn't turned abruptly, Grant would be dead.

One more thing in a whole list of things to be thankful for.

"Is that why you said you loved him?" Bryan stepped closer, gaze flicking from one eye to the other as if trying to read the truth there. "Do you really care for him? Because if you don't—"

"I really care for him."

Bryan didn't move. Just watched her, eyebrows lifted.

"I'm in love with him, Bryan. I'm not...I'm new at this. I've never even had a serious...boyfriend." The word felt weird in her mouth. "But I'll do everything in my power not to hurt him."

It was a long, tense moment before Bryan nodded. "Good. Because Grant is head-over-heels for you. You have the power to make him happy—or rip his heart out." He started walking again. Up ahead, Golinski stood beside a dark sedan, wearing an expression that told her he felt impatient but was trying to hide it.

"I had that kind of power over Grant for a long time." Bryan didn't look at her as he spoke. "And I exploited it. And hurt him. Now I'll do anything to keep him from being hurt. So just... don't be fooled. His body is tough, but inside, he's anything but."

Summer didn't plan to hurt Grant, but she wasn't always careful with people's feelings, focused more on actions than sentiments. *Help me to be kind, Lord. Show me how to love him.*

Because she did love Grant. But not like he loved her, not yet.

Maybe that was the kind of prayer God answered. Come to think of it, knowing what she knew about God, she figured it was exactly the kind of prayer He answered.

She sat in the front seat beside Golinski as he navigated out of the parking lot, turning away from the bright sunshine peeking over the eastern horizon. "How did Ramón get there? I thought you guys had him under surveillance."

"They were surveilling the hotel lobby. He must've gone out a side door."

"He knew they were there."

"Evidently."

"What happened on shore last night? We missed everything."

"Talked to Hughes. Your friends took up positions all around the property. They blocked the road, keeping the van and all the smugglers there until the police showed up. They'd lost touch with you three. One of them searched the land on the south edge of the inlet looking for you and found Misty instead."

"I can't believe Ramón dragged my sister into this." She'd worried about her sisters, but she hadn't really believed Ramón would find them, much less get to them. "Do you know when she was taken?"

"Yesterday afternoon," he said. "When you called, they forced her to lie to you."

Summer should have considered that. She should have had some kind of panic word. She'd know for next time.

Lord, let there never be a next time!

"We're still investigating Ramón and his operation," Golinski said. "I'm thinking he must've greased some palms somewhere, to figure out as much as he did—about you and your family, your cousin and where he lives. Not sure we'll ever get to the bottom of that. What I want to know is, was his sister involved."

"I believe Maritza Hidalgo is innocent. Ramón told us that on the boat last night." She glanced behind her at Bryan, thinking he might add something, but his eyes were closed, his head resting against the back of the seat. "And her husband doesn't know anything, either."

"If he was telling the truth."

"He thought he'd won," Summer said. "I don't know why he'd lie to us."

Golinski wagged his head back and forth. "Okay, we'll keep that in mind." Golinski turned into the hospital's drive and pulled over at the main entrance. "I'm headed to the FBI field office. Call if you need me. Otherwise, I'll be in touch."

"Thank you. For intervening. And for...everything you did."

The man's smile bunched his pudgy cheeks. "Glad you got a happy ending. You sure earned it."

After Golinski drove away, Summer preceded Bryan through the glass doors. This small hospital was nothing like Mass General, where she'd been guarding the Hidalgo family, but still, surfaces gleamed, the air held the faint scent of disinfectant, and men and women in scrubs bustled from place to place. It brought back memories of the days she'd spent there.

She was scanning the lobby for a desk where they could find out Grant's room number when a blur hurtled toward her and crashed into her

Misty wrapped her in a hug. "Thank God. Thank God. When I saw you in that dinghy..." Her voice was awash in tears. She clung to Summer like she hadn't since they were children. "It was the scariest thing, getting kidnapped, all alone without you beside me this time. And then getting shoved on that yacht. I thought...I don't know. That they'd take me back to Mexico, that I'd end up like before. But then Grant—the same soldier as before!—and I know you work with him, but still, bizarre that he was my rescuer again. He showed up in a wetsuit, all sleek and gorgeous, and got us out of there."

From far away, a chair scraped roughly against the linoleum floor, and a man approached, then stopped a few feet away. Six feet, sandy blond hair that curled at his nape, hazel eyes focused on Misty. Whoever he was, he was handsome. Was this a boyfriend?

Misty kept talking. "But nothing, nothing was scarier than when I saw you in that dinghy, headed toward the yacht we'd barely escaped. I was so cold I couldn't even speak. But Grant just shoved a gun in my hand and dove back in. It was the craziest thing I've ever witnessed. I could barely see him in the black water, and then he was at the boat. You guys were already on, but he just...just took out the dinghy driver. Let the little boat go, and then hung from the rails! The boat was headed out to sea, and there he was clinging to the side like Spider-Man! I've never prayed so hard in my life. It was nuts. I was so scared I'd never see any of you again."

Her sister hadn't said so many words to her since she was in elementary school, back when Misty used to follow Summer around like a shadow. Back when she thought Summer hung the moon. Before she became an angry teenager and then a haughty model and then a damaged survivor.

This was the Misty Summer had spent her childhood trying to protect.

"Sorry. Sorry." Misty stepped away, wiping her eyes. "I'm just happy to see you."

Summer pulled her in again. "Don't apologize to me. I'm the one who got you dragged into this. I never meant—"

"It's over, though, right?" Misty backed away to see Summer's face. She wore hospital scrubs and a sweatshirt that swallowed her. She had on bright pink sneakers that, Summer knew, couldn't belong to her stylish little sister. But her skin was clear, her eyes bright. Her blond hair was tangled and wind-blown. She looked healthy and whole and perfect.

"You're okay?" Summer asked.

"They didn't hurt me. It was always about stopping you and

Grant. It was the same guy who kidnapped us in Mexico, right?"

"His name was Vasco Ramón."

"Was? Oh. Oh." Misty hugged her again. "Thank God you're all right."

"Summer!"

She stepped back at the name, shocked to see her older sister running her way. "You're here. Thank God."

Misty gave her an apologetic look. "I should have warned—"

"Omigosh, omigosh." Krystal wrapped both Summer and Misty close. The oldest sister was the shortest at only five-seven, taking after their dad. She carried more weight than her little sisters, especially after three kids, but that only made her more formidable.

Summer couldn't remember the last time the three of them had been together.

It'd been years. And they'd never done the group-hug thing.

When Krystal backed away, she wiped tears. "This is absolutely ridiculous. Can't you get a real job, one where you're not constantly in danger?" Before Summer could answer, Krystal looked at their younger sister and snapped, "And you! The next time Summer offers you protection, you take it!"

The stranger behind Misty smiled, though he hid the expression quickly.

But Krystal barreled on. "Both of you out fighting bad guys. Gonna give me a heart attack. It's time for it to stop." Krystal looked stern and angry, glaring at them in turn. "I'm serious."

Summer cracked up. "I don't think you have that kind of authority over us."

Krystal planted her hands on her hips, the anger in her expression softened by tears dripping off her chin. "Well, I should. Normal people don't tangle with drug smugglers and kidnappers."

Summer caught sight of Bryan hovering beside the sandy-haired stranger. "You can lecture us later. I need to see Grant."

"We're coming with you." Misty slipped her hand into Summer's. Krystal took the other.

Bryan headed toward the elevator, and they walked behind him.

The other man followed. He was straight-backed, and though he was dressed casually—jeans and a long-sleeved polo—the clothes were crisp and expensive-looking. They were waiting for the elevator when Summer turned to figure out why he was there.

Before she said a word, Misty said, "Oh, sorry. Summer, this is Tate Steele. He's a colleague, works in my office."

Tate smiled and stuck out his hand to her. "Nice to meet you, Summer."

She shook Tate's hand. "Glad you're here." It was nice to think Misty had a friend who cared enough to drive to Maine to check on her. Though, Misty had called him a colleague.

Interesting.

In the elevator, she introduced Bryan to her sisters—and Tate, who barely spoke but somehow seemed to dominate the small space.

A couple of nurses looked up as they passed the nurses station on Grant's floor, barely acknowledging them.

Finally, Summer knocked on the wide hospital room door and stepped in.

She'd barely gotten two feet when she was enveloped in a soft hug.

Peggy said, "We were so worried."

Summer was passed from Peggy to Roger, then Sam, Michael, and Derrick.

Finally, she pushed past the group, leaving them to pepper Bryan with questions.

Grant was lying on the hospital bed, pale but awake. When she approached, the crease between his eyebrows smoothed. "Hey."

"Hey." She leaned down and kissed his cheek, ignoring the conversations behind her. "How are you?"

"Ready to go home."

"They're not letting you leave today?" Surely, after a gunshot wound—

"No. I'm stuck here at least overnight." He glared at the IV bag beside his bed. "Antibiotics and fluids. Why they can't give me a bottle of water and a prescription..."

The room was packed with people, the ledge near the window littered with cups of coffee, some empty, some nearly full, not to mention food wrappers, a giant purse that had to belong to Peggy, and a duffel bag with clothes spilling out.

The Wright family knew how to fill a space.

"Were you questioned all night?" Grant asked.

"We'd still be there if not for Agent Golinski." She gave him a quick rundown on what he'd missed. "We've been asked to stay close until they wrap up their investigation."

"They came here and talked to me earlier. Trying to figure out how the four of us managed to take down so many men."

"Four?"

"Misty shot two of them." He looked past her.

Summer tried to imagine her little sister shooting people, but the picture wouldn't come.

"Where is she?" Grant asked. "She was here earlier."

"She's waiting in the hall with Krystal."

"They were terrified for you. I was sort of out of it, but Krystal was so upset, Mom had to take her outside and calm her down."

"You met Krystal too?"

"Of course. Mom's already adopted them both."

Bryan finally extricated himself from the rest of his family and stepped around to the other side of the bed. "Glad you're okay."

Grant gripped Bryan's forearm. "You risked your life to protect me"—his gaze cut to Summer before leveling it on Bryan again—"and the woman I love. I owe you...everything." His voice cracked on the last word.

Bryan's Adam's apple bobbed. "I thought we were past that, owing each other, paying each other back."

"Yeah, well... Just when I thought we were even, I'm in debt again."

"You're not. But if you insist...Red Sox tickets, first-base line, and we'll call it even."

"Done."

Peggy had been watching the exchange, but when Grant yawned, her soft expression hardened. "Okay, everyone. Out. Grant needs his sleep."

Summer started to obey, but he caught her hand. "Stay."

"I don't want to get in trouble." She glanced at the older woman, but Peggy just winked as she kissed her son on the forehead.

"We're going to let you rest, but we'll be close. One of your brothers ordered takeout to be delivered to the waiting room." She rolled her eyes. "They're probably going to kick us out of here." After a squeeze of Grant's shoulder, she backed away. "Call if you need us."

Peggy ushered the rest of her family out the door. When the room was quiet, Summer turned back to Grant.

He squinted. "How are you, really?"

"You're the one who got shot."

"All those men, Summer. All those bullets."

She knew what he was asking, picturing the bodies of the two she'd killed. "I'll get over it." She hoped, anyway.

"I'm not sure you ever get over taking a life. Even in self-defense. Even when you have no choice. You just learn to live with it."

"Have you?"

"I've learned to trust God with it. Ultimately, He's the One in control. He holds every life in His hands." Grant pushed a button, raising the head of his bed.

"Don't sit up. You need to—"

"I'm fine. You're as bad as my mother." But he softened the words with a smile. "Are you and I...? I would understand if you wanted to take back what you said last night. And yesterday. I mean, if you're having second—"

She cut him off with a kiss, felt his smile beneath her lips. His leg might be injured, but there was nothing wrong with the arms that wrapped around her and pulled her closer.

The door opened and slammed, and a throat cleared. "Do you mind?"

Summer recognized the voice and backed away.

"Ever heard of knocking?" Grant asked.

Summer sighed before turning. "You're late."

Jon crossed the room and enveloped her in a hug. "I'm sorry I wasn't here. I took the red-eye, but..."

"We had it under control," Grant said.

"Oh, yeah. I can see that." Heavy on the sarcasm, Jon held Summer at arm's length. "Are you okay? Injured? Ticked at me?"

"Yes, no, and no."

"I should have been here."

"How's Denise?"

Summer was pretty sure a smile lurked beneath the concerned expression. "Perfect. Charming the Wrights in the waiting room as we speak."

"She's here?"

"Of course she's here. My favorite cousin could have been killed, no thanks to this idiot." He turned to Grant. "The bullet...through and through?"

"Child's play."

"Grant was amazing," Summer said. "I'd be halfway to Mexico if not for him."

Jon and Grant looked at each other a long time, all amusement gone. As a fellow Green Beret, Jon probably understood what Grant had done better than Summer ever would. All the risks he'd taken. All the men he'd incapacitated or killed. "You'll tell me everything later."

Grant just nodded.

Jon shifted his gaze to Summer. "And you two...?"

Summer opened her mouth to speak, but Grant beat her to it.

"You have a problem with that?"

Jon smiled and punched his shoulder. "Took you long enough."

She wasn't sorry to see the smile on her cousin's face. He approved. Of course he approved. Grant was his best friend.

"I've been waiting for Summer." Grant winked at her when he said it. "She's a hard sell." The words finished with a yawn.

"I'm sure I've gone over my one-minute allotted time," Jon said. "I can picture your mom pacing outside with a stopwatch. Just needed to put eyes on you. Your family tells me you'll need to stay with someone for a few weeks. When I mentioned that my place was available, Bryan bit my head off. I guess he thinks you're staying with him. But if that doesn't work out, you know you're welcome in Coventry."

"I think I'll take Bryan up on his offer, for now anyway. He and I have some time to make up."

"Glad things are better there." Jon turned to Summer. "We

should let him rest. And by the looks of you, you could use some sleep as well."

She plopped down on the chair and took Grant's hand. "I'll be here."

Jon nodded once. "Denise is looking to rent some rooms nearby for the family, so we won't be going anywhere. She's already contacted our church. By noon, the whole town of Coventry will know everything and be praying for you."

Grant grinned at that. "You've become quite the small-town guy."

"I'll take that as a compliment. You should give it a try."

Grant glanced at Summer. "We'll see."

After Jon walked out, Summer lowered the head of Grant's bed and pulled the blankets up over him. "That good?"

"I never pegged you for a caregiver."

"I can learn."

He squeezed her hand. "You'll be here when I wake up?"

"I'm not going anywhere."

His eyes drifted shut, and she sat back in the chair and let her own eyes close. She needed rest. And she needed to stay with Grant, not just today, but forever.

CHAPTER FORTY-ONE

It took days for Summer to piece together the entire story of what had happened that horrible night. To discover how many of Ramón's men had died for him, how many had ended up in jail.

At least the man hadn't been smuggling people. But fentanyl—two hundred pounds of it. Nearly three million dollars' worth, all seized by the DEA.

Richard Bannister's properties had been searched. The small artifact Summer had seen Ramón pass to him in the parking garage was found at his home in Durham. She hadn't been able to identify Bannister, having never seen his face, but she'd gotten a good look at the little gold statue.

Bannister had confessed to giving Ramón access to the seaside property, claiming that he thought Ramón was smuggling more pre-Columbian antiquities into the country. He'd sworn he had no idea the man was a drug smuggler.

He was in jail awaiting trial.

It was a month before Summer's nightmares lessened and she started getting full nights of sleep again.

She'd been on administrative leave from work, and though

she could have returned anytime, she'd opted instead to stay with Denise in Coventry. She'd have stayed with her cousin, but after a week at Bryan's, Grant had opted to move in with Jon to finish his recovery.

Apparently, Bryan had been too easy on him. Jon was happy to play the role of commanding officer again, whipping Grant back into shape at the gym in town.

Meanwhile, as Summer spent time with Denise, she remembered things she'd once loved, back before the kidnapping. Like fashion and art and beauty. Things she'd discarded as irrelevant in her bid to be tough, to never be vulnerable.

To never need anybody.

She needed to fight the lie she'd been telling herself for years, that she could take care of herself.

All humans needed each other. If anything, Summer was needier than most.

She'd known Denise was a nice person, but after a couple of weeks of living in her guest house, Summer understood why Jon had fallen in love with her. There was something special about the movie star—and her sweet little daughter, Ella, who'd wormed her way into Summer's heart when she'd helped protect her the previous winter.

Summer spent most of her days with Denise and sometimes Ella while Grant focused on physical therapy, but every night, Summer and Grant ate dinner, talked, laughed. They shared their dreams and their fears. They held hands and kissed and took walks and, when Grant was able, went on hikes around Coventry. They attended Jon's church and got to know the community.

Jon wasn't wrong. There was something amazing about small-town life. Something that drew her.

But she was part owner of a business in Boston. Grant wasn't going back. He'd already resigned from GBPS and had been offered multiple jobs, from private military contracting to law enforcement. He hadn't chosen a position yet, living off his savings—and Jon's generosity—until he knew what he wanted to do next.

Maybe waiting for her to decide what she wanted.

Which she was going to have to do soon. Bartlett had made it clear that she either needed to return to work or give him the go-ahead to hire someone to replace her. It seemed the business was going strong. Summer had worried that Maritza Hidalgo would bad-mouth the company after they took down her brother. But she'd done the opposite. Once she'd been released from the hospital to return to Mexico, she'd publicly thanked GBPS for their role in her protection and in bringing down a drug cartel, though she'd left out the fact that the cartel had been run by her own brother.

Summer had been there when the authorities had given her the news. If there'd been any doubt of the Mexican governor's innocence, the way she'd nearly collapsed with shock and heart-break had dispelled it. Summer felt for Señora Hidalgo, who was grieving both her brother's death and his duplicity.

It was over. The only question was, what should Summer do now?

She mulled it over as she parked and headed toward the beach at Lake Ayasha. It was a perfect summer evening, the sun occasionally blocked by puffy clouds as it dipped toward the western horizon across the glassy lake. The temperature hovered in the low eighties. Children splashed in shallow water. Adults lounged on towels or chairs they'd hauled from their cars. A speedboat pulled tubes with riders on the far side of the lake, the low hum of its engine nearly drowned out by music and laughter.

The town was gearing up for its annual Independence Day events, which would begin in a week. Summer and Jon had been in town the previous year, guards for Josie Harrington—soon to be Josie Windham. Coventry did the holiday up big. Of course, the longer she'd been there, the more she'd learned that Coventry did every holiday big.

Today wasn't a holiday, though she prayed there'd be a celebration as she greeted people who'd become her friends. Reid—Ella's dad—stood beside James at the edge of the crowd. They gave Summer a nod as she walked by.

Jacqui held her newborn son, Ella's half brother. Cassidy, Grace, and Aspen cooed over the baby.

Tabby chased a one-year-old toward the lake, but his daddy, Fitz, intercepted the little boy before he dove into the clear water.

Braden and Andrew hauled a cooler from the parking lot, Carly following with a tray of something in one hand, the other gripping the fist of a toddler girl trying to escape.

Josie's food truck was parked at the far end of the beach area. She'd be ready with dinner when the time came. Thomas was not far, chatting with people Summer had never seen before. The man knew everybody in town.

A handful of guys from GBPS had come. Some of the younger ones were tossing a football, showing off for a group of college-aged girls reclining on the sand.

Beyond them, older people chatted on the far side of the small beach, probably Denise's parents and their friends. Oh, and there were Aunt Sally and Uncle Marshall. Even Jon's sisters, Jocelyn and Jenny, had made the trip. Summer glanced at the water where her cousins' kids played.

She was about to head toward her aunt and uncle when a shout had her turning.

"Summer!" The call came from Misty, who was walking beside Krystal, crossing the grassy park that bordered the beach.

Summer greeted them both with a kiss. "It'll mean a lot to Jon that you're here."

Misty gazed around at the lake, the park, and the charming main street just across the road. "I can see why he likes it."

"Yeah." Summer followed her sister's gaze. "Coventry's beautiful."

"There you are!" Jon's voice was strained, almost angry, as he stomped across the park toward them. "Where have you been?"

Grant walked beside Jon, his limp almost completely gone. He gave Summer an apologetic look as if Jon's attitude were his fault.

Summer made a show of glancing at the time on her phone. "We're all in place, ten minutes early."

"Yeah, well..." Jon greeted Misty and Krystal with hugs. "Glad you two are here." Then he turned back to Summer. "You remember what to do?"

"It's not that complicated. Garrett's already set up with the camera." She nodded to the man standing in the middle of the park fiddling with camera equipment. "He'll record it. Aspen's going to take photos."

Jon wrung his hands. "Okay. Okay. Sorry I'm being such a... You think it's okay? It's not... People in California do these things really big. What if she's expecting...?"

Summer wrapped her fingers around his thick forearm. "You've got this, Jon. All she wants is you."

He pulled back, clearly too antsy to be still. "She'll be here any second. I'll be over there, trying not to..." He didn't finish the sentence, just jogged across the park to the picnic table about a hundred yards away. He'd planned to drape it with a white cloth, thinking that would be enough.

But their new friends hadn't been content with that. That morning, most of the women in their little group had gathered to string lights and rope from trees surrounding the table. They'd clipped photos of the couple on the rope, along with fresh flowers and greenery. Tabby's artistic side had come out as she'd ordered the rest of them around. She'd added a beautiful center-piece of wildflowers. Somehow, she'd transformed the run-of-the-mill picnic table into a showpiece.

Grant slipped his hand in Summer's, gazing past the trees to where Jon paced. "You think Denise is going to be surprised?"

"She'll guess as soon as she sees. The surprise will be all of us."

"You think she'll say yes?"

"No doubt in my mind."

"Hmm..."

Summer turned to Grant. "What?"

"Just wondering what that would feel like, not to doubt. Obviously, Jon's terrified."

"He's just nervous."

Grant was quiet a long moment, standing beside her. Their hands linked. Two months ago, she would never have imagined falling in love with this man, being in a relationship with him. Being one half of a couple. She certainly wouldn't have known how amazing it would be to have a man like Grant at her side. To know she was loved and cherished. To know somebody believed she was worth fighting for.

Yet here she was with a man who'd somehow become the most important person in her entire world. She'd never dared to dream she could love somebody like she loved him.

Never dared to dream somebody like him would ever love her.

Denise's red Tesla whipped into a space near the ice cream shop.

Summer turned to tell everybody to look away, look busy,

but they'd all seen. The whole group suddenly seemed enthralled with the still lake.

She and Grant slipped behind a tree to watch.

Denise parked and headed for Jon, who was at the sidewalk by the time she crossed the street.

Summer peered at Garrett and Aspen, who were peeking from behind trees, catching it all as Jon greeted his soon-to-be-bride with a kiss.

Most of their crowd were watching now, but Summer didn't bother to tell them to look away. Denise only had eyes for Jon.

"Is this the kind of proposal you want?" Grant asked.

Summer considered Grant's question. "I've never thought about it."

"Are you thinking about it now?"

She shrugged, suddenly shy. Because she was imagining this scene differently. The man not Jon but Grant. The woman not Denise but herself.

"A little. But..."

"You're going back to Boston."

He stated it like fact. As if there were no question. She didn't miss the flat tone when he added, "It's okay. I can take that job with—"

"I don't think that's what I want." As she said it, she knew it was true. "I'm done carrying a gun for work. I'm done living in fear."

Grant faced her, eyes wide. "Really?"

"I don't have a plan. At all. You do whatever you want, and I'll just...follow." Had she really said that? She'd let some guy dictate her life to her?

Like her mother had done?

But Mom had made a crucial mistake. She'd trusted the wrong man.

"Not that I expect you to..." She didn't want him to get the wrong idea. "I have money, and I can sell my condo—"

He shut her up with a kiss, then pulled her into a hug. "I know we're not ready. But just so you know, I'd be honored to take care of you. And if you're serious... I have so many options, so many offers, but you want to know what I really want?"

She pressed her ear against his chest, reveling in the sound of his heart beating, and watched as Jon led Denise to the picnic table. "Oh, here it goes."

The sun was setting. The timing was perfect.

Denise slowed, gazing up at Jon with wide eyes.

She knew what was coming.

And in some ways, so did Summer.

"What I want," Grant said, "is you. And this." His words rumbled in his chest against her ear. "This town, this community. I'd like to stay right here."

His words settled in her heart as she watched the scene.

Jon and Denise reached the picnic table.

Jon fell to one knee. Summer couldn't hear what he was saying, but it seemed he'd prepared quite a speech. Finally, he lifted a small box.

Nodding, Denise held out her hand. Jon slipped the ring on her finger, and then she tugged him to his feet and threw herself into his arms.

Summer couldn't help the tears that dripped down her cheeks. She'd never been a crier. Or maybe she'd always just hidden that part of herself.

She didn't need to hide anymore.

Grant and Summer hurried across the park, the rest of Jon and Denise's friends and family joining them.

Jon finally ended the kiss, and the crowd erupted in applause and cheers—and a couple of wolf whistles.

Denise turned, shocked. Little Ella was the first to burst into the circle, hurrying to hug her mother. "I knew for a whole week, Mom! He asked me if it was okay, and of course I said yes. I knew you'd say yes!" She continued to babble as the families and friends drew close, offering their congratulations.

Grant and Summer hung back. They'd have their chance with the happy couple soon enough. From behind, Grant wrapped his arms around her and pulled her against his chest.

"I see what you mean about this place, these people. This... this is pretty perfect." She laid her hands over his, reveling in their warmth, and watched the celebration. Knowing Jon and Denise would have a beautiful future here.

She and Grant would too.

~

 Want more of Summer and Grant's story? Click here to download a BONUS EPILOGUE to find out what happens next.

~

Thank you for hanging out with Summer and Grant as they defeated her old enemies. I love a good unrequited love story. (If you do, too, you should check out Legacy Redeemed.) It's fun to see the guy finally get the girl, isn't it? I hope you enjoyed getting to know their families as well. You'll be seeing more of the Wright brothers, who'll have starring roles in future novels. And if you're curious about Camilla, Zoe, and Jeremy, whose husband and father, Daniel (Grant's oldest brother), was taken out by angry gang members four years ago, then you'll want to preorder *A Mountain Too Steep,* which releases this summer.

But first, check out the final book in the Coventry Saga, *Vengeance in the Mist.* You won't want to miss Misty and Tate's adventures. This story's got everything—enemies-to-lovers, legal drama, and a twisty mystery that's keeping me up at night as I write it. Is it wrong for me to hope it'll do the same when you read it? I really think you're going to love this story. Turn the page for more about *Vengeance in the Mist.*

VENGEANCE IN THE MIST

A routine assault conviction gone wrong. A menacing intruder. And a case that's more twisted—and dangerous—than anyone suspected.

Assistant District Attorney Misty Lake wants nothing more than to ensure Boston lawbreakers face justice, but how can she when she's faced with an increasing workload and pressure to offer plea deals? When a criminal she prosecuted is released on a technicality, she doesn't have time to worry about the threats he once breathed against her.

Tate Steele dreams of rising in the ranks at the DA's office, but idealistic prosecutor Misty is in his way. When the district attorney asks him to assist her with a few cases, he's eager to close them quickly to prove his merit. But he and Misty discover her apartment has been broken into, and this is no run-of-the-mill burglar. The intruder escapes and leaves no trace.

Either the vengeful convict Misty put away has upped his skills, or there's more at play than a defendant seeking revenge.

Every clue opens up a deeper layer of lies and corruption. Though Tate has always been her rival—more concerned with ambition than justice—seeing his protective side makes Misty's heart vulnerable to his charm...something she can't risk. Someone is bent on making sure the truth never comes to light— no matter what the cost.

Don't miss the final twisted mystery in the addictive Coventry Saga.

ALSO BY ROBIN PATCHEN

The Coventry Saga

Glimmer in the Darkness

Tides of Duplicity

Betrayal of Genius

Traces of Virtue

Touch of Innocence

Inheritance of Secrets

Lineage of Corruption

Wreathed in Disgrace

Courage in the Shadows

Vengeance in the Mist

A Mountain Too Steep

The Nutfield Saga

Convenient Lies

Twisted Lies

Generous Lies

Innocent Lies

Beautiful Lies

Legacy Rejected

Legacy Restored

Legacy Reclaimed

Legacy Redeemed

Amanda Series

Chasing Amanda

Finding Amanda

ABOUT THE AUTHOR

Robin Patchen is a *USA Today* bestselling and award-winning author of Christian romantic suspense. She grew up in a small town in New Hampshire, the setting of her Nutfield Saga books, and then headed to Boston to earn a journalism degree. After college, working in marketing and public relations, she discovered how much she loathed the nine-to-five ball and chain. After relocating to the Southwest, she started writing her first novel while she homeschooled her three children. The novel was dreadful, but her passion for storytelling didn't wane. Thankfully, as her children grew, so did her writing ability. Now that her kids are adults, she has more time to play with the lives of fictional heroes and heroines, wreaking havoc and working magic to give her characters happy endings. When she's not writing, she's editing or reading, proving that most of her life revolves around the twenty-six letters of the alphabet. Visit robinpatchen.com/subscribe to receive a free book and stay informed about Robin's latest projects.

CPSIA information can be obtained
at www.ICGtesting.com
Printed in the USA
BVHW062359190223
658797BV00008B/1075